His Lips Claimed Hers
in a Bruising Kiss
That Shocked Her
with the Raw Intensity
of Its Demand. . . .

. . . His hands moved down her body. Her own arms, with a will of their own, slipped around his neck. She returned his kiss with a mounting ardor that seemed to release in him even greater hunger. She had never before experienced a kiss that was almost an act of love in itself. Brutal and demanding, yet a force potent enough to bring her to an exquisitely agonizing peak of desire she had never felt with Jonathon or any other man.

When Darius's hands slipped under her knees and he lifted her into his arms, still kissing her mouth with increasing urgency, there was a tight coil of tension inside her that could not remain unappeased. She wanted him to make love to her, without thought of time or place or consequences, as she had never wanted anything before. . . .

Midnight Tango

KATHERINE KENT

A CHERISH BOOK
New York, N.Y.

This novel is a work of fiction. Names, characters, places and incidents are either the product of the author's imagination or are used fictitiously, and any resemblance to actual persons, living or dead, events or locales is entirely coincidental.

A CHERISH BOOK
Published By Cherish Books, Ltd.
New York, N.Y. 10018

Copyright © 1982 by Katherine Kent

First Cherish Printing—1984

Printed in the United States of America

Midnight Tango

Chapter 1

The marketplace of Marrakech was a noisy babble of activity under the sword thrust of the Moroccan sun. Sarah Latimer dodged a *djellabah*-clad juggler, side-stepped a leaping acrobat and ducked so that her wide-brimmed hat wouldn't connect with a red fez worn by a smiling hawker.

Shrill-voiced peddlers jostled closer. Persian rugs and glittering gems were waved under her nose, but she moved with urgent haste, anxious to reach the fortune-teller's alcove.

A quick glance over her shoulder showed that the tall man in the white linen suit was still following her.

Damn! Wasn't it enough that Charmain was in trouble again and she, Sarah, had to drop everything to go and find her? To say nothing of the other decision that needed facing. The last thing Sarah needed today was to be followed by an enigmatic stranger whose penetrating dark eyes sent unspoken but explicit messages.

He had appeared in the doorway of the cafe where she had dined the previous evening, his glance sweeping the crowded tables until his eyes came to rest on her. A moment later a waiter appeared at her elbow with a single dark red rose and a note. Sarah ignored both offerings and left immediately by way of the ladies' room. The white-suited man was European, she thought, with the razor-sharp look of one who knows he will control any situation. And now he was still following her through the bazaar.

To the rear of the fortune-teller's alcove was a doorway hung with strings of dust-filmed beads. As she entered, the beads tinkled with a faintly derisive sound. Inside the smothering darkness of the small room she caught a glimpse of vermilion skirts, a flash of gold earrings and the heavy scent of sandalwood. A deep contralto voice said, "Welcome, a thousand welcomes to my humble home. Please, be seated."

Sarah said breathlessly, "I was told you read the palm of an American woman a few days ago. Tall, regal-looking, dark auburn hair piled on top of her head . . . usually dresses in misty pastels—feminine floating dresses, hats with feathers. She's in her sixties, but doesn't look much more than forty. Her name is Charmain D'Evelyn."

There was silence. "You *are* Madame Fazia?" Sarah asked. As her eyes adjusted to the dimness, she saw that the woman wore a sheer veil over the lower part of her face, fastened to a jewel-encrusted tiara. Dark eyes, emphasized with dramatic strokes of kohl, regarded her with the careful appraisal her profession demanded.

"I am Madam Fazia. The Marchioness was indeed here. She is about to embark on her greatest adventure."

Sarah groaned. So Charmain had resurrected that title from three liaisons ago and not legal then. No wonder she'd been so hard to find. Aloud she said, "I'm a friend of hers. It's important that I find her— quickly."

Madame Fazia pointed to the crystal ball, set upon a carved ebony stand in the center of the red-swathed table. "Sit. I will tell your fortune. I was expecting you. In the fortune of the Marchioness I saw mysterious bonds between her and a much younger woman. I was able to describe your flame-colored hair and eyes like sapphires to her."

Sarah slid into a plastic-covered chair. She was

obviously not going to get any information about Charmain without going through the ritual. Just as well, perhaps. Give the white-suited man time to leave the bazaar.

Fingers heavy with rings passed over the crystal ball. "The past . . . shows me that you are tormented by a hopeless love affair. The Marchioness will teach you much about men. Heed her." The hands moved again, and there was a sharply indrawn breath. "A journey over water. An enemy who conspires against you. Danger in a faraway land. But you will receive aid from an unexpected source . . . ah!" She broke off, shuddering.

"But do you see me finding Charmain and, if so, where?" Sarah tried to keep the impatience from her voice. A Swiss taxi driver had once told her that Americans were instantly identifiable because of their extreme impatience. "Forgive me, but there's a crisis back home and everything Charmain has is at stake. I must speak with her." A hopeless love affair, she thought. Wasn't that the standard gambit of fortune-tellers? Fazia couldn't know it hit home for once.

The beads rattled behind her. A resonant, slightly accented voice said, "Fazia, you old fraud, you left out the bit about the tall, dark, handsome stranger; you ruined my entrance."

Sarah knew before she turned it would be the white-suited man. He stood framed by the light from the bazaar, his face in shadow, exuding the triumph of the hunter cornering his prey. "You're wasting your time here, Miss Latimer. I can take you to your aunt." He opened a slim silver card case and handed her a business card.

DARIUS DESCARTES   **Import–Export**
Cables: DARECAR, London

Resisting the urge to ask how he knew her name, Sarah said, "I'd be grateful if you'd tell me where Miss

D'Evelyn is staying. It isn't necessary to take me there."

No need to dispel the illusion that Charmain is my aunt, Sarah thought. She hadn't learned the exact relationship Charmain bore to the Latimer family until she was well into her teens, since Charmain had always been referred to in hushed tones as *"that woman."*

Darius Descartes smiled, his teeth white against a tanned skin. "You're afraid this is a ploy to lure you into white slavery, which, of course, still thrives in the mysterious Middle East. Charmain pointed that out, somewhat gleefully, the other evening. She remarked that she loves the corrupt antiquity of Marrakech; it reminds her of a faded and worn trollop who still has a few tricks up her sleeve."

An apt smile, Sarah thought. She fished in her purse and tried charitably not to think that the description fit Charmain as well. Sarah pulled a reckless number of British pounds from her wallet. She hadn't had time to change currency since the wild goose chase from London. "Madame Fazia, please . . . I must find her."

Descartes' fingers closed over Fazia's reaching hand. "She's staying at my villa. If you had read the note I sent to your table at the cafe last night, you would know that Charmain and I are old friends. You can telephone her to verify what I say, then perhaps after she has reassured you, you'll accept my offer to drive you there."

As they went through the strings of beads, Madame Fazia shrieked after her, "Beware the dark stranger!"

The Ferrari sped up the mountain road with the precision of a skimming bee. A warm breeze ruffled Sarah's hair, sending long strands whipping across her face. As she brushed it back, Descartes, at the wheel, glanced sideways.

"You have the same extraordinarily delicate hands and wrists as your aunt. Your coloring is similar too, although I suspect her titian locks are the result of Egyptian henna. Her eyes, however, haven't changed with age. They are the same vivid blue as yours."

"You can stop imagining family resemblances," Sarah admonished. "Charmain isn't my aunt. We aren't related by law or by blood."

"Ah! By more mysterious bonds, perhaps?"

She didn't reply. Better not say too much until she'd had a chance to talk to Charmain privately. He'd been at Sarah's elbow during their phone conversation.

"What do you do, Miss Latimer, when you're not chasing Charmain around the globe? Are you perhaps one of those lovely creatures who adorns the covers of American magazines? Or models clothes? Before you corrected me, I was about to say you have Charmain's slim height, although she is growing a trifle angular with age."

Sarah felt the Ferrari's wheels brush the rocky ledge at the edge of the road as the car negotiated a hairpin turn. "I'm the regional director of a number of apartment complexes." The brief statement left unsaid a wealth of duties, obligations and relationships that were too interwoven and personal to reveal to a stranger. It also brought a quizzical lifting of Descartes' eyebrows.

"You're very young for such an important position."

At twenty-seven, Sarah did not feel young.

"And your employer can spare you to chase after Charmain? If I were he, I'd keep you under lock and key to prevent someone from luring you away from me."

Sarah was silent, wondering how Jonathon was coping with the added burden of her work when he could barely handle his own. He had never been cut out for business. If he hadn't married Cecily, he probably would have spent his days on a pleasant ivy-covered campus, teaching undergraduates and turning out slim volumes of poetry or essays every few years. Thoughts of him rekindled an old pain.

"And where are these apartment complexes?"

"Scattered throughout the United States. The home office is in Chicago." With constant probing, Descartes managed to learn a lot about her without divulging anything about himself. Despite Charmain's reassurance over the static-filled phone wires that he was a dear friend and Sarah could certainly trust him to deliver her safely to the villa, she wondered again at her own recklessness. After all, an endorsement from Charmain D'Evelyn was hardly a guarantee of safe conduct.

Charmain had deftly fielded her questions as to why, since she knew Sarah was following her, she had not waited in Marrakech herself, instead of leaving Descartes to bring Sarah to the villa. Sarah decided that Charmain had some explanations to make—before she received the news Sarah was bringing to her.

They rounded a curve of the narrow road, badly eroded by the ever-shifting sands, and began a descent toward starkly beautiful dunes, a saffron-burnished world of stratified rock and adobe reminiscent of Arizona. But this wasn't America. She was at the very door of the Sahara led by a man who eyed her with all the subtlety of a hungry wolf.

A bend in the road brought the square crenellated towers of a casbah into$view. Sarah stared, caught in an almost mystic wave of awareness of a distant Moorish past.

Descartes said, "The late Pasha of Marrakech, Al Gloui, built fifteen casbahs between Tangier and Marrakech. In each he placed three wives and a mistress."

Mistress, Sarah thought. *A woman of authority, command; as the female head of family or estate or school . . . or . . . a woman cohabiting unlawfully with a man, esp. when the man supports her financially . . . as in Charmain D'Evelyn.*

Charmain had been the subject of many hushed whispers while Sarah's grandfather lived, and an excruciating embarrassment to the Latimer family since his death. Del Latimer had left his entire estate to Charmain, her reward for having been his mistress.

And in what way would it be different if she, Sarah, gave in to Jonathon, as she surely would if she continued to be thrown into close contact with him. He wouldn't have to support her financially, but their relationship would be no less illicit. The trouble was, they were together constantly. No matter how they strived to control their feelings for one another, their yearning was a palpable force that threatened to sweep them into disaster.

But Jonathon couldn't leave the company, and Sarah didn't want to. She enjoyed the challenge of supervising the giant complexes, which were run like landlocked cruise ships; he was bound to them by his marriage to Cecily. But he was mine long before he was hers, Sarah rationalized. Since her return to Chicago their love had been a spiritual joining only, but she hadn't resisted, not really, when Jonathon had at last taken her into his arms a few weeks ago. She felt a response to his sweet tentative kiss that was anything but spiritual. There had been a fragile quality to his caresses that made her want him even more desperately. And each kiss after that had been a kiss of farewell. He offered a fleeting, ephemeral kind of love. Perhaps that was why it was so hard for her to break it off. Every moment with him seemed like the last.

Descartes' voice cut into her thoughts. "I suppose you feel the Western woman's disgust at the excess of one man possessing so many women?"

She blinked the casbah back into focus. "I don't sit in judgment. I come from a family that has a puritanical fear that somewhere in the world somebody is having a good time doing something they shouldn't."

He laughed. She liked his laughter, it seemed to echo the absurdities of the human condition. It was the

only thing about him that didn't make her hackles
rise.

They stopped for dinner at the home of a district
prefect, cloaked and turbaned and magnificent. He and
Descartes conversed in Berber. Sarah didn't refuse
when her host plunged his hand into a large bowl of
food and selected a delicacy for her. *"Mishwi,"* he said,
smiling.

There was no sign of any women, but after dinner
she was taken to a primitive kitchen where giggling
women clustered together as she was introduced. They
were exotically lovely in vivid skirts, with gold coins
jingling around their throats and wrists and ankles, a
sign of the prefect's wealth and their individual worth.
Sarah pondered again on the way women were rewarded.

Returning to Descartes, who had not been permitted
to see the women of the household, she saw that he was
ready to leave. He gave her a sharp probing glance, as
though assessing her reaction. As they departed several
turbaned and cloaked Moroccans arrived, and Sarah
had the strange feeling she was the last woman left in
an alien male society. She was glad when the Ferrari
was again speeding toward Descartes' villa.

It was dark when they reached the villa, built within
the walls of a restored casbah, and nestled amid the
rustling palms of a thickly planted date grove. The
Ferrari came to a halt. The silence of the desert night
enclosed them in cool mysterious currents, as though
unseen curtains brushed them lightly as they passed
through to another dimension.

Descartes made no move to leave the driver's seat,
allowing Sarah to observe the villa for a moment.
Starlight glittered on the fortresslike walls of white
stucco, casting them in pale silver light. A night mirage,
Sarah thought, if there is such a thing.

Lost in the spell of the setting, she started when
Descartes spoke. "Supposing it was all an elaborate
scheme to kidnap you? What if I first kidnapped

Charmain and then forced her to say what she did on the phone, insisting that you join her here."

"Why? For a ransom? I hardly think you need the money."

His face was in shadow, and she couldn't see his expression. "Must kidnap always be for ransom? Could there not be a more romantic reason? Perhaps I fell madly in love with you at first sight. Being the sort of man who doesn't care to take no for an answer nor wait for what he wants—"

Sarah interjected lightly, "I believe you're the sort of man who enjoys teasing, maybe even baiting, a woman. But I'm afraid I'm not in the mood. I've too much on my mind right now."

She reached for the door handle, but before she could turn it his arm slid across the back of the seat and strong fingers caught her head, turned her to face him. "When I first saw you in that cafe—alone, aloof, like a remote goddess, yet searching her surroundings with bold buccaneer's eyes—I thought: there is a woman ready to savor all of life. A woman I would like to know, intimately."

His face was so close his breath warmed her lips, and for a second she was sure he was going to kiss her. She tensed, ready to fight him, a stirring of anger deep inside her reminding her how much she despised arrogant, domineering men. But then he said, "I wouldn't dare kidnap such a woman. Come, Charmain will flay me alive if you arrive with one hair out of place." He vaulted out of his side of the car and came around to open her door.

They passed through solid wood gates to an inner courtyard built around a magnificently gnarled olive tree. Bougainvillea vines stirred in the faintest whisper of a breeze, and the scent of orange blossoms, insistent but elusive, drifted from some hidden grove.

Following Descartes across the flagged courtyard, Sarah thought about his kidnap remarks and of her mother, who had a proverb for every occasion. She would have warned that many a true word was said in jest. And with a man like Darius Descartes it was easy to feel that those jesting remarks contained more than a grain of truth.

Chapter 2

Charmain reclined on a cream-colored satin chaise longue in the sitting room of her suite. She was dressed in a swansdown-trimmed negligee of powder blue, her hair loose about her shoulders and one tiny foot, its toenails painted scarlet peeping from beneath the froth of chiffon. Sarah was conducted to an arched doorway by a silent white-garbed servant, who vanished the moment Charmain called, "Enter."

Surveying her late grandfather's mistress across the ivory-colored carpeting, Sarah noted the subdued yet suggestive tones of this most feminine room. It struck an almost awkward contrast to the rest of the villa, especially the stone-flagged living room where she had left Descartes conversing with several other guests, all men.

She and Charmain regarded each other quizzically. Their first meeting had been at her grandfather's funeral, when Sarah alone of all the Latimers had gone to her and spoken a few words of commiseration. Sarah wasn't sure why she did it, in view of the reaction of the rest of the family. Perhaps it was just that the woman, standing alone and clad in stark white—a sharp outline against all the somber black—had presented such a gallant and irrepressible figure.

Sarah had called on Charmain when the family

decided to contest the will, and again when Charmain sent Sarah Grandmother Latimer's sapphire and diamond brooch. The rapport had been instant.

"Dear child!" Charmain now exclaimed. "It must be rather serious this time, for you to come chasing halfway around the world." She leaned forward so Sarah could kiss her cheek. Charmain's skin was still soft. Even at close range it was difficult to see where age had ravaged or even touched her fair translucent complexion. Sarah had seen young studs of twenty trip over their feet at first sight of Charmain, despite the fact that she wasn't beautiful in the classic sense.

"I'm afraid, you old rascal, it is." It had become a game, always to address one another by anything but their real names. "You've got to come home right away."

"Why didn't you send a cable? For you, my dear, I'd have come home."

"I did, but apparently you were traveling incognito."

"Oh! Yes . . . well, there was a tiresome little matter of a debt and a collection agency. I thought—but darling, this is such an inconvenience for you. What is happening to your business while you're playing Nancy Drew, girl detective? And how did you track me down, by the way?"

Sarah slid the scarlet-tipped foot under the chiffon gown so she could sit on the edge of the chaise. "Don't worry about me. I needed to get away for a while. You did lead me on a merry chase though. I thought you were staying in London, but I didn't know it would be under an assumed title. You don't pass unnoticed, however. Men remember you. Hotel clerks, taxi drivers, airline personnel—it was suspiciously easy to follow you."

"I met the most divine man. Egyptian, charming. We went on a little odyssey—managed to be at Le Mans for the races—and that's when I ran into Darius again. He was racing one of his cars."

"Descartes? I thought he was in the import–export business?"

"He is. Antiques, objets d'art. Car racing is one of his hobbies. He's one of those daredevils who must risk death to feel fully alive. He was coming to Marrakech, and the Egyptian was getting a little tiresome."

Sarah searched Charmain's guileless blue eyes. "You and Descartes—you aren't . . . an item?"

Tinkling laughter filled the room. "An *amourette* with Darius? Alas no, dear. Ten years ago, perhaps. I knew his father rather well." She gazed dreamily into space.

"What's your game, Charlie old girl? You knew I was following you, didn't you? You got my cable. It was you who wired back that there was no Charmain D'Evelyn registered at the London hotel. You knew I'd be worried enough to come after you, and you left a clearly marked trail to Morocco. Now that I think about it, the hotel clerk looked like a man afraid he'd go to hell for the lie he was telling. Did you bribe him? No, knowing you, you wouldn't have to. You'd give him some impossibly romantic reason for your subterfuge. But why was Descartes waiting for me in Marrakech? Why didn't you wait for me yourself?"

Charmain smiled slyly. "Then you wouldn't have had an opportunity to visit this lovely old villa, would you?"

"It's going to be a short visit," Sarah said grimly. So that was the old fox's game. Matchmaking. "We've got to leave right away. I've got to get back to work, and you've got to collect your ill-gotten gains. The judge found in your favor regarding Grandfather's will."

"I knew he would," Charmain said matter-of-factly. "I slept with the old goat. It was years ago, but my partners *never* forget."

Sarah bit back a smile. "You're incorrigible. But that was the good news. The bad news is that Buck is trying to get you declared incompetent and committed to a hospital."

Charmain wrinkled her nose as though warding off

noxious fumes. "Buck Latimer is the most loathsome creature. I don't know how your uncle could have produced such a son. Your uncle was rather like your father, vague and easily contented. But that rotten cousin of yours earned his nickname from the minute he was born. He bucked at everything. However, if memory serves me correctly, he can't have me committed to an asylum because he isn't related to me. Let that be a lesson, sweetie. *Never* marry them!"

"Don't dismiss Buck too quickly. The rest of the family doesn't approve of the way you live either, especially all the jaunts with men."

"I shan't be going on any more jaunts now that your grandfather's money is definitely mine. I have the most wonderful plan."

Sarah's heart sank. She had been privy to some of Charmain's plans for her inheritance. "Look, ducks, it would be better not to get involved in anything too . . . exotic . . . right now. The family—"

"Your family, my dear, is no better nor worse than most. They have as many skeletons in their closets as everyone else; they just go to greater lengths to hide them. Oh, I consider myself part of the Latimer family. Del Latimer was the only man I actually *lived* with." She paused, sighed. "You're a good deal like him, you know. The only one of his descendants with any backbone."

"Why don't you come home, live like a normal person for a while?"

Carefully penciled eyebrows arched questioningly. "Normal? Dull, you mean. Sweet child, you're the only Latimer worth a damn, and you must guard against letting them overwhelm you with guilt about my lifestyle—or your own."

"Well, for the moment, let's concentrate on keeping you out of some sanitorium for dotty old ladies, shall we?"

"Old! Do mind what you say! You know, pet, when I was a child I decided that since I was neither beautiful

nor brilliant, I was going to be indomitable. And I am.
So let's forget Buck and the rest of the family and I'll
tell you my *plan*."

"An apartment hotel," Darius Descartes repeated as
they had breakfast on a tree-shaded terrace the following morning. "Sounds interesting. But in Mexico?
What about the language problem? You don't speak
Spanish, do you?"

A crested silver fork delicately transferred a slice of
melon to Charmain's mouth, followed by an elegant pat
with a linen napkin. "I've never had any difficulty
making myself understood. Besides, most of the permanent residents are expatriate Americans and Europeans."

Sarah's taste buds were tingling blissfully from a
sinfully light crepe. She had slept soundly and awakened with more of an appetite than she'd had for
weeks. The desert air seemed to have a therapeutic
effect. She turned to her host. "Will you please explain
to her the dangers of owning property in foreign
countries? I've tried, but—"

"I wouldn't *own* it, not entirely," Charmain interrupted. "The Mexican government won't let foreigners
own land; they can only lease it. It seemed silly to own
a hotel but not the land it stood on, so I'll only be a
partner—on paper at least. A Mexican national, one
Ramon Rodriquez, will keep it in his name, but I'll
have the controlling interest."

Sarah groaned. "That's worse! How do you know
this Ramon won't take your money and then kick you
out?"

Charmain gave her a pained look. "He's a *man*.
Furthermore, he's a Latin. I've always had great success with Latins."

Darius laughed. "You've always had great success
with all men, *belle dame*." He passed her a silver platter
containing a variety of dates, their light and dark skins
arranged in cartwheel patterns. She protested she'd

already eaten enough to sustain a camel caravan. He turned to Sarah. "You must realize you won't be able to talk her out of this. But don't worry, I've been intending to visit Mexico myself to search for some Aztec pieces, and have a look at their race across the desert—the Baja 500. I'll look at your hotel and see what the pitfalls are."

Charmain bristled. "My mind is already made up, you young Turk. Lord, how like your father you are. The complete . . . what's that word the young women use nowadays, Sal dear, to describe domineering men?"

"Macho," Sarah replied, silently agreeing. "Which is appropriate, since it's a Spanish word and I understand Mexican men make it their religion."

"If you ladies will excuse me," Darius said, rising. "I have some business to attend to."

They watched him cross the terrace, walking with a long-legged stride that ate up distance impatiently. The sunlight cast a faint blue sheen on his dark hair. Charmain sighed. "Too good-looking, of course. Like his father. What woman in her right mind would want a man better looking than she is?" She gave Sarah a sidelong glance. "Of course, in *your* case . . . you really are devastatingly lovely, and you'll be even better as you age. You'd make a handsome couple."

"No way!" Sarah breathed vehemently. "Charlie, about this hotel—"

"Come and help me run it, dear. You've had all that experience with the complexes. This will be easy, and fun, for you."

"I have a job, an apartment and a life of my own I'm quite happy with—"

"Jonathon Conway is bad for you, dear. He'll use you up. Some men do. Learn to choose men who will expand your life, not contract it."

Sarah felt a flush creep up her cheeks. If she had betrayed her true feelings about Jonathon to Charmain, then who else knew? *Oh, please, not Cecily!* She moaned inwardly. She said lightly, "I came to talk about your life, not mine. There's still cousin Buck, waiting in the wings to nab your money, old girl."

Charmain winced. "I do detest that particular form of endearment. Come on, let's walk around the grounds and pretend we're captive slaves, held by a passionate pasha in his harem."

That evening Sarah spread the contents of her suitcase on her bed and frowned. She had departed for London so hurriedly, it hadn't occurred to her she would have any need for an evening dress.

Darius was giving a farewell dinner for them, since Sarah had managed to convince Charmain they should leave the following day. Sarah knew she would feel distinctly disadvantaged facing her host in a wrinkled linen suit and severely tailored blouse.

There was a tap on the door and Charmain came into the room, an emerald green slink of jersey over her arm. "I suspected as much," she said, looking at Sarah's suit and blouse on the bed. "Fortunately we're about the same size. Wear this."

Sarah held up the gown. It would bare both shoulders, drape tightly about waist and hips, then sway sensuously from just below the thighs. "You're kidding," she said. "I'll look like a vamp out of a twenties movie."

"You and I, my pet, will be the only women present. We can look like whatever we please."

"The material is gorgeous. Silk isn't it? I've never seen such quality, even though the style is out of date."

Charmain smiled impishly. "That style is never out of date." She was quiet for a moment, her eyes misting slightly as she gazed into some distant memory. Watching her, Sarah had an inkling of the fascination this woman must have held for her grandfather. Surely she represented to him feminine mystery at its most tantalizing. Yet could Charmain have loved Del Latimer in the same way? He had been a stubborn war horse, a self-made man, gruffly kind, but without the subtlety one would expect a woman like Charmain to crave in a man.

She spoke at last, her voice husky, "You know, darling, I wore it forty years ago when I stayed here with Darius's father. I found it in the back of the closet. But if you dare mention that fact tonight, I'll disinherit you."

"I didn't know I'd been *inherited,*" Sarah said, surprised.

"I owe it to your grandfather, love. You were his favorite; after me, of course. But I've got a lot of work ahead of me before you fulfill your potential. Put the dress on, sweets, just to please me."

An hour later, as they approached the dining room, Sarah was hard put not to swing her hips and bat her eyelids. The silk jersey dress looked surprisingly less out of date than she had expected, since it was cut on simple, unadorned lines. Her deep auburn hair hung loose around her shoulders. Charmain had insisted her sapphire and emerald necklace was a necessity, since it would put fire in Sarah's eyes. "I really feel I should have rows of gold coins across my chest, like the Moroccan women," Sarah had responded. "Like good conduct medals."

"Or perhaps bad conduct?" Charmain suggested with a wicked smile.

In the dining room the men rose, every eye fixed on the two women. Charmaine wore white, with an exquisite pearl necklace that glowed softly against her creamy skin.

Darius left the table to join them, offering each an arm. He escorted them to their places, his eyes sweeping Sarah in frank admiration. "I'm resisting the urge to carry you off to my tent in the desert," he whispered. To Charmain he added, "And you, rogue female, I must warn you that my guest of honor's number one wife has a reputation for scratching out the eyes of her rivals."

"I feel like Alice in Arabian Nights," Sarah said.

Charmain's sotto voce reprimand came as she took the chair Darius offered. "You'll have to resurrect the romance in her soul, Darius. The men in her life have stunned, but not quite killed it."

They dined on savory lamb and saffron rice followed by fruit and cheeses and a cool, refreshing souffle. The dining room had a beautiful inlaid ceiling and a massive fireplace built of handmade bricks. Through grilled windows a view of the garden showed jasmine and cineraria and dark cypress trees. Sarah felt a bewildering wave of disorientation, as though she were caught in the timelessness of her setting, and would forever be a part of some unwritten legend.

Darius watched her intently. "You sense a thousand years of history. Not only the enchantment and romance, but also the savagery and conquest. If you would only stay long enough to fall in love . . ." He paused for an interminable moment before concluding, ". . . with this magical place, you'd never leave. There is seclusion, but also excitement here. The desert is a seductive enchantress."

"And what would I do? Stay in the kitchen, preparing meals, or the boudoir? Kept hidden from everyone but my master?"

"No, I had something entirely different in mind—" he began, but Charmain interrupted, "Darius darling, do translate what I'm saying to this charming gentleman on my left. . . ."

After dinner they moved outside to a moonlit terrace. Hidden speakers filled the night with music, and concealed lights flickered on. The male guests, who seemed to speak every language but English, conversed in small groups as servants dispensed trays of liqueurs.

Charmain clapped her hands delightedly as the tempo of the music changed. "You sweet boy! You're playing my favorite dance. Come, I need a partner. Although I must warn you, I always promised myself I'd run away with a man who could tango like Valentino?"

"You knew Valentino?" Sarah asked.

"Of course not. I'm not old enough."

Darius led Charmain to the center of the terrace as servants quickly moved aside chairs and tables. They paused, hands touching each other lightly, as they waited for the right beat of the music, then swept across the smooth tiled floor in time with the hauntingly compelling "Jealousy."

Sarah watched, spellbound, as they danced what had to be the most erotically beautiful series of intricate steps, turns, breathless pauses. Darius led strongly, and Charmain followed effortlessly. Suddenly she would pause on a certain beat, then turn in a different direction, quickly pursued by her partner. With a final flourish, she stepped around him in a circle and he caught her waist and bent her backward, his face poised just above hers.

The dance ended abruptly, to the laughter and applause of the other guests. Sarah sat unmoving, lost in the sheer sensuality of the tango. Charmain, pink and breathless, was led back to her chair as the strains of a second tango filled the desert night.

Darius bowed to Sarah. "May I have the honor?"

Sarah hesitated, unwilling to admit to this man that there was anything she couldn't do.

As though reading her mind, he said, "Follow your instincts. I believe there's a tango in your soul. Come, Sarah, if only for the exhilaration of it. I assure you I won't see it as capitulation on your part."

The music throbbed in her ears, the cool desert breeze plucked insistently at the hem of her dress. Almost without thinking, she stood up, placed her hand in his. The masculine force of his nearness was a shock. She felt her hand tremble, and her eyes seemed perma-

nently locked with his. He exuded a powerful vitality
that threatened to make her knees buckle. I'm supposed to hate his type, she told herself in silent
desperation.

She wasn't aware of the progress of her feet. His
hands guided and she followed. When the beat of the
music seemed to indicate, she paused as she had seen
Charmain do, pulled away and went in her own direction. With a single graceful twist, like that of a mata-
dor, he turned so that they moved side by side.

After a little while she forgot the watchers. Everything receded until there was just the two of them,
dancing to that pulsating rhythm on some remote
plateau. It seemed that the dance was both a duel and a
blending of personalities, a victory and a surrender.
Just when she thought she had the advantage, he would
spin her in a dizzying turn and she had to cling to him to
keep her balance. His hand burned through the silk of
her dress, and she felt his touch all the way to her toes.
The music pulsated through her veins heating her
blood, and she thought wildly, I know how to tango.
I've always known how to tango.

When it ended and he bent her backward over his
arm, instead of stopping with his face inches from hers,
as he had with Charmain, his lips closed against Sarah's
mouth in a hard insistent kiss. She gasped, taken by
surprise, but he didn't release her. There was a rushing
sound in her ears and a taste on her lips like well-
ripened wine. She was being drawn into a cauldron of
sensation that left her limp. For a long moment she
responded, then twisted her face from his but didn't
resist the support of his arms for fear she would fall if
she did. He stared at her, raw longing in his eyes.

Above the roar of the other guests, over the sound of
a rumba bursting from the hidden stereo speakers, she
heard his indrawn breath and his low, urgent plea,
"Don't go back to him."

Then she pulled free and ran for the sanctuary of her
room.

Chapter 3

Sarah stood at the window, staring with unseeing eyes at the shadowed trees of the garden. Her flesh still burned, the music of the tango throbbed in her ears. The blood in her veins tingled with a yearning she had never wanted to feel again.

She leaned her forehead against the cool glass. Closing her eyes, although the room behind her was unlit, she fought a losing battle with the clamor of her senses. Telling herself she didn't even like Darius Descartes had no effect on the desire she felt. It was, she knew, the result of the romantic setting, the dancing, the music. But more than any of these, it was her memories of the time before she lost Jonathon. She had buried her longings deep inside her on the day Jonathon and Cecily said their vows. Tonight the floodgates of memory opened, and Darius Descartes had been the one to turn the key.

There was a tap on her bedroom door. She turned and called, "Who is it?"

"Darius. Sarah, I'm sorry! I had no right to steal that kiss and even less right to speak to you as I did. Please come back and I promise to behave."

"I'm very tired. Please excuse me. And don't worry about the kiss, I've forgotten it already." She hoped her voice didn't betray her.

There was a moment's silence, then he said, "Good night, Sarah."

She went to the bed and sat down. You're crazy, she

told herself. He's an attractive, exciting man. Every nerve in your body is screaming for him, and all you can think about is a love affair that's been over for years.

It was a point of honor that they had not physically betrayed Cecily. But oh, how much easier chastity would have been without those haunting memories. Sarah's teeth bit into her lower lip, and her hands gripped the bedspread at her sides. She was shaking so violently she lay back, feeling the smooth caress of satin against her bare shoulders, and gave in to a forbidden flight into memory. To the time when Cecily had still been a skinny junior high school kid with braces on her teeth and Sarah and Jonathon went away to college, filled with wonderful plans for a future together.

They'd known each other since fourth grade. Sarah recalled the exact moment his voice first broke, the first time she noticed there was a soft blond down on his upper lip and a slightly darker shading of hair on his lean pectoral muscles. She knew every tiny tributary of the scar on his back, printed there when he fell out of a tree. Jonathon had never been agile or athletic. He was quiet, sensitive, gentle. He understood things other boys did not. He knew how much a scribbled note, a line from a love poem or a simply expressed compliment—*Sarah, I love the way your hair blazes in the sun*—meant to her.

That had been the spring of their eighteenth year. They wandered down by the lake, alone and unobserved on a school morning when they couldn't bear to go to separate classes. They had to be together. Sarah had said, "Do you love me, really, Jon?"

He took her hand and drew her down on a sweetly fresh grassy bank. "I love you more than I love life, Sarah. We've got to be together, for always. I'll write haunting love stories, and you'll be my inspiration. Will you marry me?"

"Yes, yes. I love you so much it frightens me."

They had hurled themselves into an embrace, laughing and kissing, and filled with the sheer energy of their love and blind faith in their invincibility. They would live and love forever and nothing would ever come between them.

Sarah had felt the quickening of his desire, heard her own breath grow ragged in her throat. Before, they had fought their feelings, stopping short of consummation. But on this day there was no turning back. Liquid longing was coursing through her, reducing her body to a pliant bow that curved toward him, seeking to weld all of their curves and planes and hollows together until they no longer knew if they were one or two.

He proved stronger, for an instant, than she. He pushed himself away from her, held her face between his hands and whispered, "Sarah . . ."

She looked up at him through a misty haze. "I love you, I want you to make love to me, Jon."

His hands were gentle as he unfastened her blouse, slipped it from her shoulders. She closed her eyes and felt the sun warm against her bare skin, heard his swiftly indrawn breath as his fingers touched her breast gently, wonderingly. He traced the silken auriole, lightly pressed the taut center, then bent and kissed her, drawing the nipple into his mouth.

She felt a shudder pass through her body, rippling upward. He was so gentle, so tender, caressing her with the exquisite care of a man afraid he will shatter a delicate piece of china.

She hadn't been able to stop the soft cry that came to her lips. Her hands seized his head and pressed him closer. Everything she had ever heard about the clumsy groping and sweaty coupling of inexperienced boys was not true of Jonathon. His lovemaking was almost reverent. She had been the impatient one. She had pulled his face up to hers to kiss his lips with a feverish intensity, trying to convey to him her love and her need.

Her jeans and panties were removed with the same care as her blouse. She had expected to feel exposed and perhaps ashamed, but she opened her eyes and smiled at him. He looked at her, his eyes telling her his feelings. Then he tore off his own clothes and came to her. She parted her thighs for him, writhing as the coiled spring of tension inside her gripped more fiercely.

"Sarah . . . I love you, I'll try not to hurt you . . ."

The sudden sharp pain had been a shock. She cried out, but his mouth closed over hers again and he withdrew from her, kissing her and caressing her until she blocked out the memory of the sweet agony. Then he was inside her, and the world rushed away as she gave herself to him completely. Feelings were concentrated in isolated parts of her body, yet all was joined by hot surging ribbons. It seemed their minds had somehow joined, along with their bodies, and she knew his pleasure as well as her own.

Both had been overwhelmed by the explosive release that came moments later. Lying enfolded in each others arms, they had marveled at an experience so beautiful it could only have been ordained by the gods.

Jonathon had stroked her hair. "Sarah, you know I haven't any money. I'll have to work my way through college. But we can get married before we go. Especially if . . . well, we didn't take any precautions. . . ."

Sarah had not conceived a child. Perhaps if she had, all those terrible things that happened later would have been avoided.

Her mother had proved unexpectedly difficult when Sarah wanted to go East to school because Jon had a scholarship. "No, dear, I think it would be better if you and Jonathon went to different schools. You spend far too much time together. Why, dear, you've never really dated any other boys. This is a time of discovery for you both. You need to spread your wings, meet new people. How can you be sure you're right for each other if you've never known anyone else?"

"We'll get married before we go then," Sarah had insisted. "Then you can't stop us from being together."

"And what will you live on? Jonathon's grandparents aren't able to support themselves, let alone a boy in college." Her mother's tightly knitted brows expressed clearly that she felt the Conways' troubles were of their own making. Jonathon's father had been a teacher who had given up his position to care for his wife when she was stricken with cancer. He had outlived her only by a couple of years, leaving his aging parents responsible for Jonathon and a stack of unpaid bills.

"Sarah, we'll put you through college provided you don't get married, and go to the college of our choice."

Jonathon too had persuaded her they should wait. He could barely get himself through school, and he wanted her to get her education. They'd be able to see each other on holidays, and they'd both be working and studying so hard the rest of the year that they wouldn't have time to miss one another.

They had spent an idyllic summer, their lovemaking honed to a sharp edge of unappeased need by the impending separation. To Sarah, Jon was the fulfillment of every dream she had ever had. He was flawless, so noble of mind and perfect of body it was inconceivable he could ever exhibit a less-than-admirable trait. But there had been one, and it had grown and festered every moment they were apart. And Sarah, blithely unaware of the approaching precipice, had counted the days and longed for him to return to her.

She had been shocked, that first Christmas, to be confronted by his jealousy. He was jealous of everyone she had met, needing constant reassurance she still loved only him. Sarah had rationalized; his jealousy was the result of their absence, of his loving her too much, as she loved him. Jon had always been a little insecure, the result she thought, of having been raised by poor and elderly grandparents.

She had made love to him with great tenderness, trying to drive away the demons. She thought everything would be all right. Time would pass and eventually they would be together.

But all the while, Cecily, shy, gangly, nondescript little cousin Cecily—the most unlikely rival on earth—was quietly waiting in the wings.

Chapter 4

Buck Latimer's Palazzo Apartment complexes—Chicago, San Francisco and Los Angeles—were all cast from the same mold: three stories, balconied, built around a central garden area with pool, jacuzzi, tennis courts, barbeque pits. A vaguely Tahitian-style clubhouse stood surrounded by strips of sand, one of which was a volley ball court. The amenities were designed to distract would-be renters from the exorbitant sums they would pay for five hundred square feet of depressingly similar and uninspired living quarters.

Sarah's more luxurious apartment was in the private wing of the Chicago complex, which also housed the executive offices. She had first come to work there as a leasing agent. Her family and cousin Buck, owner of the Palazzo, lived in Palerville, a pleasant small town fifty miles from the city.

Charmain and Sarah flew into O'Hare Airport and went directly to Sarah's apartment, since Charmain protested she was not yet ready to go back to the house from which she had been barred during the contesting of Del Latimer's will. She dropped weakly to Sarah's couch. "I shall jet-lag for at least a month. Be a love and fill your tub with warm water, and a gallon of bath oil. And put a large glass of sherry within reach. Then go away and don't come back until tomorrow. Very late tomorrow."

Sarah smiled. "I'll have a quick shower and go to the office."

"Quick showers are for men and horses. A leisurely soak in the tub would do wonders for you."

But Sarah was already on her way to the bathroom. After her shower she turned the water on in the tub, then knotted her hair on top of her head and dressed in a gray Chanel suit.

Minutes later she was crossing the inner quadrangle on her way to Jonathon's office, feeling letdown as if awakening from a delicious dream to find a wet Monday stretching ahead. It wasn't raining, but there was a bite in the air, lingering after a long snow-filled winter. A few optimists were sprawled, shivering and shirtless, around the pool. The sun darted fitfully between rushing clouds. The heat of the Sahara seemed more than a jet flight away, her encounter with the enigmatic Darius Descartes even more remote. Not that she had been able to put him out of her mind. He was not a man who inspired indifference. A woman would either hate him or love him, perhaps both. Fortunately Sarah wouldn't have to see him again, since she had no intention of returning to Morocco or accompanying Charmain to Mexico.

She quickened her pace, telling herself she was longing to see Jonathon after the two-week absence. An elevator enclosed in a glass tower lifted her up to the suite of executive offices.

The receptionist looked up from her typewriter. "Hi! How was your vacation? He's in, but he's on the phone to L.A. I think that new manager is having another tenant revolt. Your messages are on your desk, along with a whole slew of pay-or-quits that Bookkeeping wants you to look at, and the maintenance manager says if he doesn't get more gardeners before the spring growth—"

When she paused for breath, Sarah said, "Patty, I'm

not here, okay? You haven't seen me. I just stopped by to say I'll be back in harness in the morning. It's the middle of the night, my time, and I'm beat."

Patty nodded solemnly, a finger to her lips. She was very young and eager and vulnerable. Sarah was suddenly tempted to say: Get out of here, you're wasting your time in a dead-end job. If you somehow manage to evade Buck Latimer's paws and if you don't enrage Estelle to fire you, then he'll make Jonathon get rid of you as soon as you're experienced enough to demand more than minimum wage. And please—don't look at me like I'm a shining example of how a woman can be successful in this business! But she said nothing, just stared at Patty's desk.

"Miss Latimer? You okay? You look sort of funny."

"Jet lag. I'm not sure if it's day or night. Let me know when Mr. Conway is off the phone. I'll be in my office."

Her office was furnished with the same stark black and white, chrome and mirrored wall tile as the other executive offices, the creation of Buck's wife, Estelle, who fancied herself as a decorator. Sarah had managed to soften the surrealism with a forest of plants. Buck objected to what he called her greenhouse, but she stood firm. Cecily, Buck's only daughter and Jonathon's wife, had backed her up. Here was an irony that Sarah resented bitterly. The man one loved, not his wife, was supposed to champion one's causes.

She looked at her desk. Stacks of file folders, mail, telephone messages and interoffice memos were anchored to the glass surface with paperweights and notebooks and paperclip holders. The buzzer signaled that Patty wanted to speak to her.

"Miss Latimer, I know you said you weren't here, but Mr. Latimer is on the line and he says—"

"That's all right, Patty. Put him on."

Buck's voice rumbled over the line. "Dammit, Sarah, I'll see you in hell for this. What's the big idea bringing that woman back here? I suppose you told her everything? Whose side are you on, anyway? Your grandmother must be spinning in her grave, knowing a granddaughter of hers is helping that woman get her hands on the old man's money. I never should have listened to Cecily and hired you. You're a renegade, a traitor. Don't you have any family pride?"

"Buck, dear," Sarah interrupted sweetly, "save your breath. If you're going to fire me, it's too late. I quit." She hadn't known she was going to say it, but once it was out, she was glad. The situation with Jonathon had become impossible, and the sooner she got away from it, the better.

There was a long silence, followed by the sound of his deep breathing. "Now, Sarah, don't be so hasty. I was going to give you a chance to explain. Let's keep the family and business separate. You know how Jonathon depends on you. But we won't be able to hold up our heads in Palerville if that woman gets away with this. Why did you bring her back here? To start spending the money?"

"I take it you were unsuccessful in starting commitment proceedings? Not a blood relative, huh?"

"How did you know that?"

"You just said Charmain could start spending the money."

"I'm not through with her yet. There's more than one way to skin a cat."

"Oh, profound. Any more gems of wisdom to drop before I leave?"

The phone clicked in her ear. She dropped the receiver. The light had gone out on Jonathon's private line, so she crossed to the door that connected his office to hers. He stood at the window, staring at the cloud-tossed sky. There was a dejected droop to his shoulders. She spoke his name softly. When he turned, one lock of dark gold hair falling over his brow and his light gray eyes lighting up at the sight of her, her heart turned over.

"Sarah! Oh, my darling, I've missed you so." He moved across the expanse of black carpet slowly, looking at her as a drowning man watches the approach of his rescuer. A moment later she was wrapped in his arms, and he was breathing into her hair and caressing her. All of her resolutions were flying out the window.

Feeling the familiar quickening of desire, Sarah freed herself gently from his arms. "I just spoke to Buck."

A shadow flickered across his eyes. He held her hands tightly, as though afraid she would run away. "I tried to cover for you, but I'm afraid you gave the game away when you checked with the Palerville travel agent about Charmain's plans. You know he practically owns that town."

"Jonathon, I just quit. I'd had it with Buck even before this latest attack on Charmain."

He caught his breath. "Oh, God, no . . . Sarah, I can't go on without you. If you're leaving, I'm going with you."

"And what about Cecily? You'll just walk out on her?"

His tortured gaze twisted the knife in her heart again. He said heavily, "Yes. Yes, I'll leave Cecily."

Sarah jerked her hands free of his. Two voices were warring in her head. The one that wanted to forget honor was shrill, honed by her need for him. She ached with wanting to make love to him. That same blind obsession he had inspired in her, so long ago, was stronger than ever. It would have been easy to say *yes*, to hell with Cecily and everybody. Let's run away together.

She said in a small hollow voice, "We can't do that to her. She trusts us so . . . completely." Unable to bear the look on his face, Sarah walked to the window and stood looking down at the gardens and parking lot below. A specially equipped van was parked in its usual spot. "You didn't say you were expecting her. Cecily is crossing the parking lot right now."

The sun gleamed on the pale silver-blonde hair that

streamed over Cecily's shoulders, and glinted on the spokes of her wheelchair as she rolled toward them.

Too exhausted and drained to sleep, Sarah drove home to Palerville and found her mother fussing about a crack in one of her best china plates. Her women's club was meeting for lunch, and Sarah knew how the members vied with one another to achieve the ultimate in elegance. It was more important than a crisis with the Soviet Union or starvation in the Far East. Maybe, Sarah thought, my problem is caring. Perhaps a more narrowly focused life, like her mother's, would bring less anguish.

Her mother looked at her reproachfully and turned away from Sarah's offered kiss. "I'm glad you're back safely, Sarah. But I simply can't understand—"

"Mother, listen, I'm too tired to argue. It's all over. Grandfather's money is Charmain's now. That's what he wanted. And after all, we don't really need it, do we? Buck certainly doesn't, and you and Daddy are comfortably off."

"But that isn't the point. It isn't the money—"

"I know. It's the principle of the thing." Sarah flopped down on a velvet-upholstered dining chair and studied the coy floret of napkin bursting from a crystal goblet.

Her mother moved a gold-rimmed plate out of reach of Sarah's elbow. "We may be living in liberated times, but Palerville doesn't tolerate the kind of goings-on of the Charmains of the world. And you, Sarah, don't know the whole story. That woman is little more than a . . . a—"

"She doesn't intend to go on living in grandfather's house. In fact, she's leaving the country permanently. Can't we just let her go peacefully? Wouldn't that end the gossip?"

The telephone rang. Her mother, lips still pursed in disapproval, went to answer it. She looked at Sarah. "It's for you."

Buck's voice was brisk. "Jonathon told me you're suffering from jet lag, Sarah. Now as soon as you've had a night's sleep, I want you to fly out to the Coast. Crazy Californians are revolting again."

"The California tenants didn't expect that you'd raise their rents after your property taxes were cut. But be that as it may, I'm not going."

"Now, Sarah, you know how high my operating costs are." His tone was wheedling. "We've had our differences, you and me, but we're still on the same team, right?"

Sarah was remembering Cecily's wheelchair crossing the Palazzo parking lot. No doubt Jonathon had told her of Sarah's intention of quitting, and Cecily had promptly called her father. The overwhelming burden of Cecily's love for her assaulted Sarah again! How much easier it would have been if Cecily had been like her mother. Estelle would have fought her with every dirty trick in the book, and Sarah would have relished the battle. But how could anyone fight Cecily—sweet and kind and bruisingly loyal to those she loved—and confined forever to a wheelchair.

"Sarah, take a couple of days, if you like. But go to California for me. It's serious there this time."

"What about Charmain D'Evelyn? Give me your word you won't try anything while I'm gone and I'll fly out there tomorrow."

There was an audible sigh of relief. "My word, Sarah. Sure."

A coolly indifferent moon played on the surface of the lake. Nestled against Jonathon's shoulder, his fingers gently smoothing the lines of fatigue from her brow, Sarah shivered in the night chill. "I feel like a high school kid. Do you remember the last time we parked here?"

"The senior prom. You wore a white dress with little green leaves scattered on some soft material, and I was the envy of every guy in the class. They couldn't understand why you passed up the entire football and track teams for—"

She stopped him with a finger to his lips. "For a guy who made me feel like the most fascinating woman alive. Who would write me love poems and was so tender. Oh, Jon, we were supposed to live happily ever after."

They were silent, remembering a stupid quarrel their last year in college. Jon's jealousy had not lessened. He demanded an accounting of every minute of her time away from him, then refused to believe she wasn't dating anyone else. Sarah had stormed back that if she was going to be accused anyway, she might as well be guilty of something. She would start dating at school.

She hadn't meant it, but Jonathon had gone home the following weekend and taken Cecily Latimer to a roadhouse only ten miles from Palerville. There had been a sudden thaw, softening the surface of the snow, then a quick freeze. The other car had spun out of control on the slick surface, and Jonathon had tried desperately to avoid the collision. No one blamed him, least of all Cecily. The lone occupant of the other car was killed.

Guilt, Sarah thought. How we let it shape our lives.

She should have stayed away, never come back to Palerville. She had left immediately after Jon and Cecily's wedding, ostensibly to take a fabulous job in New York. For four years she'd worked at a succession of more or less secretarial jobs, never really happy or fulfilled. She'd tried to forget Jonathon by dating other men, but none had measured up. There were older men, men her own age, professional men, creative men, but she eventually found that she preferred her own company to theirs. This earned her the reputation of being a loner, which intrigued men she met even more. As Charmain had once told her. If you want them to run after you, walk the other way.

Sarah supposed she kept searching for another Jonathon. A man who was tender, gentle, sweetly romantic and just a little lost. A man so filled with compassion that he would marry a women he didn't love in order to protect and care for her.

After a time Sarah realized she couldn't replace Jonathon. Then she dated men who were his opposite in every way. Ruthless, determined, driving. They weren't the answer either. She had almost despaired of ever being able to love a man completely again when her father became ill and she returned to Illinois.

While he was in the hospital, she stayed with her mother. Then, when it became obvious her father's heart attack would keep him in intensive care for some time, Sarah accepted Buck's offer of a job as leasing agent at the Palazzo.

At the time, she'd reasoned she'd have little contact with Jonathon, who was the national director and traveled extensively to the other complexes. But Sarah rose quickly through the ranks, becoming assistant manager, then manager. Slowly she assumed many of Jon's duties, due to her sheer ability to handle a greater load than he. As Buck opened new complexes, he divided responsibility equally between them.

Sarah had been so careful not to betray the fact that she still loved Jon. How rigidly formal they'd been in those early days. But there had been times when she turned suddenly to find him watching her, or she had accidentally brushed his hand as they studied some chart or other and the electricity had raced through her. She had tried to arrange to be out of town when he was in the home office, and vice versa. But Buck called so many meetings and Cecily was forever including her in their social activities. It seemed that everyone was determined to throw them together. When they had finally broken their resolve, the breathless kisses and anguished words seemed somehow inevitable.

Now in the parked car Jonathon kissed her again. His

mouth was cold. He whispered, "This is crazy. We'll freeze to death out here. Let's go to a motel. Please, Sarah . . . just to talk."

She disengaged his arms. "We're both too emotional tonight. Jon, we've got to face it, we're close to drifting into an affair. How much longer can we resist it? We mustn't be alone. No more slipping away to talk. Oh, God, I never should have come back."

"Would it be so wrong?" he asked softly. "We've loved each other, needed each other, for so long now. I never stopped thinking of you, every day you were gone from me. Do you have any idea how many letters I wrote you pouring out my feelings? I burned all the letters, but my feelings can't be destroyed so easily. Sarah, we wouldn't be taking anything away from Cecily. She can't lose what she never had."

"I can't. Jon, if we made love I wouldn't be able to bear it when you left me to go to her."

"Sarah, I don't . . . Cecily is paralyzed from the waist down. We don't make love."

She pressed her finger to his lips to silence him. "For God's sake, don't! I don't want to hear any more."

Charmain, looking refreshed and serene, sat on Sarah's bed, watching her pack. "I shall follow you to Southern California in a day or two and persuade you to come to Mexico with me. You'll be halfway there anyway, so might as well come and look at my hotel."

Sarah murmured absently, her mind still on her parting from Jonathon. She jumped as the doorbell rang. A delivery boy stood outside with a dozen red roses for Sarah. Charmain winked at her, but Sarah merely put them in water and dropped the card into her handbag unread. A moment later the intercom buzzer signaled someone at the main entrance.

"They all seem to know you're back, darling," Charmain remarked.

Sarah's heart sank as she heard Cecily's voice over

the intercom. "Sarah? It's me. Jonathon told me you were leaving for Los Angeles today, and I couldn't bear for you to go away again without seeing you. Can you spare just a moment?"

"I'm only going for a few days, but, yes, I'll be right down."

Buck Latimer had put in wheelchair ramps inside and outside his Chicago complex following his daughter's accident, although he had not been similarly accommodating at the other complexes. Sarah didn't want to embarrass Cecily by having her confront Charmain, so she hurried to the elevator.

Cecily's wheelchair was near the window of the main lounge. She twirled a tiny pot of African violets in her hands, and Sarah thought guiltily of the red roses upstairs in her apartment. At Cecily's side, in a protective stance that suggested a queen's archer ready to lay down his life for his sovereign, was Cecily's chauffeur, Danny. Although he was only in his early twenties, he had the blank, hard look of a man who had seen the dark underside of life. Danny's faded blue eyes always seemed to regard Sarah with open contempt. "Wait outside, Danny," she said, "I'll call you when Mrs. Conway needs you."

He hesitated, hovering uncertainly over the wheelchair. His expression softened when Cecily nodded that it was all right to go. Giving Sarah a disdainful glance, he sauntered toward the door.

Sarah frowned. "Did your father ever check on his background? He's just not the chauffeur type somehow —too educated by far."

The color flooded Cecily's cheeks. "Sarah, please don't tell Daddy, but I told him *you'd* checked on Danny's references. I spend so much time with him. It's such a pleasure to have a chauffeur I can talk to. I'd hate to go back to some taciturn creature like the last driver I had. Please?"

Sarah sighed. When Cecily fixed that imploring gaze

on you, how could you resist? Especially when you were torn apart with guilt over her in the first place. "Okay, but listen, as soon as I get back from the Coast I *will* check up on Danny boy, for real."

"I wish you weren't going away again so soon. I wanted to hear all about your vacation. How was London? Oh . . . these are for you." Cecily handed Sarah the violets.

Pulling a chair close to the wheelchair, Sarah sat down. She placed the violets on an adjacent table. "They're lovely, thank you. I didn't stay in London after all. The weather was terrible, so I flew to Morocco." She was thinking that she should have picked up a souvenir somewhere along the way for Cecily. "I'm sorry I didn't bring anything back or send you a card. Everything was so hectic and unplanned."

"You met a man!" Cecily said, her light brown eyes shining. She had delicate features, not pretty, but so luminously serene that other people felt ashamed of their petty problems when they looked at Cecily. "Did you? Oh, do tell."

Sarah thought of Darius Descartes and felt herself shiver. "Well . . . yes."

"American? Is he nice? Is he coming to see you?"

"Whoa!" Sarah laughed. "Don't start planning a wedding. I'm not sure I even like him. He isn't American."

"I suppose I just want you to have what Jonathon and I have." Cecily stretched out thin arms to seek Sarah's touch. Sarah squeezed her fingers briefly, wanting to drop into a black hole. "We'll have a nice long leisurely lunch when I get back from the Coast. I've really got to run now, my plane leaves in two hours. Can I take you up to Jonathon's office?"

"No, I don't want to interrupt his work. Danny is driving me downtown for some dress fittings. You know mother is giving us an anniversary party next week?"

"Yes. I got an invitation," Sarah answered, wondering if she could stay in California long enough to avoid it. Through the window she could see Danny standing motionless, his eyes fixed on her accusingly. I'm getting paranoid, she thought, imagining everyone knows about Jonathon and me. She said, "I really must run, Cecily. Take care."

Hurrying back toward the elevator, Sarah knew that if she looked back over her shoulder Cecily would be following her progress with adoring eyes. If I wasn't obsessed with your husband, she thought, would I resent that adoration so much?

Charmain had finished packing for her and had a cup of coffee waiting. "I've decided to accept your invitation and stay here for a day or two until I can get what I need from Del's house. Then I'll fly to Mexico by way of Los Angeles. I'll call you, Sal love."

Sarah checked her handbag to be sure she had her airline tickets. When she pulled them out, the card that had accompanied the roses dropped to the floor. She picked it up and opened it. Instead of an incredibly poignant line from a poem—Jonathon's usual message to her—she found two lines of bold black script. *I do mean to have you. One way or another. Descartes.*

Chapter 5

Sarah parked her rented Ford in the reserved parking space marked Staff Only. The largest of the Southern California Palazzos was a Frisbee throw from the ocean, caressed by sea breezes that kept the smog at bay. It was built exactly like all the other complexes, but was kept lush by a profusion of palms and semitropical plants. The benign climate attracted a young and upwardly mobile clientele who craved outdoor living. Most tenants were of the swinging singles variety, and many of the Palazzo's organized activities served as a thinly disguised dating service.

Today, however, the usual array of trim and tanned bodies cavorting in the pool and on the tennis courts was ominously missing. Anywhere else Sarah would have put it down to being a workday, but in California there were always people of leisure. She crossed the quadrangle, automatically making a note to mention a couple of patches of unkempt grass and missing tiki torches to Maintenance.

The absence of sunning tenants was explained when she entered the main building. The lounge was jammed with an angry, noisy crowd being addressed by an intense-eyed young man in cutoff jeans and a T-shirt that read *Fight The S.O.B.'s.*

"If we all stick together, if every last one of us refuses to pay our rent," he was saying as Sarah slipped unnoticed through the door, "they can't evict all of us. Not before we've called the media and gotten coverage!"

There was a shouted chorus of agreement and upraised fists. The excitement of rebellion surged through the group. Sarah had seen similar meetings end in smashed furniture and broken windows. She noted that the doors and windows to the staff offices, including the tenant service window, were closed. Probably locked too.

She moved through the crowd, aware that her tailored clothes and briefcase marked her as an outsider. Several people turned to stare as she approached the table their leader was using as a platform.

When she was close enough to look him square in the eyes, she said, "And what will that accomplish, besides a few minutes air time on the six o'clock news?"

He turned in her direction, seeking the only dissenting voice he'd heard all afternoon. His eyes flickered over her, but before he could reply, she went on, "The vacancy rate in the beach area is less than two percent. They could fill up this entire complex within a month, even if they lost every tenant living here now. The news media may hang around a day or two, but after that we're stale news. Wouldn't it be better to get management to sit down and talk about grievances?"

"Where did you come from, lady? You a tenant here?" His eyes took in her clothes and briefcase. "You're no tenant. If you were, you'd know we've talked to management until we're blue in the face."

"Local management, I presume? What about the home office in Chicago? You haven't tried going to them."

"And what about you butting out? Who the hell are you, anyway?" The question brought an instantaneous wave of hostility from the people around her. Sarah felt an elbow jab her side sharply. She fought back a rising tide of panic. Stepping forward, she turned her back on the young man to address the others directly. "I'm a representative from the Chicago office. You see we do care. We want to solve any problems we may have."

"Sure you do! You want us to pay up and keep quiet," their leader said.

She looked back over her shoulder at him, "Tell me, how far behind with your rent are you personally?"

Her shot in the dark hit home. His jaw worked, but he didn't answer. Sarah pressed her advantage. She raised her hand to the crowd. "Please! Give me a chance to go over your grievances with the manager. Go back to the pool or your apartments. Meet me back here tonight at seven. I promise I'll have answers for you then." She fixed her gaze pleadingly on a husky young man near the front of the crowd and gave him a hopeful smile. He said, "Come on, everybody, let's give the lady from Chicago a chance."

Hoping the deep sense of relief she felt wasn't showing all over her face, Sarah walked toward the closed office door. It was opened by a frightened-looking clerk. "Keep this door open and get the tenant service window open. And smile!"

The manager, looking sheepish, appeared at the door to his private office. "Hi, Sarah. I tried to break it up—"

Sarah's attention was distracted by an olive-skinned young man trying to hide behind the potted palm he was carrying as he made a beeline for the staff exit. She called after him, *"Señor, habla inglés?"* His dark eyes went warily to the manager, then measured the distance to the door in the way a hunted animal seeks escape. Sarah sighed and waved her hand, dismissing the man and the question.

Inside the manager's office she said, "You're using illegals again. I thought we agreed that we weren't going to employ undocumented aliens?"

The manager's eyes focused on a spot just above her head. "Mr. Latimer called and said it was all right. I couldn't find any gardeners—"

"You mean you couldn't find any who'd work for the pittance you pay the illegals. We'll get to that later. Now, where are the tenant grievances—theirs, not your watered-down report."

He rummaged through a desk file marked Urgent–Action. "I sent copies to Mr. Conway, but Mr. Latimer called personally to tell me to serve notice on all tenants who'd been here before rent controls went into effect. He said we couldn't live with the seven percent a year increases."

Sarah gritted her teeth. "So you started getting rid of tenants on trumped-up excuses and promptly rerented their apartments at a higher rate. What else?"

"We had to cancel the Sunday brunch because the entertainment director quit, and that meant no dances either. Sarah, I can't hire a director at what Mr.

Latimer wants to pay. We cut back on pool maintenance too. Some of the tenants complained there was a
ring around the jacuzzi. We also reduced the parking
lot lighting, and some of the women are afraid it's an
invitation to muggers. There was no other way to
handle the budget cuts."

Sarah sat down at his desk. "In other words, the
revolt I just witnessed was thoroughly justified?"

"Well . . ."

"Would you ask your secretary to get Chicago on the
line for me, please?" She opened her briefcase and
took out an indexed notebook, thumbing through to
the Caliornia section.

Patty's voice, breathless with excitement, came over
the line. "Miss Latimer? I was just going to call to relay
your messages. Your office is absolutely filled with red
roses! And a gentleman was here a little while ago, a
Mr. Darius Descartes."

The sound of his name brought him instantly into
Sarah's mind. She could see his dark penetrating eyes,
the arrogant way he stood and moved, his slightly
mocking smile. "He's in Chicago? In the office?"

"In the flesh. Mmm, what a hunk! He seemed very
disappointed when I told him you'd flown to the Coast.
He said to tell you he'd be flying to New York but
would try to make it back to Chicago before he leaves
the country."

"Okay, Patty, thanks. Put Mr. Conway on, would
you?" Sarah tried to bring the notebook into focus, but
saw instead the stark grandeur of the desert, the clean
simple lines of the dunes against a hot blue sky and the
image of a man who would have been equally at home
riding a camel over the unadored rim of the earth as
behind the wheel of a Ferrari.

Jonathon sounded distant, strained. "Hello, Sarah. I
suppose Patty told you about your visitor? He threw
the staff into a state of utter confusion. Who the hell is
Darius Descartes?"

The note of jealousy in Jonathon's voice brought an apologetic reply. "Just a friend of Charmain's. I don't know why he came to the office, Jon. Perhaps he couldn't find my apartment. You know Charmain's staying there." She was denying Darius and his interest in her, and she wondered fleetingly if she were trying to reassure herself more than Jonathon. "The situation is serious here. What's all this about budget cuts? Did you know Buck ordered the manager to get rid of all the long-term tenants?"

There was a pause. "Yes, I did know. Buck was adamant."

"Is he there?" She tried to conceal her disappointment in him, but it crept into her voice. Jonathon had never been a match for his father-in-law. No doubt Jon had pleaded in his restrained gentlemanly way, but he just wasn't a fighter. "Jon? Is Buck there? I must get some answers right away or we're going to be on the late news tonight."

"He took Estelle to the lake. They'll be staying at the cabin for a couple of days."

Of course he would! "Okay, Jon, then I need your okay to withdraw the thirty-day notices that were served without real cause. And we've got to get an entertainment director and reinstate the services we cut. We can trim the advertising budget and cancel the replacement landscaping and we'll skip the outdoor painting until fall. That should balance the books."

"Sarah, you know I can't overrule Buck. The budget cuts, yes, fine, do what you like as long as we keep within the limits. But the notice to the long-term tenants—I can't. And I can't authorize the kind of salary entertainment directors out there demand."

"Then you'll have to drive out to the lake and get Buck to okay it. I've stalled until seven tonight California time, so you've got to get back to me by then. Jon, this is no handful of troublemakers. This is the whole complex!"

"I'll drive out to the lake. Sarah . . . ?"

"Yes?"

"I miss you."

She replaced the receiver and said to the manager, "We'll walk through the entire complex for a maintenance check. Then we'll have a staff meeting."

She was so busy all day she had little time to wonder about Darius's unexpected arrival in Chicago other than to hope Jonathon understood she hadn't invited the attentions of Charmain's good-looking friend. Questioning herself as to why she worried about Jon's jealousy brought only the old answer: she simply couldn't bear his distress. It was easier to hide things from him than to deal with his reaction. Jon's emotions were always close to the surface, and Sarah had long ago accepted the fact that she felt his pain as keenly as her own.

Jonathon called back only minutes before her seven o'clock meeting with the tenants to say that Buck had reluctantly agreed to her proposals. Breathing a sigh of relief, she went into the main lounge to make the announcement.

She met the sea of inquiring faces with a level gaze, hoping no one realized how much her heart was pounding. She was nervous addressing any kind of assembly, let alone an obviously hostile one. A hush fell as she appeared. She cleared her throat. "I'll have an entertainment director by the end of the week. Pool service and parking lot lights will be brought up to former level."

"What about the tenants who got notice to quit so their apartments could be rented at higher rates?" the leader asked.

"As long as there are no arrears in rents," she paused, smiling, "and all visiting cats are sent home . . ."

There was a murmur of laughter, followed by a cheer

as she continued, "There'll be a combo here for a dance tomorrow night, if I have to run it myself!"

When the meeting ended, she went up to the apartment reserved for her, feeling tired but something like a hero. The job had its occasional rewards. She called Jonathon to tell him what transpired, then took a shower and flopped gratefully into bed. She was almost asleep when her phone rang.

Considering the lateness of the hour, Charmain's voice was animated. "Hello young Sal, did you hear about your visitor? Darling, he must have been quite smitten to travel this far. I can't imagine Darius seeking out a mere woman so far from his usual ports of call. Sweetie, are you there?"

"Charlie, you old reprobate, it's nearly midnight here, so it's two your time. Are you still on Greenwich time or what? Yes, I've heard from more than one source that Darius dropped by. I don't expect to see him, I'll be here for at least a week."

"I'm calling from Del's house," Charmain said slyly.

"Oh, God! I thought we agreed you'd use my apartment until you leave for Mexico?"

"I'm not really *in* to apartments, dear. Too confined. Besides, I decided I couldn't let some stranger dispose of all our things. Then too, it's difficult to put up a house guest unless one has a house . . ."

"Darius is staying with you," Sarah said, trying to picture his impact on small-town life. They'd probably have him arrested as a spy.

Charmain's voice was a soft purr. "Who else? He's going to be such a help, cataloguing the furniture and so on. I'm so lost without a man around. "I'm delighted he's here—all thanks to you, love."

"I suppose the family knows you're there?"

"We just arrived this evening, but we did see your mother leaving the country club."

Sarah's head dropped back on her pillow. "Try to keep from getting murdered, old bean. I can't possibly get back there before the weekend. You're on your own."

"Oh, not quite. I have Darius. Good night, dear."

Sarah dropped the receiver into its cradle and fell asleep, only to dream of a cloaked and turbaned figure wielding a rapier to fend off hordes of rampaging tenants.

Chapter 6

Sarah wrapped up all of the Palazzo business and returned to the Midwest the following Friday. Spring was now rollicking through the countryside in extravagant splendor. When she arrived at the complex, a crocodile of prospective tenants wended, wide-eyed, through banks of peonies and marigolds. Sarah resisted an urge to tell them all to go home before they were enticed into Buck Latimer's web, and went directly to the executive offices. She was anxious to see Jonathon, yet dreaded being with him.

Away from him, she knew the only way to end the relationship was never to see him again, but her resolve evaporated the moment she saw him. He could conjure up youthful passion with a quick glance, a small gesture, a word. Perhaps that was the fascination: he represented a carefree time of her life, one she'd never have again.

She told herself resolutely she *would* leave the Palazzo, and Jonathon, no matter how devastated he was. She'd have to break the news to him privately, so they'd have time to search for a replacement for her without letting Buck get into the act. But, knowing Jon, she dreaded the outburst that would surely come and might be overheard in the office. There was nothing else for it, they'd have to meet somewhere away from the complex.

They had fallen into the dangerous habit of slipping away for a few minutes of private conversation. At first they pretended they had to talk business, but rarely did. Fingers crept across restaurant tables and touched. There was a quick kiss of hello or goodbye, and Sarah's senses flamed. She wanted him so desperately, but hated the thought of surreptitious sex. They deserved something better than furtive lovemaking. Why should they go on paying for the rest of their lives because Jonathon had taken Cecily for a drive on those icy roads?

Her honorable self always reminded her that no matter what had happened in the past, in the present Jonathon was Cecily's husband, not hers. Yet, loving him as she did, it was comforting to know that his feelings for her had not diminished. Those brief moments when they were alone seemed so little to ask. Sarah sometimes pretended to herself that he had never married Cecily, that they were all young and indestructible again and wanting something badly enough was all it took to make dreams come true.

She pressed the elevator button, wondering how to get Jon alone without him expecting a rendezvous of a different kind. What could she say to him besides *goodbye, Jon*. If only she really *wanted* it to end!

If only! Those two tiny despairing words were never far from Sarah's thoughts. If only Jonathon hadn't rushed into marriage with Cecily. If only he'd known exactly what he was getting into: that he'd have to give up his dream of becoming a writer in order to take the position his new father-in-law decided he was to have. Jon had tried to write, part-time, but hadn't produced anything salable. How could he? Drained and exhausted from running the Palazzo, or attending those ever-lasting musical evenings Estelle was always arranging because the only thing Cecily could do any more was play the piano. Where was the inspiration in that kind of life?

Cecily told her, privately and with great pride, that Jon wrote beautiful poems and wonderful philosophical essays and that it wasn't necessary for a writer to be published in order for him to be fulfilled. Inwardly seething, Sarah had thought that if he'd married her he would have published his novel by now.

How could Cecily know the soul-destroying regimen of their days at the Palazzo? Cecily lived in a pampered and insulated world of luxury, even if she was confined to a wheelchair. Sarah herself often longed to provide people with luxury, the kind of comfort and recreation the Palazzo promised but didn't deliver. She had often dreamed of running a resort hotel where she could institute all the special touches she, as a traveler, craved. It wasn't hard to see where Charmain had gotten the idea of investing in a hotel, as Sarah had mentioned her goal often enough. But she hadn't envisioned running one in some wilderness in a foreign country. The old girl was mad. Luckily Charmain grew quickly bored with any kind of routine, so this latest escapade would be fleeting.

The glass elevator in the Palazzo shot upward. A fellow passenger smiled at her. He was freshly scrubbed and earnest-looking, probably a salesman. He looked a little like the police officer who had come that night, bringing the news that wrecked her life.

Oh, God, Cecily, didn't you know Jon was marrying you out of pity? Couldn't you have refused? Everyone knew Jon and I . . .

The feeling of resentment brought on another attack of guilt. By the time she reached Patty's desk a small knot between Sarah's eyes threatened to erupt into a full-blown headache. Patty held the phone between shoulder and chin as she juggled a steno pad, pencil and bulging file folder. She managed a pathetic grin at Sarah and wiped the beads of perspiration from her brow with the pencil eraser.

Noting that the light on Jonathon's line was out, Sarah decided to spare Patty the chore of announcing her and went directly into his office. Wearing her warmest smile to disguise her mood, she flung open the door in a show of enthusiasm and said, "Hello, dar—" Mercifully the word *darling* was not completely out of her mouth when she saw that Jonathon's mother-in-law, and not he, was seated at his desk. Sarah finished, "*Darn*, I forgot to bring the reports up from my car . . . oh, hello Estelle."

Estelle Latimer was a small raven-haired woman whose girlhood prettiness was now marred by an expression of self-absorption, as though she had somehow managed to turn her face inward to admire herself and her self-acknowledged talents. The only time her pale green eyes looked outward was when they sensed a discrepancy needing correction, as at this moment. She regarded Sarah with budding suspicion in her glance. Sarah said brightly, "How was the lake? Is Cecily here?" She never ceased to wonder how the dark and selfish Estelle had produced a golden-haired and self-less daughter.

"It rained at the lake. Cecily's gone to an afternoon concert," Estelle replied, her eyes still adding up the sum of Sarah's appearance and discomfort. "I'm making final plans for the party tomorrow night."

That explained Patty's added burden. Sarah had forgotten the anniversary party Estelle intended to give Cecily and Jon. She should have stayed on the Coast another day. And she certainly should have known better than to burst through his door with an endearment on her lips. Had Estelle realized what she had been about to say? Sarah said, "I have to report to Jonathon on the California situation. Is he around?"

"Buck called a meeting. Sarah, you never responded to my invitation. Are you coming tomorrow night or not?" Her eyes were still narrowed, speculative.

"Oh, sorry about not responding. I meant to, but then I left so unexpectedly—"

"To go chasing after that woman. I know. I promised Buck I wouldn't mention that episode, despite the fact that it was unforgivable of you, Sarah. Well?"

"Well what?"

Estelle tapped her ceramic fingernails on the desk impatiently. "Are you coming?"

"Oh, yes. Of course, I wouldn't miss it."

"With . . . or without an escort?" The cat's eyes gleamed.

"With, of course," Sarah replied impulsively, wanting to clear the air of suspicion and also determined not to let Estelle hang an old maid tag on her at one more family gathering. Estelle loved to point out that both she and her daughter had been married at twenty-one and how slim a woman's chances were as she approached thirty. Sarah, at twenty-seven, had a moment's satisfaction as she saw the pitying look fade from Estelle's face. She recovered quickly and went on with the attack. "I'm so glad. Your poor mother is beginning to despair that she'll ever have a son-in-law. Then, too, it would be so much better for the family if you settled down with a man of your own. People still remember that childhood infatuation you had for Jonathon. Of course, although everyone knows how he adores Cecily, well, you two do work together and Palerville is a small town. There's bound to be gossip about unmarried women."

Sarah swallowed hard. No use trying to read Estelle's thoughts in those opaque green eyes. Did she suspect? Sometimes Sarah was afraid she wore her love for Jon like a banner. She had to get away from him, and soon. "There are alternatives to marriage available for a woman nowadays, you know, Estelle," she said lightly.

Estelle picked up the phone and buzzed Patty. At the

same time she played her last card. "I know, Sarah. There's the type of liaison that woman had with your late grandfather when he was in his dotage. Patty? What happened to my call to the caterer? And did you get a definite answer from the florist? Have you called the jeweler yet? Do hurry up. You know, when my son-in-law hired you, there were twenty-three applications for the position . . ."

Sarah beat a hasty retreat to her own office, wondering where she was going to find an escort for that blasted anniversary party.

She began to wade through the week's accumulation on her desk, and made several phone calls. An hour later a drained and weary Jonathon came into her office. He had the battered look of a man who had been folded, spindled and mutilated by an expert. The look of utter defeat in his eyes made her ache to take him into her arms to comfort him, but she nodded toward the connecting office doors in a glance of warning. "Estelle," she mouthed, pointing.

"Still here?" He sighed deeply, perched on the edge of her desk beside her so that his hand could touch her fingertips spread over the report. He looked down. "That the report from California? Don't bother to have Patty type it."

"Why not?" A cold fist closed somewhere inside her. She had an idea why not.

"Because Buck has reneged on all of the promises you made to the California tenants."

The room revolved slowly around Sarah's head. She came up out of her chair wanting to scream. She said, "*All* of the promises?"

"Virtually all of them. The entertainment director you hired can stay on if she'll take a cut in the salary you promised, and she'll have to plan her soirees within a practically nonexistent budget. And the only reason he relented on that was to preserve the illusion of the swinging singles image for incoming tenants . . . *no more entertainment expenses . . . nothing to pay but the rent . . ."* he quoted from one of their advertising slogans.

"Jon, do you realize he had the manager trump up all sorts of reasons to give notice to tenants whose rents were fixed by the controls? Accused them of after-hours jacuzzi parties or vandalism or keeping pets. He even put stray cats into a couple of apartments. Jon, we can't be a party to this. We've got to go to the stockholders—"

He grabbed her arms and held her. She was shaking with rage. "Wait a minute, Sarah, you're not thinking clearly. The stockholders are all Latimers, at least the ones with enough stock to have any clout. My stock and your folks' stock isn't enough to swing any votes, even if we could get your folks to vote our way, which I doubt. It's the old story of the bottom line: profits, dividends. Listen, Sarah, we don't have to be a party to it. We can quit. I should have done it years ago. I'm sick of sneaking around. I love you. I want the world to know—"

She wrenched free of his grasp. "Jon, for God's sake! Are you out of your mind? Talking about *us* here, now. Someone might hear."

He bit his lip. "I'm sorry. It's just that I have a strong hunch this California fiasco is going to make you leave—and if it does, I want to go with you."

"No," Sarah said. "No, you can't—we can't. Jon, I'm too angry to think clearly right now. I gave my word to those people."

The connecting door opened suddenly, and Estelle stood on the threshold. Her darting eyes went over them in swift appraisal. They were standing only inches apart, but were not touching.

Jonathon said, "Sarah's rather upset, Estelle. Buck has reversed his California decisions."

Sarah muttered, "Upset isn't the word. Why did he send me to the Coast in the first place?"

"To forestall bad publicity," Jonathon said. "The

new entertainment director got the dances and brunches going again and distracted everyone from the evictions. The human animal is a selfish beast, Sarah. Not many are concerned with issues that don't threaten their own well-being and pleasure."

Estelle said, "Look, leave me out of this, will you? I just came to tell Sarah she'd better use her influence on that woman at Grandfather's house. No one in Palerville is going to make a bid on Del Latimer's effects, Sarah, so tell her the sooner she ships everything to Chicago and herself out of town, the better." She closed the door and went back into Jonathon's office.

Sarah looked at him. "That was too close for comfort. You'd better go in there. We'll talk about California later."

He gave her one of his helpless, imploring looks. "I have to see you alone. Can you drive down to the lake about nine? I can't stay in town tonight because of the party tomorrow. Besides, you'll be home for the weekend too, won't you?"

She nodded and he went into his office like an inmate returning to his cell.

Sarah returned to the mountain of work on her desk. She wasn't aware of the passage of time nor of the departure of Estelle and Jonathon. Patty buzzed to say she would be working late if Sarah needed anything.

Darkness fell. Sarah, shoulders aching, stood up and stretched. She picked up her notes for memos and letters to dictate to Patty and, wanting a change of scenery, took them to the reception area.

Patty was pinned to the desk by Buck, her face pink and tear-streaked as she fought off his hands. "Please, Mr. Latimer, *please!*"

"Come on now, honey, you've been giving me those come-hither looks right along. Admit it, now." Buck was a big man, tall enough to carry his excess weight. He'd unbuttoned Patty's blouse and got his hand on her breast. He tried to capture her mouth, but she twisted her face away.

Sarah said loudly, "I have some dictation for Patty, Buck."

He turned, red-faced with frustration, and let go of Patty. "What are you doing here?"

"I work here," Sarah said acidly, wanting to punch him in the mouth. Patty, biting her lip to keep back the tears, retreated to her desk and fastened her blouse with shaking fingers.

Buck shrugged and gave a little-boy grin. "Just horsing around, Sarah. We've all had a hard day."

"Yes, I know. It must have been tough, reversing all those decisions about California."

His sandy brows came down threateningly over deep-set eyes. "There'll be a meeting to discuss it on Monday morning. I don't want to talk about it now." He looked at Patty. "Good night, Patty. I'll see you Monday morning. Get the conference room ready." He didn't look back as he headed for the elevator.

Patty raised tear-filled eyes to Sarah's sympathetic gaze. "I didn't give him any come-hither looks."

"I know, Patty. What he did just now was sexual harassment. If you want to bring charges—"

"No! Please, I just want to keep my job. I guess I shouldn't have stayed after everyone else left, but I got so far behind because of all that stuff I did for Mrs. Latimer this afternoon."

"Come on, we're both going home. My dictation can wait. I'll go down to the garage with you." Sarah dropped her notes on the desk.

They collected their coats and purses and Sarah locked the outer doors.

"Are you going to the big party tomorrow night?" Patty asked as the elevator reached the underground parking area.

Sarah fumbled in her purse for her car keys. "Yes. I'm driving to Palerville tonight." And meeting your boss for a secret tryst, she thought, and tried to overcome the stabs of conscience by promising herself that she'd also look in on Charmain. She bid Patty good night and climbed into her car, recalling that she also had the problem of finding an escort for the party.

The only two unmarried men she could think of in Palerville were the dentist and the mortician, neither of them thrilling prospects. Jonathon was the only Palerville man she'd ever been involved with. And the other men she'd dated—college friends, business acquaintances, the men she met in New York—were too far away to be any use at all.

Her parents were engrossed in their Friday night bridge game when she arrived. They looked up with the baffled expressions they both wore whenever they regarded their only child. Sarah had long ago decided they couldn't fathom how they'd produced her.

By the same token Sarah couldn't fathom how her parents, so thoroughly Midwestern, could have allowed themselves to be surrounded by the carefully color-coordinated ultramodern furniture Estelle had used to "decorate" their ruggedly Colonial house.

"Hello, Sarah," her father said. Her mother asked vaguely, "Have you eaten, dear?"

Planting kisses on their cheeks and greeting their partners, Sarah said, "Don't let me interrupt the game. Yes, I've eaten. I'll just put my bag in the guest room and then I'm going out."

"Do you have a date, dear?" her mother asked hopefully.

Sarah made noncommittal sounds as she backed out of the room. After depositing her suitcase and combing her hair, she slipped out of the house and got into her car.

The lake was narrow at the end bordering the town, flaring to a width of about five miles where it disappeared into the woods of the state park to the north. The Latimer's summer cabin was built on the last stretch of privately owned beach, an hour's drive on the winding single-lane road. But there wasn't time to drive there even if it hadn't been too risky. Sarah was to meet Jonathon closer to town, at the local lovers' lane, a narrow pebble beach screened by a whispering row of maples.

Sarah was dismayed to find that the balmy spring evening had brought forth many of the town's teenagers. Car radios dueled for predominance of the air waves: country rock pulsed in a battered pickup truck; punk rock blared from a sleek sports car; oldies rocked out of a vintage Chevrolet.

She braked, threw the car into reverse and backed up. She parked on the approach road and glanced at her watch, Nine-fifteen. She was late. Perhaps Jonathon had left after seeing the other parked cars? It wasn't like her to be late. Perhaps he hadn't waited?

A carload of high school boys came shrieking up the dirt road, burning rubber, and slowed as they saw she was alone in her car. She was given a chorus of yells and whistles. "He stand you up, babe? Hey, I'm available."

Sarah turned the key in the ignition and drove away. She was too old for this. Never again. Please, she thought, give me the strength to end it! Okay Charmain, I guess it was written that I visit you tonight. She could call Jon from there on the pretext of speaking to Cecily to let him know she'd been late.

Grandfather Del Latimer had built his house on what was the very edge of town back in the twenties, but the expanding surburban housing tracts had spread like a stain over the surrounding farmland, engulfing the house in the process. Fortunately old Del had taken the precaution of building the house on six acres of land.

Surrounded by maples, elms, grape arbors and flower-punctuated lawns, the white frame house had a full porch, and wooden shutters flanked all of the windows. Sarah drove around the circular driveway and parked in front of the two garages over which were long-unused maids' quarters.

Walking back to the house, Sarah thought about all those years he lived here with Charmain, ostracized by everyone in town. Yet he hadn't cared, and neither had she. His wealth insulated them. Of course, they'd traveled much of the time, but the stubborn old mule kept the house in Palerville, knowing full well how it infuriated the family. And why hadn't he married Charmain? Rumor had it that she'd been his mistress before the death of his wife, but they had lived together openly after that event.

Charmain insisted it was she who would not marry him, or any other man. Afraid of drifting into a similar relationship with Jon, Sarah found it hard to believe that any woman who really loved a man wouldn't want the total commitment of marriage.

As a child, Sarah had caught glimpses of Charmain through the smoky windows of the black limousine she always rode in. Sarah hadn't known then who that mysterious woman who lived in her grandfather's house was, nor why she could never visit the big house behind the trees. Her grandfather would come to their house and to cousin Buck's house, but always alone. He was generous and a bit gruff. When she questioned her mother about Charmain, there had been awkward pauses and angry flushes. Sarah was told the woman was a housekeeper, and Sarah wasn't to listen to any rumors to the contrary. But even as a child she knew housekeepers were not driven around in chauffered limousines.

She paused for a moment before ascending the veranda steps, musing how it would be if she and Jonathon had such a hideaway, seeing them sprawled before a burning log in the fireplace as he composed poetry and read it aloud to her. She sighed. No doubt after the sale, some developer would tear down the charming old house and chop up the six acres into tiny lots.

Charmain answered the doorbell herself, swathed in

yards of flame-colored chiffon. "Dear child! What exquisite timing! We just opened a bottle of vintage sherry."

Until the moment she saw him, rising from a chair by the fireplace, Sarah hadn't considered the possibility that Darius would still be with Charmain, a week after his arrival in the Midwest. He looked darkly handsome and completely out of place amid Charmain's delicately feminine Sheraton furniture. He navigated a graceful path to her side, took her hand in his and kissed her wrist. "You came, at last." He looked into her eyes with a glance she felt all the way to her toes.

Sarah pulled her hand back, confused by the old world gesture of the kiss and at a loss how to handle his open admiration. He said, "I hope you realize I've neglected my business while I pined away for you here? Forgive me, Charmain, not that your company hasn't been delightful."

Charmain gave him a conspiratorial smile. Sarah said, "I don't remember inviting you to wait around for me." Before he could respond, she turned to Charmain. "How long do you think it will take you to dispose of the house? I'm afraid the Latimers see your residency as a direct insult. I don't know what Buck can do about it exactly, but I'm worried."

"Oh, Darius and I have decided the fate of all my possessions. I'll be on my way to Mexico next week. Tell me, Sal, are you home for the soiree tomorrow night? What are you going to wear? Who will be there?"

The eagerness of the questions saddened Sarah. She accepted a glass of sherry and sat down to sip it, thinking of all the parties and social gatherings Charmain had missed because she chose to be a mistress rather than a wife. Darius was regarding Sarah with silent intensity. She said, "Yes, I'm going. It's a command performance and, besides, I'm fond of Cecily and . . ." she hesitated a fraction of a second, afraid to say his name as always, in case she gave away her feelings, ". . . and Jonathon."

Darius leaned forward. "Jonathon is your business colleague, son-in-law of Charmain's nemesis, the infamous Buck Latimer?" The innocent interest in his tone didn't mask the probing of his eyes as he waited for her reply.

Reading the innuendo in the question, Sarah felt like a butterfly impaled on a pin. "Yes. I work with Jonathon, and his wife is my dear friend," she said carefully.

"Ah, I see. I was curious about small-town life in America and about people who successfully combine family and business attachments. A rare accomplishment."

Over the rim of her wineglass, Sarah studied his wide forehead, sculptured cheeks and clefted chin. As Charmain had pointed out, he was almost too handsome. Almost irresistible. With his European-styled clothes and aristocratic bearing and charming courtesy—You, my friend, Sarah thought, would wow them if I turned you loose on Palerville society, and I could certainly use an escort for the party. But if I invite you, would that be the proverbial inch you'd need before taking a mile? She met his stare with one she hoped was equally bold and said, "One has to know where to draw the line between personal and business relationships. Or those that are purely for convenience' sake."

"Ah, but between certain individuals there's the problem of chemistry," he replied softly. "A volatile mixture can upset the equilibrium of a tightrope walker. You and I, for instance, generate enough electricity to light up the city."

Charmain laughingly excused herself to go and bring refreshments. Sarah tried to think of a suitable remark to douse the fire she could plainly see burning in Darius's glance, but the pause lengthened. She couldn't even disengage their eyes, which seemed locked in a way that was both tantalizing and disturbing. She was losing the struggle and didn't really care.

The trouble was, he was right. She also believed that a certain attraction can erupt, inexplicably, between two people who don't even particularly like each other: an intense interest that has nothing to do with the mind or heart or soul, but is simply a wildly primitive call of flesh to flesh. Even across the room, she felt the power and virility he exuded. Sex, she thought, pure and simple. How easy to fantasize tearing off our clothes and flying at each other's body in frenzied passion.

She was astonished at the journey her thoughts had taken and hoped they didn't show in her expression, but he was watching her with a knowing look. If she'd been sitting there naked, she couldn't have felt more exposed.

He said, "So, you've decided to treat that remark with silent contempt. We're always outraged by the truth, aren't we?"

"Truth is relative. It has to do with how we perceive life." She hoped she sounded profound, but suspected she didn't. The air in the room crackled. The tension between them was a coiled spring that threatened to fly apart. Somewhere, in some long-sealed part of her mind, was the certain knowledge that the cool and controlled facade she was trying to present was a myth. She *was* attracted to him. But there had been other attractive men, other romantic interludes that flared to life and just as quickly died. All of their appeal had been on the surface. None of those other men had possessed the mystical and endearing layers to their personalities that Jonathon had. She thought, with a slight pang of regret, that Darius would also prove to be a physical being only, lacking Jon's nobility of mind and spirit.

Why was Charmain taking so long in the kitchen? But, of course, Sarah knew why.

Darius said, "And what is today's truth can prove to be tomorrow's lie. Don't you agree? Particularly in human relationships. Forgive me for getting personal again, but have you ever noticed how many people who clash at first later become fast friends?"

Sarah murmured something noncommittal and glanced in the direction of the door. He added quickly, "Wouldn't it be fun to find out if such would be the case with you and I? Or, rather, with you, since I'm already sure we're destined to be much, much more than friends."

There it was again, that look in his eye she could feel all through her body. There was, she knew, a perfect excuse for prolonging what was fast becoming an interesting encounter.

She said casually, "If you haven't anything better to do, you could accompany me to the Conways' anniversary party, observe small-town society firsthand. My escort came down with a virus and can't make it, and Estelle will be furious if she has an odd female unbalancing her seating arrangements." Sarah hoped the excuse didn't sound too obvious.

Darius rewarded her with a smile that seemed genuinely pleased by the invitation, but there was a mocking note in his voice when he replied, "Why, I should be delighted, my dear Sarah, to accompany you into the arena."

Chapter 7

Sarah had just finished breakfast when her mother, standing at the window overlooking the tree-shaded street, called to her, "Cecily's van just arrived. That strange young man is still driving her, I see."

Danny . . . I was going to check on him, Sarah thought. She went to open the front door. The chauffeur had parked the van and was carrying Cecily in his arms up the steps to the house. Looking at the fragile bundle in his arms, Sarah chided herself for not looking into Danny's background earlier. Cecily was the daughter of a very wealthy man. But if Danny were a kidnapper, wouldn't he have done it by now? Cecily looked sheltered, safe, nestled against his chest.

"Good morning, Cecily," Sarah said, gesturing for Danny to carry her into the living room. His eyes met Sarah's over the top of Cecily's pale gold head with his usual cynical glance. Cecily smiled and raised her cheek for a kiss. Sarah would have preferred to wait for Danny to depart, but dutifully brushed the delicate cheek with her lips. The expression on Danny's face made her feel like a Judas, but everybody kissed Cecily. As Danny put her on the couch with tender care, she said, "We can't stay more than a minute, Sarah. No, Danny, don't go."

Sarah's mother came into the room, kissed Cecily and insisted on going to make fresh coffee. Cecily gave Sarah a helpless smile and said, "I just wanted to know who you're coming to the party with. Jonathon thought you were coming alone, but Mother said—" she broke off, breathless.

"I'm bringing the man I met in Morocco," Sarah said. "He's in town for a few days. His name is Darius Descartes."

Cecily clapped her hands. "He followed you halfway across the world! No one is 'in Palerville for a few days!' Oh, how romantic."

Danny positioned himself by the door, behind Sarah, but she could feel his eyes on her back. She made small talk until her mother brought the tray of coffee and helped with the conversation. They chatted about the party until Cecily announced they must leave to pick up her dress.

Sarah immediately went to her room and placed a call to the Palazzo executive offices. The phone was answered by the weekend relief manager. Sarah said, "Would you unlock the personnel files and look up Danny Cowan, Cecily's chauffeur. I want his last place of employment. Yes, I'll hold."

The manager gave her the name of a family in Connecticut, a Mr. and Mrs. Danielson. Her call was answered by Mrs. Danielson. When Sarah asked about their former chauffeur, there was a long pause.

"Did you dismiss him?" Sarah asked. "He said you would give him a good reference."

"Miss Latimer, Danny, as he calls himself, is my son. His name is Cowan Danielson, not Danny Cowan. I promised to say he'd worked for us as a chauffeur if anyone called, but I can't lie for him."

Sarah felt fear run in cold rivulets along her veins. "Why? Why did he ask you to lie? And why is he using a false name? Please, Mrs. Danielson, we've entrusted a handicapped young woman to his care—"

"Danny won't hurt her," his mother said quickly. "Please don't worry about her safety. Give him a chance, I beg you, he just needs time to find himself."

"I really don't think we want a chauffeur with personal problems—" Sarah began.

"He hasn't broken the law or anything like that. Please don't fire him, he's been so happy driving Mrs. Conway."

"He keeps in touch with you then?"

"Well, he calls once in a while. I believe he changed his name because he didn't want anyone to find him. We called him 'Danny' as a nickname because his father is Cowan Danielson too. You see, his best friend died while they were roommates in college. Danny couldn't seem to get over his grief. He left school, traveled around the country. Became a drifter. But he was never in trouble, not really. Oh, please don't discharge him. When he called to ask us to give him a reference, he sounded almost like his old self again. We hadn't heard from him for a couple of years before that."

Sarah murmured that she would have to see what Cecily's husband wanted to do, then replaced the receiver. She wondered where Danny's years as a drifter had taken him. There was nothing to do but to tell Jonathon what she'd learned, dump the whole matter in his lap.

An hour before Darius was to pick her up, a florist's van delivered a box for her. She went downstairs in her robe, still undecided what to wear. Perhaps Darius's corsage would offer an inspiration.

The box contained a single orchid, which at first glance appeared to be black but was actually a deep purple. There was a realistic dewdrop stone on one petal—a rhinestone, carefully placed. Or was it? She squinted at the brilliance of the stone. It wasn't a rhinestone. No artificial stone had such fire. It was a diamond, she was sure.

Several emotions hit her simultaneously. Astonishment at the extravagance of the gift, anger at his presuming to give her a jewel both valuable and symbolic, awe at the beauty of the combination of flower and precious stone. The gesture put their relationship immediately on a commercial basis, making her think of the gold coins worn by the Moroccan women. She could afford to buy her own trinkets. Still, she could not take her eyes off the diamond dewdrop, mesmerized by its sheer beauty. From any other man it would have been a tribute to the beauty of the woman receiving it, but she remembered the note Darius had sent with his first gift of roses: *I do mean to have you, one way or another.* Well, she wasn't for sale. She telephoned the florist and asked them to send their messenger back to pick up the orchid. There had been some mistake.

She went upstairs to choose which of the two evening dresses she'd brought to wear. There was the dark green with matching jacket. No! Estelle would be certain to wear green to set off her eyes. The black then. A simple sheath with one bare shoulder and one long tight sleeve. Dramatic, different. She'd sweep her hair back and fasten it with the jade comb Charmain had given her. No other jewelry. No flowers.

Her parents left early, as she knew they would, and she was alone in the house when Darius arrived, prompt to the minute. Sarah reasoned that her mother wouldn't put him through the usual ritual if he were introduced at the party. Her mother interrogated Sarah's men friends as if Sarah were still in high school.

Darius arrived in a silver Rolls Royce. From her bedroom window she watched him stride toward the house, carelessly elegant in a perfectly tailored dinner jacket, looking as though he should be dressed in a burnoose, astride an Arab stallion. Sarah went downstairs to let him in. As she murmured a greeting and led him into the living room, she saw his eyes flicker over her dress. "You look lovely, but I'd hoped to see you wearing an orchid. Perhaps the color was too intense for a black gown?"

"The orchid—and the dewdrop—went back to the florist. Look, just so we understand one another. I needed an escort tonight, and although Palerville society isn't the most exciting on earth, I thought you'd like to get out, if only to give Charmain a night off to do her hair—"

"Do you have to be so brutally honest?"

"Yes, I think I do. Would you like a drink before we go? There'll only be punch tonight, nonalcoholic. My parents don't drink either, but I've got a bottle of wine in my suitcase and a flask of brandy."

He smiled. "I don't need to fortify myself. But if you would care for one, of course I'll join you."

Sarah would have liked a glass of wine, but she picked up her coat instead. He came to help her with it. She was acutely aware of his presence behind her, his faint masculine scent, and the warmth of his hand as he brushed her bare shoulder. He said, "This is a charming house. Built in the thirties I'd guess. But it seems to cry out for American Colonial furniture, some handsomely sturdy maple pieces or uncluttered oak as solid as the Midwestern agricultural belt. Your parents prefer ultramodern, I see."

"Yes," Sarah said shortly, not wanting to agree with him aloud.

They went out to the chauffeur-driven Rolls Royce and settled in the back. The car glided away. Darius remarked, "I brought a gift for the anniversary couple. I trust it will be suitable. It's just a small jade piece I picked up in the Orient recently."

Sarah gave him a sidelong glance. "It wasn't necessary for you to bring a gift. I have one for them. You know, it's considered somewhat crass here to give expensive gifts to acquaintances. People get the idea you're calling attention to your wealth."

"Perhaps I'm trying to impress you more with my thoughtfulness? I *am* trying to impress you, you know."

"I'm afraid you wouldn't understand the qualities that impress me in a man."

"Tell me anyway. Perhaps I can acquire them."

He was joking, of course, but Sarah had a sudden image of Jon, in those early days before Cecily came between them. Sarah felt a tear prick the back of her eye. "Gentle, sensitive, understanding. Everything you are not. You flaunt your power, your money. Your good looks too. I prefer the hidden beauty of a man's mind, his caring, compassion."

"I see. And who is this paragon you describe? If my rival is the Archbishop of Canterbury or the Pope, then I'll concede."

"Oh, you're impossible," Sarah cried, turning to look out of the window and immediately regretting having made the standard retort. Fortunately the chauffeur was approaching Buck and Estelle's house, a massive brick structure Sarah had dubbed "Buckingham Palace" and which was about as architecturally appealing as a barracks.

They went into the vast marble-floored hall and joined the receiving line.

Estelle was resplendent in sequined green, Buck looked as if he'd been poured into his tux and overflowed. Jonathon was a quiet, brooding presence beside Cecily's wheelchair. Only Cecily, fragile and gently appealing in a delicate pink gown, wore an expression of genuine welcome for her guests.

When Sarah and Darius reached their hosts, Sarah sensed in Darius an immediate warm respect as well as deep compassion for Cecily. He lingered over their introduction, cradling her hand. His reaction surprised Sarah. So he was capable of treating a woman like a human being, rather than an object to be possessed or conquered in some way. But, of course, Cecily was hardly a sexual object, confined as she was to her wheelchair. Sarah could hardly count the times she had rationalized that if she gave in and slept with Jon she would not be depriving Cecily of his sexuality, since Cecily was incapable of having sex with him. But there had always been the knowledge that those other areas of Jon's total being upon which she trespassed were sacred to Cecily. And the mere fact that she trespassed on them was a severe deprivation for Cecily.

Estelle slipped her arm through Darius's. "Let me take you around, present you to the guests already here." She swept him away, gushing up at him, obviously determined that this particular social catch was to be displayed as the hostess's personal coup. Either Darius's connection to Charmain had not been mentioned to Estelle, or she chose to ignore it in the face of Darius's suavely handsome presence.

Buck avoided Sarah's eyes as he too decided he'd stood in the receiving line long enough. No doubt he was still feeling sheepish about Sarah catching him with Patty. Sarah looked at Jonathon over the top of Cecily's head, saw the hurt in his eyes. There'd never been a moment to call him to explain why she hadn't met him at the lake.

Cecily grasped Sarah's hands and pulled her down for a kiss on the cheek. "Oh, Sarah, you look stunning. You make every other woman here look overdressed, overjeweled and, oh, I don't know, just overblown, I guess. Doesn't she look lovely, Jon?"

"She always does." There was an edge to his voice, but Cecily didn't notice. She went on, "Your Darius Descartes is absolutely charming. You didn't say he was devastatingly good-looking. He looks a lot like that old-time movie star, what's his name?"

"I've no idea," Jonathon said. "Not being addicted to the late late show as you are."

Cecily flushed. Sarah wanted to snap at Jonathon. He shouldn't take out his anger with Sarah on his wife. Instead Sarah said quickly, "Am I dreaming, or do I hear real live dance music drifting this way?"

"That's my big surprise," Cecily said, her smile widening. "I persuaded Mother that the best present she could give me would be to have music and dancing and champagne, not one of those dreary evenings when everyone divides into cliques and gossips all night."

"Champagne? Why, we haven't had champagne at a family function since . . ." Sarah's voice trailed off and she wanted to kick herself. Jon had been drinking the night of the accident. No charges were filed, but Sarah had a suspicion Buck Latimer might have fixed things with a payoff at Cecily's request.

With her usual tact, Cecily covered the awkward pause. "Jon, I want you to dance with Sarah. Right now, this minute. Go on, you probably won't get another chance after Mother's finished with Darius. He didn't look like the kind of man who'd relinquish Sarah to anyone, not even her second cousin's husband."

Sarah declined nervously. "Oh, not right now. I haven't said hello to anyone yet."

"Then the next dance after this," Cecily said firmly. "Jon, push me into the living room. I believe everyone's here now. I want to be surrounded by music and laughter tonight. I may even get a little silly on champagne."

They went into the Latimers' Olympic-sized living room where the hardwood floor had been uncovered and buffed to a high gloss. A dais had been erected in the window alcove to accommodate a five-piece combo.

Sarah stood on the sidelines, nodding and smiling to various relatives and friends. An admiring knot of guests moved with Estelle and Darius as she ushered him around the room. The champagne fountain was sparkling under an amber light.

When Cecily again insisted that Jonathon dance with Sarah, he took her arm and led her onto the floor. The musicians played a pounding disco beat that called for individual choreography rather than intimate dancing, but Jonathon took her into his arms and merely swayed in time with the music. She said, "I know you don't like dancing, but break away, for God's sake, and *move*. Don't hold me so close."

"I want to hold you close. Where were you last night? I waited half an hour, surrounded by kids."

There was a hint of liquor on his breath that was not

champagne. "You must have arrived fifteen minutes early then. Listen, we can't talk now. Break away from me, turn me, people are watching."

His eyes went suddenly to something over her shoulder and he said, "Not any more. Look—"

Turning, Sarah saw that Darius had escaped Estelle and was steering Cecily's wheelchair into the middle of the dancers. Cecily was laughing and protesting, while Darius spoke to her in a determinedly earnest way. The other couples fell back, allowing them to approach the musicians on the dais. Darius spoke to the pianist, and a moment later the disco beat gave way to a waltz.

Darius now held one of Cecily's hands, while she turned her wheelchair with the other, moving in small circles to the strains of music. The other couples began to dance also, but every eye was fixed on the dashingly handsome Darius gallantly leading Cecily, whose pale oval face was lighted by the glow in her eyes. Sarah felt her throat constrict, partly at Cecily's joy and partly because it should have been Jonathon who made that gesture, although she admitted to herself he would never have thought of it.

Jonathon said, "What the hell does he think he's doing?"

"Go to her. Cut in," Sarah urged.

He hesitated, then let go of Sarah. Darius saw him coming, and raised his hand in some signal to the musicians. They immediately switched to *"The Anniversary Waltz."* There was a smattering of applause as Darius handed Cecily to her husband, and the floor cleared to allow them to dance alone.

Jonathon was tense, awkward. A smile didn't hide the annoyance in his eyes, and he didn't move with Darius's natural grace. Sarah could feel Jon's embarrassment at being placed on display in such a manner. Darius had crossed the floor to her side and whispered, "Come on, let's join them now."

Knowing it would be better if everyone danced, rather than watched, Sarah placed her hand stiffly on

Darius's shoulder and allowed him to swing her on to the floor. He regarded her with a level gaze. "In my circles it's customary for a husband to dance first with his wife. Since Mr. Conway instead danced with you, I assumed it was correct for me to dance with his wife."

"Cecily doesn't dance—" Sarah began, but Cecily was so obviously enjoying herself that the rest of the statement seemed pointless. Sarah felt her irritation grow. Darius was an outsider. He had no right to show Jon up in that way, treating Cecily as though she were . . .

As though reading her thoughts, Darius said, "Her wheelchair doesn't prevent her from moving to the music, being a part of the festivities instead of a spectator. Since I understand her husband married her *after* her accident, one concludes that he is not intimidated by the wheelchair."

"I'd like some champagne," Sarah said shortly, dropping her hands from his and turning to leave the floor.

For Sarah, the evening progressed at a snail's pace. There was the call to dinner, mercifully served buffet style, then more dancing. The anniversary gifts had been piled on a table, and the ritual of opening them was speeded up by several guests helping to untie ribbons and open boxes so Cecily and Jon could make the appropriate comments and thanks. Sarah had brought an arrangement of delicate china roses in a filigree basket. Cecily exclaimed and shed a tear over the beauty of the workmanship. Sarah had chosen the gift to please Cecily more than Jonathon. But it was Darius's gift that caused a stir.

He had brought an exquisite jade statuette of the Buddhist Goddess of Mercy, her face in serene repose, hands folded over a tiny fan. Cecily said, "Oh, you shouldn't have!" but at the same time her fingers caressed the small statuette reverently. Everyone crowded closer to see the gift.

Sarah found herself at the back of the thronging

guests. Since Darius's gift was the last to be opened, she took the opportunity to slip away to one of the bathrooms to repair her makeup. She lingered before a gilt-framed mirror, thinking that Darius Descartes had managed to eclipse everyone and everything around him.

Jonathon would never shove himself into the limelight in such a manner, he'd be content to retire quietly into the background. Sarah had always felt this showed strength of character, but tonight found that she admired the way Darius had taken command of the situation.

For weeks to come people would be talking about the gift he gave Cecily. Not the exquisite statuette, but the simple gesture of dancing with her. Sarah had believed that Jonathon was protective, caring, but now she realized he had insulated Cecily from many small pleasures, as well as possible wounds and embarrassments. In one brilliant flash of insight, Darius had seen that Cecily wanted to feel like an attractive, sought-after woman. He had given her that moment on the dance floor.

Recapturing the image of Cecily's glowing expression, Sarah felt grateful to Darius and at the same time experienced a twinge of some undefinable emotion. What stayed in her mind was that gentle solicitous look on his face when he regarded Cecily—a look of respect and appreciation, as though he were saying, you're lovely and brave and I admire you. Sarah almost envied Cecily that look. The glances he had bestowed on Sarah were little more than pure lust, and she suddenly wanted him to see her as more than a conquest. Why, she didn't know. Surely she wasn't actually responding to him?

When she stepped into the hall, she heard the music filling the improvised ballroom. Estelle, a whoosh of green chiffon, whirled by the double doors in the arms of Darius. Good, that would keep him occupied for a while. Needing a breath of air, Sarah retraced her steps.

There was a patio off the solarium at the side of the house. None of the other guests was likely to go there. Estelle had enclosed it with a white-painted trellis draped with vines and there was wicker furniture, but Sarah remained standing, too restless to relax. She needed to confront Buck about reneging on the promises she'd made to the California tenants. And she had to tell Jonathon she could no longer stand the deception. But neither of these conversations could take place tonight and postponing them was becoming torture. She wondered if Darius's presence was adding to her impulse to self-castigation. That was the difference between him and Jon, she decided. Jon made her feel needed, wanted, while Darius made her feel like she was not quite living up to her own ideals. But surely that was in her own mind. She hardly knew the man, so why was she comparing him to Jon?

There was a slight sound behind her. Her spirits fell even lower when she saw that Jonathon had followed her. "Jon, no! Go back. I just needed a minute by myself. Please—"

"They won't miss us for a moment. Sarah, what's wrong?" He moved to her side, reached for her hand, then let his fingers slide up her arm.

Steeling herself against that vulnerable look on his face, Sarah said, "This isn't the time to talk. But you might as well know, I'm resigning from the company. First thing Monday."

He caught his breath. "What will you do?"

"Look for another job. Travel. Go to a nunnery. I don't know yet."

"Sarah, I could set you up in a place, perhaps in the city. I could come to you—"

"No! You won't set me up anywhere. I'll take care of my own living arrangements. I'm not going to be this generation's Charmain D'Evelyn."

His hand tightened on her shoulder, pulled her closer. "You know I didn't mean . . . oh, God, Sarah, I love you so!" He bent over her face and she turned her head to try to avoid his kiss, but he clung to her and she felt his breath against her hair. He said in a ragged voice, "Your escort tonight—should I be worried about him? Is he the reason for this change in you?"

"Darius has nothing to do with my decision. It's one I've been thinking about for some time. Jon, don't you see, there's no hope for us. We live in the past and snatch minutes in the present, but we've no future—"

Before she could stop him, his mouth covered hers, shutting off her words.

Almost instantaneously, there was a sudden harsh explosion of light around them, striking them with the impact of icy water.

They broke away from each other, blinking against the sudden flood of lights. Sarah heard a sharp exclamation and knew before she turned that it would be Estelle who had caught them.

Darius Descartes stood at Estelle's side, his dark eyes angrily reproaching Sarah.

Chapter 8

Charmain came to the door in her robe in response to Sarah's frantic ringing of the bell. Peering through the darkness, Charmain cried, "Good heavens, what happened to you?" She held the door wide for Sarah to enter.

Breathless, Sarah said, "I walked—ran—from

Buck's place. My heel's broken and my stockings are wrecked. Pour me a drink, would you?"

Her hair had come loose and flopped over her eyes. She hadn't stopped to pick up her wrap. The shortcut through the grounds of her grandfather's house had left tears and snags from tree branches on both her dress and her bare flesh. She followed Charmain into the living room and dropped to the nearest chair, kicking off her ruined shoes.

Charmain brought her a glass of cognac. "Where's Darius? What on earth *happened?*" She perched on the arm of Sarah's chair and brushed her hair back out of her eyes. "You look as though someone dragged you through a hedge backward."

"Darius is still . . . back there. I ran. Like an idiot, I just ran! Estelle began screaming, and Darius just stood there staring at me. Jon didn't say a word. I couldn't stand the thought of facing Cecily—" Sarah gulped the cognac, choked and coughed.

"Calm down," Charmain urged, thumping her on the back. "And tell me from the beginning."

Sarah told her, not sparing herself. Charmain stood up and paced slowly in front of the fireplace. "I see. So now you want the earth to open and swallow you, I take it?"

"Something like that. I can't stand—"

"Yes, you told me. Cecily's heartbreak. You are in a unique position, my pet, in that you care for your lover's wife almost as much as you care for him. I was never faced with that situation because I loathed and detested your grandmother. She was a frigid old harridan. But that's a different story. Now, what to do with you."

"They'll all be wondering where I went," Sarah said miserably. An awful possibility occurred to her. "Oh no! Do you think Darius will come here?"

"Undoubtedly, as he's staying with me. But not until he's searched everywhere for you, I'm sure." Charmain paced more slowly for a moment, then whirled around in triumph. "Of course! We'll crank up Del's car, and you shall drive into Chicago. Get a room for the night and be on the first plane south in the morning. By this time tomorrow you can be in Mexico at my hotel. *Voila!* Two birds with one stone. A new position, a new address. You can even change your name if you wish."

The protest died on Sarah's lips. Why not? She was never going to be able to look anyone in Palerville in the eye again. Her parents would disown her, Cecily would never forgive her. It was Cecily's disillusionment that affected Sarah most. She would have given anything to have prevented that.

Charmain urged, "Come on, let's go up to my room and find some traveling clothes for you. We'll have you on your way before Darius comes storming in here."

Sarah shivered. She wasn't ready to face him either. It was much later, when she was speeding toward the city in her grandfather's old barge of a Buick, that she realized in all of her consternation she had never once given a thought to Jonathon and what he must be feeling.

En route, Sarah made a brief stop at her apartment at the Palazzo, flung clothes into a suitcase and grabbed her passport and savings passbook. She wrote a quick note to tell her parents she was safe, then was on her way again in less than ten minutes, dropping the note in the first mailbox she passed. She spent the night at a motel with paper-thin walls, a revolving and amorous clientele and pillows that reeked of tobacco.

Arriving at O'Hare Airport, she was luckier. There was a plane to Los Angeles holding a vacant seat. She didn't let out her breath until they were aloft. Halfway to California she asked herself why she was acting like a fugitive. But, of course, she knew the answer. At Los Angeles International Airport she was able to connect with a commuter flight to San Diego. But in San Diego she ran into her first problem. Charmain's hotel, the *Casa Brava*, was not near an airport, not even near a town or village. When Sarah unfolded the map Charmain had given her, the only directions proved to be a red X and an arrow pointing to a small cove about halfway down the Baja California peninsula on the Sea of Cortez. She was advised by airline personnel to check with a travel agent to see if there were any chartered buses headed that way.

The pretty Latina travel agent shook her head. "Sorry, I know of no way for you to get there other than drive yourself. There's a good road down the Baja, although you have to cross the desert to get to the Sea of Cortez. You can follow the road to here—" she pointed to a spot on Charmain's map. "I don't know what the road's like from there to that particular spot. Do you know anyone who has a four-wheel drive vehicle? That might be your best bet. By the way, *Casa Brava* means brave house. I guess you'd have to be brave to build a hotel there . . . so isolated."

Sarah considered her choices. Since she intended to stay, at least for a while, renting a four-wheel drive vehicle didn't seem too practical. She spent most of the day prowling car lots and, upon learning the cost of new vehicles, quickly switched to the used car dealers.

By late afternoon she was the somewhat nervous owner of an ancient jeep, and the graduate of a twenty-minute course of instruction from the dealer, a hyperactive man with glazed eyes set like poached eggs upon a permanently smiling face. He called one piece of advice after her as she left, "Hey, take it easy on the curves; these old jeeps will tip over if you go too fast." It wasn't the most reassuring news. Sarah decided to get a hotel room and cross the border first thing the following morning.

Fortunately the new day brought a renewed sense of adventure, and she was soon on the freeway heading south, a Mexican auto insurance policy and a Spanish-English phrase book tucked in the side compartment of her bag.

The phrase book seemed unnecessary in the dusty and bustling streets of Tijuana, where every vendor of gaudy pottery and vivid paper flowers spoke flawless English. She ran the gauntlet of the body and upholstery shops, each one quoting a lower price for "fixing her car." After that she went around the interchange twice and finally found her way to the toll road to Ensenada.

The coast was a serendipity of lace ruffles on a deep indigo sea, covered by endless clear skies and dotted with sheltered coves lined with clean surf-washed sand. In Ensenada she lunched on fresh-caught abalone and a wonderful mellow wine served by an English-speaking waiter. He advised her that she must obtain a visa from the Mexican authorities in order to proceed south of Ensenada. This was easily accomplished upon presentation of her passport. Spirits high, she followed the excellent road south. When she stopped for gas, she found that the Pemex station attendant didn't speak English. But it was easy to point to the pumps, and the car was soon filled and ready to go. Turning off the coast road to cross the peninsula, she found herself in a strangely beautiful cactus garden stretching up an incline. Tall saguaros reached reverently for the heavens, and the sunlight sparkled on golden cholla. Barrel cactus wearing flaming blossoms huddled beside heat-baked rocks.

The heat increased as she drove east, despite the waning of the afternoon sun. She was glad she had dressed in cool cotton and worn a sun visor over a protective head scarf. She was getting used to the jeep, but it wasn't the most comfortable mode of transportation. Dropping suddenly into a valley, she felt as if she had entered a blast furnace. There were few other cars on the narrow road, and she drove for miles without seeing any sign of habitation. Once a large coyote appeared at the side of the road and she jammed on the brakes, but the animal turned and sauntered back into the rocks.

After two hours she had a raging thirst and pulled over to open one of the cans of juice she'd bought in San Diego. She got out of the jeep to stretch and sip the already warm grapefruit juice. The sudden silence that enclosed her brought a sense of total isolation. She had a moment's panic. What if she couldn't get the jeep to start? She'd heard that people could die of heat prostration and thirst in a matter of hours. No, don't think of that, she admonished herself. You've got five more cans of juice and you haven't wandered from the road. As if to reassure her, a Volkswagen camper went by in a flurry of dust and a tow-headed tanned Californian waved in passing.

The jeep started easily. There were still several hours of daylight, so she would at least reach the other coast before dark.

The vegetation became even more sparse, the heat more intense. Mirages floated in the distance, and she blinked and took her eyes off the road to regain perspective. Her shoulders ached and her fingers seemed permanently bonded to the wheel. Still the road stretched endlessly through bleached rocks and drifts of empty sand.

A sudden bend in the road around a towering rock formation revealed the most breathtaking sight. Slashed across the horizon was the vivid blue of the Sea of Cortez. Sarah braked, coming to an abrupt halt in a cloud of dust.

She stared at the wild contrast of desert and sea, wanting to give a triumphant yell into the cracklingly dry air, but her parched throat constricted in protest. Her eyes gulped in visions of a vast, impossibly brilliant landscape, painted by an artist magician in colors too bold to be real.

The gulf was farther away than she realized. The desert deceived the eye, bringing distant objects close in the absolute clarity of the air. She drove at top speed now, anxious to reach the cooler air near the water.

Throughout the remainder of her drive to the coast she wondered about her destination, putting aside thoughts about the people she had left behind. Since leaving Palerville, she had pondered deeply on her relationships with the Latimers and the Conways. Even while she bitterly regretted the manner of her departure and the humiliating incident that had triggered it, she knew she had been right to leave. Buck's business practices had grown increasingly crooked. The more money he made, the more he wanted. And Jon . . . dear, sweet Jon who had been her love for so long. It seemed she had been born loving him, but he belonged to Cecily. Perhaps he always had. They were really more alike than Sarah cared to admit. Both enjoyed the quiet pursuits of reading, writing poetry, music, raising flowers and plants. Jon had once told Sarah he loved her zest for living, her willingness to try anything, go anywhere. He said he wished he had her ambition and her ability to accept any challenge. He preferred his adventures to be quests of the mind, inward journeys seeking answers to imponderable questions. All he asked of life was a quiet place in which to think and dream and write.

"And you shall have it," Sarah had told him. "Darling, don't you see, there are the dreamers of the world and we who must take care of them. We're opposites, yes, I'll grant you that. But hasn't the attraction of opposites always been one of life's great mysteries? We're two parts of one whole. You're everything I'm not."

"And you, my sweet Sarah, are brave and fearless in a way I can never be. Will you open your eyes one day and see all my timid reticence? You were never meant to live as a recluse yet, given the chance, that would be an idyllic existence for me. Odd, isn't it, that the dull gray churchmouse seeks the company of the brilliantly plumed flamingo.''

Sarah remembered those words as the offshore rocks of the gulf came closer, wondering if he had been telling her that although opposites attract, they seldom make each other happy. Despite her disagreements with Charmain's philosophy on men, Sarah had to admit that she and the older woman were kindred spirits.

Once, in a burst of indignation, Sarah's mother had referred to Charmain not as Del's mistress, probably due to her reluctance to say the word, but as an "adventuress." Sarah liked the word. It conjured up a woman who sought adventure, not of an amorous nature, but excursions into the unknown, and possibly dangerous, places of the world. Why was it that if a man were an "adventurer" it was an admirable trait, whereas an adventuress . . .

A small village appeared at the end of the road, a ragged clump of buildings around a craggy cove. She reached the only street, flanked by houses, vegetable stands and a couple of cantinas on one side and rickety boat-lined docks on the other.

An old man with a sun-parched face that scowled beneath a sombrero stepped unexpectedly into her path, waving her to a stop. Seeing a large pistol strapped to his side, Sarah complied with his wishes.

She was greeted with a burst of Spanish too fast to follow, then an outstretched hand. She promptly offered him her visa, although he was not wearing a uniform. He shook his head and repeated his question, more impatiently. He seemed to be saying something about a number, she caught *numero* in the rapid stream of Spanish.

Reasoning that the number he wanted must be the number of days she was staying, she opened her phrase book and nervously translated that she was going to the Casa Brava for an unlimited stay. She wished now she had shopped for one of those computerized translators, but she hadn't thought of it until she was purchasing insurance at the border and by then her only alternative was a phrase book.

The man with the pistol shook his head angrily and bombarded her with more Spanish. One eye on the gun, Sarah gave him her birth date, the horsepower of the jeep and every other number she could think of. Eventually, with a sigh of exasperation, he waved her on.

She drove out of the village as fast as she could, although she had planned to stop for dinner.

The sun was now setting. The travel agent had been right about the deterioration of the road leading to the Casa Brava. Soon there was no road at all, merely a rutted path beaten through the creosote and cactus, meandering as close to the water as the rocks and cliffs would allow. Twilight cast its long shadows, sharpening her uneasiness. Surely she should have reached her destination by now. But, of course, she was making much slower progress than on the paved road.

A dark shape loomed ahead. An impassable rock! She braked, sending up a cloud of sand. Straining to see through the fading light, she realized she had come to the end of the trail. There was simply nowhere to go. To her right was the sea, and all around her rocks and cliffs too steep even for the jeep to scale.

Damn Charmain's map! Damn her own stupidity. It was too late to go back to the village. She shouldn't have let that man with the pistol scare her. Someone in the village would have been able to direct her to the Casa Brava.

There was nothing for it but to spend the night here. She shut off the engine and contemplated the warm grapefruit juice that would be a poor substitute for dinner.

"*Hola . . . hola?*" A soft voice came out of the darkness. "*Señorita?*"

Two figures materialized. She caught a glimpse of crossed bandoliers, the gleam of a rifle barrel, a shiny peaked cap. *Federalis!* Thank God. She babbled in English that she was looking for the Casa Brava, then handed them her visa.

The visa was taken from her shaking fingers and examined under the beam of a flashlight. "Señorita, it is all right, you are not lost. The place you seek, see—"

The officer took her arm and turned her toward the dark cliff. He pointed to crude steps, barely distinguishable in the rock, then to the rocky point of the bluff where it jutted into the sea. She could just make out the silhouette of a building and wind-bent trees, the amber glow of lanterns.

"Casa Brava, señorita. You are there. Señor Rodriquez asked us to look for you, but we did not believe you would be so foolhardy as to travel after dark. Fortunately we heard in the village that a *gringa* with bright hair had passed through. We followed you to be sure you found your destination."

Sarah wanted to embrace him for being there, for speaking English. He and his silent companion helped her get her bags out of the jeep, then carried them up the steps hewn into the cliff. She was panting with exertion, but asked, "How on earth do they get supplies in to the hotel. Is this the only way in?"

The officer laughed. "No, señorita. It is not even the *preferred* way in. This way leads to the back door. There is a more civilized front entrance. But to reach it you would have to drive inland, away from the water, making a long detour around the hills. It is one of the difficulties of the Casa Brava."

Sarah climbed the remaining steps, wondering what other "difficulties" she would find.

At the top of the cliff, by the faint light of a wrought iron-lantern, Sarah got her first glimpse of the old hacienda: vine-covered stucco and red tiles, a long terrace marked with Spanish arches, flowers spilling from enormous clay pots.

As the silent *federalis* pulled a bell cord at the iron-studded door, the one who spoke English said,

"You must understand, señorita, that we patrol this area infrequently. This is an isolated place with no law enforcement as you understand it. There are no other dwellings nearby. The village is seventeen rough miles away, as you know. The people here choose to be alone, away from what you call civilization."

"Yes, thank you. I understand. I'm grateful that you came to show me the way."

"We are in the vicinity now only because of an unfortunate incident. Yesterday the bodies of two men were found in the hills. We are trying to determine who they were and how they died."

Chapter 9

The solid oak door of the Casa Brava yawned open before Sarah had a chance to respond to the *federalis'* startling announcement. A slim, dapper Mexican with silver hair and matching handlebar mustache stood on the threshold. "Señorita Latimer! Ah, you followed Charmain's map!"

Laughing heartily, Ramon Rodriquez introduced himself, shook Sarah's hand warmly and greeted the *federalis*. Sarah returned the greeting and found herself being ushered into a spacious adobe-floored kitchen. Intricate blue and white tiles decorated the walls, and a mammoth wood-burning stove with a black hood caught her eye at once. Through an archway at the far end of the room she caught a glimpse of massive Spanish Colonial dining tables, flanked by high-backed chairs.

Realizing the two federal officers had not entered the

room with her, Sarah turned as Ramon started to close the door behind them. "Wait, what did you say about finding bodies?"

But it was too late, the *federalis* were gone. Ramon, who appeared to be in his fifties, although he moved with the vigor of a much younger man, threw out his hands in a gesture of exasperation.

"Those *federalis!* They frighten you with stories about bodies, eh? Do not worry. No doubt the two were hunters who accidentally shot one another. Or perhaps fools who went into the desert without sufficient water. There is no reason to suspect foul play. No need to worry about *banditos.*"

It hadn't occurred to Sarah to worry about bandits before that moment. Nor was there time to dwell on the possibility. Ramon was intent on showing her to her room so that she could bathe away the dust of the journey and enjoy the meal he had prepared for her. He had been expecting her since Charmain's phone call.

She followed Ramon along a narrow hall, lit by wood and iron wall lights, each bearing three red glass globes. When Sarah admired them, she was told they were called *triangulos.* As Ramon opened the door to her room, he pointed with pride to the thickness of the adobe wall. "Two feet thick, Señorita Latimer. The Casa Brava is built to stand forever. Withstand any storm."

"Please, you must call me Sarah," she said as he placed her suitcases on a hand-braided rug beside a comfortable bed covered with a striped quilt. The many colors in the room vibrated with a pleasant warmth.

Ramon replied suavely, "Thank you, Sarah. You will call me Ramon. Come to the kitchen when you are ready and I will feed you royally."

After he left, Sarah went to the window. As she'd hoped, it faced the sea. Outside the French doors, a narrow flagged terrace abutted a strip of grass marking the edge of the bluff. The dark mass of the Sea of

Cortez lay beyond. The hotel was not perched too far above the beach, she guessed, judging by the closeness of the soft lapping of waves against sand. No doubt the bluff was higher on the inland side. The old hacienda had probably been built on that spot in order to have the protection of both sea and rocky cliffs. But when Ramon converted it to a hotel, he had disregarded the fact that the terrain that had discouraged marauders would also hamper the arrival of guests.

Sarah turned her attention to the adjacent bathroom. There was an enormous old-fashioned tub surrounded by the same pretty blue and white tiles she'd seen in the kitchen. No shower.

The water proved to be only tepid and she didn't linger. Bedroom and bath cooled rapidly as night fell over desert and sea. Sarah dressed quickly, not wanting to close the windows. She put on a long-sleeved cotton madras dress, tied a scarf around her waist as a sash, threw a shawl over her shoulders and went back to the kitchen. It was filled with mouth-watering aromas. Ramon had set two places at a small wrought iron tile-topped table in a corner of the kitchen near the archway. The dining room beyond was still dark and deserted, but the light from the kitchen showed an antique upright piano on one wall, and a handsome brick fireplace nestled in one corner. An enormous carved mahogany sideboard added a homelike touch certain to appeal to dining guests.

Ramon had eyes the color of ripe olives, with a rogue's sparkle in their depths. He pulled out a chair for her. "Tonight I enjoy your company alone. I feed the others early. I want to hear all about my new partner. I am fascinated by the señora. Forgive my rudeness, but I have so many questions about Charmain."

Sarah smiled. She could almost hear Charmain's admonition, "Retain a little mystery, darling. Never tell all."

There was a delicious paella yielding all sorts of

surprises, from plump shrimp to crisp vegetables, followed by tamales both savory and sweet. Sarah enjoyed the food and Ramon's company. He was so obviously bowled over by Charmain, whom he had met years previously on a Hawaiian vacation, that Sarah wondered if he'd really wanted a partner in his hotel or had simply wanted Charmain.

After she had fielded numerous questions about Charmain, Sarah asked about the Casa Brava and learned that it had indeed been a hacienda in the old days.

Her host refilled her wine glass. "All the land you can see belonged to the *padrone* who lived here. Cattle and horses roamed where the desert now claims the land. Some of my more educated friends tell me that deserts are growing, living things, continually seeking to enlarge their borders. I do not know. I found this place, abandoned, nothing standing but the stout adobe walls. In the morning you will see there is an arroyo close by, and there I found the ruins of many peons' huts. I think those huts can become cottages, the many rooms of the hacienda guest bedrooms."

He smiled ruefully. "I was a young man then. There was never enough money to . . . what do you call? Ah, restore, as I wanted. I fix two cottages, some of the hacienda rooms. Not many people come. A few fishermen. One or two wanted to stay permanently. There are now three permanent residents. Sometimes we get overnight guests, but the road is bad. The new road is far to the south, so tourists go that way."

Ramon got up and went to the stove. Opening its door, he threw in several logs and soon a blazing fire warmed the room. The firelight danced on the patina of smoothly worn adobe tile and painted a mellow light on the brightly colored clay pots from which the food was served. "Charmain has great plans for the Casa Brava," he continued. "She will invite her friends, bring many new guests. When the cottages are finished and the plumbing is fixed . . ."

Sarah was too sated with food and wine, warmed by the fire and sleepy from the journey to note the ominous reference to the hotel's poor financial status and faulty plumbing.

The following morning Sarah awakened to the sight of the sun rising over the black hills on the far shore of the Sea of Cortez. She stood at the uncurtained windows and gazed in awe as the first radiant shafts of light pierced the darkness, probed the skies, then slipped over the edge of the earth and bathed the water in gentle morning sunlight.

As she had concluded, the hacienda was built close to the sea. The main building sprawled on a plateau just above sea level, but at some time a valley had been carved inland, perhaps by flash floods. The sand had eroded away from the base of the rocks so that a portion of the land was actually below sea level. It was to this point that she had driven the jeep.

There were several terraces and patios. Breakfast was served on a sheltered brick patio overlooking the sea. Small tables were set around a triple-tiered stone fountain made lively by a profusion of red and pink geraniums in clay pots.

Two elderly men, eating together, lowered yellowing newspapers to look at her and say, *"Buenos días, señorita."* Their dark skins contrasted with white hair, their expressions were contented.

A very old lady sat alone, sipping thoughtfully from a gold-rimmed teacup. A tiny apricot-colored poodle waited expectantly for her to drop crumbs of *pan dulce*. The woman didn't look in Sarah's direction and ignored Sarah's greeting.

"Mrs. Jerome," Ramon explained, placing a dish of melon balls on a table and pulling out a chair. "Very deaf. She'll speak to you when she sees you. Her husband was a famous author; he wrote under another name, I don't remember what it was. His books were not translated into Spanish. He came here to write years ago. After he died, she stayed. The two old gentlemen are retired merchants from Mexico City, lost their wives in the same plane crash. Now, Sarah, you must try my *rancheros huevos.*"

Sarah devoured the spicy eggs, contrasting the leisurely breakfast to her usual fast orange juice and coffee. The mellow air here seemed to preclude haste in any activity. She thought of Morocco and the similar soothing quality of the desert air there, but that thought brought Darius Descartes to mind and disturbed her tranquility. She remembered the look on his face as he surveyed her and Jonathon in each other's arms. It had been the angry, stricken stare of a man betrayed. Damn Descartes, what claim did he have on her? What right to judge? And why, for heaven's sake, did she care what he thought about her? The odd thing was, she did. She wanted him to respect and admire her, although she couldn't imagine why.

As Mrs. Jerome left the patio she peered in surprise at Sarah, then smiled. The tiny poodle trotted behind her. Ramon, bringing a pot of rich Mexican coffee, bellowed an introduction. He came to Sarah but she shook her head. "No, no more, thank you."

"There are a couple of other guests who will be down soon. I cannot leave just now, but when Margarita or Consuela arrive—they are my nieces who help me with the housekeeping—I'll show you around. I want everything just so for Charmain's arrival, so you must point out whatever offends the eye."

"I can't imagine anything here offending the eye," Sarah said fervently. "But I'd love to explore on my own, if I may." She wasn't sure of her status. If she was going to help run the place, there was much she needed to know. But perhaps it would be better to await Charmain's arrival before pressing Ramon for information.

In the harsh daylight, she saw that much of the ancient adobe and tile was in need of repair. Ramon had lovingly restored his kitchen and several other rooms. The bathroom in her room was in working order, but the others had reluctant toilets and the water heater couldn't keep pace with the demand for hot water. Ancient pipes grumbled and wheezed alarmingly, despite the lack of guests. If all the rooms were occupied, the plumbing simply wouldn't be able to cope.

But there were delightful discoveries too. A huge banquet hall was dusty and unused, but perfect for dancing and shows. The long row of peons' huts in the adjacent *arroyo* would make perfect cottages. Ramon had restored two of them to their original adobe and tile design, but Sarah saw that it would be faster and cheaper to tear down the ruined adobe walls and re-build with frame and stucco.

After converting two of the peons' huts, Ramon had no doubt run out of money. Well, he'd have to learn to make compromises. It would be too expensive and time-consuming to restore the hacienda exactly to its original splendor.

The most pressing need of all was for a direct route to the Casa Brava. There had to be some way for guests to avoid the long detour from the main highway now required to skirt the fortresslike rocks. Sarah eyed the indigo waters of the sea thoughtfully, wondering if ferry boats from the village were the answer.

By noon Sarah had covered most of the Casa Brava. The sun now blazed with debilitating fury, and she gave in to the silent call of the blue waters of the gulf. The beach below the hotel was deserted. Under foot the sand was fine as chalk, almost white, marked with tufts of hardy grasses scattered among the rocks at the base of the cliff. The high tide mark was more than halfway up the bluff upon which the hacienda was built.

Sarah plunged into the warm sea, floated, then swam away from shore. Despite its temperature, the water was refreshing. She lay on her back and admired the serene bay. The hacienda sprawling across the rocky bluff was exactly right for its setting. In her mind's eye, she placed one of the Palazzo monstrosities on the same spot and shuddered.

Swimming back to the shore, she was astonished at the variety of shells scattered on the beach. It was a veritable gift shop for the picking. Some were totally unfamiliar, others exotic cousins of familiar sand dollars and sea urchins. She wandered around the tide pools for a while, then placed her towel on the sand and lay down. She closed her eyes and absorbed sun and air into winter-starved skin.

A deep male voice said in English, "I thought only mad dogs and Englishmen went out in the midday sun."

The sun blinded her as she opened her eyes and looked up through a funnel of exploding prisms at the silhouetted figure standing over her. Her first thought was that the hard-muscled body, deeply tanned, clothed only in brief swim trunks, was poised in a threatening stance, as if ready to fling itself upon her. Darius Descartes had the body of an athlete, all sculpted planes and hollows, exuding strength and vitality and the illusion of forward movement even when motionless.

Shielding her eyes with her hand, she sat up. "What are you doing here?"

Darius dropped to the sand beside her. "I brought Charmain. She's exhausted and taking a siesta. She insisted she had to get out of Palerville immediately or run the risk of going after Latimers and Conways with a broom. Apparently she once gave her word to your grandfather that she would never do battle with his family."

Sarah was silent, uncomfortably aware of the closeness of his thigh beside hers, of the hand he placed on the sand behind her. He wasn't touching her, yet his body sent messages that made her skin burn and her ears ring. She was also excruciatingly aware of how she had fled, leaving him at the party. That thought brought a stinging flush to her cheeks.

"By the way," he said lightly, "the Cinderella scene at your cousin's house was ill-advised. When caught red-handed, it's always better to brazen it out. Running away merely confirms everyone's worst suspicions."

"Why don't you just mind your own business?" Sarah jumped to her feet, snatched up her towel and wrapped it around her.

He was on his feet instantly, his hand snaking out to catch her wrist to prevent her from leaving. "You *invited* me to accompany you to that party. It was not only ill-bred to make love to the guest of honor in his father-in-law's house, but also ill-mannered to leave your escort stranded. We won't even go into the morality of stealing the husband of a woman confined to a wheelchair."

"Damn you! How dare you judge me! Let me go! You don't know what you're talking about."

He jerked her wrist, pulling her closer. "You were in love with the melancholy-looking Mr. Conway when you were both children. He married Cecily after accidentally crippling her, no doubt expecting her wealthy father to support both of them in a life of leisure. But Buck Latimer put the would-be poet to work instead. And you, my lovely, went away but couldn't forget your lost love. You want him now only because you can't have him. Believe me, it's a dilemma I understand well."

Sarah wanted to hit him. Instead she pulled her wrist free and ran. Over the sigh of the sea and the whisper of a breeze, the sound of mocking laughter followed her.

Charmain emerged from her siesta, refreshed and radiant in a pale lilac silk gown, to find Sarah hiding out in her room. The older woman's eyes took in Sarah's bathrobe and bare feet in shrewd appraisal. "Hello, sweets, what do you think of our hotel? Isn't it wonderfully eccentric, like its new owner?"

"I don't think old Del left you enough money to fix it. How long is Darius staying?"

Charmain sat on a carved mahogany sanctuary bench that stood in the window alcove. "Ah, I see. You're too embarrassed to face Darius. Well, he was angry, of course, but not dismayed. I doubt anything dismays him. Tell me, what do you think of Ramon? Isn't he divinely handsome? Wait till you see us tango!"

Sarah pressed her fingers to her brow. "I've a vile headache. I don't think I'll come to dinner tonight."

"And will you have a headache tomorrow too? And the day after that? Darius plans to spend some time in Mexico. He'll fly down to Mazatlán for a couple of days, then come back here. You might as well face him now."

"Fly? Where's the airport?"

"It's more of a clearing really, a two-hour drive down the coast. Darius has a private plane. He flew us in, then we drove up here. I'd have suggested you wait and come with us, but I thought perhaps you wouldn't want to travel with Darius."

Sarah was tempted to announce that if he stayed, she was leaving, but that seemed too childish. After all, he was a friend of Charmain's. "What about Ramon, old bean? How is he going to feel if a couple of females start running things?"

Charmain shrugged her slim shoulders and smiled seductively. "You leave Ramon to me. Come on now, pet, get dressed. Wear your most flamboyant gown and bold makeup and put on a don't-give-a-damn smile. If you're going to play the part of the scarlet woman, you might as well enjoy all of the advantages."

"Scarlet woman? Come on now!"

"Why, you told me yourself you were caught in the arms of Cecily's husband. Darius saw you. You can hardly pretend it didn't happen. So you should smile secretively and drive Darius wild with jealousy."

"Charlie, you old reprobate, I don't want to make

Darius jealous. I just want him to go away and leave me alone."

"Of course, dear." Charmain got up and went to the closet, ran her hand along the short row of dresses. She turned away. "Which atrociously antifeminine couturier persuaded you these rags were designed for a woman's body? I'll fetch you something pretty to wear."

"Those are designer originals—" Sarah began, then shook her head in exasperation as Charmain disappeared through the door.

Sarah went to dinner wearing a fuchsia skirt of sheerest gauze, flounced and full, with a delicate off-the-shoulder blouse of palest lavender. A vivid yellow sash cinched her waist. A younger, more carefree Sarah had regarded herself in the mottled dresser mirror, and it didn't occur to her until later in the evening that the outfit was not something Charmain would have bought for herself, nor even worn. Not to mention that the woven sandals were Sarah's size seven rather than Charmain's size five.

Dinner was in the main dining room tonight, served at a massive mahogany table. The silverware and pewter dishes glowed in the candlelight, and wonderful aromas of spicy *salsa*, marinated beef and freshly baked rolls wafted over the room.

Ramon had prepared enough food for a small army. Including himself there were only seven diners, and Sarah wondered what would happen to the large portions that were sure to be left over. But these thoughts could not distract her from Darius's warm breath in her ear as he pulled out a chair for her and murmured, "You look enchanting, as always. Do you have any idea of the effect you have on a man?"

Sarah was more concerned with the effect he was having on her. She was still seething from his remarks on the beach about Jonathon, yet despite her anger, she found all of her senses more finely tuned when Darius was near. There was an excitement in the air. Probably akin to that of a swordsman about to begin a duel, she decided.

Rather than responding to his remark, since she certainly didn't want him to think she'd forgiven his earlier taunts, she turned to Charmain and whispered, "We're going to have to speak to Ramon about preparing so much food. The refrigerators don't stay cold enough to keep what's left. I think maybe the generator's on the blink."

Charmain gave her a reproachful glance. "Oh, let's not hurt his feelings. He's putting on a show for us tonight. I'm sure he doesn't usually prepare so many dishes."

Darius said, "I, for one, intend to eat like a Persian pasha."

Ignoring him, Sarah said in her best executive tone, "We must have a business meeting. First thing in . . ." She faltered under the onslaught of an outrageously teasing glint in his eyes and a cheeky smile that made her feel pompous.

Raising his glass to her, he said, "To the loveliest businessman I know."

That did it. Her first assessment of him was correct. Women belonged in the boudoir and the kitchen where they could be maneuvered and manipulated by men. She remembered with sudden aching clarity why she had loved Jon. Still loved him. . . .

Dinner proceeded at a leisurely pace. Sarah answered remarks addressed to her with a monosyllable. The many glasses of wine consumed by the diners sparkled almost as much as the conversation between Darius and Charmain. Both were fully informed on everything happening everywhere in the world. But underlying their pronouncements and observations there was always that banter—teasing and flirtatious. They had fun with each other.

Darius kept trying to draw Sarah into the conversation, but she resisted his efforts. If she didn't keep her distance, she would be lulled by the sheer charm of the man and would be caught offguard again when he delivered one of his rapier thrusts. Several times, though, she couldn't help smiling at his wit, and once she had to smother a laugh.

After a while he gave up trying to include Sarah in the repartee and concentrated on Charmain. Sarah felt curiously left out, like a child who in pouting punishes only herself. The food was delicious, but her palate was dulled by her mood. All his fault. What right did he have to sit in judgment of anyone? If only Darius hadn't seen her in Jon's arms!

When the meal ended, Ramon tore his adoring gaze away from Charmain and unhooked a guitar from the wall. He began to play softly, serenading Charmain in a rich baritone. The haunting Spanish song needed no translation. Sarah stood up and excused herself curtly. No one pleaded that she stay.

The sadly sweet notes of the love song followed her along the twilit corridor to her room. She paced the floor restlessly for a moment, then opened the French doors and stepped out onto the terrace. The sea was almost too beautiful, moonlight playing on the waves like floating quicksilver. She turned away, searching the gaunt outline of the rocky coast with eyes that were suddenly misted by perplexing tears, longing for something that could have been hers, but was not.

A flash of light, gone almost before she could be aware of it, penetrated the inky darkness of the bluffs on the other side of the bay. A second later another finger of light swept the cliff—almost as if someone were signaling.

Chapter 10

Charmain swept regally into the kitchen as Sarah finished taking inventory of the china. "My dear child, I do hope you haven't been counting the plates." Her aristocratic nostrils wrinkled with distaste. It was embarrassing enough when you badgered Ramon about his account books. After all, sweets, you don't even read Spanish."

Sarah looked up from the inventory sheet. "Numbers are the same, old bean. I can read pesos as well as dollars, and I've seen enough to know we're in trouble if you've inherited all of his unpaid debts—which I suspect you have."

A velvet-eyed maid, little more than a child, was scrubbing pots at the sink. She was one of Ramon's numerous nieces. Charmain smiled sweetly at her, then hissed between her teeth at Sarah, "I won't have you acting like a badly brought up *gringa*. Manners are important anywhere, but especially so here. We are not going to sacrifice courtesy for Yankee business acumen."

Sarah looked her straight in the eye. "Just how much did you actually pay Ramon for this so-called partnership."

Charmain regarded her shoe, arching a high instep between stiletto heel and pointed toe. When she looked up at Sarah, her eyebrows were also arched in an expression that clearly indicated she considered the question in poor taste. She tapped her toe again and said, "I thought we might go sailing this morning. Ramon has a nice little boat. We can make some tiny sandwiches, chill a bottle of chablis."

The exasperated expulsion of Sarah's breath was lost on her. She continued, "I'll wear the white eyelet with my straw boater; I can tie a chiffon scarf over it to keep it on if the breeze freshens. Darling, please don't wear shorts or trousers. Ramon is of the old school, and he'll be shocked by anything other than a dress." She added encouragingly, "We shan't be expected to work as deckhands or anything like that."

"You've come a long way, baby," Sarah muttered. "Look, your ladyship, I don't know how long it will be before you fire me, or your friend Darius infuriates me enough that I quit, but before I go, believe me, this place will be paying its own way."

Charmain's china blue eyes expressed regret. "You're much too intense, pet. Life has a habit of smoothing out the bumps for those who don't fight it."

"Very profound, Charmain *chérie*," Darius uttered from the doorway. Sarah turned to find his dark eyes on her. She was uncomfortably aware of her faded jeans and scruffy shirt, but she had been rummaging through a dusty storeroom, working while the two of them slept late.

Darius went to the coffee pot and poured himself a cup. The young maid stared at him in open admiration. He wore a light tan safari shirt and matching slacks that looked cool and comfortable and softened by wear. He gave Sarah a one-sided smile that was part questioning, part mocking. "*Buenos días, señorita, como está?*"

"Good morning," Sarah responded. "I'm busy, thank you." She studied the inventory sheet.

"We're going sailing, Darius darling," Charmain announced gaily. "As soon as Ramon comes back from his fishing expedition."

"Fishing!" Sarah repeated simmering with indignation. "He went fishing when there is so much to be done in this white elephant?"

"Sweetie, there isn't any hurry, is there? Can't we just relax and let matters take their course?" Charmain appealed to Darius. "Speak to her, darling. She's rather like you in that she must live every moment as if it were her last."

"If it were my last," Sarah said, "I wouldn't spend it working."

"I believe what Charmain means," Darius commented, "is that your sense of urgency makes it difficult for you to take advantage of some new and promising possibility. In that respect we're quite unalike. I'm always ready to explore new experiences."

"So I've noticed."

"Look at you. Here you are in this exotic and beautiful country and instead of reveling in your surroundings, you're counting spoons. Charmain, my love, it might just be Sarah's form of penance. That wonderful old guilt complex at work. If our dear Sarah can find absolution in the monotonous task of taking inventory, perhaps we shouldn't interfere?"

"Guilt? I don't feel guilty about anything," Sarah snapped, despite her resolve not to get into an argument with him.

"Oh? Then why did you beat such a hasty and ignominious retreat from the Conways' party?"

Sarah felt a flush start up her cheeks. She was about to say that the incident with Jonathon had been misunderstood, that they'd been saying goodbye, when she remembered something Charmain had once told her, *"Never* explain anything, darling. It just confirms suspicions."

Turning to Charmain, Sarah said, "If the housekeeper shows up, tell her I'm going through the linen supplies. That is, if she speaks English, otherwise I'll need Ramon to translate. But only until I get the computerized translator I'm ordering from San Diego."

Darius said, "You should learn the language. Spanish is a musical tongue. Punching phrases into a hand-held computer can't possibly replace the human voice, no matter how halting and clumsy its mastery of a foreign language."

"There's one human voice I can do without at present," Sarah said, still smarting under his taunt, "yours."

She tried to slam the door as she left the room, but the heavy carved wood swung silently behind her.

The corridors of the hacienda were empty, despite the lateness of the hour. There were no hurrying maids pushing carts of fresh linens, no clean-up crews or maintenance people, no bellhops ushering new guests. But why should there be? Sarah had determined as best she could from Ramon's haphazard records of the past three months that only one party of guests had stayed for more than a single night. Without the three permanent residents, there would have been virtually no income. Casa Brava was run more like a private home than a hotel.

She had just located the first linen closet when Darius caught up with her. She didn't need to look around to know who was at her side. She felt his presence in the sudden warmth of the surface of her skin, the tingling sensation down her spine. As she reached for the door, his hand closed over her wrist. To cover her confusion she snapped, "Must you keep touching me?"

His index finger gently stroked the back of her hand before releasing her. "Yes, I'm afraid it's becoming a compulsion. Every time I see you I want to sweep you into my arms."

For a split second she had the wild desire to be swept into his arms. She didn't dare challenge his gaze in case he realized the impact he was having on her. "What do you want—no, don't answer that. What is it you wish to say to me?"

"Before you wear yourself out trying to turn this place into a model of American efficiency, let me take you somewhere. There's something I want you to see."

"I can't imagine—" she began.

He placed his hand solemnly over his heart. "I swear

by all that's holy to me, I will be a model of decorum. Further, I shall not mention Jonathon Conway or his plucky young wife all day long. Come on, Ramon is back and he's taking Charmain for a sail around the bay. You can't communicate with anyone without him."

Sarah hesitated, looking at her clothes.

"You don't need to change. Please, come with me. You see, Charmain is very dear to me. If she weren't, I'd simply let you rush headlong into a frenzy of organization. But I feel extremely protective toward Charmain and am compelled, therefore, to set you straight on a few matters. There's something I can show you that might make you look at the Casa Brava with clearer vision."

"All right," Sarah agreed grudgingly. "I suppose it is Charmain's hotel."

They left by the front doors, which opened onto a brick and tile plaza built around another magnificent stone fountain. An ancient gardener was lovingly tending an olive tree almost as gnarled as himself. Sarah glanced in his direction, thinking of the drying chaparral she had seen dangerously close to the former peons' huts. It could go up in flames at any moment, and there were more weeds than grass in the strip of lawn at the edge of the bluff.

As though reading her thoughts, Darius said, "I understand he is Ramon's elderly uncle. He volunteers his services and is rightly more concerned with an ancient and venerable tree than in manicuring lawns. I've traveled extensively in Mexico, Sarah, and can tell you that what may appear to be lethargic procrastination is more likely to be an awareness of what is important and what isn't. Priorities, I believe you'd say."

There was a rugged-looking vehicle parked on the hard-packed dirt at the bottom of the terraced steps. Darius opened the passenger door for her and assisted her into the seat. "Why do I get the impression that you find my habits and standards a source of amusement? Old world contempt for American know-how? What nationality are you, anyway?"

The engine roared to life. Darius eased the car away from the plaza slowly, apparently not wishing to create a dust cloud. "I'm a dual citizen, French father but born in England of an English mother. I consider myself a citizen of the world, though. I travel constantly and maintain three permanent residences—the villa in Morocco, a charming cottage in Surrey, a house in the south of France. I also keep apartments in Manhattan and London."

Of course, Sarah thought. Filthy rich. Probably never had to worry about a balance sheet in his life. "How far are we going?" she asked.

He flipped on the air conditioning. "Not far. Your seat reclines, if you'd like to relax. And the refrigerator behind you is well-stocked with cold drinks."

She looked around. "What kind of car is this?"

"I believe it was originally one of your American Ram Chargers. I bought it in San Diego from a dealer who said it had been 'customized,' whatever that means, for a client who didn't take delivery. It seemed suitable for the terrain, so I had it driven down to the village before Charmain and I left Palerville."

The uneven ground was miraculously smooth under the Charger's wheels, and she drew an air-conditioned breath, remembering her own blistering drive in the old jeep. "It must be nice simply to issue orders and have things placed exactly where you want them."

He glanced at her out of the corner of his eye. "If I had that kind of power, I'd have ordered you placed in my sole custody. Oh, Sarah, to have been born a couple of hundred years ago. I could have simply carried you off."

"You *are* carrying me off," she pointed out. "How much farther?"

They drove along the ridge of rocky hills, then turned south. The bleached, glittering desert dazzled beneath ultramarine skies. A jackrabbit scurried out of their path for the cover of a clump of sagebrush. "Where are we going, Darius, and what has it to do with the Casa Brava?"

"Isn't one picture worth a thousand words? Be patient. If I could have explained, I would have. You must see for yourself."

He turned the wheel, and they skirted a towering rock formation shaped vaguely like a crouching gorilla. A moment later the sea came into view. They followed the coast, sometimes on the remnants of a road, but mostly on a rutted path of packed sand.

Seeing the gulf in daylight, from the comfort of an air-conditioned car, was a revelation. The delicate hues of the offshore rocks, pale shrimp blending with soft beige and creamy yellow, were reflected on the clear calm surface of the water. Darius sensed that she was now ready to lose herself in the unadorned beauty of desert and sea, and he was silent. She marveled silently at the sweeping symmetry of the sand dunes, at the power of the sea slowly carving its will into the rocks.

They came to a sandbar, dark gray and forlorn, and crossed it cautiously. Another cove came into view and, rising from the beach like a misplaced outpost on an alien planet, was a domelike structure of concrete and steel. Its vast proportions dwarfed the companion cliffs.

Sarah stared in amazement as Darius brought the car to a stop before a wide ramp leading to a gaping doorway. An eerie stillness hung about the huge building. There was no sign of life.

Taking Darius's hand as he helped her down from the car, she thought of stories of lost desert fortresses, of Beau Geste using dead legionnaires to create the illusion he was not the last man alive. The size of the abandoned structure was mind-numbing. She craned her neck to look up to its pinnacle.

"Makes one feel a little like Gulliver arriving in Brobdingnag, doesn't it?" Darius said as they ascended the ramp.

Feeling more like an anthropologist coming upon the totem of an unknown tribe, she said, "What on earth is it? Who built it? It seems modern yet old. Is there anyone here? It looks deserted—"

She broke off as they reached the top of the ramp and stepped through the wide doorway. The moment they were under the great dome her voice echoed with a thunderous roar, startling her. Darius slipped his arm across her shoulder reassuringly. "You sound like the voice of doom," he whispered, smiling. "It was to have been a hotel and casino. Investors gambled millions on a dream that never became reality."

They stood for a minute, looking at the mammoth circle that was designed to be the casino. Something indistinguishable fluttered high above their heads. Sarah shivered. Feeling her tremble, Darius led her outside to the comforting warmth of the sun. She looked back at the ruins of a mad fantasy, wondering how long the sturdy dome would last. Centuries, perhaps, so that future generations would come to wonder at its purpose. Would they recognize it as a cathedral in which to pursue the myth of easy wealth?

"I'd read about this place," Darius said in his normal voice. "It was a relief to find that Charmain had invested in a converted hacienda. Think how much worse it might have been if she'd bought a monstrosity like this."

"I still don't understand why you wanted me to see it."

"The Casa Brava is at least in tune with its setting. And Ramon is living an uncomplicated and remarkably happy life. I don't think you should make too many changes. Charmain fell in love with the Casa Brava as it is, and as it is it will outlast other vainglorious efforts that have been defeated by the Baja."

"Have you ever visited a resort hotel like the ones

that are springing up in the most unlikely spots? I see no reason why the Casa Brava can't be as successful. There's fishing, sailing, a wonderful beach. After we've finished the restoration, we can get some entertainers down here—a combo so we can have dancing in the old banquet hall. Maybe buy some catamarans and scuba equipment to rent. Charmain's hotel doesn't have to end up like this nightmare. I wouldn't change the appearance of the Casa, it's perfect for its setting. But so much can be done to attract more business—"

His eyes rolled. "That's exactly the kind of thinking I was hoping to circumvent. Let's get our lunch and take it down to the beach. It's a trifle warm for such grandiose plans."

Annoyed by the amusement in his tone, she said, "I agreed to come and look, not spend the day with you. I'd like to go back, I have work to do."

"I have chilled crab salad and papayas in the fridge. Couldn't you spare half an hour? The chef will be hurt otherwise."

There seemed no gracious way to refuse, so Sarah agreed. They walked down to the crescent of beach, and Darius spread a checkered cloth on the white sand. "I thought Ramon went riding. Which chef prepared this?"

He regarded her solemnly. "I did."

"So," she said lightly, "you speak several languages, drive race cars at Le Mans, deal in imports and exports, tango and cook. Is there anything you don't do?"

A beach umbrella was driven into the sand with a single sure motion. He dropped down beside her in the circle of shade. His eyes were dark mirrors reflecting his surroundings rather than offering any glimpse of his feelings. "I suppose I've done everything but the one thing I want most to do."

"And that is?"

"Oh, no, I don't believe the time's ripe to divulge my most heartfelt desire. It would leave me too vulnerable, perhaps even prey to your amusement."

"Heaven forbid that anyone would laugh at you. But it's all right for you to belittle other people's dreams. Especially if they're mere women."

He looked genuinely surprised. "But I adore women. I always have."

"I was referring to your attitude toward my plans for the Casa Brava. That infuriating, oh-the-little-woman-is-off-on-another-tangent—"

He leaned closer. "As you surmised, I'm quite wealthy. With the right incentive, I could restore your crumbling hacienda, convert it to our Baja retreat, and you'd never have to reduce it to a mecca for tourists with peeling sunburns and dangling cameras."

His fingers slid up her arm, pushed a strand of hair back from her face. The touch of his hand, even through the material of her shirt, was disturbingly intimate. "You're the most exciting and attractive woman I've ever known, and I'll admit to knowing plenty. I don't know what it is about you that makes me want you with such utter disregard for the consequences, because you're a tigress likely to cause a man many sleepless nights."

His hand had lingered, rubbing her chin lightly, as he spoke. She pushed it away. "You're wasting your time. Now if we're going to talk instead of eat . . ."

He opened the container of salad, produced two china plates from inside the hamper he'd brought from the car. There were wineglasses, linen napkins and silver fish forks. He turned a corkscrew in the wine bottle, and gave her a glass of delicately dry white wine. Sarah half expected a butler to appear to serve them, but Darius accomplished this as smoothly as everything else. They ate in silence, and she was surprised both by her appetite and the excellence of the food.

As hunger was appeased, she wondered why she had not found his words more infuriating than she had. He was a man who should not be given an inch. He'd made another blatant pass, this time practically offering financial rewards in return for sexual favors. And all she'd done was suggest they eat lunch. It must be the heat of the desert and the remoteness of the setting that tempered anger with caution. She could hardly walk home.

She finished a fragrantly delicious slice of papaya and said, "Charmain told me you'd be flying to Mazatlán. Soon, I hope? I'm not sure how long I'll be able to maintain a mask of politeness for Charmain's sake. I find your manner offensive and your presence irritating. I don't know how to put it any more clearly than that."

His eyes met hers in a glance that seemed to plumb the depths of thoughts she wasn't aware she harbored. "You feel that electricity we generate together. You've felt it since we first met."

"Is that what it is? I thought it was intense dislike."

"Are you ever going to get over your lost love, Sarah? Do you really believe the somber Mr. Conway would have made you happy? He'd have made you miserable, and he, poor fool, wouldn't have known what he had in you. You'd have wasted valuable time being bewildered by one another."

She jumped to her feet, almost knocking the umbrella from its mooring. "Damn you! You swore you wouldn't mention Jonathon. Take me back this minute, or I'll . . . I'll—"

"Walk? There's no need. I'll take you back." He stood up, his expression mocking. "And in regard to your question, I'll be leaving for Mazatlán this afternoon, so you will not have to endure my intolerable presence for much longer. Come on, help me pick up the remnants. After all, I did prepare lunch."

She gathered plates and cutlery, her fingers trembling with anger. Dariuus said softly, "You should have had an affair with him. It would have gotten all those childish passions out of your system and made you realize how much you've both changed since the days you were childhood sweethearts."

Enraged beyond endurance, Sarah scooped up the hamper and ran toward the car. She had just reached a cluster of rocks shaded by a wizened mesquite bush when Darius called out sharply, "Stop! Don't move. There's a snake under that bush."

Sarah froze. She heard the rattle then, close. The snake was coiled, head rearing, only a few feet away. Her heart hammered in her throat. Almost instantly, Darius was at her side. She felt his hand push her firmly away. He stepped in front of her. "Very slowly now . . . step backward. No sudden movements."

She complied, her knees shaking. Darius looked back at her over his shoulder. When she was safely back on the beach, he began to inch one foot down the rocky slope, unhurried, eyes fixed on the rattlesnake.

When he was at least beside her, she said hoarsely, "Why didn't you kill it?"

He gave her a chastening glance. "Why? This is his home, not ours. We're the intruders. Why should he die because we chose to invade his territory? Come on, we'll walk around the other side of the rock. And in the future we'll remember that reptiles prefer the shade during the heat of the day, just as we do."

Chapter 11

After Darius left for Mazatlán, Sarah set about making a list of items sorely needed by the Casa Brava, including the crucial plumbing equipment. She sent her order to a firm in California that had been one of the Palazzo suppliers. Then she went to work planning an advertising campaign to attract guests. Later on, when we're in the black, she thought, I'll get an agency to handle that end of the business.

Charmain and Ramon were so wrapped up with each other that Sarah was left to her own devices. She threw herself into her work and was grateful she was busy enought to put Jonathon out of her thoughts most of the time. But late at night she found herself agonizing over what Cecily's reaction must have been to their betrayal. Poor sweet Cecily, stabbed in the back by the two people she loved most on earth. If only, oh, if only it hadn't happened. Yet nothing had happened, and that made it all the more unbearable.

Funny how she missed Cecily. Ever since Cecily had married Jon, Sarah had lived with the belief that they were rivals, enemies even. Yet now she realized that Cecily had always provided a quiet haven when Buck or Estelle or even Jonathon exasperated her. Cecily had offered a brand of loyalty that was irreplaceable.

Several times during those sleepness nights Sarah thought she saw signal lights across the bay. Once when she asked Ramon about them, he looked a trifle taken aback and replied quickly that it must have been moonlight reflecting on something, a car windshield perhaps.

A party of fishermen arrived, noisy and boisterous in the evening after their quiet hours on the sea. When they left, the Casa Brava seemed silent and empty. Sarah waited impatiently for the shipment of goods from California, anxious to get things moving. Ramon's staff, which seemed to consist mainly of his relatives, smiled encouragingly when Sarah tried, with the aid of her phrase book, to get them to perform various tasks, but she usually ended up doing them herself.

She fell into bed exhausted most nights after vigorous cleaning and weeding and reorganizing. Ramon promised that a work crew of strong young nephews would arrive the moment they had the plumbing supplies and lumber to convert the peons' huts. Sarah had finally won a long argument with Ramon about the proposed cottages. He wanted to restore the crumbling adobe, but she insisted that wood frame and stucco would be faster and cheaper.

One evening, as they were finishing another of Ramon's incredible dinners, Sarah heard the back door thud, as though someone had shoved it with great force. She looked up, "Did you hear that?"

Ramon tore his eyes reluctantly from Charmain, who looked tonight like Marlene Dietrich in *The Blue Angel.* "Pardon?"

"It sounded like someone came in the back door."

"No one comes up those cliff steps at night," Charmain declared.

Ramon said, "My friends the *federalis* have traveled south, and they are the only ones who would enter my house unannounced."

"Someone just came in the kitchen door," Sarah insisted. "It's too heavy to blow shut. Besides, it's protected from the wind by the outer wall." She rose, placing her napkin beside her plate. "I'll go and see who it is."

Ramon jumped to his feet. "I will go. Please, finish your meal."

After he departed Charmain said, "Probably just one of his visiting relatives."

"They always come in the front doors, they all live to the north. There's no reason for them to travel all that way inland to go around the hills."

"Didn't you tell me you came up the cliff steps when you first arrived? Perhaps we've another guest—" Charmain broke off as the dining room door burst open.

Ramon, his eyes flashing a silent warning, was pushed into the room. Behind him two men in dust-covered ponchos prodded him with large handguns.

Charmain stifled a gasp. Sarah leaped to her feet. There was a rapid burst of Spanish from the taller of the two men, who wore an almost comically exaggerated drooping mustache and Vandyke beard. Ramon translated quickly, "Don't move. Put your hands on the table in front of you."

He was shoved to one of the high-backed chairs. The tall man pushed his gun into his belt and reached under his poncho to unhook a coil of rope from his shoulder. He began to tie Ramon to the chair. The other man, short and powerfully built, grinned at the two women, revealing tobacco-stained teeth and intensifying a deep scar running from his lower lip to the point of his chin. He reached for a roll and stuffed it, almost whole, into his mouth. At the same time he pushed up the brim of his hat with the barrel of his gun. His eyes traveled slowly up and down Sarah.

After the initial shock passed, Sarah was able to consider the condition of the invaders' clothes, the mud-spattered boots, the unshaved face of the man with the scar, the straggling mustache and beard of the tall man. She thought of the flashes of light she'd seen in the hills and of the *federalis* finding the bodies of the two hunters. Then she took a quick mental count of the

people in the hotel. The two elderly gentlemen had
ordered dinner sent to their cottage, as had Mrs.
Jerome. Ramon's young niece, Consuela, was still here
cleaning the kitchen. One able-bodied man, a couple of
old ladies and gentlemen, a child and herself. How
many bandits were there? These two seemed uncon-
cerned about the occupants of the rest of the rooms,
indicating there was at least one more man with them.

Sarah looked at Ramon. "What do they want?" she
whispered.

"To hide here. They've been watching and know we
are few. We must—"

The man tying the rope struck him across the mouth,
momentarily silencing him. Roman, glaring, spat out a
Spanish oath. He was given a second blow that left a
smear of blood on his lip. The bandit reached for his
gun and it leaped into his hand.

Charmain rose majestically. "Stop that this instant!"
A pair of silver tongs lay on the platter of *pan dulce* and
she picked them up, parrying with her weapon as she
advanced on the man abusing Ramon. "How dare you
burst in here like this? You great lumbering beast!
Don't you dare strike him again."

The man backed off in amazement as she prodded
him with the tongs, deflecting the gun barrel with a
ringing sound. Sarah held her breath, not daring to
move, but the man was so completely nonplussed that
he turned the gun away and tried to ward off the tongs
with his other hand.

The second bandit's mouth dropped open, spewing
forth bread crumbs. The sight of his companion held at
bay by a wisp of a woman proved too much for him. He
roared with laughter. His companion glared at him,
then shoved his gun back into his belt and grabbed
Charmain's wrist with one hand as his arm went around
her, lifting her from the floor.

She struggled and continued to berate him, his
ancestry, his hygiene and his lack of chivalry. Sarah
was surprised by the saltiness of Charmain's invectives

and grateful the two bandits didn't seem to understand English.

Sarah stepped forward and clutched the bandit's arm that imprisoned Charmain. *"Señor, por favor . . .* don't hurt her—"

"Don't you dare grovel to these animals, Sal!" Charmain snapped. She jabbed her stiletto heel into the knee of the man holding her. He shouted with pain and dropped her. Sarah flung her arms around Charmain to restrain her.

Ramon cried, "Please, do as they say. These are desperate men."

"I will not be intimidated," Charmain said, quivering with rage.

"Listen, old girl, save the heroics for later," Sarah hissed between clenched teeth. "Those aren't water pistols."

The two bandits now closed in, roughly pulling the two women apart. Fingers bit into Sarah's arms, and she was propelled through the dining room door and along the hall. From the indignant and breathless protests behind her, Sarah knew Charmain was hard on her heels.

They were taken to the nearest bedroom. Sarah's heart lurched at the sight of the bed and its implications. She went sprawling on the floor as the bandit released her. The second man, with Charmain in his arms, strode across the room and dropped her on the bed. At the same moment there was a heart-wrenching scream.

Consuela, Sarah thought, closing her eyes in silent prayer. As she'd feared, there was at least one other bandit. Rolling over onto her back, she looked up at the man who had shoved her into the room. He looked at his partner and grinned, jerking his head in the direction of the scream that now seemed to hang in the air with terrible finality.

Out of the corner of her eye she saw the bedside table. It held a telephone. But many of the extension lines weren't working, and the men had surely cut the outside wires. She inched backward across the floor. Her back connected with the bed, and she cautiously pulled herself up beside Charmain.

The two bandits were speaking to each other, their heads close together. The voice of one rose and the other interrupted. They were arguing. Beside her, Charmain whispered, "Don't despair. Perhaps one of the others phoned for help. They may not know about the cottages."

Sarah nodded, admiring Charmain's optimism.

"Besides," Charmain added, "Darius is due back any moment."

One of the men turned and shouted at her, *"Silencio!"*

The other was gesturing with his hands and pleading some unknown cause. Seconds later the door was kicked open, and a third man entered. Crushed against his chest was a terrified bundle. Consuela's eyes sought Sarah in mute pleading as she was dumped on the bed.

The third man was as trail-dusted and ferocious-looking as the other two. In the instant before he spoke, Sarah had the wild impression that the trio was almost too fierce in appearance, as if they'd been costumed and made up by some central casting agent.

"Amigos," the newly arrived bandit said, waving his hands and pointing to each of the women in turn. *"Uno, dos, tres . . ."*

One for each of us, Sarah translated silently. Oh, God, no, please, no.

Darius Descartes turned away impatiently. "Fakes. All of them. You're wasting my time."

The antique dealer shook his head vehemently. The tropical heat had turned the small store into a steam room. A ceiling fan lazily stirred the clammy air. Every inch of space was jammed with pottery and statuary. Glass cases housed onyx and jade and an array of silver pieces that gleamed persuasively. Over all hung the odor of ancient dust and the musty smell acquired by long unused objects. But there was no sign of the genuine Aztec pieces Darius had been assured he would find.

He moved carefully through the obstacle course toward the door, annoyed that he'd wasted his time. The dealer's protests followed him outside to the damp heat of the deserted street. Summer had come and the tourists had departed, wisely awaiting the return of autumn's gentler climate. The waiting taxi driver regarded him disinterestedly from beneath the brim of a handsome straw Panama hat. *"Señor?"*

"Take me to the airfield," Darius said in Spanish.

The trip hadn't been entirely wasted. He'd found a genuine gold lip ornament in the form of a serpent, as well as stone sculptures of Huitzilopochtli, the war god, and Tlaloc, the rain god. A certain Arab collector would pay handsomely for the three pieces.

Although his trip down the Baja Peninsula had ostensibly been prompted by his search for the Aztec pieces, Darius would have found some other reason to leave the Casa Brava. He was uncomfortably aware that if he didn't get away from Sarah Latimer for a while, he was in danger of making a complete fool of himself. The traditional Descartes pride forbade such loss of face, particularly over a woman.

At the airfield he had to wait while his twin-engine Cessna was washed free of dust and refueled. He paced in the shade of a rusting hangar, sipping rich Mexican beer, telling himself he should fly straight back to San Diego, pick up his Lear jet and put as much distance as possible between his lust and the object of it.

Charmain's so-called hotel would probably stumble along for a while, with Sarah's efficient help. Both women were obviously ready for the adventure and challenge of converting the rambling old hacienda into a real hotel. After all, Charmain had only recently been turned loose after years with Del Latimer. And Sarah . . .

Darius frowned and absentmindedly crushed the beer can before tossing it into a refuse container. Sarah was in love with Jonathon Conway and desperate to get away from the temptation to drift into an affair with him. It was just as simple and as agonizing as that. It hadn't taken a genius to fill in the missing pieces of Sarah's story, even though Charmain had adamantly refused to discuss Sarah's past with him.

"Dear boy," Charmain had cooed, "Sarah is *unattached*. What more do you need to know about her than that? Your father wouldn't have cared if she'd been a sultan's wife, guarded by an army of eunuchs. *He* would have known what to do and wouldn't have hesitated a second."

The conversation had taken place in Del Latimer's house while Sarah was in California. Darius had surveyed the French antiques Charmain had imported after the death of Del's wife. "Were you happy with him, *chérie?*"

Charmain shrugged. "There are degrees of happiness."

"Does Sarah know . . . any of your past? I mean, before you met and entranced her grandfather."

"No. And I would advise you not to tell her. At least not until—"

"When?"

Charmain had given him a veiled and mysterious glance and murmured, "You'll know when the right time comes. Or perhaps I shall tell her myself. For now I don't wish her to be influenced by nostalgia. She will think I'm foisting you upon her in order to relive my affair with your father. An old woman's yearning for lost youth."

"What about Conway? How formidable a rival is he? I understand they were engaged while they were in college and his marriage to Cecily took place suddenly and unexpectedly after the accident that paralyzed her."

Charmain had shaken a finger at him reprovingly.

"Life, my young friend, is lived *forward*, not backward. Which makes it marvelous, because we can make it up as we go along."

The Cessna was now ready, and Darius climbed into the cockpit, turned on the radio and waited for clearance to take off. He hadn't confessed to Charmain how deeply he'd been affected by Sarah. At first he'd been amused by the way Charmain had contrived to get them together and merely curious about the young woman being championed by one of the greatest courtesans the world had ever seen. Darius had long ago forgiven Charmain for destroying his father. She hadn't been able to help herself—any more than the flame was guilty of the moth's death.

How blithely he, Darius, had agreed to the little charade of inducing Sarah to visit his villa in Morocco. Why hadn't he known that Charmain would choose her successor with great deliberation and care?

No, by God, history would not repeat itself. Another Descartes would not love a woman unable to return his adoration in equal measure. Sarah Latimer would not be allowed to insinuate herself into his thoughts and senses this way. It wasn't too late to turn away from that folly. Only when her feelings matched his own would he allow her to become an irreplaceable part of his total being.

The Cessna roared aloft into the brilliant sky, its course resolutely set for San Diego rather than the primitive airstrip south of the Casa Brava.

Chapter 12

The third bandit wore a red shirt and, having dropped Consuela, turned his attention to Sarah. Seizing a handful of her hair, he jerked her face upward. She forced herself to look him straight in the eyes and tried not to shake in terror. Deep-set eyes, almost black, matching his hair, squinted down at her. She said, "*Habla inglés? Por favor, señor . . .*" She stumbled over the most elementary Spanish phrases.

Behind him, the other two were discarding their ponchos. It was evident that red shirt was their leader and they'd been waiting for his permission to proceed with whatever plans they had for the women. He grinned at Sarah. "*Si.* I speak *inglés*. You are one pretty *gringa*. Tell Carlos how much you love him, *si?*"

His accented English was almost comically bad, and his complexion seemed too pale to match the black hair. But there wasn't time to speculate on this.

Glancing out of the corner of her eye, Sarah saw that Charmain had gathered the sobbing Consuela into her arms and now held her protectively. Sarah forced herself to smile at Carlos. "What's the hurry? Can't we get to know one another first? There's food and wine in the dining room. Why force a woman who might be more exciting if you courted her a little?"

She lay perfectly still. Carlos leaned over her, his hand still tangled in her hair. She could feel Consuela's sobs shaking the bed, and smell Charmain's perfume faintly, almost lost under the onslaught of Carlos's unwashed clothes and sweat. Only minutes had elapsed since the bandits shoved Ramon into the dining room, yet Sarah felt as though time had slowed to a nightmare crawl. Her brain functioned in slow motion too. She tried to clear her mind and think. What could be done?

Try to talk them out of it, an inner voice whispered urgently. At the same time the worry grew over what Charmain would do. She'd fight tooth and nail, of course. She's old and frail, but she thinks she's a match for anyone. What will they do to her?

"Carlos?" Sarah said, using his name, trying to make him accept her as another human being. "Please don't rush things. There's no need. I understand, I really do. You must have been driven by desperate circumstances—" No! she suddenly thought. Don't use English words that might be unfamiliar to him, that will just enrage him. His expression was tightening again. "I mean, I'm sorry, for whatever caused you to feel pain, hurt."

He blinked rapidly, as though he had something in his eye. The feeling that he wasn't what he was pretending to be surfaced again, but just then the taller of his two accomplices approached the bed and grabbed Consuela's cotton dress. There was a hideous tearing sound, accompanied by the child's panicked cry. Charmain shrieked at him to leave her alone, batted at his hands, but he was too intent on ripping away the dress to notice.

"Carlos! Please, she's only a child," Sarah begged, struggling to sit up. "Have pity—"

The telephone rang with sudden startling clarity.

Everyone froze into instant silence. The shrill ring was repeated; insistent, demanding. Sarah was ridiculously grateful for the interruption, brief though she knew it would be. She knew she must formulate some plan, but her mind was a frightening blank.

Carlos let go of her hair and thumped the shoulder of the man tearing at Consuela's clothing. Shouting angrily in Spanish, Carlos pointed toward the ringing telephone. The other bandit looked sheepish, muttered a reply.

He was supposed to cut the wires, Sarah thought, but somehow had not. Now for the first time she looked around the room. The half open closet door revealed several of Ramon's embroidered shirts. This was his room. Ramon had a private line, an intercom hooked up to the kitchen and the cottages housing the retired men and Mrs. Jerome. When they cut the main lines, they'd missed it. Not that it would do them any good, since the elderly guests could hardly come to their rescue.

Sarah said quickly, "They'll be suspicious if we don't answer. The person on the other end of that line will know the phone is ringing. The *federalis* were here recently; they said they'd call to check on us." If the bandits had been watching the hotel, they'd know this was true.

Carlos dragged her to her feet. She was pushed over to the telephone. He kept one hand on her throat, ready to choke off any unauthorized conversation. She had to hold her head at an uncomfortable angle in order to bring the receiver to her ear. Her voice was hoarse. *"Hola? Casa Brava."*

Mrs. Jerome's voice shrieked, "Well, of course it is. Who is this? Is this Miss D'Evelyn?"

Sarah wondered only fleetingly at the implication of the question. She said, "No, it's Miss Latimer. Ramon is . . ." She thought, tied up right now, but said, "Not here. Is there something I can do for you?"

"Yes, there is. I was promised a bottle of wine with my dinner and I didn't get it. Chesney needs a glass of sherry before retiring. It really isn't too much to ask, is it?"

"Chesney?" Sarah repeated faintly.

"My little companion. Will you please bring the sherry yourself, Miss Latimer? It's so hot and sticky tonight I've already undressed. I don't want Ramon to bring it. I have my reputation to consider. Besides, Chesney is a bit out of sorts tonight and when he is he can't stand his own gender."

Chesney, her poodle. Sarah blinked, the conversation seemed grotesquely humorous but she didn't feel like laughing. She didn't remember ever seeing Mrs. Jerome, or Chesney, partake of wine. The deaf old lady had shouted so loudly that Carlos must have heard what she said. Sarah turned the receiver away from her mouth and looked at him questioningly.

He nodded. Sarah said, "Someone will be along with the sherry in a few minutes, Mrs. Jerome."

"Not 'someone'—you—" the old lady bellowed, but Carlos snatched the phone from Sarah and slammed it down.

Sarah said, "Let Consuela take the wine to her."

Carlos turned to the man holding Consuela and spoke in Spanish. For a moment Sarah thought he was agreeable to letting the child go, but Carlos said, "*You* will go, pretty *gringa*. But first, who is that woman and who is Chesney and where are they?" His Spanish accent was slipping, she noticed.

"She's a guest, Chesney is her dog." There didn't seem to be any point in lying. "There are some old peons' huts in the arroyo. We're converting them to cottages for guests."

"How many people there?"

Sarah hesitated. His Spanish accent was definitely less noticeable. She stared into his black eyes, a suspicion forming. "There's just the old lady and her poodle," she lied. Would there be some way to warn the two old men? Could they go for help? What was the Spanish word for help . . . *socorro?*

Carlos shouted, "Miguel, *vamos.*"

The taller of the bandits drew his pistol from his belt and gestured for Sarah to lead the way. She flung a reassuring glance at Charmain and Consuela. Carlos was ripping the telephone wire out of the wall.

Heart thumping, Sarah led the way to the dining

room. Ramon made muffled sounds behind a napkin that had been stuffed into his mouth as a gag. She saw his arms strain at his bonds. She went to the mahogany sideboard and selected a bottle of sherry, placed it on a tray with a glass. She assumed Chesney drank from his bowl.

Bottle and glass rattled nervously as Miguel followed her outside. They crossed the brick terrace to the path leading down a rocky slope to the cottages. Sarah prayed that the two old gentlemen wouldn't have their lights on in the front room of their cottage. She was lucky; it was dark and silent, apparently unoccupied, as they passed.

The door to Mrs. Jerome's cottage was illuminated by the soft glow of an amber lantern. Miguel drew back into the shadows, pistol in hand, as Sarah knocked on the door. Sarah had decided her only chance would be to write a note for the deaf old lady, but now there seemed to be no hope.

A tiny grilled window, permitting guests to observe visitors, was slid back. Mrs. Jerome's voice yelled, "It's about time. Chesney wanted to retire early. Put the tray down on the doorstep and I'll get it. But don't leave yet. Stand over there in the bushes in case you brought the wrong wine. Chesney is particular about his sherry. Go on, I'm not dressed."

The old lady seemed excessively modest about being seen in her bathrobe, But Sarah was too distracted to consider that Mrs. Jerome was acting strangely. Sarah hesitated, unsure what to do, and looked at Miguel. He motioned for her to obey the order.

Placing the tray carefully on the brick step, Sarah moved back toward the bushes.

Instantly all was confusion. Blurred images, sharp sounds. Sarah blinked as the door was flung wide open and a dark shape hurled itself outside and tackled Miguel. Two silhouettes blended, broke away, crashed at each other again. The barrel of Miguel's pistol gleamed in the dim light. There was the sickening thud of bone meeting flesh and the clatter of the gun falling to the brick step. The two shadows fell after it, one of them crashing against the adobe wall. The lantern over the door went out, plunging everything into inky darkness.

A beam of light flooded the scene. Sarah looked up to see Miguel flat on the ground, Darius astride his back. The two *federalis* emerged from behind the cottage, their powerful flashlight blinding Darius, who shielded his eyes. "It's about time you two arrived," he said, keeping his knee in Miguel's back as one of the officers snapped on a handcuff and hauled the bandit to his feet. Darius leaped up and came to Sarah. She was swept into his arms in a fierce embrace. "Are you all right? Did they hurt you?"

She shook her head, feeling herself tremble as reaction set in, grateful for the comfort of his arms. She leaned against him, clinging to him, and felt his lips press a kiss to her forehead. She gasped against his chest, "Charmain and Consuela! Two more of them— in the main building."

The officer who spoke English approached. *"Señorita,* you've had a frightening experience. But you must show us which room."

"No," Darius said, his arms tightening about her. "You should never have let these damned *banditos* get this far." He looked down at Sarah nestled against him. "They've been tailing them for days. I'd like to know how the hell they got into the Casa Brava."

Sarah nestled closer to him, feeling fear evaporate, luxuriating in the sense of being safe, protected.

The officer added in a low, urgent tone, *"Señorita,* if you can get them to open the door, perhaps we can avoid further shooting."

"Yes, of course, I'll go." Sarah lingered for one more comforting moment in Darius's arms, then pulled away reluctantly. Darius said, "I'll go too."

"No, *señor,"* the agent said firmly. "You will be more valuable here keeping an eye on him." He pointed to Miguel, now handcuffed but looking anything but cowed.

A moment later Sarah acompanied the two officers up the path to the terrace, leaving Darius guarding Miguel with the bandit's own gun.

As they hurried back toward the main building, Sarah thought about the phone call from Mrs. Jerome. A ruse to get at least one of the women free. She marveled at the old woman's acting ability and presence of mind. Darius must have put her up to it.

The officer said, "When we reach the room where the other ladies are, you will call out that the other *bandito,* Miguel, has fallen and has broken his leg. Then get out of the way and let us do the rest."

Carlos and his henchman were apparently so surprised Sarah had returned alone that they opened the bedroom door and walked into the hands of the two federal officers.

Charmain, looking unruffled, led Consuela from the room and went straight to the dining room to release Ramon.

Minutes later they were all assembled in the front of the Casa Brava as the federal officers prepared to load the three handcuffed bandits into their car. Darius was still angry that the women had been placed in jeopardy by men who had been under surveillance. Piecing together what had happened, Sarah understood that Darius had landed at the airstrip earlier in the day and had driven to the Casa Brava. At the bottom of the steps hewn into the rock he had been stopped by the two *federalis,* who had seen three men climbing the steps in a suspicious and stealthy manner and wanted to investigate before proceeding. The federal officers had been tailing the bandits who killed the hunters earlier.

"Those men," one officer explained to Darius patiently, "had escaped from prison in Tijuana. We captured them early this morning. So we wondered who was sneaking into the Casa Brava."

Darius looked from him to the three handcuffed men. "You don't know who these men are? How did you know they were up to no good?"

"Law officers learn to recognize certain signs." He smiled. "And the two old gentlemen went looking for a nightcap. They found Ramon tied up in the dining room, and he persuaded them to leave him, so as not to arouse suspicion, and go for help. He knew we were scouring the hills for the two escaped prisoners and weren't far away."

His partner, who had been studying the bandits, suddenly held up his hand. *"Por favor!"* He walked over to Carlos and reached up to grasp his black mustache. It came away in his hand. A moment later the sombrero and curly black wig lay on the ground. Without them, Carlos proved to be dirty blond with squinting black eyes.

"Norteamericanos," the agent said, his suspicions satisfied.

The other officer moved closer to stare at Carlos. "I believe the eyes will be a different color without the contact lenses." He flashed a triumphant glance at Darius.

Chapter 13

The following morning sunrise brought tranquillity back to the Casa Brava's mellow adobe walls, but not to its occupants. Darius confronted two obstinate women when he insisted the previous night's incident proved the danger of remaining in this isolated place.

Charmain, looking cool and lovely in pastel pink,

calmly selected a slice of fresh mango and placed it on her breakfast plate. "Nonsense, darling."

Sarah, chin jutting, declared, "If anything, the incident proved how safe we are here. The three men were Americans. The *federalis* came in time. Nothing happened to us."

"By what twisted reasoning do you arrive at that little gem of wisdom?" Darius demanded. "You were manhandled, almost raped, and you feel *safe?*"

"Safer than facing a mugger on the streets of any American city, or European city for that matter," Sarah exclaimed. "It was unfortunate, but it isn't going to drive us away. Right, Charlie?"

Darius swore soundly in Arabic, which was the only language adequate to express his feelings.

"Darlings!" Charmain interrupted. "Let's not quarrel on such a lovely morning. Do sit down, Darius, you're towering over us like an avenging god."

"I'm leaving for San Diego. I was on my way there when some instinct told me to stop over and check up on you."

"If you're inferring that you came to our rescue, it seems to me that the two *federalis* didn't really need your help. You just couldn't resist showing off your unarmed combat techniques," Sarah challenged, her warm feelings of the previous evening vanishing under his obvious scorn. She'd always loathed men who flaunted their physical superiority over women. "All you did, as far as I'm concerned, was to exhibit recklessly foolish bravado—tackling a man with a gun."

"Now, now, sweets," Charmain chided. "Never, ever, belittle a man for making a gallant gesture even if you do think it was foolhardy."

"What about his belittling us? Suggesting we're two crackpot women who have no business being loose without a keeper?"

Sarah was secretly grateful to him and more than a little impressed by his courage. But he hadn't changed his imperious attitude toward her and that annoyed her no end. Her mixed feelings were baffling. She supposed it was impossible not to find him dynamic, but she still harbored the suspicion he was the kind of man who relished the chase more than the conquest, and she was loathe to let him win.

Ignoring her, Darius said to Charmain, "I have some business to attend to in the States. My answering service can find me if you need me. Meantime, here's the name of a reliable pilot in San Diego. He can be here two hours after you call him." He dropped a card on the table, then bent and brushed Charmain's cheek with his lips. "Take care and treat poor old Ramon gently."

Darius straightened up, dark eyes searching Sarah's face. Then with a single swift movement he seized her face between his hands and kissed her full on the mouth, as hungrily and demandingly as if they were alone.

For an instant she responded, unable to stop herself. There was spontaneous combustion when his mouth closed with hers. Every nerve in her body flared to life and her voice of reason was momentarily stilled. When it made itself heard, she pulled away, furious with herself for giving in, if only for a second.

He regarded her with a mocking lift to his eyebrows. "Some day, my dear Miss Latimer, you'll discover that while it's true he travels fastest who travels alone, it's more fun in tandem. *Au revoir.*"

Charmain smothered a giggle as Darius ran lightly down the terrace steps. Sarah wiped her mouth angrily on her napkin, picked up her glass and choked on the orange juice.

"Sal, sweet love, you're never going to prevail in any encounter with a Descartes. And who'd want to? Life can be delicious for a woman when she allows a man like Darius to take care of her."

Sarah's eyes rolled upward. "I don't believe I'm

hearing this. Not in the enlightened eighties. But we've more important things to discuss. He was right about our vulnerability. We've got to keep that back door locked. And we need to hire some regular help. A night clerk, for one thing. Once we've filled the place with people, staff and guests, we won't be so vulnerable. When Ramon gets back with the phone repairman and our lines are hooked up, I'll call San Diego and see what's holding up our order."

Charmain regarded her quizzically. "Aren't you the least bit attracted to him?"

Sarah stared at her untouched plate. "Look, ducks, I've never lied to you, so I won't now. Descartes *is* a hunk. But this isn't the right time for me to get involved with *anyone*. Especially not a man who makes me feel like a female Judas."

Charmain leaned forward. "You've heard that rebound romances are often illusions. Is that it?"

"No," Sarah said shortly, not wanting to hear Charmain point out Jonathon's shortcomings, since she always confused his gentleness and sensitivity with weakness. "It's simply that I don't want to be another notch on Darius's gun. Charlie, you of all people should recognize a seduction scene when you see one. I want something more lasting from a man."

"Like Jonathon Conway has given you? An everlasting state of limbo?"

Wincing inwardly, Sarah excused herself and left. She spent an exasperating day. By the time Ramon returned in the late afternoon and the telephone lines were repaired, all of the San Diego offices were closed. She went into the bathroom to wash her hair, but as soon as she was covered with lather, the water dwindled to a trickle.

Wrapping a towel around her head, she went in search of Ramon. He gave an apologetic smile. "Bad leak in main pipe. When the new connections come, I fix."

"And what do we do for water in the meantime?"

"Open the old well, bring in buckets."

Within a few days, Sarah looked back on this inconvenience as being the merest ripple on the surface of a sea of woes that rose rapidly into a tidal wave. The firm in San Diego who were supposed to send the plumbing fixtures and other sorely needed materials kept fobbing her off with excuses for delayed delivery. Then the phone lines died again. Charmain brought her the news that taxes were due on the hotel and that their food and wine suppliers had not been paid. The final catastrophe came when the electricity went out.

"The generator," Ramon explained sadly. "She is old."

"Charlie," Sarah said grimly, "time for a war council. Come on, Ramon, you too." She ushered them into the dining room where they settled around the long table.

The situation was even more bleak than Sarah anticipated. They needed money for taxes, a new generator, plumbing supplies, past due bills. Not to mention materials for finishing the renovation and building the cottages. Sarah had believed the small balance in Charmain's checking account could be augmented by an infusion from her savings account. But Charmain didn't have a savings account.

"But . . . grandfather's estate . . . all the money you inherited," Sarah cried weakly, "what happened to it?"

Charmain studied her shell pink nails carefully. "Darling, it's extremely *gauche* to discuss money with such bald-faced abandon."

"Tough bananas, old girl. What happened to the loot?"

The graceful hands waved airily. "If you must know, it's gone. Used up, darling."

"But how? Where?"

"Well!" Charmain frowned. "My little excursion to

Europe and Africa was mostly on credit. Then too, I had a few debts before I left. Quite a few, actually. I bought the Casa Brava, of course. Sal, love, try to understand. Del was extremely generous, but all those years I lived with him, I was always the *recipient,* if you know what I mean. There were so many dear friends I wanted to give to, not just little gifts, but tokens of what I really felt for them."

Sarah thought of the sapphire and diamond brooch she had received. Charmain had claimed it belonged to Sarah's grandmother, but her grandmother, who had died when she was a small child, had been a plainly dressed woman who made a religion of frugality. She was not the type of woman who would accept or even wear such an expensive ornament. Charmain had bought the brooch herself and given it to Sarah. How many similarly extravagant gifts had been bestowed to reduce an inheritance of at least a million dollars to a few hundred in a checking account? But even Charmain couldn't have let that much slip through her fingers.

"What about Del's house in Palerville? You'll have proceeds from that. With all that land right in the middle of town, it should be worth—"

"Sweets, I deeded it to the town to be used as a museum and a park. It was always Del's dream to have a museum of early Americana in Palerville. And I felt so guilty I put all of his beloved pieces in storage or away in the attic. Perhaps you don't remember, but your grandfather had all of those machines—nickelodeons, slot machines, early phonographs. I was fascinated by them, but I couldn't *live* with them. So I've arranged to have them all cleaned and restored and put on display. It seemed a fitting epitaph."

"A museum takes money—maintenance and a curator," Sarah said. "I suppose you had to set up a trust?"

Charmain nodded. "Don't be cross, dear."

"I'm not, Charlie," Sarah said. She was thinking of

Darius's visit to Palerville. It had been to help Charmain set up a museum. He must have known how little working capital she'd have left to run the Casa Brava. He probably intended to bail her out, but that was before Sarah moved in. "I'm just a bit worried about how we're going to operate the hotel without capital. Didn't you put anything aside for that?"

"I thought—" Charmain waved her hands vaguely. "The rent money from the permanent guests, the fishing groups and tours that would come, we could pay our way out of that."

Sarah groaned. "I think I'd better make up a complete financial profile. See exactly where we stand. I have a little in my savings."

By the end of the month her savings were gone too. Mrs. Jerome was threatening to leave unless the electric service was restored, and the only overnight guests who had made the torturous journey over the desert road had refused to pay their bills because there was no hot water.

Even Charmain's optimism was fading. The San Diego company was still stalling with their order. Repeated phone calls never got Sarah past the president's secretary, despite the fact that a twenty percent deposit had been sent with the order.

Sarah paced restlessly in the small room adjacent to the kitchen, which Ramon referred to as "the office." Charmain came in with a tray of aromatic coffee and freshly baked *pan dulce* as Sarah glared resentfully at the telephone.

"Darling, I can't let you worry like this. We shall simply have to sell the hotel."

"To whom? Do you think rich *gringas* with more money than sense grow on trees?" Immediately contrite, Sarah said, "Oh, God, I didn't mean that, old bean. Forgive me."

"It's all right, dear." Charmain offered the tray of *pan dulce*. "Have a sweet roll, they're scrumptious."

Sarah bit into a cinnamon-sugared delight, not really tasting it. "You know, if we could get the plumbing working properly and the parts Ramon said he needs to patch up the generator, we could keep going. Damn that company—I've given them seventy-five percent of their Southern California business over the last five years—" She broke off. "Of course! Jonathon is still giving them business. I'll call him, get him to use his influence. If they're threatened with losing the Palazzo account—"

Charmain said quickly, "I don't know, love. About calling Jonathon, I mean. Do you really want the family to know where we are?"

"Especially Jonathon? Is that what you're inferring? I know you find it hard to believe, but Jon and I didn't *do* anything. It was a bum rap, as they say in the old movies."

"Yes, but, well, I've a premonition that a call to him would be an invitation . . ."

Sarah wasn't listening, she was already dialing the long distance operator.

Jonathon wasn't in his office. Patty, sounding harried, promised to have him call back.

His call came early the following day. Sarah was so glad to hear his voice, concerned, caring, that she found herself blurting out all of their misfortunes. She broke off at last. "Jon, I'm sorry to unload on you like this. I haven't even asked how you are, or how Cecily is." She wanted to add, and has the gossip about us died down? But she resisted probing old miseries.

"We're fine. Don't worry about anything. I'll call San Diego and find out what happened to your order. What do you need mostly desperately? Is there an airfield near by or can you wait for a truck?"

"Jon, we needed everything *yesterday,* but no, don't fly anything down. As long as we know it's coming, we can hold out."

"Good. Now give me directions to the Casa Brava.

Perhaps the truck driver got lost with the first delivery."

They waited expectantly for almost a week. Mrs. Jerome had been placated and had promised to stay out the month. There was no further word from Jonathon or from San Diego. As the weekend drew near, Sarah began to worry that perhaps Jon had paid lip service to his promise with an ineffectual call to San Diego and then put her out of his mind. No, he wouldn't do that. But why hadn't the truck arrived? She was too proud to call Jon again, and there seemed little point in calling San Diego.

Charmain kept up a brave front, assuring her that their supplies would certainly arrive. She wrote scores of postcards to everyone she knew, announcing that the hotel would be ready to receive guests by late summer. Privately Sarah wished she felt as confident.

On Saturday morning she had just returned from a quick swim before breakfast and was contemplating washing off the salt water with a meager amount of cold fresh water from the well, when Ramon came to her door. His swarthy face was wreathed in smiles. "Come! See what I see?"

They went onto the bluff where they could survey the desert plain below, stretching forever in the clear air. Two clouds of dust approached, one larger than the other. "A very big truck," Ramon said, "and a smaller one. They will be here in an hour. Then we fix pipes, mend generator, and have big party to celebrate."

Sarah said a silent prayer of thanks and raced for her room so she would be washed, dressed and have eaten before the trucks arrived. This would be a busy day. Good old Jonathon, he hadn't let her down after all. Later, when the supplies were unloaded, she would call and thank him.

She and Charmain, as well as Ramon and some of his relatives, were waiting on the terrace when the truck, having detoured around the cliffs, came grinding to a halt at the front of the Casa Brava. But Sarah was not looking at the delivery truck. She was watching the approach of a smaller vehicle that had somehow crossed the Baja Peninsula and negotiated the last miles of rough road. Danny Cowan looked at Sarah through the dust-filmed windshield of the specially equipped van, giving her his usual disapproving frown.

Sarah stood quite still, a small numbing tension growing between her eyes, her feet rooted to the spot, as the truck door swung open and Jonathon climbed down. A moment later Danny was operating the lift gate that allowed Cecily's wheelchair to descend to the ground.

Chapter 14

When the confusion of greetings, hugs, expressions of surprise slowed to the point where Sarah could speak, she asked Ramon to supervise the unloading of the supplies while she and Charmain ushered their visitors into the hotel.

Cecily looked pale after the long journey, but she bubbled with barely suppressed emotion as she explained their unexpected arrival. Sipping the cold fruit juice Sarah offered, but declining the offer of a room to rest, she said, "There's so much we have to tell you that just can't wait."

Sarah couldn't look Cecily in the eyes, nor could she fathom the excitement bursting from her cousin. Sarah could imagine, however, what Estelle had told her about finding Jon and herself in each other's arms. No doubt the story had been embellished, and Sarah's flight had confirmed her guilt.

Before that nagging worry could fester any further, Cecily burst in, "First I want to apologize to you, Sarah, for my mother's reprehensible behavior. I knew she was jealous of you, but I didn't think she'd sink so low as to make up awful stories about you and Jon."

Jonathon's expression was carefully blank. He watched his wife, letting her hold the floor. Cecily's eyes burned with a fierce determination that seemed out of place in her frail body. "As though anyone would believe such a thing of you and Jon! Why, you're both the most honorable, dear, wonderful people in the world. Sarah, please don't judge mother too harshly. You know how devastated she was by my accident. It made her overprotective of me. I suppose she could never understand why the most handsome, intelligent and charming man in town would want to marry me. I think that's why she worried about you working with Jon. You're so beautiful, so bright and clever, she thought I simply couldn't compare and I'd lose him to you. She doesn't know you two as I do. We have to make allowances for her."

Sarah swallowed a lump in her throat. She didn't look at Jonathon. "Cecily, I should have stayed, explained, but—"

"You didn't want to expose Mother's pettiness," Cecily finished for her. "And I love you for it. You'd rather go away and let people think the worst of you than let everyone know Mother lied."

"Oh, Cecily—" Sarah exclaimed, unable to stand Cecily's rationalization. But Charmain instantly rose to her feet and moved between them, flashing Sarah a warning look that clearly said: don't you dare shatter the poor child's illusions.

Charmain bent to refill Cecily's glass. "Sarah's integrity is more important to her than silly rumors, dear. Besides, she realized that your husband would have explained to you what really happened."

Taking his cue, Jonathon said, "I told Cecily we were just saying goodbye, Sarah. And about your reasons for quitting—the California fiasco and Buck's broken promises."

Cecily bit her lip. "Sarah, I'm afraid Father has done some horrible things. You see, all of your troubles—the supplies that didn't come, even the bandits who terrorized you—it was all my father's doing."

"What?" Sarah thought of the three men hauled away by the *federalis*. They *had* been Americans. And they had certainly known how vulnerable the Casa Brava was—and how to find it.

Jonathon said, "It's true, Sarah. After you called and told me about the bandits and all your other problems, I remembered seeing a memo on Buck's desk: a phone number and the notation Baja California, Mexico scrawled with a heavy square inked around it. It didn't mean anything at the time. The phone number had a Chicago area code. Maybe it would prove to be a pool hall or storefront where your *banditos* were recruited. And the San Diego firm, it seems, received instructions from Buck not to ship your supplies. By the way, I canceled the order and bought everything from another supplier. Everything you need is in the truck."

"Sarah, dear, I'm so sorry," Cecily exclaimed fervently. "We confronted Father and he admitted he'd had you and Charmain followed."

"I can't believe Buck would go to such lengths," Sarah muttered, aghast.

Jonathon said, "It wasn't only because you walked out on him, although God knows he was angry enough about that. You never realized it, but you were the main reason for his success these past few years. It sure wasn't my doing! I think what really frosted him was losing the suit against Charmain, then looking like a fool when she deeded old Del's house and land to the town. I don't believe anything else she did enraged him more than that one magnanimous gesture. It showed she was a bigger person than any of them, including

Buck. Funny how our good deeds sometimes cause us more trouble than our transgressions, isn't it?"

"So," Charmain mused, lips pursed, "Buck Latimer not only wanted us to fall on our faces here, but he also wanted to frighten us to death. I've always felt we don't fully recognize the adversary position some people will take in order to avenge what they consider to be slights."

"I still don't understand," Sarah queried, "why you and Cecily brought the supplies in person—not that we're not delighted to see you, but why?"

Cecily smiled happily. "I did so want to hear you say that. You see, if you don't mind, we'd like to stay. Dear, please don't look so dismayed! Danny has agreed to stay too. He's an experienced handyman, and there'll be lots he can do. And Jon will at last be able to write full time. You know he always wanted to. I shan't be any trouble, I promise. I could help out too. I'd make a good desk clerk, wouldn't I?"

Sarah hoped her feelings weren't showing. She glanced in Charmain's direction, but didn't get any help.

Cecily went on, "Sarah, we won't accept any of Daddy's money, even if he offers any, which he probably won't. We do have a little put away, enough to live on until Jon starts selling his work. We won't be a burden—"

Jonathon's eyes met Sarah's imploringly and he put in quickly. "We can't go back. I hope you'll allow us to stay as paying guests. I swear I won't try to run things, but I don't have to tell you that. You know how much I hated dealing with the Palazzo and all the tenants."

Sarah nodded weakly, feeling as though all of her limbs were caught in a sticky sweet syrup that would surely rise and choke her.

Danny proved to be an unexpected boon. He helped Ramon and his relatives restore water and electricity to the hotel, then pitched in with the work of restoring the main building and constructing the new cottages. Ramon shook his head sadly as the old adobe was broken up and hauled away to be replaced by wood frame. Only the two cottages he had restored, one occupied by Mrs. Jerome and the other by the two elderly gentlemen, would still boast thick adobe walls and solid tile roofs.

As the Casa Brava hummed with activity, some of Sarah's misgivings evaporated. Jonathon made no attempt to see her alone. Charmain, however, was frankly dismayed by his presence.

"Listen, pet, you've got to find a tactful way of getting them to leave. Yes, I know I agreed to let them have rooms, but what else could I do? I certainly don't want to be nasty and order them out. They're paying guests, and heaven knows we need all of those we can get. But I'm worried. Jonathon makes calf's eyes at you when he thinks no one is looking, and I know what it does to you to have him around. You play a good part, but it's tearing you up, isn't it, love?"

"It's your hotel, old bean. You have the right to refuse service to anyone you choose. If you want me to boot them out, I'll have to tell them the order comes from a higher authority than a mere manager, or whatever my capacity is."

"Oh, sweetie, you can be exasperating. It's your problem, but you're making it mine."

"What would we have done without Danny? Ramon's a charmer, and he tangos divinely, but Danny gets the work done," Sarah said pointedly. "And if Cecily goes, Danny goes. Besides, you won't have to worry, we're going to be so busy there won't be time for calf's eyes or anything else. I just spoke to that travel agent in Chula Vista, and she's sending us a large party. A company weekend with wives and kids."

Charmain clapped her hands. "I knew you could do it! Congratulations, Sal. We're in the hotel business, love."

When the chartered bus arrived late the following Friday, Charmain was less thrilled. The bus was hours late, due to the bad road. The detour around the shardlike gray rocks, with the hacienda in full sight, had further enraged the disgruntled guests. Children were tired and fretful, wives wide-eyed with fear at the remote location, so the men immediately began to find fault with their accommodations.

"I think they were expecting the Club Med," Sarah whispered to Charmain as she hung up the phone after listening to another complaint. "Maybe Ramon's cooking will pacify them."

"He's been keeping dinner warm for hours," Charmain said, "and half of them want it served in their rooms because it's so late. We don't have enough staff to wait on them."

Cecily wheeled into the kitchen after a long and harrowing session at the desk. Overhearing Charmain's last remark, Cecily declared, "I can help serve dinner. I can stack a couple of trays on my wheelchair, or I could push a serving cart."

The three women worked at a killing pace until the last tray was delivered. Sarah wondered where Jonathon was. She hadn't seen him all evening, but she didn't ask. Danny was busy hauling in luggage. When the guests were at last settled for the night and Cecily and Charmain had gone to their rooms, Sarah flopped down on a leather couch in the lobby. She kicked off her shoes and leaned back, feeling drained.

Around the walls of the stone-flagged room were small alcoves housing stone statues of various saints. Ramon thought the room had once been the hacienda chapel. It made an impressive lobby after he installed a carved wood desk and several sanctuary benches. Sarah closed her eyes wearily.

Ramon was locking up, a precaution Sarah now insisted upon. She could hear him coming along the passageway from the back door, speaking to someone.

The words were indistinguishable, muffled by the thick adobe walls. A moment later footsteps crossed the stone floor. She opened her eyes and looked into the questing gaze of Darius Descartes.

Chapter 15

Darius's glance flickered over her slumped body, taking in the tendrils of hair escaping from the knot on top of her head, the way her cotton shirt clung damply to her body. Sarah thought, in the instant before he spoke, that she'd never before met a man who appeared to read every line of a woman's face and body with his eyes.

"The bad penny turns up again, I'm afraid. You look exhausted. There's a bus outside with California plates. I assume business is booming at the Casa?"

"I suppose you want a room? I'm not sure we have one, at least not a finished one. You should have called for a reservation." She sounded rude, she knew, but she was past caring. There were too many other problems without having to deal with Darius's compelling presence. With him around she'd be fighting that undeniable chemistry instead of concentrating on the guests.

"No word of greeting? No question as to why I'm back when I swore never to darken your doorstep again?"

"Did you swear that? I don't remember. I'm too tired to play games with you. I'll get you some linen, point you in the direction of a room, then you're on your own."

She stood up, swayed slightly on her feet and immediately found herself in his arms. He held her in a gentle embrace that was more comforting than passionate. She was tempted to relax against him, but said, "Take your hands off me."

He withdrew at once. "I was offering temporary support, nothing more. I wouldn't take advantage of a woman about to collapse on her feet."

He gave her a slow smile and the room behind him swam dizzily. "Sarah, sweet Sarah, did you miss me, even for a second? I've had you on my mind constantly. I can't go on like this. I can't concentrate on anything but how to maneuver you into an all-encompassing relationship with me."

She steadied herself with one hand on the back of the couch. "You know what, Darius? Your choice of words speaks volumes. Maneuver, relationship. Back in Charmain's day, I would have been a conquest, right?"

"Alas, my obsession is far deeper than that. The all-encompassing relationship I had in mind . . . lord, I'm incoherent as a schoolboy around you, but—"

He broke off, his eyes darting to the doorway behind her. Jonathon's voice interrupted, "Sarah? Oh, sorry, I thought you were alone. Well, now, it's Descartes, isn't it?"

Darius's expression hardened visibly. "Mr. Jonathon Conway, not merely in the spirit but in the flesh. Forgive my intrusion. I had no idea you and Sarah were planning a reunion in Mexico. It seems I'm more of a fool than I realized."

Sarah said breathlessly, "It's not what you think, not a reunion. Jon and Cecily kindly brought the supplies we needed from San Diego."

Jonathon glared. "I don't know what you're inferring, Descartes, or who gave you the right—"

Darius ignored him. Turning to Sarah, he said, "I'll find sleeping quarters for myself. I don't need a woman to take care of me. Good night." He walked quickly from the lobby, not looking at either of them.

Sarah said, "I thought you'd gone to bed hours ago, Jon."

"I was working. I had to stop typing when Cecily fell asleep. I came out for a drink and heard voices in here."

"Your wife worked like a Trojan tonight. I hope she didn't overdo it. How's the novel going?" Sarah remained standing, wanting more than anything to go to sleep.

"It's going well. Or it was, until all the commotion tonight. As soon as one of the new cottages is complete, I was thinking Cecily and I could move in, get away from the noise and activity of the hotel guests."

Sarah murmured something, she wasn't sure what. Jonathon was giving her a comfortingly familiar look of longing, and she indulged in a moment of imagining what it would be like to curl up against him, feel his arms around her again and his breath against her face. She blinked the image away.

"I'm dead on my feet, Jon. Can we talk about it tomorrow? Help yourself to anything you want."

She started for the hallway leading to her room. When she reached the door, he put out his hand and touched her arm, stopping her. In the softly lit room his hair was the deep gold of old wine and in his face was etched a hopelessness beyond words. He looked, Sarah thought, like a doomed Viking, sailing out to sea aboard a vessel that would be his funeral pyre. She immediately felt guilty she'd been so absorbed in her own problems she hadn't considered the yoke he was bearing. Trying to take care of a crippled wife, trying to eke out a living at writing, that most precarious of all occupations. He looked even more tired than she felt.

He whispered, "Sarah, oh, God, I missed you so. It was supposed to be you and me forever. Why should we pay for one mistake for the rest of our lives?"

Although she ached to take him in her arms and comfort him, she stepped backward, steeling herself against feeling pity for his misery. "You shouldn't have come here, Jon. Now we'll have to go cold turkey all over again."

"I had to come to you, Sarah. I couldn't stand being away from you."

"But you brought Cecily. Jon, I can't share you, and you can't abandon her."

He ran his hand through his hair in a gesture of despair that brought tears to her eyes. "Estelle would have destroyed me. By the time she was finished exaggerating what she'd seen, we were making sweaty love on the floor, naked. Buck—"

"Buck believed Estelle," Sarah said. "Thank God Cecily didn't."

"Cecily wouldn't believe it if she caught us in bed together." There was a trace of bitterness in his voice. "I tried to tell her, but—"

Sarah felt faint. "Oh, no! You didn't."

"I mean I tried to tell her she'd be better off staying home with her parents. I thought after I got here, we could call and break it to her."

We, Sarah thought. You mean *me*. Jonathon had always avoided unpleasantness. She'd been the buttress between him and irate tenants, between him and a rampaging Buck Latimer. She could yell and scream like a fishwife to defend his rights, but Jonathon always remained the gentleman, soft-spoken, courteous.

Her thoughts must have been written on her face, because he gave a strangled sob and tried to take her into his arms. "Sarah, I love you!" He grabbed her hand when she pushed him away, and began to rain kisses on her palm.

She said quietly, "Jon, let me go."

He dropped her hand and walked over to the adjacent cocktail lounge, which was unfinished, but housed a well-stocked sideboard. Sarah followed. He poured two drinks. Wine for her and for himself a stiff whiskey without soda or water. "Buck wanted me to leave alone. Then he and Estelle would have their little girl back. Every time I gave an order, he countermanded it.

One humiliation after another! The staff began to act as though I were already out. I dreaded going to the office. Cecily was a tower of strength, of course."

"Oh, Jon, I'm sorry I ran away and left you to pick up the pieces."

"When you called and we found out what he'd been up to, what he'd been doing to you and Charmain, I told Cecily I was personally going to deliver the supplies you needed. She didn't hesitate. She said she was coming too, that she'd never forgive her parents for what they'd done. I tried to talk her out of it, I swear, but then Danny said he'd come. What could I do?"

"Jon, I understand. But we can't push our willpower beyond the breaking point. One of us has to move on and soon."

He sighed and drained his glass. She was surprised to see him refill it. He hadn't touched hard liquor since the accident. "Charmain needs you here, and you obviously love the place. I'll get myself out of your hair as soon as I sell my novel. I've an agent interested in it."

"How long do you think that will take?" Sarah felt faint. "Do you have enough to live on in the meantime?"

"If I can finish it within six months, maybe. Cecily has a trust fund, but she refuses to touch it. She has this blind faith in me, that I'll be able to support her."

"How are you paying Danny?"

"He hasn't been paid. Perhaps you could find him a job?"

Sarah thought of all the work Danny had done and of Cecily's contributions. "He's found one already, Cecily too. I'll put them both on the payroll, as soon as we have one. In the meantime, the least we can do is provide your rooms and meals free of charge. As soon as we get paid for this weekend group, I'll pay you for all the supplies you brought too."

Jonathon's ardor and her own fatigue seemed to have fled in the cold light of financial reality. "There, you see," he said, "we need each other in more ways than we realized."

They said good night and went to bed, Sarah to toss restlessly, too tired to sleep. It seemed she had only just closed her eyes when she was roused by a piercing shriek.

One of the newly arrived guests had found a tarantula on the wall above her bed. Explaining that it was a harmless variety was useless. Husband and wife, looking ridiculous in his and hers nightshirts, yelled and screamed about poisonous insects. Sarah was looking around for a container in which to capture the spider when Darius appeared. He marched over to the wall, slid the tarantula onto the palm of his hand and took it outside.

The incident proved to be the least of the day's problems. The patched-up generator balked under the increased load and died. Water diminished to a trickle as guests, unaccustomed to the heat, took repeated showers trying to cool off after searing sojourns on the beach. By evening most of the guests were sunburned and ill-tempered.

Ramon's dinner, perfectly cooked traditional Mexican dishes aromatic with spices and herbs, was met with a chorus of requests for alternate menus. "We don't want Mexican food," somebody whined. A small boy demanded hamburgers, and a little girl was afraid of the candlelight and kept flipping the impotent light switches off and on.

"There's an excellent choice of dishes," Sarah tried to explain. "We thought you'd like to dine as the *padrone* and his family did in the hacienda days."

They wouldn't. Nor did they want to hear Ramon play classical guitar to accompany the meal. They milled around the dining room, waiting for Sarah to give them what they wanted. Some of the men were drinking too much. The only thing they didn't complain about was the fishing. Everyone who had taken rod in hand had caught scads of fish, but with the generator dead, the refrigerators were defrosting rapidly. Sarah was afraid most of the fish would spoil before Danny, who was working on the repairs, could get them going again.

Sarah hadn't seen Darius all day, but had a brief and stormy confrontation with Charmain amid the numerous crises. Sarah wanted Charmain to ask Darius to leave and Charmain, bristling, refused.

"Come on, old love, he can't stay while Jon's here."

"Then send Jon away. Darius is my guest and he'll stay as long as he wishes. This is *my* hotel, pet."

"It sure is. So why am I knocking myself out to make a go of it?" Sarah broke off, hating herself.

"I'm sorry, love. I didn't mean to criticize. You've had so much to contend with—the Conways, then all this mess today. But Darius is like a son to me. It's such a treat for me to have him here. He's so witty and stimulating."

Just when Sarah despaired of pleasing any of the disgruntled guests, Darius appeared. Urbane, sophisticated, flirting outrageously with the women and speaking easily with the men, he took charge. Now that the furnace of the sun was shut off, it was a pleasantly cool evening. All of the men had caught fish. Why not have a barbecue and fish fry on the beach, he suggested. Afterward they could put the children to bed and move indoors to the banquet hall for dancing.

Sarah thought of the unrefrigerated fish and silently blessed him for his ingenuity. Charmain flashed her an I-told-you-so glance. Jonathon and Cecily appeared just as the group was moving outside. Cecily, who was apparently seeing Darius for the first time since his arrival, greeted him like a long-lost brother. Jonathon gave him a blank stare.

On the beach, cool night air caressed sand still warm from the sun. An almost-full moon painted the sea silver, and driftwood crackling in fire pits cast a golden glow on eager faces. Ramon set up a trestle table and brought some of his dishes outside. Everyone began to nibble as they waited for the fish to be cleaned and cooked. It was soon obvious that, having tasted Ramon's food, few could resist going back for more.

Danny carried Cecily down to the beach and placed her reverently on a blanket. He gave Sarah a hard stare and said laconically, "Generator's fixed." Then he went to fill a plate for Cecily. Jonathon was deep in conversation with one of the other guests.

By the time the party moved indoors, the atmosphere was relaxed but festive. In the long unused *sala,* which Darius called a banquet hall, chairs lined the walls and an ancient but serviceable record player had been found. The hall was soon filled with dancing couples.

Sarah gave a sigh of relief and found a chair in a corner, settling back to listen to the music. There were Spanish love songs and old American dance records that must have dated back to the forties. The records had probably arrived in the trunks that had accompanied Charmain to the Casa Brava.

Cecily and Jonathon watched from the sidelines, while Charmain and Ramon whirled gracefully about the floor. Sarah saw Darius, standing on the far side of the room surrounded by guests, chatting amiably. The memory of the night in Morocco when he had insisted she tango with him came forcefully back to her. She wished he would come and ask her to dance, but he didn't look in her direction.

Later he danced with Charmain, then several of the other women. Sarah watched until she couldn't stand the feeling of being shut out. She stood up and picked her way through the dancing couples to the door. Darius was angry that Jonathon was here, of course, and was punishing her by ignoring her. Darius's actions were easy to fathom. But Sarah was troubled by her reaction. It shouldn't have bothered her so much. Just as she reached the door the record ended. There was a split second pause, then a familiar piece of music began its insistent beat. It was the same tango she had danced with Darius in Morocco: "Jealousy."

Chapter 16

Sarah held her breath as Danny inched Cecily's wheelchair along the top of the gray rocks extending inland from the Casa Brava. Cecily had asked to see the view of the desert plain from the highest mesa. Sarah stood on the terrace watching their progress.

Darius's voice beside her made her jump. "He has the look of a fiercely loyal Sherpa guiding his master to some Himalayan peak, doesn't he? An interesting young man. I feel a certain empathy with him."

Sarah turned to look at him. He had a travel bag slung over his shoulder. "Checking out?" she asked, avoiding comment on his remark. She too had noticed that Danny's devotion to Cecily went deeper than anyone else realized, particularly Jonathon.

"Yes. But I'll be back, never fear. I'm curious to see how you'll resolve your burning passion for the melancholy Mr. Conway."

Sarah ignored the taunt. A breeze rustled the bougainvillea vines, sending a shower of deep pink blossoms whirling around their heads. The fronds of the fan palms slapped together like clapping hands, the olive tree's branches stirred. A second gust of wind whipped Sarah's hair around her face.

Darius said, "I'd better go before the storm grounds me. I've got a promise of a genuine Tlaloc. That's the

Aztec rain god, which seems appropriate, because you're going to get some." He looked up at the sky, now an ominous white. The air had an oppressive quality. "But you shouldn't get a severe storm this time of year. I'm sure Ramon will batten down the hatches. Meantime, I suggest someone goes up there and tells Danny to bring the wheelchair down."

But Danny, feeling the wind rise, was already turning back. Sarah said, "And I suggest you stop dictating what everyone should do. You're the most domineering, overbearing, conceited, self-centered—"

Darius held up his hands in mock surrender. "I get the message. I'll be on my way as soon as I can tear my eyes off you. Charmain knows how to reach me if you need me."

"I will never, ever, need you," Sarah declared.

He stared at her for a moment, as though searching for something he couldn't find. Then his shoulders dropped slightly in a gesture of resignation. "Yes, I believe you're right. You won't ever need me. You've stood up to bandits and recalcitrant generators and uncooperative plumbing, to say nothing of a howling mob of guests. You're not the kind of woman who seeks a male shoulder to lean on, are you? Is that why you pine for Jonathon Conway? So you can mother him? He strikes me as a man who would let a woman look after him, make his decisions, eliminate his problems."

"If you tell me that what I need is a 'real' man, I think I'll throw up."

He smiled. "You need a man who, while not trying to run your life for you, won't allow you to walk all over him either. A man like yourself, who knows what he wants and goes after it. Not a vacillating, timid groveler who takes everything life dishes out and tells himself there's nothing he can do about it because he's just unlucky. Conway doesn't even have the courage to choose between two women, so he keeps you both dangling."

Sarah glanced around. They were alone on the

terrace, but Danny was easing Cecily's wheelchair down the last slope toward the retaining wall at the edge of the terrace. "I've asked you before to mind your own business. I'm not going to defend either Jonathon or myself to you. Think what you wish about us." She turned and walked toward the path leading to the new cottages, now a buzzing hive of activity.

As she watched workmen install interior wallboard, she thought about Darius's assessment of Jonathon. At least part of it might be correct. The part about him not being able to give all of his love to one woman. Sarah had felt a nagging suspicion for some time that what Jon really wanted was Cecily as wife and herself as mistress. Just like old Del Latimer had her grandmother and Charmain. The irony was that only one thing had kept Jon from achieving his goal: Sarah's friendship with Cecily.

A stray piece of tar paper blew against her leg in the rising wind and she bent to remove it, trying to rid herself of the feeling that perhaps, like Charmain, she was one of those women destined to be forever lusted after but never truly loved. Darius might appear sincere, but Sarah was convinced his intentions toward her were even less honorable than Jon's.

Cecily smiled gratefully at Danny as he slid her wheelchair to level ground. He said, "I'll take you up again for a better view when the wind drops. I've heard that some of the summer storms that whip up the gulf can be vicious. By the look of the sky, we're in for a blow."

"Thank you, Danny, for taking me where I'm sure no wheelchair ever went before. The view was breathtaking. I could learn to love the desert, its peace, the feeling of timelessness. Knowing those dunes and great silent rock formations were there long before man got up on his hind legs and walked is sobering. Jon says that the uncluttered beauty of the desert has a therapeutic effect on the mind, and I do agree. He's writing with a clarity and insight he could never manage before."

She couldn't see Danny's expression, since he was behind her, pushing her wheelchair. His voice was carefully expressionless. "I'm glad to hear it. I guess you plan to stay here then?"

"You don't sound too enthusiastic about the idea. Don't you like it here?"

"I don't like some of the company we keep."

"Danny! I do hope you weren't one of those people who listened to spiteful gossip back home." She looked over her shoulder reproachfully. He'd never said anything, but she knew he became edgy in Sarah's company. Cecily supposed it was just that some people's chemistry didn't mix.

"No, ma'am," Danny said. "I always form my own opinions. Do you want to go to your room and rest?"

"No. Jon's working, I don't want to disturb him. Would you take me to the *sala*? There's a marvelous view of the bay from the windows on the bluff side. We'll see the wind whipping the sea. I promised Sarah I'd go over the account books, but I feel restless this morning."

"It's the storm," Danny said. "Electrical disturbances in the air. Affects sensitive people like you."

"What about sensitive people like you, Danny? Oh, I know you're a sweet kind person under that tough exterior."

They had reached the doors leading to the lobby and he still didn't answer Cecily. Minutes later he pushed her chair into the vast empty hall. He opened the shutters over the arched windows, and they looked across the Sea of Cortez, already white-capped and slate gray.

Still feeling the peculiar sense of bravado that overcomes even shy people just before a storm, Cecily urged, "You didn't answer my question, Danny."

He looked down at her, his expression frozen into the

brooding, don't-come-close mask he always wore. "I didn't know it was a question. I thought you were just making an observation."

He always gave a warning signal if she trespassed too close to personal matters. This time she wasn't going to be put off. "Danny, you know it's time we talked things over."

His expression was guarded. "What things?"

"Sarah spoke to your mother just before that disastrous party. She told Jon, but I begged him not to bring up the subject of your past with you. Then when you said you'd come with us to Baja, I . . . we . . . well, things aren't quite the same now, are they? You pretend you're still being employed to chauffeur me about, but we both know you're not being paid at all and you've been doing hard physical work here."

"I have a room, my meals. What else do I need?"

"Danny, are you running away from something? The law, perhaps? I know it's none of my business, but I care about what happens to you and it's difficult for me to accept that someone of your intelligence and education is content to live like—"

"A drifter?"

"No. I was about to say, like you have no one in the world you care about. Not many people would cross a continent on the spur of the moment."

"I have someone I care about."

Cecily lowered her eyes from his. For an instant there had been a look there she hadn't seen in a man's eyes since before her accident. She thought she must have imagined it.

Sensing her discomfort, Danny said, "I'd like to tell you what happened. Why I left home and don't want to go back."

He perched on the dusty window ledge, silent for a moment as though wondering where to begin. Cecily waited patiently, knowing that whatever he was about to tell her would be wrenched from some locked place inside him. She felt she knew Danny, better than her husband sometimes, in that way one person knows exactly how another will react to any set of circumstances or what they'll say at any given moment. Danny was strong and courageous and good, she was sure, yet there was something in his past of which he was deeply ashamed. She'd been able to talk easily with him right from the start, and there had been times when she was sure he wanted to tell her what troubled him, but he always held back. She leaned forward, willing him to feel her compassion.

Danny started slowly. "I had a friend. Since fourth grade. We did everything together. We were closer than brothers." He gazed at some distant point in time and memory and brushed his fist across his eyes. "Everything," he repeated. "In college we were roommates. I thought I knew him better than I knew myself." He hesitated, and Cecily saw his fists clench and unclench at his sides.

"I was a psychology student, not my major, but I thought I understood the workings of the human mind. Enough at least to help a friend. In our second year away from home, my friend began to change. He was depressed, then off on some wild high, then down in the depths again. I suspected drugs at first, but it wasn't that. He began to talk about the hopelessness of life and ask what was the point of going on. He'd been dating a girl who dumped him. I figured that was the reason. That he'd get over it."

There was a tremor in his voice, and Cecily felt his agony as he tried to collect himself and go on with the story. "He seemed to be okay after a while. Sort of withdrawn, but not obviously depressed. I didn't think much about it because we were both studying hard. Then he started up again, not with the highs and lows, this time sort of quiet and rational, but talking about suicide."

Cecily caught her breath. She wanted to hear a different ending to the one she knew was coming.

Danny said bitterly, "I got an A in psychology, right?

I knew it all. Every time he mentioned falling asleep and not waking up, I told him suicide is a permanent solution to a temporary problem. Cecily, I blithely disregarded the deep depression even a temporary problem can bring. I played with the most delicate mechanism of all—the human mind."

"He killed himself?" Cecily whispered.

Danny nodded. She saw a lump ripple slowly down his throat as he swallowed.

"Jumped from the top floor window of the dorm one night. He was lying on a grassy bank below. People walked by him all morning, thinking he was asleep. I saw him about noon and went down and touched him. Oh, God, Cecily, it was like touching jelly. Everything inside him was smashed—"

She had turned the wheels of her chair, closed the short distance between them before his voice broke into dry sobs. She reached out and grabbed his hands, pulled him down so she could hold him. He knelt on the floor, his face cradled on her lap, and she stroked his soft brown hair and murmured soothing words that later she could not recall. But they came from her heart.

Chapter 17

The early summer storm that swept the Sea of Cortez was gone by nightfall, leaving a trail of torn palm fronds, broken bougainvillea vines and dust devils dancing on the desert plain.

For Sarah, the cool respite after the rain seemed to mark the last tranquil hours before the onslaught of a long troubled summer. That first storm was a mere warning breeze compared to the first of the winter storms that came, unseasonably early, in October.

On the morning of that day Sarah sat staring at the balance sheet in front of her, trying to make the figures come out differently. She'd believed if they could get through the summer doldrums, when few guests braved the heat, they would put the hotel in the black by attracting winter visitors to the refurbished rooms and by renting the cottages to permanent residents. But costs had exceeded her direst predictions. Charmain's money was gone, and Sarah's own savings had also been swallowed. Now that they were ready to bring hordes of guests to the hotel, there was neither money to advertise, nor funds to stock the food and wines they'd need.

Sarah tapped her pencil against the rough-hewn wood of a refectory table she'd had brought into her room to use as a desk. She looked through the windows at the bleak scene outside.

The sky was a sullen white, the sea slate gray. She remembered the last gale they'd had, on the day Darius left. It seemed appropriate to think about him and the storm simultaneously. Both were dangerous and unpredictable.

There had been regular phone calls from Darius. Friendly inquiries as to how they were withstanding the rigors of the summer. Postcards from various parts of the world, usually addressed to Charmain with a postscript to give his love to Sarah. There had also been a gift for Sarah on her birthday. She'd been annoyed that Charmain had given him the date.

His present to her was a heavy gold bracelet, an antique with ornate designs and lettering worked into the precious metal and an ingenious clasp of locking teeth. The accompanying note read: *I'm assured that a birthday gift cannot be misconstrued. I hope this is true. This bangle has been in my possession for some time awaiting the right recipient, and has a rather interesting legend attached to it. Perhaps some time you'll be curious enough to ask me to tell you the story? Darius.*

Charmain had exclaimed, "Of course you must accept a birthday gift. It would be in the most ghastly taste to refuse." She fingered the beaten gold, slowly tracing the scrolls and roses and barely discernible hieroglyphics. Her eyes filled with tears.

Sarah was surprised by the glimpse of deep sadness behind Charmain's doughty facade. She was always so much in command of her feelings that her distress was more moving than it would have been in a less controlled personality. Sarah had gone to her and hugged her. "Don't upset yourself, old love, I'll keep his blasted slave bracelet if it means that much to you. Sooner or later he'll get tired of the chase and give up."

She tossed the bracelet into the bottom drawer of her dresser, where it glinted wickedly among no-longer-worn hosiery, fancy belts and designer scarves. Sarah found a cotton skirt and blouse, bare legs and sandals, more in keeping with the climate, although she longed for the freedom of shorts and skimpy halters on days when the temperature soared over a hundred and the humidity dropped to scarcely measurable percentage points. Charmain assured her that such attire would shock Ramon and the other local gentlemen.

The thick adobe walls and heavy tiled roof of the old hacienda helped Sarah and Charmain withstand the fierce heat, but they learned to emulate the Baja natives and work only in the cool of the morning and late evening. Cecily and Jonathon had moved into one of the new cottages and felt the heat more, but Cecily stoically refused to comment on it. Sarah saw little of Jonathon, who was now deeply involved in his novel.

Danny had proved to be a jack-of-all-trades and could turn his hand to any task. His attitude toward Sarah didn't change, but he was so transformed in Cecily's presence that Sarah learned to ignore his baleful glances. Cecily told her she knew all about

Danny's past and there was nothing in it that need worry them. She didn't elaborate.

Sarah had said, "Cecily, you have talked it all over with Jonathon, haven't you? Whatever you learned about Danny, I mean."

Cecily avoided her eyes. "Oh, yes. Don't worry. Well, no, I haven't exactly told Jon. Don't be angry, Sarah, but I've learned there are times when it's better not to disturb Jon. He's very sensitive, so highly strung. He gets more upset about things than ordinary people do. I try to shield him from unpleasantness as much as I can, not that there's anything in Danny's past, but—"

She'd looked so flustered that Sarah said quickly, "Okay, don't worry, I'm not going to bring it up. I haven't seen Jonathon anyway. He must really be working on his novel."

For an instant a shadow flitted across the back of Cecily's eyes. "Yes, he's driving himself to get it finished. At first he seemed so happy, being able to devote all of his time to his writing, but now it seems more of an agony to him and his temper is shorter. He's quicker to find fault."

It was the first hint that Cecily's admiration for her husband was fading. Sarah had always felt that Jonathon treated his wife with casual, sometimes almost cruel, indifference, but Cecily had never appeared to see it. Sarah noticed too that Cecily spent as much time as possible away from the cottage she shared with Jonathon, often lingering in the dining room until very late at night, playing the piano or talking with Danny and Ramon and Charmain.

Sarah was startled from her reverie as a vine lashed the window pane. A moment later she heard the howl of the rising wind. She stood up as rain began to pelt the glass. Ramon appeared outside, his hair plastered to his forehead, and gave her a damp grin before slamming the shutters over her window.

By midmorning it was obvious that the storm's

increasing ferocity was causing even Ramon concern. He brought Mrs. Jerome and Chesney, as well as the two elderly Mexicans, to the main building. He told Sarah, "Danny is bringing *Señora* Conway. The *señor* says he will come soon. The walls of the Casa have stood up to such winds many times, but the new cottages . . ."

His voice trailed away, and Sarah felt a stirring of apprehension. The cottages were her pride and joy. They were modern and efficient, self-contained homes for the permanent tenants she hoped to attract. "The cottages will be fine, but I think it's a good idea to have everybody together."

They gathered in the dining room, and Ramon promised his special version of *chiles rellenos* for lunch. Outside the trees bent almost to the ground under persistent gales, and the cold rain rattled like machine gun fire.

Danny wheeled Cecily into the room, positioned her by the inside wall and glared at Sarah as though the storm were her fault. Charmain swept into the room amid a cloud of delicately embroidered wheat-colored gauze. "Isn't it lovely?" she sighed, whirling to show the fullness of the skirt. "It's a Mexican wedding dress. It belonged to Ramon's mother. The dear man insisted I wear it. Today seemed as good a time as any. One can face anything if one feels pretty."

Mrs. Jerome bellowed, "Chesney gets nervous in stormy weather. I hope lunch won't be late."

Sarah asked Danny to light the logs in the grate. "It's cool enough for a fire and it will cheer us up."

Cecily clapped her hands. "Lovely idea, Sarah. It's rather exciting, isn't it? The storm, I mean. After all those hot, still days, it's like winter is waking up with a vengeance."

"What's keeping Jonathon?" Sarah asked, placing a tray of tortilla chips and *salsa* beside Mrs. Jerome. Chesney sat up and begged.

Cecily said, "Jon's working on the last chapter of his book and doesn't want to leave until it's finished."

Sarah poured wine for the two old gentlemen, who beamed and chorused, *"Muchas gracias, señorita."*

"De nada," Sarah murmured, remembering her manners. She was thinking that if Jonathon sold his novel, perhaps he could start paying rent on his cottage, perhaps even make her a loan. Apart from a brief article on the Baja Peninsula that he had sold to an airline magazine, there had been no income from his writing, or any other source, since they arrived. Sarah rationalized that Danny's services and Cecily's bookkeeping and attending to the desk more than made up for Jonathon's free ride, but Charmain's feelings of disdain for him were clearly expressed. Sarah didn't want them to leave. She'd become accustomed to having them around. Although Jon's conversation was directed at all of them, Sarah felt that often he made particularly poignant remarks meant for her alone. They loved each other wordlessly, chastely, and it was beautiful in a heartbreaking way.

Jonathon came into the dining room just as Ramon was serving lunch. Jon's eyes found Sarah. He wore a euphoric smile and looked boyishly youthful for the first time since Cecily's accident. He said, "I just wrote those magic words. *The End. Finis.* Triple asterisks."

"Which?" Sarah asked, laughing.

"All of them. I'm done with it. Of course, it's only the first draft, I'll have a lot of revision and rewriting to do, but the worst is over—the bridge that must be built in thin air. Now I'll go back and put in the pilings."

Sarah's dream of a publisher's advance evaporated, but she said, "Congratulations, Jon."

Cecily said, "How wonderful you must feel, dear. I'm so proud of you." She looked around the room and added, "I've read every word and it's a masterpiece. Jon's characters are so real and so intricately woven into the fabric of his narrative, into the world he created for them, that you couldn't pull them out and put them anywhere else." She colored slightly, as everyone quieted to listen to her. "I'm not expressing this very well. I mean, I think the sense of drama in a novel has to do with people in a particular time and place." She looked at Jonathon for help.

"I believe Cecily means my characters couldn't be plucked from my story. But I'm sure the others aren't interested, dear. Listen, let's open a bottle of champagne and celebrate."

Some of Cecily's joy faded. "Isn't it a bit early in the day?"

"Come on, love, a glass of champagne isn't a drunken binge. Is it, Sarah?"

Sarah looked awkwardly from one to the other.

Ramon said, "Sarah, *por favor,* I need you for a moment in the kitchen."

Surprised by the request, Sarah followed Ramon into the kitchen. He closed the door. "I didn't want to say anything, because the *señor* is a friend of yours. But I have been taking much wine to his cottage. I think perhaps he is drinking too much, but it is not my business. However, now I see his lovely wife is also worried about this." Ramon spread his hands expressively.

Sarah said defensively, "He's been working hard—"

Ramon's expression was carefully impartial. "The bill for his wine is now considerable, and we are running out."

Sarah muttered something about speaking to him and that she had to get back to the lunch table. After all, it had been years since the accident. The fact that Jon had been drunk that night didn't mean he couldn't ever have another drink, did it? Sarah felt almost as much guilt as he did, since it had been their quarrel that caused him to drink too much the night his car skidded.

Champagne glasses were brimming when Sarah returned to the dining room. Cecily stared at hers as though it were a crystal time bomb. Danny was standing beside the fireplace, as usual making no move to join the guests. He always ate in the kitchen. Sarah said, "Danny, please join us for lunch." He hesitated, eyes on Cecily. She said, "Oh, yes, please do."

He strolled with elaborate indifference to the table, pulled out the chair next to Cecily's wheelchair and sat down. Sarah made a mental note to ask Cecily to insist he have his meals with them from now on. It was ridiculous for Danny to maintain his chauffeur status in view of their small number. They were more like a family than staff and guests.

The wind moaned in the chimney, sending a hissing cloud of smoke gusting into the room. With all the lights turned on and the shutters closed, it could have been night instead of noon.

Before they finished lunch, the cacophony of raging wind and pounding seas made conversation almost impossible. Despite the champagne, the sense of uneasiness grew each time the group heard the thud of a windblown object striking the walls and roof.

When dessert had been served, Sarah slipped out to the kitchen to peer through the cracks in the shutters. Through a blur of heavy rain, she saw uprooted trees and a tangle of debris all over the terrace. She ran to the other side of the building where her room overlooked the sea. The shutters formed a solid screen and she couldn't see out, but the roar of the waves smashing against the rocks painted a clear picture of the storm's violence.

Returning to the dining room, she found a nervous knot of people around the fireplace, oblivious to the fact that the fire had gone out. Cecily's wheelchair was pulled up to the piano, and she began a rousing rendition of "Singing in the Rain," which she sang in her sweet soprano voice. Charmain stood nearby, leaning elegantly against the carved wood of the piano, providing a slightly off-key contralto accompaniment.

At the end of the song, Charmain picked up the hem of her dress and her tiny high-arched feet executed a passable soft-shoe routine.

There was a chorus of applause, almost drowned by the roar of an explosion. The lights went out.

Sarah fumbled in the darkness for the candles she kept on the mantelpiece. A match flickered to life nearby, illuminating Danny's chiseled features. His hand cupped the tiny flame as Sarah lit a candle. The wind now rushed down the chimney, rain crackled and spat on the still-warm logs.

"What was that?" Jonathon exclaimed.

Ramon said, "Everyone stay here, please. I will go and see."

After he left there was a panicky silence, broken only by the roar of the storm. It seemed to Sarah that the din of rain and wind was even louder than before, almost as if it were now inside the building. "I'll be back in a minute," she said and ran from the room before anyone could protest.

She found Ramon in the kitchen, battling the wind and rain blasting in through the gaping window. Remnants of smashed shutters flapped uselessly against the shattered glass. Horizontal sheets of wind-whipped rain blinded Sarah and she stumbled, feeling the crunch of broken glass under her feet.

Ramon was trying to hammer a nail through a blanket to form a makeshift screen, but Sarah could see that the effort was futile. She clutched his arm. "It's no use, come on, let's get everyone into the *sala*." If the other windows blew in, the size of the great hall would offer some protection.

There was another crash, followed by an earsplitting shriek of wind. Another window was gone, somewhere close. Sarah didn't wait for Ramon, she ran back to the dining room.

At the door she almost collided with Danny carrying Cecily. Behind him Jonathon helped Charmain remain upright in the vicious gusts of wind now rushing through the shattered windows. The two old men flanked Mrs. Jerome, who clutched Chesney in her arms. Sarah pointed in the direction of the *sala*. "Far end of the hall, no windows," she yelled. Danny nodded and led the way. Sarah hung on to Charmain's arm, wishing for the safety of a good old-fashioned Midwestern storm cellar. But the Casa Brava was built on solid rock, with no basement. Still, that rocky base had protected the hacienda from the sea in the past, and the sturdy walls had withstood storms like this one.

They huddled against the inside wall of the vast room the rest of the day and most of the night, without light or food, as the raging forces of nature tried to reclaim the bluff by eliminating everything man had built. When Sarah saw Ramon cross himself and begin to pray, she knew they were experiencing the worst storm he had ever seen.

Just before dawn the wind dropped, although the rain continued to batter the roof and pour in through smashed windows. As the first gray light of the new day pushed tentative fingers through the shutters of the *sala,* miraculously still intact, Sarah uncoiled stiff limbs and went to the doors leading to the inner corridor. They refused to budge.

Danny and Ramon came to help her shove them open. Jonathon lay sprawled in a corner, sound asleep.

A heavy wood and wrought iron lantern had fallen from the wall and was blocking the door. Sarah stepped over it and looked at a scene of utter carnage. All the doors and windows must have blown in, as well as part of the roof. There was water everywhere. Inner doors hung on broken hinges, furniture had been blown over or shoved against the walls by the force of the wind. Tapestries, draperies, rugs, bedspreads . . . all soaked and ruined. There was mud and sand in many of the rooms.

Sarah moved trancelike through the devastated hotel to the lobby. All the statues had fallen from the alcoves, shattering, and breaking furniture. She went through the gaping front doors. The entry plaza was unrecognizable. All the flowers and shrubs were gone. The ancient olive tree Ramon's uncle had so lovingly nurtured was now a blackened ravel of leafless branches. The metal umbrella tables had been swept up and hurled into twisted tangles, as if they had been made of strips of dough.

Someone was speaking to her, but the words didn't penetrate the numbed state of her brain. She picked her way over piles of driftwood blown in from the sea and stumbled over tiles toppled from the roof. The handsome fountain was gone.

Scrambling up the spilled dirt and broken bricks that had once been the planter at the edge of the plaza, she looked down the inland arroyo where the cottages had stood. Except for the two adobe cottages, restored by Ramon, all that remained of the others were a few forlorn sticks and strips of tar paper. A child pounding a Tinkertoy house would have been left with more to show for a summer's work.

A sob rose in Sarah's throat as she stood transfixed, unable to believe there was nothing left. They were ruined. All of Charmain's inheritance, all of Sarah's savings were gone. There wasn't a single habitable room in the entire hotel. At her side, Ramon murmured, *"Madre de Dios!"*

Sarah fought down a rising tide of panic. "We'll rebuild. Somehow we'll hold out until we can rebuild. This time I'll listen to you and build with adobe, not frame. The insurance will pay for the cottages and maybe we can salvage—"

Ramon's hand closed over her arm. "Sarah!" he said in a small broken voice. "No. We cannot rebuild. The insurance premium . . . the notice came from Mexico City just days ago. The policy was canceled because we did not pay the premium."

"But I gave you the money! You said—"

Ramon hung his head. "My old uncle is very sick. I

send him to hospital. I did not think the insurance company would cancel so soon, just a few days overdue."

For Sarah everything went out of focus for a moment. Jonathon's voice, rising with hysteria, aroused her. "My God! What happened to the cottages? Oh, no, Sarah! My manuscript was in there!"

He went crashing down the rocky slope and began tearing through the pitiful broken sticks. Watching him, Sarah wanted to laugh and weep at the same time. All of his work was gone too. Unable to bear his anguish, she turned and walked back to the hacienda on feet that seemed to drag her into the depths of the earth.

Charmain was in the littered kitchen, examining the broken coffee maker. She still wore the Mexican wedding dress, it's hem now torn and trailing, and her hair, usually so elegant, stood up in untidy spikes. "A bit of a mess, Sal girl. Looks like we've really been and gone and done it this time. We've lost the whole bloody lot." She tipped the broken glass off the only whole chair left in the room and sat down. "What now?" She looked up at Sarah.

Sarah pushed back her hair from her eyes in an angry gesture. "Damn it, I won't be beaten like this."

"Listen toots, I think it's time to give up. I didn't dare tell you, but Ramon didn't send in the insurance premium."

"I know. Charlie, we can't give up. We've both invested everything we've got. Besides, I've grown fond of this place. It's wild and bleak and probably untamable, but I don't think I can ever go back to something like Buck's Palazzo apartments again."

"I know what you mean." Charmain sighed. "Ramon's heart will be broken too. I don't know how I'll console him."

Sarah remembered Jonathon, scrabbling through the rubble in search of manuscript pages that couldn't have survived. He and Cecily were penniless. Where would they go, what would they do now? They couldn't go crawling back to Buck and Estelle. It would be the ultimate humiliation.

Then there was Charmain and Ramon and all of his relatives. Sarah suddenly felt like the matriarch of a large family who depended on her for survival. "We can't just abandon the Casa Brava," she declared.

Charmain sighed. "You're just as stubborn as your grandfather was. Darling, look around you. It will take a small fortune to get this place back to the way it was when we came here—never mind all the rebuilding we did. Where could you raise so much money? You saw the great abandoned monstrosity that was to have been a gambling casino. If no one could raise enough money to complete it, what hope do we have? No one in their right mind would lend us enough to put the Casa back together."

Sarah stared unseeingly into space, then she said slowly, "There *is* someone who may help us. But I've got to get to him right away and plead our cause. He mustn't come here and see how desperate we are. Charlie, where was Darius the last time you heard from him?"

Chapter 18

A chill autumn rain misted the canyons of Manhattan as Sarah stepped from the taxi to the shelter of an umbrella held for her by a uniformed doorman. She paid the taxi driver, frowning at the diminishing number of bills in her purse. It was a good thing she'd had to fly only to New York instead of one of Darius's far-flung residences.

Across the street in Central Park a lone hansom cab pulled by a bedraggled horse disappeared into dripping trees of muted green. There would be a spectacular view from Darius's penthouse.

Sarah felt nervous. She stood stiffly in the elevator, thinking she'd been an idiot not to bring more suitable clothes. It had been hot when she left Baja, and even hotter in Los Angeles as a Santa Ana wind breathed its dragon breath from desert to sea, devouring every drop of moisture in the air. How quickly one forgot the dramatic arrival of autumn on the East Coast. She wore a linen dress of pale green with matching jacket. There was a spattering of mud on her high-heeled sandals. A dark suit and closed pumps would have been more in keeping with the weather, to say nothing of a raincoat.

Her clothes were the least of her worries, however. She wasn't sure she could keep from blurting out her desperation. She felt like an actress about to step on stage without having seen a script. She reminded herself sternly of all the people back at the Casa Brava who were depending on her.

The elevator stopped, the doors yawned open. She was standing in a semicircular foyer, thickly carpeted, a fortune in paintings and sculpture scattered tastefully about. Her attention was immediately caught by a bronze sculpture of a rearing stallion placed on a handsome marble table near open double doors on the far side of the foyer. Through the doorway she could see Darius, lounging on a leather chair, a telephone tucked into his shoulder as his hands busied themselves with calculator, pen and pad. He looked up at her, smiled and motioned for her to come in.

The feeling that she was making a big mistake intensified as she walked into the room. She took a chair near the window and waited for him to finish his conversation.

". . . yes, I agree. But with current interest rates that investment is hardly worth the effort. Get rid of it. What? No. Beirut is a city that's slowly killing itself. Now, about the Maori pieces for that collector in Paris . . ."

Sarah felt a raindrop run from her hair down her forehead. She tried to smooth the wrinkles from her dress, but they sprang back when she moved her fingers away. Darius was making no effort to curtail his business call. Yet he'd seemed genuinely delighted when she called him from Kennedy Airport and said she'd be in New York for a couple of days and would like to see him.

By the time he'd finished discussing the value and availability of primitive art works, Sarah's throat was dry and her palms damp. A picture of the devastated Casa Brava and the desperate expressions of its occupants contrasted sharply with the luxury of Darius's apartment. She managed a smile when at last he hung up and rose to his feet.

"Sarah! How wonderful to see you. I was afraid I was dreaming when you called. Forgive me, but now that I've taken care of that call I can devote the rest of the day to you."

He crossed the room, took her hands and drew her to her feet, his eyes fixed on her face, reading every nuance of her expression in the way she found so disturbing, especially now. "You're lovelier than ever. What a treat a tanned skin is amid the pallor of the city. I suppose the sun is still warm on the walls of the Casa Brava?"

There are no walls of the Casa Brava, she thought, envisioning the wreckage she'd left behind. She hoped her expression was enigmatic as she nodded but said nothing.

"You definitely look different," he remarked. "The role of hotel mogul seems to have brought out the buccaneer in you even more. I've seen eyes like yours across a baccarat table."

"Oh, I'm just wary in your presence, that's all."

"Afraid I'll force you into my harem?"

She withdrew her hands from his. "Oh, so you do have a harem? I suspected it, of course, but . . ."

Smiling, he slipped his arm around her shoulders. "Come on, let's have cocktails before lunch. There's a wonderful view of Central Park from the living room."

There were French doors opening to a balcony. Sarah walked toward them, saying, "Could we step outside for a moment?"

"Of course. We'll get drenched, but I've wondered for some time what it would be like to kiss raindrops from your eyelashes." He opened the door for her, and she stepped outside.

She told herself she should be glad he was flirting with her. It would make it easier to approach him about a loan. Or would it? And why did she enjoy his banter so much? He was good-looking and somehow unattainable despite his heavy come-on. Maybe that was it. A woman who became involved with him would never have an exclusive claim on him, though he'd cater and flatter and tease. The woman would have to be content with a fraction of his time and attention once the chase was over. There was absolutely no reason for him to marry, when any woman in her right mind would welcome his advances, even invite them. Lord, *she* was inviting them, wasn't she? Laughing and teasing and flirting with a shamelessness that would have surprised even Charmain.

They stood in the rain, looking at the panorama below—park and city streets all washed with the delicate watercolors of a gentle rain. A scene far different from the torrential rain, frenzied surf and gale winds that had lashed the Casa Brava to near destruction.

"Will you spend the evening with me, Sarah? I can get tickets to a show. What would you like to see?"

Sarah hesitated. Originally she had planned, if he proved cooperative, to be on her way back to Mexico by evening. But now she savored the prospect of an evening in his company. It would be fun to have someone pamper and adore her, if only for a few hours. Not to have to worry about bills or feel guilty about anything. Just to laugh and enjoy life with a forceful, exciting man who would take command and not allow her to think about anything but the exhilaration of being together. She wavered, though, afraid of where such an evening might lead. He was just *too* attractive.

"I'm not sure I can. I've a couple of other appointments." She shivered, unsure if the chill in the air or the proximity of his body was the reason.

"Don't decide yet." He smiled and brushed a raindrop from her eyelashes with a gentle fingertip. "Give me a chance to show you what a gentleman I can be. Not that I've ever cared for gentlemen, but if that's what you want . . ." Fingering the light material of her lapel, he commented warmly, "You're soaked to the skin. Come inside." Drawing her back into the warmth of the room, he queried sympathetically, "Don't you own a raincoat? You really do need someone to take care of you, don't you? Come on, I'll show you where you can change while I make some cocktails. Then you can tell me what mysterious business brings you so far from your desert outpost."

The bedroom to which he took her was furnished with a satin-covered circular bed and delicately curved Queen Anne dressers and chairs. A blue velvet caftan lay on the bed beside a pair of ostrich-trimmed mules. Sarah knew they would be her size before she picked them up. "Are you clairvoyant, or do you just see around corners?" she asked lightly. "How did you know I'd arrive *sans* raincoat and in need of dry clothes?"

"I know how disorienting a change of climate can be. Why don't you have a nice warm shower to thaw out? I'll be in the dining room. Unless you'd like me to stay and help? No? Spoilsport! Hurry and change, I can't bear to let you out of my sight."

At the door he paused and gave an elaborate sigh.

"You can't know what it means to me to have you here of your own volition. How many times I've imagined this! Thank you for coming, Sarah."

Feeling guiltier than ever, Sarah shrugged off the creased linen jacket and dress. She decided to pass up the shower. The blue velvet caftan felt sinfully soft against her skin. Turning back the hem, she saw it was fully lined with pure silk. She surveyed herself in the dressing table mirror, tempted to unpin her chignon and let her hair hang loosely over her shoulders. But that would be too obvious. What was she thinking of? Seducing him? She was beginning to regret coming to New York, using up the last of their meager funds. How could she have forgotten the impact of his dark good looks, his dynamic charm, his élan that defied description? And, above all, his blazing honesty and what it did to her. She was no longer sure she could keep from telling him the truth. And she doubted that he wouldn't see through her, even if she was able to pretend the loan she needed was for expansion, not disaster aid.

When she rejoined him in the dining room, his long glance of appreciation told her how she looked in the blue velvet, which revealed her every curve, despite the caftan cut. His interest in her was obviously stronger than ever, but there was also a wary watchfulness in his gaze, as though he suspected she had an ulterior motive for being here. But perhaps that was her guilty conscience talking. He offered her a frothy concoction in a mint-trimmed glass. "My own invention. Guaranteed to fade inhibitions."

She took the glass to the dining table, admiring the cool perfection of white bone china and plain gold cutlery. A high-backed dining chair seemed the safest place to sit. "What makes you think I'm inhibited?"

He smiled. "I recognize a code of honor when I see one. For a woman like you, it's all or nothing. A physical relationship with a man must be accompanied by the complete commitment you call true love. Unfortunately your style of true love is misdirected. Perhaps your life would be more fun if you'd let go and have a fling with some dashing fellow, whether you loved him or not."

"I suppose you're volunteering?"

"Of course. I've never concealed my deep and abiding lust for you, my dear Sarah. I believe you'd find me an accomplished lover."

"I've no doubt of it." She looked at the gold-plated dishes. "What's for lunch? I'm starved."

He rolled his eyes toward the ceiling. "So much for my romantic scenario. Very well, gorge yourself. We'll worry about honing another palate later. Would you like a glass of wine?"

"Whatever you put in this cocktail, it's dynamite. I think I'd better eat something." The memory of Ramon's warning about Jonathon's drinking flashed into her mind as Darius replaced the decanter on the table.

"You're frowning. Is something wrong?"

"You don't miss a thing, do you? Nothing's wrong. The pâté is wonderful."

"Tell me, how's Charmain?"

"Feisty and incorrigible as ever. She's practically reduced Ramon to gibbering idiocy with love for her."

Darius laughed. Then his face became serious. "I suppose she told you about my father?"

"Only that she knew him. Back during the forties, wasn't it? Wartime?" He nodded. Sarah waited for him to elaborate, but he quickly changed the subject, making small talk about the current shows on Broadway, a new cafe he'd found in Greenwich Village that made a passable *tajine*.

When he paused to serve the next course, Sarah asked, "What did you think Charmain might have told me about your father?"

His dark gaze was impenetrable, as though a door marked 'don't enter' had slammed into place. "My father died rather tragically, perhaps foolishly. Charmain sometimes becomes exasperated enough with me to predict a similar end."

"Your penchant for car races, I presume?"

"Actually, no. It's my penchant for dangerous women."

"Count me among them. I'm here on business, Darius. I'm sorry I let you think this was a social visit. I'm not usually so devious. I guess I've been listening to Charmain too much. She believes every encounter between a man and a woman should be a flirtation."

"She's right. It makes life more intriguing." His tone was light, but there was a cautious edge to it.

Sarah decided to plunge ahead. "I'm in town to talk to several prospective . . . investors. Well, no, not exactly investors. Lenders. I'm trying to raise a loan." She waited for a moment, hoping he would come to her rescue, but he merely watched her silently.

Sarah cleared her throat. "The Casa Brava has terrific potential. The Mexican government plans a new highway that will pass within a mile or two of the bay, and I've been thinking of a ferry service from the airstrip. I believe we can attract not only fishermen and sailing enthusiasts, but also the Club Med type crowd, as long as we offer entertainment and dancing—thanks to your idea of using the *sala!* Well, you know the climate in winter is ideal, the beach glorious—" She broke off, her confidence waning.

Still he remained silent. She forged ahead, "We need to expand, we need enough rooms for large crowds. We need to put in air conditioning. Oh, the main building is cool, thick adobe walls, but the cottages . . ."

Her voice trailed off, remembering there were no cottages now except the two adobe ones.

"But you were rebuilding the cottages when I left. Surely you put in air conditioning. You were building wood frame."

Sarah twisted the napkin on her lap into a tight ball. "Yes, but, uh, we were hoping to build more. Enough to accommodate a large tour group. We need working capital too to attract big-name entertainers, hire more help and so on." She wondered if her voice sounded as brittle to him as it did to her. She reached for her water goblet.

His hand came across the damask cloth and caught her wrist. "Look at me," he said and it was a command.

She raised her eyes and gave him what she hoped was a cool, level gaze. He studied her face for a moment, then his mouth twisted into a sardonic smile. He said, so softly she barely heard him, "Don't ever lie to me, Sarah. I can forgive almost any other transgression up to and including murder. But a liar sends me into a frenzy of anger."

"I'm not—" she began, but the glint in his eyes stopped her. She pulled her wrist free and stood up. "All right. There was a storm, we had some damage. The cottages aren't habitable." It was a slight understatement, but she salved her conscience by telling herself he wasn't going to help her anyway. She turned and walked from the room into the bedroom where she'd left her clothes.

He caught up with her as she reached for her still-damp dress, hanging on the back of a chair. He turned her around to face him. "I haven't refused to lend you the money."

His face was inches from hers, she could feel his breath. For a second he stared at her, into her soul it seemed, then his arms were hard against her back, crushing her to him, and his lips claimed hers in a bruising kiss that shocked her with the raw intensity of its demand.

She was too surprised to do anything but sway dizzily on her feet, neither cooperating nor resisting.

His tongue forced her teeth apart, explored the inside of her lip, touched her tongue lightly. She closed her eyes to shut out the paralyzing impact of his hypnotic stare. There was an invisible clash of wills, his determined to make her respond and hers struggling to maintain the illusion of an indifference she didn't feel. She was shocked by the feelings he brought to life. His lips and tongue and hands excited her beyond reason. She felt as though she were spinning on the edge of a cauldron of molten longings. Her body demanded fulfillment whether or not her mind accepted her desire.

His hands moved down her body. Her own arms, with a will of their own, slipped around his neck. She returned his kiss with a mounting ardor that seemed to release in him even greater hunger. She had never before experienced a kiss that was almost an act of love in itself. Brutal and demanding, yet a force potent enough to bring her to an exquisitely agonizing peak of desire she had never felt with Jonathon or any other man.

When Darius's hands slipped under her knees and he lifted her into his arms, still kissing her mouth with increasing urgency, there was a tight coil of tension inside her that could not remain unappeased. She wanted him to make love to her, without thought of time or place or consequences, as she had never wanted anything before.

As he laid her on the bed, she opened her eyes and looked up into his face. The smokescreen was gone from his eyes. She could clearly see much more than lust there.

Chapter 19

The blue velvet caftan was slipped from her shoulders, exposing her breasts. Darius inched the soft material down her body slowly, kissing her nipples, then each part of her, with lips that burned her skin and lit each nerve ending until it seemed the imprint of his mouth was both outside and inside her body.

Somewhere on the edge of rational thought a warning beacon flashed. The look of utter worship in his eyes frightened her. With a jolting clarity she knew she was playing with a force whose power she could only guess at. She struggled to overcome the sweet lethargy she felt, wanting to submit, but knowing she must not.

As he straightened up and began to unbutton his shirt, showing hard pectoral muscles lightly shaded by fine black hair, she forced her heavy-lidded eyes fully open and whispered, "No . . . no, I can't do this."

She sat up, reaching for the caftan he had tossed on the bed beside her. Clutching it to her breast, she swung her feet to the floor. "I'm sorry. I don't know what came over me. I didn't mean to lead you on, give you the impression I wanted . . ."

"My lovemaking?" His hand dropped from his shirt. There was a frozen look on his face, as though she had flung cold water at him. He made no move to stop her as she stood up and backed away from him, holding the blue velvet shield in front of her. "You little fool. Of course you wanted me to make love to you. Why do you deny me, and yourself? Are you still carrying a torch—"

"Darius, I came here to ask you for a loan. If I let you make love to me, it will seem like some sort of payment on account."

His jaw moved slightly. "And wasn't that exactly what you had in mind? I'm a man of the world, Sarah, not a gullible schoolboy. You came willingly to my apartment, removed your clothes, batted your eyes at me throughout an intimate meal. My dear Sarah, there's an ugly word for women who behave as you've behaved today."

She felt a flush stain her cheeks. "My clothes were wet, I certainly didn't mean to invite . . ." she trailed off, feeling angry and foolish and wishing she were a thousand miles away.

He sat on the edge of the bed, watching her. "When you report this episode to Charmain, she's going to chastise you for not paying closer attention to her tuition."

"That's not fair, Darius. To Charmain or to me. I didn't come here to sell myself to you. I wanted a legitimate loan, properly and legally drawn up, with appropriate terms and interest." She stopped retreating, turning to attack in the face of his scornful amusement. The mirror behind her reflected the naked length of her back, but she didn't care. "I *told* you I came for a loan, before you—"

"And what did you propose to use as collateral? A ramshackle hotel without guests? I'm a businessman. If I made such foolhardy investments, I'd soon be bankrupt."

Feeling severely handicapped by her lack of clothing, Sarah grabbed her dress from the back of the chair and went into the adjoining bathroom. When she was dressed, she found he was no longer in the bedroom. The crumpled bedspread told its silent story. She looked at it for a moment, feeling acute regret.

Darius was waiting for her in the sitting room. "I've got some coffee ready. Sit down. If you're ready to be honest with me, I've a solution to both your problem and mine."

She sat stiffly on the edge of a chair as he poured coffee into demitasse cups and brought a tray to her. He sat opposite her, looking cool and controlled. Watching him, it was difficult to realize that only moments earlier he had been as lost in the madness of desire as she. "*Your* problem," she repeated. "I didn't know you had one."

"Oh, yes. I'm faced with a dilemma I've never had before. I want a woman who won't let herself want me."

"Did it occur to you perhaps that's the reason you want her? Simply because you can't have her. If she capitulated, you'd probably lose interest immediately."

"No, I don't think so. You see, the Descartes men have an Achilles heel. We admit to being noted womanizers. We learn to enjoy the fair sex at an early age and must have female companionship at all times. Had you been interested enough to inquire, you'd have been informed that the name of Descartes is indelibly branded into feminine hearts the world over. But our punishment is that when we eventually fall for a woman, our passion is irrevocable. Our penance for a trail of broken hearts is undying devotion to one woman, no matter how badly she uses us. If you don't believe me, ask Charmain to tell you the real story behind her romance with my father."

I will, Sarah thought. Aloud, she said, "I don't know what you're driving at. Look, you wanted me to be honest, so I will be. Charmain and I need money. I doubt anyone will lend it to us. If you won't, then I'll be on my way. We'll survive. The Casa Brava will survive. I let myself get carried away for a moment because you're a damned attractive man. But you know that. I didn't plan what happened, no matter what you think."

He held up his hand. "Please! Spare me. You came

to see me, in person, knowing the impact your presence has on me. If you'd wanted nothing more than a loan, you could have phoned."

"I thought it would be easier to explain. Besides, I was coming to New York. Oh, what's the use! Believe what you like. May I please use the phone to call a cab?"

"You haven't heard my proposal yet." The wary look was back in his eyes.

A small hope flickered. Sarah said, "You mean you'll lend us the money?"

"On one condition."

"Yes?"

"Please, sit down again for a moment. You just said, I believe the term was 'damned attractive.' Did you mean that?"

Sarah sat down. "Don't play coy, Darius. You know you are. Unbearably conceited and domineering, but damned attractive."

He smiled, teeth white against his tanned skin, but there was a small undecipherable flame in his eyes. "Then perhaps you will be amenable to my proposal, after all."

"You should watch your terminology. Wouldn't 'business proposition' be more apropos? If you're worried about security for the loan—"

"Proposal *is* the proper word, Sarah. I want you to marry me."

There was a moment's silence so intense it seemed to drum against her ears. She was aware of the scent of roses in the silver vase on the table beside her, of the muted patter of rain against the windows, of her own heartbeat as she began to breathe again. His face was serious, but unreadable. "Why?"

"The lady asks *why*. Why, indeed!" His expression changed to amused tolerance. "Because, Sarah, my love, I don't know any other way to woo you. As my wife, you would be more, shall we say, accessible?"

"You're mad."

"It would seem so. But that doesn't answer my question. No, wait before you say anything. Let me point out a few advantages to assuming the role of Mrs. Darius Descartes."

He rose and slowly paced back and forth in front of her. She thought of a caged panther silently plotting the fate of his keeper after the escape. Darius said in a conversational tone, "There's the obvious advantage of my wealth. You'd never again have to go searching for business loans. And I would promise not to interfere with the operation of the Casa Brava. That would be up to you and Charmain." He paused. "Unless, of course, you couldn't make a go of it. I wouldn't be inclined to allow you to throw my money away on another foolish investment. You would be allowed one financial disaster only. After that, you'd have to carve out a career without capital, if a career you must have."

Sarah said slowly, "I still don't understand why you're offering marriage. You must think you can buy me. Why not just offer a loan in return for cohabitation?"

His eyes darkened. "I want collateral, I told you that. I want you bound to me by a more durable tie than that of being my mistress. Besides, I shall expect you to do more than simply decorate the boudoir. My residences would benefit from a woman's touch. There will be hostess duties from time to time. I'd like a wife to cheer me on when I race my cars. To say nothing of the tiresome matter of husband-hunting females. A man of my age and position is expected to have a wife. I want you, and your present misfortune seems tailor-made. I may not get another chance to bargain with you."

"It doesn't matter to you that I don't love you?"

A ghost of a smile hovered about his sensual lips. "You might learn, given time and the right circumstances."

"Don't count on it. I think not, Darius. I'm not sure whether to be flattered or insulted."

"Oh, come on, it wouldn't be so bad. You might even enjoy it. Where else are you going to find a man who can tango?"

Sarah smiled in spite of herself.

In a quick change of tactics, he said, "You might as well settle for me. Your true love will never leave Cecily and even if he would, you wouldn't let him. So the elusive Jonathon Conway is never going to be yours. Did it ever occur to you that he might settle down and realize what a gem he has in Cecily if you were no longer available?"

She bit back a denial, thinking of Jon anxiously awaiting her return to the Casa Brava. He had been demolished by the loss of his manuscript, although Cecily encouraged him to begin again. Sarah's argument died on her lips. Darius was right, her love for Jonathon was hopeless. What better way to insulate herself against further hurt than by marrying Darius? Besides, if it hadn't been for her, Jon never would have brought Cecily to the Casa Brava and they wouldn't be destitute now. Sarah owed them a new start.

But the thought that obliterated all other considerations was the quickening of her senses that accompanied the sudden image of herself and Darius, locked away from the world in a romantic hideaway.

Darius, watching her closely, said, "I see you're at last weighing advantages. That's a good sign. But don't say yes or no just now. Give me twenty-four hours. See if you can stand my company that long. Then tomorrow at midnight you can tell me whether or not you'll marry me."

Sarah hadn't realized she was agreeing to spend the most breathlessly exhilarating twenty-four hours of her life. It began with a ride through Central Park in a hansom cab as the rain gave way to fleeting rays of sunshine. Darius assured her that the rainbow arch under which they seemed to pass was the best of omens.

They returned to his apartment where she found a smiling maid laying out a lovely sea green evening dress. Sarah looked questioningly at Darius, who said, "I wanted to see you in that particular shade of green again. You'll never know how many times I've dreamed of you wearing Charmain's dress at the villa, dancing the tango like you'd been born to it."

When Sarah hesitated, he said, "I'm sorry for presuming. Perhaps you have an evening dress with you you'd prefer to wear?"

A quick image of her ruined clothes at the Casa Brava flashed into her mind. "I'll wear this one, thank you."

The evening whirled by. Certain pictures clicked into place in Sarah's mind. The way every head turned when they entered the most exclusive French restaurant in town. The maître d' and waiters treating Darius as though he were visiting royalty. His crowd-dominating presence made her wonder how his wife would feel about being envied by every other woman who crossed his path. Yet he was impeccably attentive, apparently so wrapped up in Sarah that he never even saw anyone else.

"That shade of green is a devastating foil for you," he whispered after giving the waiter their order. "You look like Aphrodite rising from the warm tropical sea. The color makes your eyes even bluer, and your skin glows like ripe peaches."

Sarah smiled her thanks for the compliment and twisted the stem of her wineglass. On Darius's lips such extravagant words of praise sounded completely spontaneous and natural, yet a nagging suspicion that this was all a preseduction charade persisted. But if that were the case, why bother to propose marriage? And what about her loan?

Later she wondered at the ease with which he conjured up the best seats for Broadway's number one hit, booked solid for weeks in advance. After a late supper they danced until it was nearly dawn and they were the only couple left amid deserted tables and yawning waiters.

Where had the hours flown? They were gone faster than minutes. Conversation ranged from pre-Columbian art to the latest Superman movie, which Darius freely admitted seeing and enjoying. Sarah teased him that such movies were aimed at twelve-year olds. He wasn't fazed. "They're aimed at audiences tired of antiheroes and unrelieved gloom. They're for people who want to see courage prevail and the villain get his just deserts. And speaking of villains, I understand the three wretches who terrorized you at the Casa were put away for a long stretch by the Mexican judicial system."

Sarah nodded, thinking that the real villain of the piece had got off scot-free. But perhaps Buck Latimer had been punished enough in losing his beloved daughter and knowing why he had lost her.

As Sarah leaned sleepily against Darius's shoulder for one last dance, she felt both a sense of time rushing by and the comforting continuity of a well-seasoned relationship, as if she had known Darius for a long time. They talked easily, each understanding the other's remarks instantly. Sarah found that when she dropped her defenses, he was warm, keenly aware of the world around him, compassionately concerned with the people he knew. She felt as though he had slipped off his mask, allowing her to see that the man beneath was more complex and interesting than she had imagined.

"Come on, you're asleep on your feet," Darius said firmly. "You're going home to bed." When she tensed in his arms, he added quickly, "I'll be the perfect gentleman. It will kill me, but you have my word. I just want to watch you sleep, be there when you wake up. Will you come back to my apartment?"

She thought of the run-down hotel at which she had registered, perilously close to Times Square and its nocturnal subculture. She would stay at his apartment.

When they reached the bedroom door, she turned and looked up at him. The evening had been perfect. She felt as carefree and happy as a young girl who sees the world opening before her like an oyster. Darius had the ability to blot everything from her mind but his own electric presence. Looking into his face, she wanted him to kiss her, wanted to return his kiss in a way that would thank him. There were no words to express what she felt.

But he merely smiled down at her, an odd regretful smile, and touched her cheek lightly with his forefinger. "Good night, Sarah." He held the door open for her.

Feeling suddenly bereft, she went into the large empty bedroom.

She awakened to the scent of flowers. Opening her eyes, she saw they were strewn all over her bed. Roses, carnations, orchids, gladioli, even exotic blossoms that looked as if they had been flown in from a distant tropical island. The room was filled with baskets of flowers on every inch of the floor, covering the dressing table and nightstands. Garlands of flowers hung from the chairs and draperies. Beside her head on the pillow was a bunch of violets tied with a white satin ribbon.

As she sat up, tiny lilies-of-the-valley and forget-me-nots slid from her hair. She inhaled their fragrance, wondering if she were dreaming. She picked up the violets and surveyed Darius over the soft velvet petals.

He sat in a chair near the bed, smiling at her reaction.

Sarah tossed a handful of rose petals in the air, and they fluttered over her head in a perfumed cloud. She laughed, swept away by the sheer extravagance and sensuality of the gesture.

Darius came to her as she rose from the bed. He took her into his arms and he looked at her, his dark eyes nakedly adoring her. There was no pretense in that gaze. She knew now that his feelings for her ran deep and true. The knowledge was both exhilarating and frightening. God help the woman who played fast and loose with feelings that intense. A small warning voice was vying for her attention, deep in the rational part of her mind. It whispered, *run!*

"It isn't quite twenty-four hours, but I can't wait another moment. Patience isn't one of my virtues, I'm afraid. Say you'll marry me and we'll fly to the most romantic spot on earth and say our vows. Then we'll go away on a honeymoon anywhere you choose."

He didn't wait for her answer, his lips traveled lightly down her forehead and he kissed her eyelids, then took her mouth in a tender lingering exploration that sent a surge of longing through her. The inner warning voice was forgotten. She wanted him to make love to her there amid the flowers, with the heady scent in her nostrils and the lean hard warmth of his body fused to hers.

"Sarah?"

"Yes," she whispered, her voice liquid. "Yes, I'll marry you. Here, now, whenever you want."

He seized her and lifted her into the air, spinning her around in an exuberant pirouette. When he put her down, still holding her close, he kissed her again, firmly, possessively, but with an unspoken promise of devotion that needed no explanation. She felt it in his touch, even before he said softly, "I'll spend the rest of my life making you happy, Sarah. Tell me what you want and I'll get it for you. We'll be married as soon as we can arrange it. Then we'll go away. Where do you want to go?"

"Somewhere warm and sunny."

"Not your Casa Brava?" he asked in mock alarm. "With Charmain leering at us knowingly?"

Sarah thought of the condition of the Casa Brava and shook her head quickly. "How about your villa in Morocco?"

"Later, not now. I want to make some changes in the

staff and furnishings of my former bachelor quarters before we go there. I know a wonderful South Seas island, remote, romantic. After our ceremony here we could have a native wedding in one of the most beautiful spots on earth."

"Perfect." She paused. "Darius?"

He was kissing her hair, nibbling her ear lobe. "Yes?"

"Could I wire some money to Charmain before we leave?"

He held her at arm's length, studying her with amused resignation. "Whoever started the rumor that women are romantics was sadly misinformed. It's we foolish men who forget practical matters at moments like this. Yes, my dear Sarah, we'll send whatever funds are needed to shore up your hotel."

Chapter 20

They were married by a justice of the peace, yanked from his sleep at dawn the day after they were issued a license. Sarah wore a simple white suit and Darius wore the awed expression of a man who reaches for the stars and captures a comet.

"I won't feel you're really mine until we reach our island," he told her. "But I want to make you legally my wife before you change your mind."

His private jet was waiting to take them to the West Coast and from there to Honolulu. A smaller island-hopping plane took them on the last leg of their journey.

That evening Darius took Sarah's hand and led her into an immense unspoiled fern grove, cool and green and more beautiful than any cathedral. They walked toward the wedding cave along a path sprinkled with flower petals, yellow and white ginger blossoms and plumeria. A sparklingly clear waterfall descended from black volcanic rock, and the sound of the water was more musical than any wedding march. The air had been recently cleansed by warm tropical rain, and gentle trade winds brought the scent of a million blossoms. Each of her senses delighted in the magic of the island.

The wedding cave, ringed with ferns and flowers, was little more than a hollow in the side of the verdant hill. Sarah took her place at Darius's side, moved by the beauty of the setting. Tears sprang to her eyes as a long row of dancers swayed slowly, their sarongs splashing color against the deep green backdrop, chanting the traditional wedding song.

Darius placed a *lei* around her neck, and she stood on tiptoe to slide a garland of flowers and shells over his head. They repeated their vows. Then Darius gathered her into his arms and kissed her slowly, tenderly. He whispered so that only she could hear, "I'll love you until I die."

She couldn't speak, her throat was tight with tears. She looked at him through a misting over her eyes, thinking that everything was perfect, only a little voice whispered that she was marrying the wrong man.

There was a *luau* on the beach with fire dancers and a wild hula. An enormous roast pig was pulled, steaming and aromatic, from an underground pit. Sarah drank a strong island brew until she felt light-headed.

At the height of the feasting, Darius took her hand and they sped away through the soft purple twilight to the wedding hut built on a black sand beach, sheltered from view by a thickly planted cluster of coconut palms.

Darius swept her into his arms to carry her through

the open door. He put her down slowly so that she slid against his body. Then he took her mouth and kissed her with rising passion.

She felt his fingers slip the white embroidered gown from her shoulders. His lips followed the curve of her throat. "I had them bring in a modern bed. I hope you don't mind foregoing the traditional reed mat?"

Shaking her head, she thought, it's a dream. An erotic fantasy I've conjured up. A moonlit tropical island, a handsome stranger about to make passionate love to me, surrounded by the scent of flowers and the whisper of surf breaking against a coral reef. Odd how she now thought of Darius as a stranger when she'd felt so close to him in New York. But that was before they were married. Before he began to take these physical intimacies. Perhaps thinking of him as a stranger added to her excitement, or perhaps it was simply too much liquor. Whatever it was, she abandoned herself to an unexpected and surprising sense of joy.

She lay back in his arms as he carried her to the bed. He finished undressing her, then removed his own white slacks and matching tunic. The outfit reminded her of the white linen suit he had worn the day he pursued her through the marketplace, the Djemaa el Fna in Marrakech, looking like a Berber prince intent on plunder.

Tonight in the warm stillness of the tropical night, his body seemed to be sculpted from bronze, muscular, alive, a fine-tuned instrument. She shivered as he pressed close, feeling his strength and virility, overwhelmed by his masculine drive, trapped by the strength of his passion.

Long ago in her youth and innocence Jonathon had made love to her. It had been a tentative joining, hesitant, tremblingly awkward, she realized now. Then she had thought no other man would ever be able to awaken desire in her, but the raw power of Darius swept everything from her mind. Only the sensations his lips and tongue and hands brought to her flesh were real. Everywhere he touched her, a long-dormant volcano erupted into lava flows of response, until she writhed beneath him and wanted him to enter her more than she had ever wanted anything before in her life.

Darius whispered her name, over and over, pressing his lips to her eyelids, her hair, her breasts. "Sarah, oh, Sarah, my darling," until his voice was a litany, expressing his love and yearning for fulfillment that brought down the last barrier of her reserve. She opened herself to him and he was part of her and she gasped because he reached some inner core of her being she hadn't known existed.

Afterward she lay in his arms, feeling a euphoria that was part sensual satiety, part wonder that she could have been so lost in passion with a man she had thought of as a stranger only moments before. It was as though the intensity of his feelings had been enough to encompass both of them. She felt a twinge of guilt that her body had responsed so fully to his lovemaking, while a part of her mind held back, still loyal to her first love.

She pressed her face into the hollow of Darius's neck and hoped the pale silver moonlight hid any outward expression of her thoughts. He kissed her lingeringly and searched her face as if trying to read her feelings. Was that a shadow that flitted across the moon, or did she see disappointment in his eyes when he looked at her?

They swam and surfed during the day, walked on the beach at night under a sky studded with a thousand stars. Once they went to a tiny cafe and danced to throbbing rhythms that soon sent them back to the privacy of their beach retreat to seek frenzied fulfillment of their desire.

Whether in blazing sunlight or cool darkness, their passion threatened to erupt at any moment. Sarah thought she would never get used to his intricate and varied approaches to lovemaking. On the rare moments she was alone she blushed at the memory of some of the kisses and caresses they had shared, yet the second he took her into his arms and began another of those slow erotic journeys, her inhibitions vanished.

He made love to her on the beach, in the shelter of a sand dune, with the sun still high in the sky; on a bed of ferns while a tiny white bird fluttered over their heads. Each time she closed her eyes and lost herself in a feast of sensual delights, her guilty memories grew dimmer and dimmer. But one night as they lay in bed he suddenly swore and pulled away from her.

He snapped on the bedside lamp and she blinked, looking up at him in surprise as he stood up and began to pull on his swim trunks. "Darius? What's wrong?"

His voice was ragged with emotion. "You hold back. You don't give all of yourself. Why?" Anger and hurt burned in his eyes.

She sat up, cold with dread. "I don't know what you mean. Have I denied you anything?"

"You deny me what I crave most. Your body is mine, available, neither willingly nor grudgingly given. I've had whores who feigned more joy in my arms than you."

A surge of resentment flowed through her. "You got what you wanted. Why isn't it enough?"

"Because I want all of you."

"I'm here, your wife, in your bed. What more do you want?"

"Your love." The words were whispered like a prayer.

She turned away from him, staring at the open window that framed an empty silver sea and a rising moon that looked lost and lonely in the blackness of the night sky. "So that your conquest will be complete? Darius, it's time you learned there are some things you can't buy or take or demand. They have to be freely given."

The instant the words were out she regretted them. She had attacked him to defend her own guilty conscience, because he had given more than she.

He was silent for a moment, then he sat down beside her on the bed. "I deserved that. I shan't bring up the subject again. I'll just have to try harder to earn your love. I'm sorry, Sarah. My impatience has always been my undoing."

She ached to pull him into her arms, to cradle his head to her breast and whisper to him that she couldn't imagine falling asleep without making love to him. Why didn't he know that without her telling him? Her body responded to him easily, instantly, but perhaps some lingering loyalty to Jonathon did remain in her mind, and that made her hold back. She said in a small voice, "You put on your swim trunks. Are you going swimming?"

He pulled off the trunks. "No, no, I don't think so." Then he wrapped her in his arms and made love to her with fierce urgency.

All of the adjectives Sarah had applied to Darius seemed to belong to some other man as the days of their honeymoon sped by. Where before she had seen him as ruthless, mocking, domineering, conceited and self-centered, he began to emerge as a different person entirely. He was tender, attentive, so aware of each of her whims and moods that it seemed her every wish was granted before she had time to realize she had made it.

He was generous to a fault. She learned never to admire anything or he would find a way to buy it for her. Even so, his gifts came almost daily, each one more extravagant than the last. A perfectly matched pearl necklace, a stunning pendant, a whisper of wicked black lace, a tiny shell-encrusted box. Flowers every day.

But more than these expressions of devotion was the giving of himself. He was a witty and stimulating

companion, quick to laugh and see the ridiculous or
amusing side of a situation. Behind his handsome
exterior Sarah found a mind keenly intelligent, an
awareness of the world and knowledge of humanity
that left her awed. If he weren't so physically attractive,
she thought, I'd have liked to have him for a friend. As
the days passed she began to think that perhaps wild
sexual attraction along with the security of a solid
friendship with a man was better than love. She wondered about that old saying that a woman loves only her
first lover, after that she's in love with love. What
would it have been like if Darius had been her first
lover?

They spent a week on the island, then flew back to
Oahu and boarded a gleaming white yacht he had
chartered. The leisurely sail across the serene Pacific
was a period of deepening their knowledge of one
another, of making love under starlit skies and forget-
ting that any other world existed outside of their
floating love nest.

Darius constantly delighted her with his lovemaking.
He led her so delicately into acts of love that sometimes
the wildfire was in her veins before she realized they
were making love. His nearness could inflame her
senses, and sometimes her knees felt weak when he
simply looked at her across their cabin.

There were moments when she found herself melting
and she almost wanted to tell him that she was happy
being Mrs. Darius Descartes, that he had brought a
heady excitement to her life and made her feel like a
complete human being. But an inexplicable caution
stopped her. Her words might appear to be only a salve
for his wounded pride. If only he hadn't accused her of
holding back. If only he'd been patient enough to wait
for her feelings for him to form. What she felt for him
wasn't the joyous and innocent first love she'd felt for
Jonathon, but perhaps it was more enduring. Not quite
love, but a certain bond that was the next best thing.

When the yacht docked in San Pedro, California, Darius had already announced that their honeymoon was far from over. He wanted to take her to Paris so she could buy a belated trousseau, then spend Christmas with her at his cottage in Surrey. There was nothing that couldn't be delayed until the first of the year— neither his business nor the Casa Brava. Ramon and Charmain could handle things, couldn't they?

When he brought the subject up, Sarah was too sated with lovemaking to argue. When he caressed her, kissed her, lay with her pressed to his chest, nothing was more important than the consummation of feelings too overpowering to allow anything mundane to intrude.

Afterward, as she lay in his arms, he said, "We could stop off in Illinois to see your parents for a couple of days. I've felt guilty they didn't attend their only daughter's wedding, but we were a trifle impetuous about it, weren't we, my love?"

"They were too relieved I was getting married to worry about it," Sarah said, laughing. "They were afraid I was going to be an old maid. There are such creatures in Palerville, believe it or not, even in the enlightened eighties."

"Then, too, I'd like to meet your cousin Buck Latimer again," Darius added. "Perhaps invite him to dine with us. We could serve crow."

Sarah grimaced. "Why crow? Why not arsenic?" She nestled closer to him, relishing the knowledge that she'd never have to worry about Buck again.

"Because, my dear, you've proved that he and his frightful wife were wrong about you. You married *me*. You didn't steal their daughter's husband."

Sarah was silent, remembering that Cecily and Jon were still staying at the Casa Brava. If she had to answer Buck and Estelle's questions about them, it would mean Darius would find out. "You know, perhaps it would be better to postpone our visit to

Palerville. If I know Mother, she'll want to arrange parties for us and a couple of days wouldn't give her enough time. I'll phone them again and promise a long visit in the spring. After all, we *are* on our honeymoon."

Next morning she awakened to find he was already dressed. He bent to kiss her. "I've ordered your breakfast tray. I'm going to make arrangements for our flight to Paris. I'll be back soon."

The moment he left Sarah picked up the phone, hoping she would be able to complete a call to Mexico before he returned. She wasn't supposed to be thinking about the Casa Brava on her honeymoon, but she'd invested all of her own money in the hotel, as well as a generous amount of her husband's. She was now more or less an equal partner with Charmain and Ramon, and she was anxious to know how they were handling her investment.

Charmain's voice crackled over the long distance line, fading at times. "Darling! We were shocked by your wire, I mean, stunned! Do you really think you should have gone that far? Marrying him . . . hope you know what you . . . didn't I warn you not to . . ."

"Hey, old bean, yell a bit louder, the line's bad. Listen, I've only got a minute. You got the money okay? Tell me about our hotel."

"You realize every woman on earth envies you . . . what? Oh, yes . . . Ramon and I . . . yes, we got the generator going and we'll start . . ." There was a burst of static, concluding with a faint, ". . . but don't worry . . ."

"Charlie, old girl, I can't *hear* you. Don't worry about what?"

"I can hear you fine, love. Tell me, are you ecstatically happy with Darius? Of course you are! You—"

Sarah couldn't make out the rest. She would have liked to ask about Jonathon, how he was taking the loss of his manuscript, but didn't dare for fear Darius would return to the hotel room. Charmain said they didn't need any more money for the time being. Sarah asked if they'd started rebuilding the cottages, but couldn't decipher the reply.

The fragmented conversation had told her little about what was happening at the Casa Brava, but Sarah reasoned that they wouldn't really need her until the rebuilding was well under way.

She and Darius stayed in Los Angeles long enough for Sarah to buy clothes for the journey to France. She was astonished when the Rodeo Drive saleswoman asked shyly if she were on her honeymoon.

Sarah blushed inexplicably. "How did you know?"

"You've got a certain glow. It's in your eyes and your smile, even the way you walk." The woman's eyes crinkled with memories of her own. She slipped a heather-colored coat over Sarah's shoulders. "This will be perfect for the cold weather and will look marvelous if you layer it with the matching shawl." She paused, smiling, and added, "You must love your husband very much."

Sarah was disconcerted for a moment. Darius was certainly a lusty, virile male and his rampant sexuality made life with him excitingly complete. But to mistake this for love . . .

Darius and Sarah joined the "Mile High Club" when Darius made love to her aboard his jet as they headed east toward Paris. As he nuzzled her breast and stroked her inner thighs, she murmured, "I'm turning into a sex maniac. How did I ever manage to live so chastely before you came along?"

He laughed and pulled her over on top of him, looking at her with eyes that openly worshiped her. "You're a perfectly normal warm-blooded woman, as I knew you would be, and I'm your slave. Can you begin to imagine how I adore you? I want nothing more than to be with you every second of every day. It's a good thing I made several fortunes before you came along, the way I'm neglecting my business now. I don't even have any interest in racing."

"Is it true that men who drive race cars have a death wish? If so, I'm glad you've lost interest."

"I never told you this, but I had planned to enter the Baja 500 last summer while you were slaving away over your hotel. I'd been thinking of starting a similar race through the Moroccan desert. But I didn't enter the Baja 500. I waited around like a fool for you or Charmain to call that pilot's number in San Diego. I didn't want to be away in case you needed me. I kept thinking about those bandits."

"But all those postcards we got, from all over the world!"

He smiled sheepishly. "Easy enough to arrange when you have as many shipping agents as I do. I merely wrote them myself and had them posted from different countries. I only returned to New York when it became obvious you two very gutsy ladies were handling things nicely without my help."

"Gutsy ladies?" Sarah came close to giggling. "That sounds so unlike your precise European speech, Darius. Am I corrupting your semantics too?"

"I love the American language. It's vital and alive, constantly changing. Like you, my love."

She felt him stir beneath her and responded by bending to kiss his lips and draw him into her moist warmth. She moved against him in a shameless sensual dance. Everything seemed so natural in their lovemaking. At times they were equal partners, but there were occasions when he commanded and other moments when she was the aggressor. He lay still for a minute, allowing her to advance and retreat, to tease and promise greater delights to come. Her hair trailed over his chest. He reached up to run his fingers through the soft waves, then allowed his hand to drift back to the throbbing point of her breast. Her desire grew until she was lost in it, exploding into a climax that sent aftershocks shuddering through her body. She floated, mindless, in a soft dark pool of contentment.

He rolled her gently to her back, kissed her mouth and her throat and her still-taut nipples and said, "And now, my darling, that you've again awakened the sleeping gods . . ."

Sarah had been to Paris before, but she'd never really seen it until she saw it with Darius. Surely the Arc de Triomphe had been less grand before? The fountain in the Place de la Concorde less beautiful? The stairway to the Basilica of the Sacre Coeur, with its winter-bare trees and lampposts almost lost in a pale blue mist, had never been so romantic as it was when she and Darius climbed it and looked down at the Seine far below.

Darius's flawless French eased their passage around the lovely city, procured for them the finest meals and best seats in the theatre and opera. Sarah was aghast at the number of gowns he insisted she buy. She knew the couturiers by reputation but he knew them personally. She laughingly protested that she'd need to rent the *Queen Elizabeth* to ship all of her purchases home.

As they were dressing for dinner and the theater one night, Darius apologized profusely that he would have to take some time to check on his business investments. He would also need to inspect a new racing car that was being built for him. After that there were one or two social engagements they really should attend, since his friends were all eager to meet Sarah.

Sarah didn't hear anything he said after he mentioned the racing car. "Oh, no, you aren't going to race it yourself?" She had a cold knot in her stomach as she remembered, too vividly, visiting Cecily and Jonathon in the hospital after their car had crashed.

Darius gave her a quizzical glance. "You sounded almost like a wife then. Don't tell me you really are concerned about my skin?"

Sarah looked at his reflection in her mirror. He was

darkly handsome in his dinner jacket, but there was a certain reckless gleam in his eyes when he mentioned his racing cars that was at odds with his dress and quiet manner. He has so much unleashed energy he must find ways to expend it, she thought. "I don't know what anyone gets out of speed for speed's sake, danger for no real purpose. Besides, I had some close friends who were badly hurt—" she broke off, realizing she was about to say the one name she had promised herself never to mention to Darius. Sarah stood up quickly and went to the bed to pick up her dress. "It's your hide, Darius. I won't nag about your racing."

She stepped into the white jersey gown, and he came to help her zip it and fasten the clasp of her necklace. "But I love it when you nag. It gives me the illusion that you worry about me. Unfortunately there's no need. I haven't any races scheduled this time of year. Actually the car I'm building is designed for desert racing where stamina is more important than speed. I understand there is a Baja 1000 in addition to the Baja 500. If you're busy with your hotel next year, it might be a diversion to try out my cars."

"When do you have to check on your investments and the car?"

"Tomorrow. You can rest if you like. There's going to be a gala party tomorrow evening."

He pressed a kiss between the silken strands of her hair at the nape of her neck. The imprint of his lips went far beyond the surface of her skin, touching the intangible part of her that was the spirit and essence of her whole being. It was like a musical chord that reverberates far beyond the instrument strings. She shivered and turned to face him, then pressed herself into the warm circle of his arms. She was on the brink of making some declaration, she wasn't even sure what, because she was so overcome by the force of her feelings.

Before she could speak, he looked down at her and said wryly, "From the suddenly intense look in your eyes, I assume my mentioning business had reminded you of the Casa Brava? Ah, Sarah, how I wish I could inspire such a look in your eyes. Why don't you call Charmain and see how they're faring?"

For once, Sarah was acutely sorry he'd misread her mind. To tell him she'd been experiencing a wave of intense feeling for him rather than the Casa Brava would now seem like an afterthought. Nonplussed, she offered a denial rather than an explanation. "Mexico was the last thing on my mind," she said. Then, to cover her confusion, she kissed his mouth. As always, she felt the surge of his manhood, his immediate desire for her. He began to caress her body as he explored her mouth. After a moment he whispered, "I'm afraid, my darling, you've just made us miss the curtain, perhaps even the entire performance."

Later, basking in sweet contentment, she tried to recapture the earlier moment, but it drifted out of reach as elusive as the starlight glinting on Darius's perfect profile. She thought perhaps it was the small gesture—a quick kiss, or a squeeze of her hand, or the brushing back of her hair—she found so endearing. However, she'd found similar gestures touching when they came from Jon. Perhaps that accounted for her wave of feeling. Perhaps unconsciously she was trying to find some of Jon's qualities in her husband.

The following morning, after Darius left to take care of his business, she put in a long distance call to Mexico and waited in an agony of suspense because the circuits were busy.

She told herself she was being ridiculous, keeping the calls to Mexico secret. After all, if it was necessary for him to keep an eye of his investments, why shouldn't she do likewise? But she knew the real reason was that she had neither told him the full extent of the storm damage to the Casa Brava nor informed him that the Conways were still in residence. Not that he'd inquired about them, but in not volunteering the information she felt guilty of a sin of omission.

The phone rang and she snatched it up, expecting Ramon to answer in Spanish. She was surprised when she heard Jonathon's voice.

"Jon? It's Sarah. Yes, I'm fine, how are you and Cecily and everyone?" She was uncomfortably aware that the announcement of her marriage to Darius had been relayed to him secondhand via her wire to Charmain from New York. "Jon? Can you hear me?"

"Yes. We're all right. At least, everyone but Ramon is. He had an accident, fell from one of the rocks and broke his leg. Charmain's taking care of him. Where are you?"

"In Paris. We're leaving in a few days for England. I expect it will be the first of the year before I get back to Mexico. I'm sorry about Ramon. Give him my regards. I hope his accident isn't causing a problem with all the clean-up and repairs. Is Danny handling Ramon's relatives all right?"

There was a long pause. "Danny isn't here. He had to go home because his mother was ill."

Oh, no, Sarah thought. Both Ramon and Danny out of commission. She was immediately ashamed of the thought. "I'm sorry about his mother. Does he plan to return to the Baja?"

"Yes, I think so. He calls Cecily occasionally."

He sounds distant, Sarah thought, and not only in miles. My marriage to Darius must have been a shock, and Jon's too much of a gentleman to mention it. It seemed more gracious, somehow, than hearing empty congratulations. Jon must have realized why she had entered into the marriage. She waited for him to elaborate, but there was another silence. "Cecily okay?"

"She's like the flower in Gray's 'Elegy,' blossoming in the desert air."

Wasting her sweetness on the desert air, Sarah thought, wasn't that the line? Just as Cecily wasted a lot of love on a meaningless marriage to you.

"We both love it here, Sarah, despite everything. The peace and tranquillity of the setting, the air itself, seems therapeutic. I believe if I'd been anywhere else on earth I'd have gone out of my mind. First the loss of my manuscript, then losing you, imagining you in the arms of that slightly sinister foreigner—"

Sarah interrupted. "Jon, I haven't much time. Will you bring Charmain to the phone?"

She waited a long time for Charmain's voice to come on the line. "Is this Mrs. Darius Descartes? Sal, old love, what a wonderful sound that title has. I know I warned you never to get married, but I believe in your case it was the only way to go. I hear you're in Paris. Are you having a most magnificent honeymoon? But of course you are. Darius is driving you wild with sweet madness . . ."

Sarah wondered, as Charmain trilled on, whether Jonathon was still in the room, listening to her conversation. Charmain was laying it on thick for somebody's benefit. She'd sounded more dismayed about Sarah's marriage to Darius during their last call and now there was an unnatural brittleness to her voice. Perhaps it was the distortion of the long distance wires. Charmain assured her that Ramon was all right, but couldn't work until the cast came off his leg, and his relatives did little without his personal direction.

"But you did get them started on cleaning up the hacienda rooms? Did you order the supplies for re-building the cottages? Do you have any guests at all? Do you need more money?"

"Sweets, not so fast! *Más despacio, por favor!* I can't possibly answer a dozen questions at once. Can't all this wait until you come back? You *are* coming back? I've missed you both so. Especially with Ramon laid up. I feel that all the lights in my life are suddenly dimmed."

She was imagining it, there was a definite wistful note in Charmain's voice. "Are you okay, old bean? You sound sort of funny."

"Just a little headache, dear." Charmain giggled. "I who never had a headache in my life! Too much sun, I expect."

"Listen, love, we're going to England for Christmas. I'll see you some time in January."

Darius came into the room and kissed Sarah on top of her head, then nuzzled her throat as she replaced the receiver. He kissed her lips with hungry precision, then gave her a probing look. "Did I just overhear you commit us to a visit to Mexico?"

Her cheeks grew warm and she looked away. "You don't have to go with me if you've business to attend to. I could look in on Charmain and see how she's managing."

He studied her carefully. "Once you've set yourself a certain goal, nothing stops you from achieving it, does it? So I suppose you won't be able to rest until your Casa Brava is a paying proposition. All right, my love, you shall go to Mexico. But if you think I'm letting you out of my sight, you're mad."

Although he captured her lips again in a demanding kiss and then pushed her back onto the bed and proceeded to make them very late for the party, Sarah couldn't help remembering a warning light that had shone briefly in his eyes when he said he would go with her to the Casa Brava.

Chapter 21

At the party given in the elegant town house of one of Darius's Parisian friends, Sarah was introduced to a glittering group of jet-setters who dazzled but did not intimidate her. She felt confident in a striking jade green dress set off by an exquisite emerald and silver necklace, a gift from Darius.

But the knowledge that more than her appearance was right contributed to her sense of ease. She was supported in this crowd of strangers by the adoration of her husband, which she saw reflected in the envious glances of the other women and the approving smiles of the men.

Darius hovered at her elbow, introducing her, parrying any conversational thrusts he felt might be lost on her, swiftly breaking any threads of recollection she couldn't share. He was announcing to all present that his life had begun when he met Sarah and he would brook no excursions into territory with which she was unfamiliar. When someone began, "Do you remember . . ." Darius would immediately point out to Sarah some interesting facet of their surroundings or mention their forthcoming departure for England.

The crowd was a cosmopolitan one, with many nationalities represented, but the language spoken was English. Sarah was sure this was also Darius's doing. A scarcely concealed air of respect for him hovered in the room. He was not the host, but he was more than the guest of honor. Sarah enjoyed the flaunting of his power almost as much as if it were her own.

They dined and danced and mingled with various knots of animated conversationalists. Only once, when she went to the powder room, did one of the guests corner her alone.

A regal-looking woman of indeterminate age with an upper crust British accent and quick darting eyes approached her. Sarah couldn't remember her name but was sure a title preceded it. "My dear, what a coup! Every woman here both admires you and hates you. You did know that Darius was the most elusive bachelor on earth? How did you manage to reel him in?"

"Actually," Sarah said, touching her lips with a dab of gloss, "It was *he* who reeled *me* in. I still can't believe I'm married."

The woman smiled faintly in disbelief. "I'm being a beast, forgive me. The gangly girl with red hair is my daughter and she's been pining for Darius for years. We all knew the second we met you what he saw in you. Not just your good looks, dear, but you seem to be as dauntless as Darius. It's perfectly obvious now, but none of us guessed he wanted a wife who was his equal in every way. And in spite of that, you've passed the test tonight with flying colors."

Sarah turned from the vanity mirror and looked the woman full in the face. "What do you mean? I didn't know I was taking some sort of test tonight."

"Darling, my tongue always run away with me. It's just that you seem like a woman with a mind of her own. Possibly a career of your own. Yet here you are, charming his friends and business acquaintances, so you've obviously, and wisely, decided to place his interests above your own. Darius loves to entertain, so important to his business. With all of his residences he's been sorely in need of a hostess. The stir you've created tonight must surely make him certain he's made a wise choice in you."

Turning back to the mirror, Sarah tightened one of

her earrings. She gave a small smile to the woman's reflection, hoping to end the conversation.

Undaunted, the woman went on. "You'll winter in Morocco I suppose? Spring in Paris, summers split between London and New York and heaven knows how much travel in between. Of course he bought that Lear jet, didn't he? Then there's the race at Le Mans and all those other races where you'll have to watch him risk his neck. I do hope you're as strong as you seem, Sarah, and don't have any regrets at leaving your old life behind."

Sarah snapped her evening purse shut. "I have a career of my own, as you surmised, but I haven't given it up. I'm part owner of a hotel in Mexico and I'll be spending at least half my time there."

The woman's mouth fell open as Sarah walked to the door.

Entering the drawing room where the floor had been cleared for dancing, Sarah went into Darius's arms and he held her tightly as they swayed together, waiting for the beat. When he was this close, smiling down at her and adoring her with his eyes, it was easy to dismiss the possibility that her obsession with the Casa Brava might become a problem in what was fast turning into a perfect union.

After the blur of parties in Paris, Sarah enjoyed the quiet serenity of the frost-silvered English countryside where Darius owned a four-hundred-year-old cottage with a thatched roof. Its low sandstone walls around the flower garden kept the last of the Michaelmas daisies from spilling over to a rolling meadow that disappeared into the woods.

"I haven't changed a thing here," Darius said as he lifted their bags from the Jaguar. Sarah no longer wondered at the fact that he had a car waiting at every airport. He went on, "This is—was—my mother's home when she was a child. I bought it and restored it years ago. There's a housekeeper, Mrs. Mason. She's a timid soul but she'll cook us a traditional English Christmas dinner that will have you thinking you've stepped into a Charles Dickens novel."

Sarah was looking across the meadow toward the woods, feeling the air bite her cheeks, enjoying the quiet restfulness of the winter-slumbering scene. "I can't see any other houses. How much of this land do you own?"

He started up a pathway to the front door, a suitcase in each hand. "To the other side of the woods. I suppose the value of the land somewhat eclipses the value of the house, but . . ."

She fell into step beside him, reaching out to give his arm a slight squeeze. "Don't apologize for being sentimental. The house is charming."

Mrs. Mason blushed and stammered and escaped to the kitchen to make tea as soon as Sarah was introduced. Darius led her into an old-fashioned parlor, cluttered with Victorian furniture, and her attention was caught immediately by a pair of portraits over the fireplace. The man in the picture was Darius's father, she knew without asking. The same startlingly bold black eyes, dark hair emphasizing a well-shaped head with high forehead and sensual mouth. A lovely woman with sad eyes and Darius's smile regarded Sarah gravely from the other frame.

"Your mother was beautiful, Darius," Sarah said softly.

He looked up at the pictures, a furrow of tension appearing between his eyes. "Yes," he said shortly. "I wish my father could have loved her in the same way she loved him."

Surprised, Sarah said, "How do you know he didn't?"

"My mother died a few days after I was born, so I never really knew her. They tell me she became ill with a toxic fever. But I think she probably died of a broken heart. I believe she knew my father loved Charmain."

"Oh, Darius! Are you sure?"

"Quite sure."

"Yet you don't hate Charmain. You seem very fond of her. Why?"

He turned and looked at her, his handsome features ravaged with emotions that seemed too strong for old regrets. He touched her cheek lightly with his fingertip, traced the line of her chin. "How can anyone hate Charmain? She's as blameless as a child. I never knew my father either, but I think he must have been obsessed by her." He paused, his lips coming together as though to bite back feelings he knew he should keep hidden. "As I'm obsessed by you," he added, resigned. "At last I understand how my father felt."

Sarah looked away from his searching gaze, wishing she could reassure him that she would be faithful forever, but back in some corner of her mind the question formed again: *what if Jonathon were suddenly free?*

It was a question she had asked herself more than once since her marriage to Darius. Her memory of her first love lingered, hauntingly, yet she had never felt more alive than when she was with Darius. She wondered, with a guilty thrill, if she was a female incarnation of old Del Latimer, who needed two loves to make her happy.

"I'm not Charmain," Sarah said abruptly. "And you weren't married to another woman when we met."

"But you, my lovely bride, were bound to another man. And I don't seem to be able to free you from that fixation, do I?"

Mrs. Mason knocked on the door and entered the parlor carrying a tray of tea and hot buttered scones. Relief flooded over Sarah. She had wanted to know more about the love affair between Darius's father and Charmain, but decided not to ask since Darius appeared determined to find parallels in their relationship. She would just have to wait and get the story from Charmain.

They settled down in front of a blazing log in the

fireplace to enjoy the delicious scones. There was a sheepskin rug in front of a shiny brass fender, two matching coal skuttles, a row of horse brasses and copper warming pans to reflect the dancing flames. Darius looked at Sarah and said, "The firelight makes your skin look like churned cream, vibrantly alive."

Sarah nestled closer to him on the big chintz-covered sofa and vowed not to invoke any unhappy memories again if she could help it. Mrs. Mason's arrival with the tray had interrupted a dangerous line of conversation.

Darius, however, was not to be detoured around it. "You didn't answer my question, Sarah. You still think of him, don't you? You thought of him a moment ago when I told you about my father and Charmain."

Sarah sat up abruptly. She reached for the teapot under its bright knitted cozy. "Darius, don't do this to me, please. It's unfair. I can't wipe out the past and everyone in it."

He sighed, leaned back against the sofa and watched her carefully. "I don't want you to wipe out the past, Sarah. I just want you to let go of your illusions about it."

She handed him a steaming cup of tea. "It seems to me that you're the one with the ghosts on your mind tonight. You're casting us in the roles of a long-ago triangle, but you're not really sure of the facts, then or now."

"Perhaps not. But I *am* sure that I pressured you into a marriage you didn't really want. There's a great deal of insecurity in that knowledge."

"Darius—"

"No!" he said sharply. "Don't say something you don't really mean. I couldn't bear to find out you were humoring me. Come on, let's have the scones while they're still warm. If you'll lift that silver lid, you'll find some delicious homemade raspberry jam."

They spent a quiet but festive Christmas, Darius cut a fir tree in the woods and they decorated it together.

Mrs. Mason strung paper streamers and bells across the beamed ceiling. Shiny-leafed holly with clusters of fat red berries was tucked around picture frames and doors. Darius fastened bunches of mistletoe all over the cottage. Sarah laughingly protested that if he didn't stop kissing her under it—sending Mrs. Mason scurrying, pink-cheeked, for the kitchen—they were likely to lose a perfectly wonderful housekeeper because of their antics.

Sarah made a couple of not very illuminating calls to Mexico on the pretext of wishing them *Feliz Navidad*. She had insisted Darius start teaching her a little Spanish in preparation for their return. Charmain sounded vague, slightly off-key. No, Ramon wasn't able to work yet, no they hadn't done too much in the way of restoration because the weather was bad, there had been flash floods in the desert and the road was still too muddy for trucks to get through with heavy building supplies. Charmain cut her short and left her feeling distinctly uneasy about the progress being made during her absence from the Casa Brava.

A second call was answered by Cecily, who said Charmain wasn't feeling too well, but not to worry, it was just indigestion.

"Don't fret about a thing, Sarah," Cecily said. "I had a call from Danny this morning and his mother is fine again. He's coming back right after Christmas. We'll get things put together then."

She went on to speak of Ramon and Consuela and added that Jonathon hoped to try to reconstruct his lost novel. Sarah was left with two distinct impressions when the long distance conversation ended. One, that without Danny and Ramon, nothing had been accomplished, and two, that Cecily seemed excessively happy Danny was returning to the Baja. There was a lilt in her voice when she spoke of him that wasn't there when she mentioned Jonathon.

Cecily had once confessed to Sarah that she had been "in love with Jonathon . . . chastely, from afar . . . all my life." But she never dreamed she had a chance with him because he was older, unaware of her existence and had gone steady with Sarah through high school. With her usual shining-eyed innocence, Cecily had added, "I know now that was just puppy love, Sarah, so please don't think I'm jealous of you. I'm just glad the two people I love most on earth like each other."

What an unlikely *menage* we are, Sarah thought. Cecily and I are both so dedicated to protecting Jonathon from the slings and arrows of outrageous fortune that perhaps we both need to have a male friend more than capable of withstanding life's hard knocks. The lilt in Cecily's voice when she spoke of Danny was clearly admiration for the way he found a way to do anything asked of him, no matter how difficult. She probably had her work cut out for her with Jonathon, consoling him about the loss of his manuscript and, unknowingly, for the loss of Sarah to Darius.

After the call to Mexico Sarah began to worry about the lack of progress on the repairs. It was no use, she couldn't count on Charmain to bully the men into working. Sarah would just have to get back there herself.

On Christmas Eve Darius asked her to accompany him to the village church. "I'm a confirmed sinner and not much of a churchgoer, but there's something about this time of year that cries out for some sort of affirmation. It's a lovely old church, which has stood there for eight hundred years. In light of the fleeting nature of our lives, it's comforting to know certain things last."

There was a hint of sadness in his voice again, a soul-deep regret that Sarah wanted to assuage but didn't know how because she wasn't even sure of the nature of his pain. Perhaps it was the time of year. Many people were depressed at holiday times. She resolved to coax him into his former *joie de vivre*.

She was deeply moved by the services in the old

church with its age-darkened steeple and cascading bells. Darius introduced her to the vicar and his wife and most of the members of the congregation. Sarah marveled again at the way Darius managed to blend with so many diverse groups of people.

At midnight they sat on the sheepskin rug in front of the dying embers of the yule log and drank a toast to their first Christmas together. The firelight threw his face into relief, accentuating chin and cheekbones but masking the expression in his eyes. He raised a sturdy mug containing hot toddy and said, "No regrets?"

"None," Sarah assured him. He was silent for a moment as though expecting her to say something else. When she didn't, he asked if she wanted to open her gifts then, in the Midwestern manner, or wait until morning. She decided she couldn't wait to see what was in an enormous box decorated with sassy red-breasted robins and plumply happy Santas. Ripping away paper and ribbons, she unearthed the largest, floppiest, saddest-eyed teddy bear she'd ever seen. Clutched in one outsized furry paw was a velvet case containing an antique gold locket.

Snapping it open, she said, "You should have put a miniature of yourself in it and a lock of hair. It's lovely, Darius, thank you. And I adore old Melancholy Mort."

Darius smiled as she cuddled the bear. He reached around the drooping head to pick up her wrist. "I see you've at last started to wear the bracelet I sent you for your birthday. Do you want to hear the legend that goes with it?"

"I thought you'd never tell. But first, here's my gift for the man who has everything."

"Not quite everything," he murmured as he opened a slim leather-bound book.

"It's a first edition; I found it in that little book shop in the village. It's a list of wifely virtues—do's and don'ts for the new bride, circa the eighteen hundreds. I really wanted to get one for husbands, but it looks like I'll have to write that one myself."

Darius turned the yellowing pages carefully, grinning at admonishments to wives not to interrupt their husbands with idle chatter, not to forget to warm cold sheets with a warming pan or their bodies if nothing else was available. Nor was she to disturb her husband's sleep as she went about her early morning chores of lighting the fire and churning the butter. Darius sighed. "Those were the days."

"Now tell me the legend of the slave bracelet," Sarah urged.

Darius leaned back against the sofa and stretched his long legs to the side of the brass coal skuttle, then pulled Sarah onto his lap. "It was the gift of a wealthy sheik to his favorite concubine. The goldsmith was ordered to beat a message of undying devotion into the design. Here, see the Arabic letters, here and here. But the original bangle was too large for her slender wrist, so the goldsmith was brought back to make it fit. Somehow he kept making it the wrong size, either too small or too large. Consequently he spent an inordinate amount of time with the sheik's lady love. Since the sheik was old and the goldsmith young and handsome, alas, nature took its course. Unfortunately for all concerned, she fell in love with the goldsmith."

"And?" Sarah asked, enraptured.

"And what?"

"What happened? Who won her in the end?"

"The sheik, of course. He was rich and powerful and the goldsmith no match for him. Especially after the sheik had the poor wretch castrated and sold to a Bedouin chief, condemned to spend the rest of his life in endless wandering."

"Darius! What a perfectly awful story." Sarah plucked at the gold bracelet on her wrist, trying to get it off. Darius's hand closed over hers. "Don't take it off, I was just joking. The goldsmith decided discretion was the better part of valor, and fled. The girl pined for him, but allowed the sheik to console her, and eventually she forgot the young man. Legend has it that the woman who is given the bangle will belong forever to the man who gives it to her."

After a while, the bracelet and everything else Sarah wore lay on the sheepskin rug in the fading firelight as Darius kissed every inch of her naked body, then made love to her with unexpected urgency, almost as if he sensed their tranquil time together would soon end.

Sarah swore she would never eat again after Mrs. Mason plied them with roast turkey, sage and onion stuffing, succulent slices of boiled ham, an array of fresh vegetables and the best gravy Sarah had ever tasted, topped off with a Christmas pudding swathed in blue flame from burning brandy, then doused with rum sauce. There were mince pies and trifle and Banbury tarts and Eccles cakes and "Maids of Honor." Darius assured Sarah she would be as fat as the sheik's favorite wife by New Year's Eve.

They traveled to London for a New Year's Eve party, and some of the people Sarah had met in Paris were there. London was cold and damp but bright with Christmas cheer. As January arrived with a slushy snowstorm, Sarah began to long for the sight of sunlight dappling the blue waters of the Sea of Cortez.

Chapter 22

Even in the private jet, the journey from England to Mexico was long and exhausting. There was a brief stopover in New York, another in San Diego where they transferred to Darius's Cessna for the last leg of the journey. The tiny airstrip on the Baja Peninsula south of the Casa Brava couldn't handle a larger aircraft.

Sarah was disoriented. They flew into endless daylight on the trip west and there was a nine-hour time difference between Mexico and London. Her inability to sleep unless it was dark caused trancelike feelings of unreality that persisted even after they landed the Cessna and climbed into the four-wheel drive vehicle for the last rugged miles over the washed-out road.

Darius had suggested they should break up the journey again, get a room and sleep for a few hours, but Sarah wanted to keep going. "I can't explain it. I'm dying to see the desert and the Casa. It's almost like going home. Ramon's old hacienda seems to have been sending me silent messages ever since I left."

Darius gave her a wry smile. "Do you suppose I'll ever inspire such feelings in you?"

Sarah replied lightly, "Of course I'd miss you if I were away from you."

"That isn't exactly what I meant."

"Oh, look, Darius, the sky!"

The desert sky at sunset was splashed with gaudy strokes of scarlet and vermilion and gold. Looking up at Darius's profile, Sarah saw there was a tight line to his jaw, visible even in silhouette; but she was too weary to worry about it.

She dozed, in spite of the bumpy road, and awakened when he nudged her gently. "Come on, love, we're at the back door to your inn. Think you can walk up the cliff steps? I'm too tired to drive inland around the hills."

He kept his arm around her as they went toward the glow of the amber lantern. Seconds dragged by after Darius pounded on the door. Sarah waited, her tiredness disappearing in the face of rising excitement. During the months she had been gone—even allowing for Ramon's broken leg and Danny's absence—they would have been able to do great things to the hotel. Darius had been more than generous with money. It was now the first of March, and there would be time for lots of guests before the summer heat set in.

Then she remembered the two guests who would be a big surprise to her husband. Sarah had tried to find the right time to tell Darius that Jon and Cecily were still at the Casa Brava, but somehow the moment had never presented itself. She decided to wait until they arrived, perhaps feign surprise that the Conways were still there, and explain she'd been sure they would leave. Sarah hated the deception, but couldn't think of any other reasonable explanation why she hadn't mentioned their continuing residence before. In the first days of their marriage, she hadn't anticipated Darius would accompany her when she returned. She had a vague idea that she'd go and take care of her business while he took care of his.

But more than that was the precarious nature of her relationship with Darius. Somehow they hadn't managed to get into sync with their feelings. When he expressed his love for her, she felt unsure, defensive. And when she wanted to tell him she felt they were rapidly approaching a state of harmony that no misunderstanding or outsider could threaten, he seemed to back away, afraid she would lie to him about her feelings.

Waiting for someone to respond to the pounding on the door, Sarah rationalized that by now there would be other guests and Cecily and Jon would be lost in the crowd. Besides, they had been there when Darius left, so their presence wouldn't be a complete surprise.

The door creaked open slowly, and Consuela peeked out at them. She looked tired and greeted them wearily, ignoring Darius's polite inquiry as to her health. She led the way into the kitchen. Sarah looked around. The room looked comfortably lived-in, but it had been the least damaged of the rooms during the storm. The broken windows and shutters had been replaced, but Sarah saw at once that the archway leading to the dining room was covered by a disreputable-looking rug.

She crossed the room and lifted a corner of the rug. The dining room wasn't lit, but even in the darkness it was obvious it hadn't been used since she'd left. The broken shutters hung at the windows, allowing dank night air to seep in. The furniture smelled musty and mildewed, as if the intruding salt water and rain from the storm had been allowed to remain.

Letting the concealing rug fall back into place, Sarah said to Darius, "Would you ask Consuela to make some coffee while I go and find Charmain and the others?" As he translated her request, Sarah went into the hall.

There was little need to tour the hacienda to see that very little had been done in the wake of the storm, but Sarah moved from room to room in dazed disbelief. Except for boarding up some of the broken windows and repairing the outer doors virtually nothing had been done during her absence. The hotel had been desperately neglected, mortally wounded in the storm and then left to die. She was appalled at the dust and cobwebs and dried mud that adorned empty rooms. She looked through doors hanging at crazy angles on rusted hinges, stepped over piles of debris, unwashed laundry, trays of dirty dishes. There were several trash cans at the end of the hall, as if someone had made a halfhearted attempt to pick up. It was clear that the Casa Brava was in worse condition than it had been on the day she'd left for New York.

Flinging open the doors to the guest lounge, Sarah looked across the water-stained floor to the small solitary figure in the wheelchair. Cecily's face was cupped wearily on her hands as she contemplated what appeared to be several empty prescription bottles on her lap. It seemed to take a supreme effort for her to raise her head as Sarah entered. "Oh, Sarah!" Cecily's voice was a sob of relief. "Thank God you're here!"

Before Sarah reached her side, tears were slipping down Cecily's pale cheeks. Sarah's arms went around pathetically thin shoulders. "Cecily, what happened?"

"Ramon broke his leg and Danny had to leave. We tried to get his people to work, but they were afraid when Charmain became so ill. Oh, please don't be cross, she wouldn't let us tell you how sick she was when you called, because she didn't want to spoil your honeymoon. She said, well, never mind what she said. Almost at once, everybody else got sick. We think maybe the water was contaminated after the storm. We all got high fevers and the most frightful stomach cramps like food poisoning. We came down with it one after the other."

Sarah was shocked by Cecily's thinness. Her pale blonde hair straggled over shoulders a skeleton would have been ashamed of, her hands were little more than claws. She looked as fragile as a stick figure, her china doll face ready to shatter at any second. Sarah drew a breath and tried not to let her shock show in her face. "Where is everyone else. Are they still ill?"

"Charmain and Ramon are quite weak. Jon got it last and he's really in the throes of it now. Danny is taking care of them. Several of Ramon's relatives were still sick when he first came back. He was marvelous— never gave a thought to catching it himself. Mrs.

Jerome and the two Mexican men left as soon as they were well again, but they promised to come back after we repaired their cottages."

Sarah said, "Well, at least we seem to have electricity."

"Danny fixed the generator. We did order a new one, but it hasn't come. And he fixed the water pipes too. But there was just too much to be done. I'm sorry everything is such a mess."

"But why didn't you send for help? You should have had a doctor, gotten a clean-up crew in."

"We tried, Sarah, we really did. But the Casa Brava is so remote. Apparently word of those bandits got out and no one wanted to come from the village. They told us to go to the hospital, but we didn't have anyone well enough to drive. Then when Danny came, the old people were too weak to move."

"All right, Cecily, don't worry. I'm here now. Come on, let's get you to bed, you're done in. Where are you sleeping? I couldn't see any habitable rooms. I don't suppose any of the cottages have been rebuilt?"

Cecily shook her head. "Danny cleaned up Charmain's room and yours. Jon and I took your room. I'm sorry what a horrible welcome this is. Do you mind? Jon's too ill to be moved—"

Cecily's eyes moved over Sarah's shoulder as she looked at the doorway. Darius stood on the threshold, thunderclouds racing across his eyes.

Sarah faced Darius in one of the empty rooms amid the depressing remnants of waterlogged furniture. Anger simmered behind his hard blank look, and he kept his distance from her. "I once told you that I could forgive everything but a lie. You lied to me, Sarah. Pretended you needed a loan to repair some minor damage and to expand, when all the time the place had been practically destroyed. You played me for a fool, but I suppose I asked for it. I wanted you so blindly, I would have taken you on any terms. It's my own fault you struck the bargain you did."

"No, Darius, please, you're wrong—"

He stared at her, forcing her into silence with eyes filled with unrelenting fury. "If you lie to me again, God help me, I may strike you. Don't say another word until I've finished. I've been talking to Consuela, so I know the whole miserable story. Perhaps if you'd come after my money only out of ambition and stubborn pride, I could have accepted it. But there was more, wasn't there, my dear wife? There was the former lover struggling to write his great American novel in penniless exile while he supported his crippled wife. Without the Casa Brava, what would have happened to your beloved Mr. Conway?"

"Darius, please, let me speak," Sarah's voice was shrill with fear. "All right, I admit things were worse here than I let you believe. But be fair! I came to you to borrow money, I never pretended otherwise. I never asked you to marry me. That was your idea. You spelled out the terms, not me. The Conways were here when you left. I never said they were leaving, you simply assumed they would. This is a hotel. Guests are our business, and they were paying guests. I don't try to run your business for you. Why should you tell me who I can rent rooms to?"

He surveyed her silently for a moment. "Very well, Sarah. I've been had. I won't be again."

There was an icy finality to his tone. Sarah suddenly wanted to fling herself into his arms, but was held at bay by his palpable anger. She stepped back as though shoved away, but tilted her chin and asked, "What do you intend to do?"

Faint respect showed briefly in his dark eyes, and she was glad she hadn't begged or pleaded for forgiveness. "First I'm going to find a dry place for us to sleep. Everything else can wait until tomorrow."

Chapter 23

Sarah awakened the following morning, stiff and unrefreshed after a night spent on a blanket on the hard floor of the kitchen. Darius was gone.

He returned late that evening with a crew of workers and an ancient truck filled with boxes and a garishly new brass bed with paper-wrapped mattress. "This is the only bed I could find. It's a double bed, but if you prefer to sleep on the floor that's up to you," he said in a tone of supreme indifference as he directed the men to begin unloading the truck.

After a long day of cleaning and washing clothes, Sarah collapsed gratefully into the bed the minute it was set up.

During the first few days there wasn't time to argue with Darius or really speak to anyone. There was simply too much to be done. Sarah felt she was pitted against a clock that rushed forward at an accelerated pace. She stumbled from one task to another and never met the schedules she set for herself. She and Consuela supervised the cleaning and repair of the main building, while Darius and Danny watched over the outside crew. Their paths crossed infrequently. She was too grateful he had remained to help to provoke him in any way. Jonathon was still too ill to leave his room. Cecily, relieved of her other chores, now took care of her husband.

Charmain was a wan shadow who rose from bed in the morning with false vigor, made ambitious plans for all she would do during the day, then collapsed onto her pillows before noon. "Sal, love, if that was Montezuma's Revenge, I'll take dysentery any time. And I had it once, in Egypt! But God, nothing like this! Look at me, I'm too thin, at last! I thought it wasn't possible to be too thin. You know, I feel like I'm lying in my own bones. It hurts to roll over in bed."

Sarah helped comb Charmain's matted hair, noting it was sorely in need of a henna rinse. "Ramon will fatten you up, soon as you're up. He's feeling fine again."

"Tell me, darling, are you and Darius wildly in love? You could have knocked me over with a feather when I got your wire. Married yet! I think I expected everything *but* that."

Feeling her stomach knot when Charmain asked if they were in love, Sarah felt an acute sense of loss. There was no question that her marriage to Darius was all but over. If this hadn't been Charmain's hotel, he probably would have left immediately. They lay next to each other in the double bed, carefully avoiding contact each interminably long night. Had there been another halfway usable bed, Sarah was sure he would have taken it.

Two weeks after their arrival, Sarah awakened one day to find Darius standing beside the bed, watching her. A gray dawn drained the colors from the room, adding its bleakness to the glacial expression he wore. "All right, Sarah, enough is enough. This spartan lifestyle can now mercifully end. I believe Charmain is strong enough to travel. We'll fly her to—"

"No, Darius. I don't want to leave yet. You can take Charmain away if that's what she wants."

His eyes narrowed. "You can't reopen the hotel until a great deal more work is done. It could take months."

"I know. But I want to be here, see it done right."

"You agreed to be my wife. Your double-dealing doesn't relieve you of certain obligations you undertook. Especially if you expect me to pay for rebuilding this disaster you call a hotel. We incurred social obligations. I have business to attend to that requires the presence of a hostess. You can come back here in a month or two."

She sat up in bed, reached for her robe and slipped her arms into the sleeves, shivering. A bone-chilling dampness had invaded the rooms of the old hacienda that no amount of fire in the grates would drive away. Ramon said it was an exceptionally cold and wet winter and that the heat would be retained better when all the windows and doors were repaired and the roof retiled. Her feet touched the icy cold adobe floor as she said, "Are you telling me you still want me to play the part of your wife?" *Damn, she hadn't meant to say it like that.*

His mouth curled sardonically at one corner. "That's what you've done from the start, isn't it? Played a part. Oh, how you must have been laughing at me behind my back. There I was, laying my heart and mind and soul at your feet while you schemed to use my money to sponsor your lover's literary efforts."

She pushed her feet into her slippers, tied the sash of her robe. "What would you have had me do? Throw Cecily and her wheelchair out into the desert? Do you know why they came here? They came because her father paid those bandits to come and scare us to death. Then he blocked the shipment of the supplies we needed. He wanted revenge on Charmain because he has to live with that museum you helped her set up in Palerville. And on me because nobody walks out on Buck Latimer. He fires them."

It was clear from the look of surprise on Darius's face that this news was more than he had bargained for.

"Are you sure about the bandits?" he asked at length, his voice escaping from his mouth like steam. When she nodded, he said, "I'll kill the swine."

"Don't bother. We can't prove anything, and the three men are in a Mexican jail. They haven't even been brought to trial yet. This is *mañana* land, remember? Besides, the best way for Charmain and me to get even with Buck Latimer is to succeed in spite of him. We're going to make a go of this hotel. Some day we're going to own a chain of hotels and I'll buy out Buck's Palazzo Apartments and convert *them* into hotels too."

Darius stared moodily into space. "Then you won't even need my money, will you?"

"Look, Darius, I'll be glad to entertain your friends, go anywhere you wish. But could we at least stay a few more days? I've got to be sure things will get done when I'm gone this time, and I've an idea how to accomplish that—"

"How? Chain the galley slaves to the bulkheads?"

"Don't ask me how. Let me see if I can arrange it. You didn't anwer my question as to whether our marriage is to continue."

"Of course it is to continue. Do you think I'd let you make a fool of me to my friends? We'll make a business arrangement. You'll preside over my parties, entertain my business acquaintances, see to my houses. You'll wear Paris gowns and gaze at your husband with adoring eyes, making him the envy of every man we meet. If you play your part well, I'll loan you the money you need, and deduct a portion of the loan—plus interest—in monthly installments."

His eyes moved with slow deliberation across the room and then to the window, which offered a view of the broken fountain. "I'd say you'll only have to keep up the pretense for, oh, let's see, what's it worth to me to have the wife of my dreams? Five years, ten? Con artists have been known to draw longer sentences, love."

He isn't saying these things to me, Sarah thought in numb horror. This is all a ghastly dream. The contemptuous look on his face, the sarcasm in his tone, the awful coldness in his eyes—this isn't Darius, he loves me.

As though reading her mind, he said, "Didn't the sage say that the cure for love was marriage? Score one for the old sage." He started toward the door, but someone knocked and he called out, "Who is it and what the devil do you want?"

"Danielson," Danny's gruff voice responded. "If I'm to get that guy over here today, I need directions."

Darius opened the door. Sarah, still smarting, shouted, "I'm in charge of this hotel, Danny. Not my husband. Bring your problems to me. And if I have any more of your insolence—"

Darius interrupted, "I'll see you at the front door in a moment, Danny."

It seemed to Sarah that Danny sauntered away with deliberate slowness. When he was gone, Darius said coldly, "Danny is the only member of your entourage who is making any real contribution to the work around here, except for Cecily, who isn't strong enough to be waiting on her husband or mending linens or trying to set up a new set of books or any of the other tasks she sets for herself."

"I resent your usupring my authority—"

"Oh, don't get pompous, Sarah. Now if you'll excuse me, I have to talk to Danny."

"Wait a minute. We haven't decided yet about leaving."

"I've decided everything, as a matter of fact. We'll stay another week. Then you'll come to Europe with me. I'm sure Charmain will want to accompany us. You can return here while I attend the trials of my new race car."

"Another week!"

His eyes locked with hers in a dueling stare. "Oh, yes, one other thing. Since you insist on spending time here, presiding over your interests, I must insist that there be no temptation in your path. I've been a bamboozled husband, but I'm damned if I'm going to be a cuckolded one. You will inform Jonathon Conway that he is to leave the Casa Brava before you return from Europe."

Chapter 24

Ramon had insisted on presiding over the grand opening of the dining room, assuring everyone that his leg was healed. To prove it, he vowed he would tango with Charmain, who was also feeling better, after dinner and drinks and the start of the dancing.

There were gray marks on the mahogany furniture, a damp bloom left by invading water, and the red velvet cushions smelled musty. But the adobe-tiled floor gleamed in the firelight, and there wasn't a speck of dust or cobweb in sight.

Sarah washed her hair and chose a soft rose-colored wool dress. As she fastened the gold bangle onto her wrist, she harbored a faint hope that Darius would see her gesture as one of conciliation. Her spirits were high. She was sure it would be a festive dinner, relieving tension and loosening feelings.

The moment she entered the dining room, she knew her hopes had been in vain. Jonathon had chosen this evening to leave the sanctuary of his sickbed, and Darius was standing with his back to the fire, surveying his rival with a look that should have struck Jonathon dead. Luckily he was listening to Charmain describe the special foods Ramon had prepared for the gala dinner.

Cecily watched everyone anxiously. Sarah was struck again by how frail she looked. Darius was right, Cecily had been working too hard. Buck and Estelle would have fainted had they seen their precious daughter sorting tattered linens and mending the rips and tears by hand.

"Ah, there you are, pet," Charmain cried, catching sight of Sarah. "Thank goodness you've discarded those tacky jeans. Designer label or not, I think blue denim makes even an attractive woman look like a ditchdigger. Darius, dear, doesn't your wife look lovely tonight?"

"No lovelier than you, *belle dame*." His dark eyes flickered briefly in Sarah's direction. He made no move toward her. She shook her head to the chair offered by Jonathon.

Feeling some of her good humor evaporate, Sarah said, "Are you feeling better, Jonathon?"

"Much, thank you. If I have to eat another bowl of rice, I think I'll break out in fluent Chinese." Jonathon gave her a watery smile. He looked haggard, Sarah thought. Dark circles under his eyes and gaunt cheekbones. On the one hand she ached with sympathy for his suffering, yet on the other she wished fervently that he and Cecily had not stayed on at the Casa Brava. She wanted to make everything right for Jon, and at the same time she desperately wanted to ask him to leave. Bewildered by her ambivalent feelings, Sarah wondered what she would do about Darius's ultimatum.

If Jon was forced to leave, Cecily had to go too, and Sarah was worried. How could Jon support and care for her? Would Cecily's frail health stand up to any kind of relocation just now?

Sarah impulsively went to Cecily and picked up her small hands, squeezing them reassuringly. "How are you feeling tonight? Did you have a rest this afternoon like the doctor ordered?"

Cecily smiled. "I'm fine, really, Sarah. You're so sweet to worry about me so."

"Your hands are like ice. Let me push you nearer the fire." Sarah pushed the wheelchair and glared at Darius, sending the unspoken message that he was cruel and unfeeling. Didn't he realize that if Jonathon left, Cecily would have to go too?

As if in answer, Darius said, "Mrs. Conway, I believe my wife is right to be concerned about you. I think you and Charmain should convalesce where you would be comfortable and cared for. I could fly you both to Acapulco. It wouldn't take long, wouldn't tax your strength, and I could be back here before my wife hardly missed me." His eyes mocked Sarah briefly.

There was a moment's silence. He had not included Jonathon in the suggestion. Sarah felt as if she were watching a wolf cut a single sheep from the herd. Darius actually intended to take Cecily to a luxury resort, while she, Sarah, kicked Jonathon out. Darius was diabolical when it came to dealing with rivals or recalcitrant wives.

Cecily said, "That's very kind of you, Darius, but I couldn't leave just now. Jon is still quite weak."

Charmain sighed. "I'm afraid I'm not feeling noble. I might take you up on the offer, darling. But don't say anything in front of Ramon, at least not yet." Ramon had gone to the kitchen.

Darius looked at Cecily. "I want you to remember that my offer is good any time, for any destination."

Jonathon looked from one to the other. "Just what exactly is going on? I know I've been ill, but I get the feeling I just walked in on the second act of a play. Why all the fuss about Cecily? She's been over the bug for some time."

"We will sincerely hope so," Darius uttered, flashing him a look that made Sarah think of pistols at twenty paces. She cast around frantically for some way to get the conversation on less dangerous ground, but all she could think of was to compliment Charmain on her dress and ask what she supposed was keeping Ramon in the kitchen.

Charmain murmured something, Sarah wasn't listening and the conversation resumed. Sarah was still watching Cecily. Something was bothering her. Not just her illness, but something else. Whatever it was, it was tearing her apart. Sarah had known her long enough to see that she was facing an inner crisis. Aren't we all, Sarah thought wearily.

Ramon suddenly appeared and announced that dinner was being served. Consuela brought a steaming tureen of soup to the table, as everyone took places. *Menuda,* Ramon said, guaranteed to drive away the last of their miseries. As Consuela began to ladle the soup into bowls, Jonathon reached for the wine decanter. Sarah looked toward Cecily but saw she hadn't even noticed. She was gazing at the door, her eyes wide and shining. Danny had just come into the room. "Sorry I'm late," he said, and took the chair next to Cecily's wheelchair.

Darius sat opposite Danny and casually asked, "How did it go?"

Watching, Sarah was sure Danny winked at Darius. But when he said, "We're going to bury the pipes at the depth you suggested and we'll have to wait for a back hoe," she decided she must have been mistaken. There was almost a smile on Danny's face, which made surprising changes in his tough countenance.

Sarah looked across the table and found Jonathon regarding her over the rim of his glass. "In all the chaos, we never had a chance to toast the happy couple. Does everyone have wine?"

He managed to make the words "happy couple" sound more like "condemned couple." Jon's eyes silently accused her. She could almost read the words there: *you betrayed our love.*

She wanted to say, *no, you did.* Why was it a crime for me to marry Darius for his money? Isn't that what you did, really? You pretended it was guilt for Cecily's accident, but when you found out she was crazy about you, had been for years, wouldn't you have dumped me anyway? She offered a life of ease, supported by Buck's money, all the time in the world for your writing. Oh, Jon, how could I have been so blind about you? When you realized Buck was going to make you work for a living, you turned to me again.

Everyone was drinking to the health of the bride and groom, but Sarah didn't hear the words of congratulations. She stared at Jonathon, seeking all the chivalry and sensitivity she had loved in him. Perhaps, she rationalized, an artist has to sacrifice everything else in order to have time to create. Perhaps they need to let others take care of their daily bread.

Darius proposed a toast to the restoration of everyone's fortune. His voice was mocking. Sarah raised her glass to her lips, wondering if her thoughts about Jonathon merely echoed Darius's charges, or if they'd been forming in her own mind for a long time and she had refused to recognize them.

After the dinner ended to contented sighs and smiles, Charmain asked Ramon to play his guitar. Darius interrupted, saying, "In a little while, Charmain. First, we have a special request for Cecily."

Cecily looked surprised. "Why, yes, anything!"

Darius smiled at her so fondly that Sarah felt a stab of jealousy. "Would you play the piano for us?

Cecily looked dismayed. "I'd love to, but it's so terribly out of tune—"

Danny couldn't contain himself any longer. Jumping to his feet, he pushed Cecily's wheelchair to the piano. His face was now wreathed with smiles. "Darius found a piano tuner, Cecily. I brought him in today from a village way down the coast."

Cecily's tiny fingers touched the keys wonderingly and she gasped with delight as an arpeggio rang out, true and clear. She began to play a Chopin piece full of trills.

So that's where Danny was going this morning, why he needed directions from Darius, Sarah thought angrily. All the work that has to be done, and Darius sends for a piano tuner. Darius's eyes locked with hers, measuring her reaction, and his jaw moved slightly. Damn him, he always manages to read my mind, she said to herself. Afraid she would explode, Sarah stood up. "Excuse me for a minute, everyone. I'll be back soon. Please, Cecily, don't stop, it's lovely."

Sarah went down the hall to the deserted lobby. She stood at the window, looking at the dark terrace, hearing the sea churn restlessly and the breeze flap the fronds of the only palm left standing after the storm. She hoped Darius would come after her, so she could tell him what she thought of him and his piano tuner. And what was that? Now that the first wave of resentment had subsided, Sarah realized that Darius had the piano tuned so that Cecily would have some much-needed relaxation. God knew she needed it, and music was the nectar of life to her. Sarah thought back to the many times she'd called on the Conways in Palerville and found Jon at his writing desk and Cecily playing softly on the grand piano. Sarah shut out the painful image that now came back to haunt her. It just confirmed how wrong she'd been to pine for Jon all these years. And he, the fool, why hadn't he realized that Sarah never could have been the wife he needed, fading into the background, absorbed in some quiet pastime, waiting for him to emerge from his make-believe world and join her in hers?

She looked around the lobby. The alcoves that had formerly housed stone statues, smashed in the storm, seemed to regard her like hollow eye sockets. There was something about these ancient walls, she thought, that washed away pretense. Everything had become devastatingly clear. She no longer loved Jonathon. The realization brought tremendous relief. Then puzzlement, because she wasn't sure why she knew this with a certainty now when such a short time ago she hadn't.

Darius, she thought. I married Darius. That was the catharsis. Her mind raced over the past months. Every minute of her marriage before they returned here had been happy. She had found fulfillment in his arms, felt incomplete when he wasn't near. It was always a sweet shock when Darius walked into a room and her heart lifted at the sight of him. Oh, Sarah, you fool, a faraway voice whispered. You love him! You were so busy carrying a torch for Jon, you didn't recognize the real thing when it came to you.

"Sarah?"

She spun around at the sound of her name, Darius's name already on her lips. But it was Jonathon who stood in the shadowy room with her. He said, "Are you all right?"

"Oh, yes. I just wanted to be alone for a moment. But since you're here, I do need to ask you something. Jon, I hate to be curt, but now that you're feeling better, what are your plans? I mean, you can't keep Cecily here indefinitely."

"Has he told you to throw me out?"

"Of course not. But . . ."

His face was in shadow, but his voice carried a hint of self-pity she hadn't heard before. "I shan't force myself on you, Sarah. Not now that you've chosen to marry him."

"I'm not worried about that. Oh, God, I might as well tell you the truth. It's time one of us was honest about things. Darius knows about us, and every minute you're here is like probing a wound."

He came across the lobby slowly and stood beside her at the window. Placing his palms on the rough ledge, he stared morosely into the blackness beyond the glass. "Yes. You're right. It's time to be frank. I don't have a dime, Sarah. Our savings are gone and I haven't earned anything from my writing since you left. I don't know where to go, what to do."

"Oh, Jon!" Sarah stifled a sigh at the utter hopelessness in his voice. "I'll lend you some money, a stake to get you started again. You could go back to apartment managing. Or get a job in a hotel. We could fake a resume for you, pretend you've been managing the Casa Brava these past months. I know it isn't what you want to do, but lots of writers hold down a job and work on their books in their spare time."

"Of course. You're right, as usual," he said stiffly. "But please don't fake a resume. I hate deception." This time there was no mistaking the accusation in his voice.

"I take it you think I deceived you?"

"You deceived Darius Descartes, that's for sure."

"You haven't any idea what you're talking about."

"No? You could barely stand the man when you left to try to borrow money from him. The next minute you're married to him. What was it, love at first sight of his checkbook?"

The last thread of control snapped for Sarah. She had raised her hand and slapped his cheek with a stinging blow before she knew she was going to move.

There was a moment of silence as they stared at each other wordlessly. Then Jonathon left, looking more defeated than ever.

Feeling suddenly exhausted, Sarah went to the bedroom she shared with Darius. She supposed she should at least go and tell everyone good night, but she was too drained to face anyone, especially Darius. She pressed her fingers to her brow, wishing she were back in the cottage in Surrey, curled up against Darius's chest in the old four-poster bed, with the winter wind howling in the chimney and her husband's comforting proximity driving away all her cares. To think she had still been thinking of Jonathon then! She supposed she had to come back, see him again, really see him. But now she'd lost Darius too, and she couldn't bear it.

Chapter 25

Sarah cleared her throat and looked at the three faces, which watched her expectantly. Jonathon's eyes didn't quite meet hers. Cecily smiled at her encouragingly. Danny tipped his chair back and looked at Sarah with hostile skepticism. They were in the newly restored office. The sun blazed on the window at Sarah's back, promising the kind of winter day sure to attract guests once all the work was finished.

"I asked you to come in here . . ." Sarah foundered, began again. "I wanted to—" She appealed to Jonathon. "Have you discussed with Cecily what we talked about last night?"

He shook his head; his eyes were bloodshot. Sarah had the uneasy suspicion he was battling a hangover.

"Cecily," Sarah said, "you've been working here for months and you've got some wages coming. There's a check in this envelope plus one for Jon to cover all the supplies he brought last year."

"Oh, Sarah, you didn't have to pay us—" Cecily began.

"Jonathon told me last night that you two will be leaving soon," Sarah said. "You'll need the money to help you get started again."

"Leaving—" Cecily repeated, looking from Sarah to Jonathon in bewilderment. "But we're so happy here. Where will we go?"

Danny had snapped forward in his chair, suddenly

alert and watchful. Sarah looked at him and said,
"Danny, I need someone to supervise the rebuilding of
the Casa Brava while I'm away. Since you're going to
be out of a job, I'd like you to take over for me here.
I've a check for back pay for you too."

He stood up, eyes fixed on Sarah as he gripped the
back of Cecily's wheelchair. "Lady, I wouldn't work for
you on a bet." He turned the chair gently, so that it was
in position to go through the door, then said, "Mr.
Conway, I suggest you take your wife out of here
because I have a few words for Mrs. Descartes that
shouldn't be said in front of an audience."

Cecily's lip was trembling and she looked up at
Danny over her shoulder, perilously close to tears.
Sarah felt as though she were drowning a kitten whose
only crime was in being born.

Jonathon got up and took the wheelchair wordlessly.
As soon as they were clear, Danny kicked the door shut
and wheeled on Sarah. "You unspeakable bitch," he
said, advancing on her.

Sarah swallowed her terror. "Stay right where you
are or I'll scream for Darius. How dare you speak to me
like that?" She was glad her desk was between them.
He stopped, leaned across it. Sarah's fingers closed
around a ruler lying in front of her.

"You—you—What kind of a monster are you? She
loves you. Like a sister, a best friend. You're her idol.
All she ever wanted all her life was to be like you. Isn't
that a laugh? She's dreamed up some sort of female
knight on a charger and substituted her for the real
Sarah Latimer, who isn't worth a damn."

"Go ahead and insult me if it makes you happy. Then
get out of here. I take it you don't want the job I
offered."

"Oh, no. You don't get off that easy. It's time
somebody told you the truth. You were happy to hang
around Jonathon Conway when it suited you. Now that
it doesn't, out he goes like last week's newspaper—and
Cecily along with him. Now you just listen to me. They

didn't tell you the whole story about leaving Palerville. Buck Latimer told them he'd never take Conway back. Cecily was welcome to come home anytime, but not her husband. You pulled the wool over Cecily's eyes, you two backstreet lovebirds, but Buck and Estelle weren't fooled."

"We weren't—"

"Sure you were. I knew it the first time I saw you together. You'll never know how many times I wanted to smash your pretty face or bust Conway for what you were doing to Cecily."

So that explained Danny's hostility, Sarah thought. She looked him squarely in the eye, knowing there was no point in lying to him. "And who appointed you anybody's keeper, Danielson? Isn't there an old adage about he who is without sin casting the first stone? Did it occur to you that maybe you weren't seeing the whole picture, from your vantage point as Cecily's chauffeur?"

"The point," Danny said, unnerving her with eyes that didn't blink, "is that Cecily is too loyal to that jerk of a husband ever to leave him. She'll starve to death along with him or try to work to support him. She won't go home to her parents."

"I really don't see that what they do is any of your business."

"She's too good, too fine—" There was almost a sob in Danny's voice and a look in his eyes when he spoke of Cecily that Sarah knew well. She had once seen a similar look in Darius's eyes. It was so clear what ailed Danny that she wondered how she could have missed seeing the truth before.

Before Sarah could bite back the words, they were out. "You love her. You're in love with Cecily."

He ignored her. "Are you really going to send them away from here?"

"Yes. I have to. Apart from the fact that it's probably best for them too, my husband won't let them stay."

"Can't say I blame him. You're a fool, you know

that? You've got a good man who's crazy about you, and you play around with a loser like Conway."

"Get out of here, get out this minute." Sarah was on her feet, shaking with anger.

"Look, please, I'm begging you. Let them stay. I'll take over, like you wanted. If you ask your husband, if you go away with him and let us take care of the place, he'll let them stay. He'll do anything you want."

"I only wish that were true. Danny, I understand how you feel, but Jonathon isn't without business skills. He can get a job if he wants one. He'll take care of Cecily."

"Wanna bet? You throw him out of here and he'll let her work for him. Don't you have a conscience? Doesn't it bother you that it's your fault they're here? Do you just use people—take all the time without giving?"

Sarah didn't answer. She didn't need Danny to call her names, she'd already used them all on herself. But she wasn't going to the pillory without a fight. She might have lost Darius, she'd certainly lost Jonathon long ago, but she wasn't going to lose the Casa Brava. And without Darius's money, she would surely lose the hotel. She walked around the desk, pushed past him to the door.

He called after her, "You're killing them, both of them."

Jonathon slammed the empty glass down on his littered desk and refilled it with tequila. The bottle was half empty. Around his feet the floor was covered with crumpled manuscript pages, the wastebasket overflowing.

Cecily sat just inside the door where he had left her wheelchair. She said again, "Please, Jon, please don't get drunk again, I can't stand it."

"Oblivion, Cecily. That's what I'm looking for. This is the only way to find it," he muttered, draining the glass again. "I didn't think she'd really send me away."

"I don't understand it either, dear. But I think perhaps Darius is the reason. He's very forceful, a dominant man. With strong emotions. I think perhaps he believed that vicious gossip mother started about you and Sarah."

Jonathon's head swiveled slowly in her direction and he looked at her with amazement. "You're a fool, Cecily. How anyone can be so naive—"

She felt her cheeks sting with a hot rush of blood. "Don't, Jon! Please don't start ridiculing me again. You're right, of course. Darius loves Sarah too much to believe she'd do anything underhanded, just as we do." She bit her lip. "Perhaps Sarah feels you'd be happier if you were working again—"

"Working! You don't think sweating blood over a novel is *playing*, do you?"

"No, I didn't mean that," Cecily said miserably. "I meant earning a salary again—"

"Oh, now we're getting down to the cold hard facts, aren't we? I'm not supporting wifey in the manner Daddy dear—"

Cecily interrupted him. "Jon, you know I was willing to go anywhere, live on whatever we could afford. I still am. But you've changed!"

"I've changed all right. My manuscript was blown away in the wind. If you had any brains at all, you'd know what that means to a writer."

"I thought you could try to write it again."

"I can't stand it!" The tequila bottle was almost empty. He tipped it to his lips and finished the innocuous-looking liquid that Cecily feared more than anything. Now the cruel words would come, and they wouldn't stop until he passed out. She supposed she was lucky he didn't beat her, as she'd heard some alcoholics did. In her despair she sometimes thought it would have been easier to take than his wounding verbal thrusts.

"Stupid little fool," he mumbled. "It isn't like sewing a quilt again or building a road again. It's capturing intangible thought processes again. But you don't know what the hell I'm talking about, do you?"

"I'm sorry, Jon. I know I'm not clever. I don't mean to make you angry."

He gripped the edge of his desk, pushed himself awkwardly to his feet and lurched across the room to her side. Grabbing a handful of her hair he jerked her face upward, making her wince with pain. "What good are you, Cecily? Just what the hell good are you. You're not a wife. Not a real wife, are you? You're nothing but a millstone around my neck."

Tears stung the back of her eyes. "Jon, it's the liquor. It's not you saying these things. Let me go. I'll get out of your sight. Then I won't make you angry—"

"Descartes might be mad as hell at Sarah," he went on, "but when they go to bed at night they can relieve the tension in ways we can't. Isn't that true? Isn't it? Answer me!"

"Jon, for pity's sake, how many times have I offered you—begged you—to let me make love to you?"

His hand fell from her hair and he stepped back, looking at her in disgust. "Don't make me ill. It would be like mugging a corpse."

"Please don't be so vile! Jon, just because I'm paralyzed below the waist doesn't mean I can't enjoy lovemaking. I can see, even if I can't feel, and I can experience the joy of closeness with you in my mind. Isn't that where our erotic thoughts begin, anyway? Please, darling, let me comfort you. My lips and my breasts and my heart aren't crippled—"

"Stop it! Shut up. Don't say another word." He stumbled back to the desk, picked up the empty bottle and looked at it.

"Jon, it wasn't like this once. Don't you remember how it used to be? We loved each other in the beginning. Oh, I know we never consummated our marriage because you were afraid of hurting me and I was too shy to tell you how I wanted us to be real lovers. I should have, I know that now. I shouldn't have waited until the problem was so great you had to drink to blot it out. Jon, I know you were devastated over the lost manuscript, but you'd begun to drink even before the storm. We've lived like brother and sister too long. It was bound to affect you."

He gave her a look of incredulous disbelief. "You still don't realize the truth, do you? You idiot! I could stand being tied to you when there was a chance she'd come to me, when she was there, waiting for me . . ."

The icy numbness was rising through Cecily's body. She felt it reach her brain and she strove desperately to speak before she was overcome by faintness. "No, no, don't say anything that can't ever be taken back. Jon, I'm begging—"

"I never loved you, Cecily. I loved Sarah. But she didn't have a rich father like you. She was just another worker bee, like me. The drones of the world have the money, so we're at their mercy. I thought she'd understand that things wouldn't change between her and me. It wasn't as if you were a real wife."

Cecily buried her face in her hands, wanting to faint, wishing she could stop the sound of his voice.

He seemed oblivious to her presence now, speaking to the empty bottle as though it were a priest in a confessional. "I thought I'd be able to write full time. My God, a year or two was all I needed. As soon as my first novel was sold, I wouldn't have been dependent on your old man. But no, he didn't have a son to put in his business, so I had to be the surrogate. Then there wasn't time, no time, and you, you couldn't work like a normal woman. If I'd married Sarah, she could easily have earned enough to support us until my book was finished."

Cecily forced her hands from her eyes, dropped her arms to the wheels of her chair and turned them. Jonathon wasn't aware that she left until the door closed behind her. She heard the tequila bottle crash against it.

Chapter 26

Cecily went blindly down the hall toward the lobby. Danny had installed a ramp at one side of the front steps so she could descend unaided to the terrace. She passed several Mexican workmen, who smiled and spoke to her, but mercifully did not see Sarah or Darius or Charmain, who surely would have seen and asked about her tears.

Outside in the hot sunlight she blinked, dazzled, and wheeled to the edge of the cliff so she could look out across the sea. The brick plaza had been cleared of debris, but the retaining walls and planters that had enclosed it had not yet been rebuilt. She stopped her chair as she felt the front of the wheel begin to roll from bricks to slippery rock.

For a moment she was afraid she had moved too fast, that her momentum would carry her over the edge. She jammed on her brake, trembling as she realized how close she had come to plunging down onto the rocks below. Almost at once, she wondered if that wouldn't have been the best thing that could have happened. After all, her husband had just told her she wasn't a whole woman. Why would any man want her? If Jonathon, who once had loved her enough to marry her, couldn't bring himself to share physical love with her, then who would?

She pushed the thought aside. She was just as guilty as Jonathon. If he'd lusted after Sarah, and she realized now that that part of his confession had been true, then hadn't she, sweet innocent Cecily whom everyone thought was so pure, hadn't she in her heart of hearts wanted Danny? Loved him, needed him, yearned for his touch for so long that she hadn't even been aware of the moment when she stopped loving Jonathon.

Yes, perhaps she should have let her chair go crashing down to those beckoning rocks. She thought back over all she and Jonathon had said to one another. It was over between them now. She'd made that one last desperate attempt to be a wife to him. If he'd taken it, she would have asked Danny to leave, and gone with Jonathon wherever he wanted to go. Yes, even knowing that he loved Sarah. Because Cecily knew that Sarah didn't love Jon. She admired his mind, was drawn to him in a way strong women are often drawn to men who will let them mother them. But Sarah didn't love him. She had never loved any man until Darius came along. Seeing the two of them together was like seeing twin comets blazing through the heavens.

Cecily idly inched the wheels of her chair forward again, her eyes fixed on the restlessly moving sea. Jon said she was a millstone. Danny had turned down Sarah's offer of a job. Funny how Danny never liked Sarah. Everything was coming apart. Cecily could go home, of course, to a life of insulated emptiness. To her mother's endless sympathy.

She didn't want to live without Danny's comforting, yet exciting presence. She didn't want to live . . .

Something was restraining her chair. It rolled back, away from the edge. Danny said, "You're too close to the rocks, Cecily. Are you daydreaming again? Look, I brought you something."

A red clay pot was placed carefully on her lap. It contained tightly packed cacti, a small army of them. Ogling button eyes had been placed on each rounded head. The cactus huddled in the pot, staring foolishly at her. She burst out laughing, but somehow the laughter dissolved into tears and Danny was down on the terrace floor, holding her in his arms and whispering against her hair, "It's all right. It's going to be all right. I love you, Cecily. I can't let you leave me. I'll take care of you always. I love you."

Sarah was awakened unceremoniously by Darius shaking her arm. She blinked open her eyes and saw the room was still dark. He was standing up beside the bed, fully dressed. "What's wrong? What is it?" She struggled to come fully awake. "All right! I'm awake. Stop shaking me, you're hurting me."

"I'd like to break your neck," he said grimly, "but I'll content myself with withdrawing from your life."

"What are you talking about? Lord, it's the middle of the night. Can't your latest attack of rage wait until morning? I had a hard day."

"Did you hear me, Sarah? I'm leaving. You're free. I understand Mexican divorces are easy and quick. Go ahead and get one."

"Divorce! What do you mean? We agreed! You said if I went to Europe with you, you'd let me have the money to fix up the hotel. Darius, you *agreed*—" Her voice rose and she was afraid she sounded hysterical. Shaking violently, she sat up and reached for the bedside lamp. It clicked on, illuminating his face. His lips curled into a cynical smile, and his eyes were filled with a venom that left no doubt he meant what he was saying.

"The agreement is off, love. As of tonight. I came to say goodbye." He turned his back on her and walked to the dresser and began to pull out drawers. She saw that he'd brought several bags from the luggage room. They stood on the rack, open and ready for the clothes he began to toss into them.

She jumped from the bed and ran to him, clutched his arm. "But why? Darius, *why*, for God's sake? Why now—tonight? What have I done?"

He paused, looked at her appraisingly. "Very good, Sarah. Almost genuine astonishment in your eyes. And

I like the pose. The seductive nightgown with one strap down so that your breast is almost but not quite exposed. Quite distracting. I could reach out and slip it down completely, get carried away by your considerable charms." He paused, his eyes raking her contemptuously. "But I'm afraid you're wasting your time."

She stepped backward, feeling as if he'd slapped her. He continued to drop shirts and socks haphazardly into a suitcase. She pulled up the strap of her nightgown, wondering if this could be a nightmare. Her mind examined all that had happened that day, searching for a clue to this sudden decision to leave her.

There'd been that confrontation with Danny this morning. After that Sarah had called a war council with Charmain and Ramon to explain to them that the Conways and Danny would be leaving. Sarah had bluntly asked if Ramon could handle the work without a foul-up while she went to Europe with Darius. Charmain had been upset with her and declared that she and Ramon weren't Sarah's lackeys and that she was not to speak to them again unless it was an apology for her rudeness. Charmain had flounced out of the room, dragging Ramon with her.

At that point there had been a commotion outside, and Sarah had rushed outside to find a fight in progress between Ramon's elderly uncle and two of the workmen who had a rope on the remaining root of the olive tree in preparation for yanking it from the ground. The old man was swinging wildly with his fists, as the two young men dodged and yelled.

By the time Ramon appeared and everyone calmed down and Sarah agreed to leave the root in the ground, since the old man was convinced the tree would grow again, another crisis was taking place in the kitchen. Consuela and one of the newly hired maids were in disagreement about who should clean the latest catch of fish.

Somehow the day had slipped into evening, Sarah

realized. Except for a hurried dinner in the kitchen when Darius joined her for a few minutes, she hadn't seen the others all day. She'd hoped they were packing.

Recalling those few minutes in the kitchen with Darius, Sarah couldn't pinpoint anything amiss. Certainly no forewarning of this sudden announcement about divorce. He was cordial, only slightly mocking, when he asked if she'd been successful in making arrangements for a whip-wielding taskmaster to take over during her absence. She'd answered shortly that she'd have to rely on Ramon. No, there was no hint there to suggest what might have happened. She'd been so tired that she came to bed early. She thought Darius and the others were probably in the dining room, perhaps listening to Cecily play the piano, although she hadn't heard it as she slipped away to her room.

Darius snapped the suitcase shut and turned his attention to his toilet articles, flinging hairbrush and razor into a bag. He methodically gathered up everything in sight. There was no doubt that he never intended to come back.

Sarah licked her lip nervously. "Where will I find you? I'm not sure how to go about arranging a divorce. Won't there be something you have to do, papers to sign, or something?"

"Oh, I'm sure you'll manage."

"Darius, I suppose you wouldn't consider sitting down and talking, really talking, about this. You see, I've been doing a lot of thinking lately and I've come to some rather startling conclusions."

"Yes, I'm sure you have. If you're going to suggest we carry on as business partners, the answer is no. I want nothing to do with this hotel. It's far enough along now that you'll be able to reopen some of the rooms. Needless to say, there won't be any more money from me. And Sarah, if you try to sue me for alimony, I'll fight you to the death. Everything I've given you up to now is yours, including the money I've pumped into this place. But now you're on your own."

He went to the closet and selected the jacket he usually wore for flying. Taking one suitcase and slinging the travel bag over his shoulder, he walked to the door. "I'll tell Ramon where to send the rest of this stuff. Apologize to Charmain for my departure, will you? I'm in no mood to see her tonight."

"I thought you were going to invite her to go with you. Darius, wait, come back!" He disappeared into the hall.

Sarah stood in the middle of the bedroom for a moment, unable to believe he would really walk out on her, then she grabbed her robe and ran after him.

She caught up with him as he was climbing into his car. "Darius, for God's sake, can't you tell me—"

He climbed into the driver's seat and slammed the door. The window was rolled down and he looked at her, shaking his head slightly. "You're amazing, Sarah. You really are. Even now, when you have everything you schemed to get, it isn't enough, is it? What more do you want, a settlement from me? You won't get it."

"I don't want your damn money," Sarah screamed. She shivered, clutching her robe closer, as the damp night air crept up from the sea. "What do you mean I have everything I schemed to get? What are you talking about?"

"You wanted the melancholy Mr. Conway, and you wanted this hotel. Now you have both. Charmain told me yesterday she's decided she's not cut out for the hotel business. She intended to let you have her share and persuade Ramon to go on a little odyssey with her, as she put it."

"I've as much of my money in this place as she has anyway," Sarah said. "But what do you mean I have Jonathon? I don't have Jonathon."

"Ah, I see, you're going to play the part to the end. Very well. They're gone, Sarah. Cecily and Danny. They slipped away some time this evening, leaving a note to the effect that Cecily was divorcing her husband in order to marry Danny. I'm not sure where Conway is. Ramon told me he thought the *señor* was off on a drunken binge. No doubt by way of celebration. Perhaps you should go and join him, Sarah."

Sarah stood with one hand on the car window, stunned and unable to speak. Darius picked up her hand and dropped it from the car. "He's free, Sarah. Your lover is free. He's all yours."

Darius gunned the engine and roared away in a choking cloud of sand.

Chapter 27

Sarah stumbled into Charmain's room, felt along the wall for the light switch, hoping that she was in her own bed and that Ramon wasn't with her.

The light flooded the room. Charmain lay on a satin pillow, a black velvet mask over her eyes. Sarah went to her bedside and patted her arm. "Charlie, wake up, old bean, I need you like I've never needed you before."

Charmain stirred, grumbling her way to consciousness. She pushed up the eye mask, blinking. "What's this, a Nazi interrogation? Switch off that blasted overhead light. What time is it? I feel as if I'd just dropped off!"

Sarah switched off the overhead light as Charmain sat up and turned on a soft pink lamp on her nightstand. Sarah said, "I'm sorry, it's a little after midnight. But it's an emergency. I had to talk to you. Darius walked out on me."

Charmain's gasp was followed by a long silence. Then she flung the sheet back and said, "Pass my dressing gown, love, then pour us both a couple of brandy toddies and tell me the whole story."

She sat on her recently recovered chaise and listened while Sarah told her everything, from the moment she arrived at Darius's apartment in New York, not sparing herself.

When she was finished, Charmain said quietly, "You love him."

It wasn't a question, but Sarah nodded. She had been walking restlessly around the room, but now she went to the chaise and sat on the end of it. "I don't know when or how it happened, but I do love him. I love him the way a woman loves a man. What I felt for Jonathon was a girl's infatuation. Oh, Charlie, I've been such a fool. Now I've lost him. It's my own stupid fault."

"Before you start flailing yourself, my pet, let me tell you that there isn't a woman alive who didn't have a schoolgirl crush on a totally unsuitable male. You're certainly not the first woman who didn't recognize a good man's love when it came along." Charmain sipped her toddy thoughtfully, her eyes unfocused, as though she were remembering something in the past rather than concentrating on the present problem.

"What am I going to do, old bean?"

Charmain blinked. "Did you ever *tell* him you loved him?"

Sarah shook her head. "There didn't seem to be the right opportunity. I mean, when he wanted to hear it, I wasn't ready to say it. And now—"

"Now you're afraid he'll think you merely want to continue with a marriage to a husband who is also your banker. That it's Darius's cash, rather than his person, you want back. Sweets, if I'd known you were going to become so obsessed with the Casa Brava, I'd never have bought the place. And to think just a couple of days ago, I was intending to deed my share to you."

"Yes, Darius told me. Are you planning to walk out on me too?"

"Frankly, love, I *am* getting a wee bit bored with the isolation. And Ramon is a sweet boy, but he's pestering me to marry him. So it is time to move on. Why can't men just enjoy things as they are? Why do they want to complicate life by getting married? If Darius hadn't insisted upon marriage, perhaps you two—"

"But I *liked* being married to him," Sarah protested. "Don't blame Darius for our problems. They're all my doing."

"You know, pet, you're telling these things to the wrong person."

"Do you think I should go after him? Tell him?"

"Of course. But first you'll have to find him. And if he doesn't want to be found, that could prove tricky and take some time. Do you want to abandon the Casa Brava."

"Absolutely not! Listen, old bean, I know you made a career out of catering to men—forgive my bluntness —but I couldn't live as you did. I need a challenge, my own dragon to slay. I want Darius. I love him, I need him, but he doesn't have anything to do with how I feel about making a go of the hotel. I love the Casa Brava in a different way. Charlie, if it's a case of choosing between them . . . but it isn't. Darius isn't that kind of man. All he wanted was for me to get over Jonathon."

"And you're sure you have?"

"Oh, yes. I'm sure." Sarah breathed fervently. "It seems Cecily has too. I wish I could have seen her, talked to her, before they left. I wish I could have asked her to forgive me."

"Cecily doesn't believe you're guilty of anything to forgive, Sal sweet, and you're not. You don't seriously believe she ran away because she thought you were trying to steal her husband? I've watched those three since they arrived. Cecily's love for her husband slowly died before our eyes. And little wonder! He's been so wrapped up in himself, shutting her out. And Danny loved her, wanted her with a sweet agony one could almost feel. I don't believe he even *saw* her wheelchair.

Oh, he moved her around in a reflex action, but he saw her as a complete and beautiful young woman, which she is. They were together so much and deeply concerned for each other. Their falling in love was inevitable."

"But Cecily is so steadfast, so loyal, I can't believe she'd walk out on Jon, even if she had fallen for Danny."

"My pet, one never knows what goes on between two people, especially married people, behind closed doors. Jonathon might have been an absolute monster. He was inclined to drink a bit too much. We all show different faces to different people, love. The Jonathon you knew might not have been the same one Cecily lived with."

"I guess not. She's gone with Danny."

"I take it you haven't yet seen Jonathon?"

"No. Darius left only a few minutes ago. I came straight to you."

"I suggest you get Ramon to drive you to the airport without any further delay. Perhaps you can catch up with Darius."

Sarah stood up again, feeling a hard lump swell and grow in her throat. "No! I tried running after him, practically hung on to his leg when he got in his car. He's in no mood to listen to confessions of undying love from me. Listen, old girl, I came to you for a few tips on feminine wiles—how to get him back. This isn't the advice I expected from you."

Charmain put her glass down with deliberate care and gave Sarah a penetrating look. "Not two minutes ago, Sal girl, you were deriding my 'catering' to men, as you put it."

"I know. Inconsistent of me, isn't it? I want him back any way I can get him. But I have a feeling that if I go after him with the kind of determination I used to keep the hotel going, I'll turn him off even more. Darius is one of those peculiar combinations of old-fashioned man and modern liberated man. He was ready to let me live my own life as long as I was faithful to him and our marriage vows. We'd have been equal partners in one perfect union, old girl, if I hadn't been carrying a torch for Jon. Now Darius probably thinks we planned this all along. He certainly thinks I'll run straight to Jon's arms now that he's free."

"Yes, I see your point. You do have a problem. You know what, sweetie, I believe it's time I told you about my own misspent youth. Perhaps it will help you make a few decisions about how to proceed from here on. Or at least deter you from making the same mistakes I made. Let's go and make some coffee. It's going to be a long night."

Chapter 28

They took a pot of coffee back to Charmain's room and locked the door. Charmain said that was to keep Jonathon out if he came looking for Sarah, but Sarah thought it might have been her signal to Ramon she wasn't receiving in case he had amorous inclinations during the night.

"You find yourself torn, don't you, love. I mean, your feelings for me are ambivalent. On the one hand you disapprove of me thoroughly, but on the other hand you can't help loving me. Don't smile! You know what I mean. No, I don't want you to say a single word. *Just listen to my story.*

"I know it's hard to believe, but I was once an innocent young virgin, waiting for the prince on the white horse like every other female of my generation, rich or poor. No one ever told us that it might be necessary for us to earn our own living. We would be pampered and adored wives, produce a child or two and live happily ever after.

"I was engaged to a young medical student. We lived near the French-Belgian border then, and he was at school in Paris for most of the year. My mother was American, my father French, so I was bilingual and had visited America with my mother several times.

"I was seventeen with nothing more in my head than the next party, my newest pretty dress and my fiancé coming home for the summer holidays. We planned to marry on my eighteenth birthday.

"Of course, I was aware that a peculiar mustached-dictator had risen to power in Germany. But what did Herr Hitler and his toy soldiers have to do with me? I was the darling daughter of loving parents, my fiancé adored me. What more could I ask, since I certainly was neither pretty nor clever.

"Sal, dear, there are some experiences we never learn to accept. No matter how much time goes by, we don't want to admit they were ever a part of our lives. Such as what happened to me when the Germans invaded France.

"Oh, nothing happened at first. We were simply occupied. We lived in a zone that the Germans decided was to be evacuated of civilians, so we were relocated to another town. My father was a doctor, and we were sent to a town in need of a doctor.

"One night some farmers brought an injured R.A.F. pilot to our house for my father to treat. The pilot had bailed out of his plane, broken his ankle on landing in a rocky field. The Germans were searching for him.

"That was my first meeting with Philippe Descartes, Darius's father.

"He had escaped to England just before the fall of Paris, joined the Royal Air Force. I thought, as I helped Mama by taking his breakfast up to the attic the next morning, that he was unbelievably good-looking and terribly nonchalant, considering the predicament he was in. He asked my name, began flirting with me at once, as though I were a great beauty. The strange thing was, I *felt* like a great beauty when he looked at me with those black, black eyes.

"I hadn't heard from my fiancé since the war began. I had no idea what had become of him. We hid Philippe for several weeks until his broken bone mended. We had an elderly housekeeper, Mme. Marquet, but Mama no longer had any other help in the household and my father had so many patients that Mama had to help him. She spent so much time in the big living room of our house, which was converted to a surgery, that Marquet and I were left to run the house.

"I'm not sure if I seduced Philippe or he seduced me. Like any young girl, I'd wondered about what it would be like to make love to a man. I'd thought about my fiancé in this way, but never with the intensity I thought about lying in Philippe's arms. Once I went up to the attic and found him naked; he had been bathing and wasn't expecting me until dinner. I'd found a book we'd talked about and taken it up to him.

"He had a cast on his lower leg, of course, but I thought he was the most perfect, beautiful creature I had ever seen. More handsome than any sculpture! I'd never imagined a man could look like that. I stood and stared at him, probably with my mouth hanging open. He didn't attempt to cover himself. He just looked at me in surprise, then he began to smile that slow delicious smile he had. All devilment. And he said, 'You've never seen a naked man before. I hope you're not shocked by our dissimilarity to your own fair selves. But you see, our bodies are designed to fit perfectly with yours. Some day your fiancé will return and—'

"He reached for a towel to cover himself, but he suddenly dropped it and said, 'To hell with your fiancé. I hope he never comes back to you. Because, sweet little Charmain, I want you for myself. But I have to go back to England. I can't live under the heel of the *Boche,* so what's to be done?'

"I think perhaps it was I who rushed into his arms. He could hardly have run to me with his cast anchoring him. The next moment we were in each other's arms. Ah, *chérie,* how right you were about our bodies fitting together so perfectly. His lips were heaven. His caresses brought a fever to my blood I'd never felt before. It was a golden afternoon.

"My hair was long in those days, longer and more luxurious even than yours, Sal. He pulled it loose, wanted to feel the silken touch of it against his skin. He always said my hair excited him. Then we were both tugging at my clothes, undressing me.

"There are no words that even hint at the ecstasy. But I see from your face that you know what a perfect fusion of two bodies is like. And I can see the unspoken question in your eyes. If it was so wonderful with Philippe, why did I have all those other men?

"The first, believe me, were not of my choosing.

"When Philippe's ankle healed, the French Underground arranged to take him to a fishing village where a boat would take him to England. We swore we would be together again when the war ended. We would wait for each other, be faithful.

"The Germans caught one of the men who helped Philippe escape. God only knows what torture they inflicted, but he broke under it, implicated my father and mother. A German officer had been killed.

"Forgive me, after all these years, I still cry. My parents were dragged from their beds and taken away. Marquet and I huddled together in the attic. She had come to me and taken me there when the storm troopers kicked down the front door. We were terrified, shaking and sobbing with fear, as we heard them search the house. Then the sound of boots coming up the attic stairs, the trapdoor raising slowly, a helmeted head coming into view—

"There were six of them. Their officer was not with them. Coarse, uncouth beasts from the slums of Berlin. I shall not tell you the unspeakable things they did to

Marquet and me. I believe they would have killed us both, had not their officer arrived. He was a gentleman —no, don't raise your eyebrows at me. You think all Germans were swine? Of course they were not.

"Karl, the officer, sent us to a hospital, came to see we were all right. He assured us his men would be punished. Afterward, after I learned my parents had been executed and I had no one to turn to, nowhere to go, what else was there for me but to turn to Karl?

"So I became one of those most despised of all women: a camp follower, fraternizing with the enemy of my country. In the long hours when I was alone— women like me were shunned, ostracized—waiting for Karl, I read books, studying the great courtesans of the past. I thought of myself as an actress, playing a part. When Karl was sent to North Africa, I was surprised at the ease with which I found another protector and how quickly I learned to accept his ardor, to adjust to his whims and desires.

"But, of course, there was a day of reckoning. The Allies invaded, France was liberated. The resistance fighters came out of the hills, and my former fiancé was one of them. It was he who wielded the scissors when they cut off my hair. His mother shaved my head.

"Philippe Descartes came searching for me. He found me living in Paris—Ah, Sal love, don't cry, please! I shan't be able to go on. It all happened so long ago.

"As I said, Philippe came. Just seeing him again was more than I ever hoped for. Handsome, sure of himself, sure of me. I couldn't tell him what happened. I kept seeing the look on my fiancé's face when the women of the town dragged me out, identified me as a collaborator. I couldn't bear to see that look on Philippe's face. Oh, I loved him so!

"We made love. We couldn't help ourselves. And in the heat of our passion he reached for my hair. Sal, dear, if the scene hadn't been so tragic, I suppose it would have been high comedy. My wig, of course, came off in his hand. He stared at me for a moment, then put the wig back on my head and gathered me into his arms.

"If he had stormed and raged at me or got up and walked out—anything but that simple silent gesture! I couldn't stand having him pity me. I knew that men despised women they pitied, it was one of the truths I learned from my fellow female sinners. So I brazened it out. I laughed about it as though I didn't give a damn. I pretended he was nothing more to me than . . . what's the word the working girls use today, Sal? Nothing more than a *john* to me. I even went so far . . . oh, God help me . . . as to suggest he leave a few francs on my dresser.

"He went crashing out into the night, cursing me and the day he met me, wishing he were dead, wishing I were dead. I cried for a week until a woman friend found me, weak and dehydrated because I'd neither drank nor eaten nor slept. She took care of me, introduced me to a kindly older man, a doctor, oddly enough, who eventually set me up in a little flat and took care of me. My role in life was cast. I would be mistress to more men than I even remember.

"But, I hadn't seen the last of Philippe. I read that he had married the daughter of a wealthy Englishman. His name appeared with increasing frequency on the lists of those men who race fast cars, climb mountains, fly airplanes. There were rumors about women, his name linked with many notorious and beautiful ones. He was also amassing a fortune in his own right. In the aftermath of war there are always those men who pick up the pieces and make a handsome profit in the bargain.

"I wanted to see him again. I plotted. How could it be arranged so it appeared to be accidental? Then I heard he had bought a villa in Morocco, the same one Darius now has. My current *amour* was a successful painter, and I persuaded him that his style would be ideally suited to painting desert landscapes.

"Once in Morocco, I fondly imagined it would be easy to get an invitation to the Descartes villa. How many expatriate Frenchmen could there be? Oh, I fully expected Philippe's English wife to be there too, but I didn't care. I just wanted to *see* him.

"Oh, Sal, my painter dragged me all over the blasted country in a battered touring car. By the time we reached Marrakech, I was benumbed by the mystery of it all. I was lucky. We ran into friends who had been invited to join Philippe and some of his business acquaintants for dinner at a well-known cafe. I brazenly suggested to my artist that we should go too. Our friends tactfully tried to dissuade me, since I would be the only woman in the group. But you know me! That was hardly the right inducement.

"Philippe had changed. I saw that at once. Where before there had been a boyish devilment, a sheer bravado and love of life, now there was cynical hardness and recklessness. He was like a man on a tightrope, trying to please the crowd by taking more and more chances that miraculously paid off. He greeted me coolly, and then acted as if I weren't there.

"The meal was a leisurely one, with long pauses between courses, and I became angrier as time went on and I was still ignored while Philippe talked with the men. Business, racing cars, speedboats—I was too angry to be bored. Why, Philippe was treating me like a *wife*. Ignoring me!

"There was a hawk-faced Arab there, fleeing his vengeful brother, and he and Philippe discussed endlessly the possibility of a desert race to be held in some remote sheikhdom. The man's father was the sheik.

"We sipped mint tea. As you know, no wine is served. There were musicians on a canopied dais, bare muscular arms and embroidered vests, splendid turbans on their heads. I concentrated on the music, feeling humiliated and angry as Philippe continued to ignore me.

"Then the heavy velvet covering a doorway near the

musicians' dais parted and a dancing boy sprang forth. He was the most sensual creature I've ever seen. He began to dance. Faster and faster as the tempo of the music increased. He moved close to our table, his eyes fixing on Philippe. He came closer and closer, hips gyrating wildly, fingers snapping, and all the time his eyes and their promise of seduction so blatant, so erotic that it would be impossible not to be aroused by him.

"The music ended abruptly and the dancing boy fell to the floor at Philippe's feet. There was a pause, as though everyone on earth were holding their breath. Then I sprang to my feet and I know my eyes were blazing and I shrieked at Philippe—something about men who played with boys not being men at all. Berating him for being afraid of women! I don't know what I said. All of it completely unreasonable, of course, because the boy had selected Philippe to dance for, not the other way around.

"I found myself outside being bundled into Philippe's car. He drove me to his villa, and the next thing I knew we were dancing on the moonlit terrace. A tango! He whispered that this was the only kind of dancing that interested him, with a woman in his arms and her skirt whirling around his legs and her scent in his nostrils.

"Oh, what a tango that was! When it ended and he bent me back over his arm and kissed me, I was sure the ground was no longer under us, that we were floating somewhere in the cosmos.

"He swept me into his arms and carried me to the bedroom. There had never been such a night. It was so perfect that when he dozed, just before sunrise, I was overcome by panic. Not knowing exactly what I was doing, I began to dress. I was filled with doubts. He had obviously changed so much, what if he no longer cared? Perhaps all he'd wanted was what I'd already given him. By the time he awakened, I'd talked myself into a fine state of nervous anticipation.

"The second he opened his eyes. I was ready for him. Cool, amused, treating the whole episode as an interlude for both of us to ward off boredom. I think I even said something as banal as, 'Darling, we must do this again some time.'

"Don't look at me like that, Sal, child. Once one has learned that attack is the best means of defense, it's a difficult habit to break. Remember that in your dealings with Darius.

"Philippe sent me back to Marrakech in his car, chauffeur driven.

"Our paths crossed several times after that, but only socially. I was desolate. I missed him, wanted him, loved him more than ever. I thought I'd die from loving him. But it seemed more likely he would kill himself first. He was still racing cars. And I read he'd bought a hydroplane, one of those super fast racing boats.

"We met again at Le Mans. I don't know if I contrived to be there because he would surely be racing. What does it matter why? I'd never stopped loving him. I'd loved *only* him. He won that year. I couldn't restrain myself. I flew into his arms, knocking aside a girl who was presenting him with a bouquet. We spent three days in a hotel, making love every minute.

"On the last evening he told me that his wife was pregnant, but that as soon as the child was born, he would ask her for a divorce so he could marry me. He didn't care, he said, what my past life had been. He loved me.

"My dear, what could I do? Had I loved him less than I did, perhaps it would have been easier, or maybe I should have loved myself more. I don't know. All at once I began to wonder if I *wanted* to marry him. I didn't want our love to end, and it seemed to me that marriage killed love more quickly than any other malaise. Hadn't I opened my arms to married men driven from their wives by sheer boredom? What if my beloved became bored with me? I wouldn't be able to stand it! Oh, what a stupid, stupid child I was . . . .

"I loved him so much I was terrified of losing him a

second time. Wouldn't it be better, I thought, to send him home to his wife and baby? To see him frequently, regularly, in some love nest where our love would always be as exciting as it had been those three days? Then he would never tire of me and I'd have him always. So I lied to him, told him I could never give up my freedom. Go home to your family, I told him, and I'll call you when next I'm in London.

"He stared at me. A frightening look on his face— acceptance, resignation and a reckless determination. A look of doom, I suppose, but I didn't know that then.

"Oh, Sal, dear, I was so sure of myself, my power over him. He would come around to my way of thinking, I was convinced of it. Why would he want to settle for the dull routine of marriage when we could have everlasting romance? I knew when he returned to his wife, he'd begin to think about the arrangement I wanted.

"Why didn't I recognize where that recklessness in him might lead?

"Philippe left for England. The moment he was gone I felt a sense of foreboding. I was making a horrible, ghastly mistake. Philippe would never take me as only his mistress. It would be all or nothing. I wrote him a long letter, begging him to come back so that we could talk.

"Philippe didn't get my letter. He was killed the day after I posted it. Racing his hydroplane on a lake in northern England. The boat flipped over at high speed. Darius was born the next day, a premature delivery, and Philippe's wife was dead of toxemia within the week.

"I will never believe Philippe committed suicide. Never. He loved life too much. If I'm to blame for his death, it's because his mind was on me instead of what he was doing. My worst crime is that I made him careless. I suppose that is what I always wanted to tell Darius. I kept track of him. When the child was taken to visit Philippe's relatives in Paris, I arranged to have a mutual friend introduce me.

"In time Darius came to regard me as an eccentric aunt, I think. It shocked me to find out that he knew about me and his father. He'd found the letter I sent Philippe among his mother's possessions. By then he'd known me for years. At first he was angry—he almost wanted to kill me—but then he said he realized that I regarded my various love affairs as a game, my lovers as a passing parade. That I couldn't have imagined anyone taking me as seriously as his father had taken me.

"God, how that hurt! Don't ever believe we get off scot-free, sweets, because there's a day of reckoning for all of us.

"Eventually, of course, I met your grandfather and he brought me to America. We visited Europe together after your grandmother died. Once again, I refused to get married. I met Darius from time to time. He was so like his father it was like being haunted. Yet I loved him too. Sometimes I fantasized he was my son.

"Then there was you, my dear. I watched you grow up, although you were never aware of it. Sometimes I'd have my chauffeur drive past your house or your school so I could see you. Perhaps it was your auburn hair, the way you carry yourself, your eyes, I don't know. You were Del's granddaughter and he told me what a spunky little girl you were, how he loved you.

"I swore to myself I wouldn't meddle in your life or in Darius's. Del would have killed me in any event. But I did secretly dream of having you meet Darius one day. It would have been a vicarious happy ending to my love affair with Philippe.

"Then when your grandfather died and you came to me at his funeral—but the rest, as they say, is history. What? No, I never told Darius the true story of my love affair with his father. I let him think I was simply one of those women who drift from one man to another, that I was incapable of real love. Darius doesn't know how much I loved his father. He only knows that I sent him away.

"Sal, I'm telling you all this because I know Darius has asked himself, a million times, did his father die accidentally or did he kill himself? Darius has repeated so many of his father's feats—the car races, the boat races, the fast airplanes. And in moments of extreme danger, I know he's asked himself if saving one's life is a reflex action. If in that split second between life and death, he would automatically do what was necessary to live.

"Darius believes you don't love him. You must tell him you do. Don't waste his love and yours for the sake of foolish pride or any other reason. Find a way to tell him how much you love him. Go to him quickly, before it's too late. Because Darius will now do exactly what his father did. He will find some death-defying thing to do, take some fearful risk. You see, the conditions are all as they were so long ago. Now, once and for all, Darius is going to find out whether or not his father killed himself for love of me or whether he simply lost control of that hydroplane and died accidentally. Even if the answer comes to Darius in the last second of his own life!"

Chapter 29

Sarah had packed, showered and dressed when Jonathon knocked on her door. She'd hoped to get away before he found her, but Ramon was having trouble getting her jeep started. She kept one hand on her bedroom door. "Hi, Jon. Let's go and get some coffee."

His face was bloated, ravaged. He followed her to the kitchen silently, with the dejected attitude of the proverbial whipped cur, anxious only to regain favor with somebody, anybody. She felt sorry for him, but even sorrier for herself and desperately anxious to be on her way.

"Sit down, Jon," she said as calmly as she could. He dropped into a chair as she poured him a cup of coffee. It was barely dawn, and they were the only ones in the large dining room.

"Your husband told you that they're gone? Cecily and—" Jonathon's voice shattered into dry wracking sobs. His head fell to his arms, sprawled on the table in front of him.

Sarah reached out to stroke his dark gold hair, but drew back. She touched his shoulder instead, feeling his grief and despair burst from him.

There was a crumpled sheet of paper in one of his hands. She disentangled his fingers and pulled the paper free. She saw at once that it was a note from Cecily. Jonathon's tears showed no sign of abating. As Sarah stood by him, her eyes turned again and again to that farewell note. At last, using one hand, she smoothed the sheet of paper and read:

My Dear Jonathon,

I'm sorry. If I stay and tell you to your face, as Danny wants to do, then I'll weaken and I won't go with him. I love him and want to be with him, but if I wait until you're sober, I'll never leave you. So forgive me for sneaking away like a thief in the night. I must go now, while I remember all the hurtful words you said to me, all the times you drank too much and I was the one who suffered for your excesses, because you never remembered afterward.

Odd, isn't it, how this wild and yet strangely peaceful place brought out both the best and worst in all of us, especially you, Jon. For I do believe in your talent. Your writing moved me deeply. I felt the pain and joy of your characters and knew that they were all part of you, the good and the evil. I do believe your folly now lies in trying to reconstruct what is irretrievably lost. You should begin a new work with a completely new set of characters and circumstances. Sometimes life imitates fiction, Jon, and I believe that in recognizing your folly, I saw my own.

For I'm going to begin a new life. I don't belong with Mother and Father, and I never belonged with you. You can only give all of yourself to your writing. You may feel you need others—me, Sarah—but you don't, not truly.

Danny and I need each other and love each other. When you've had time to adjust to the idea, you'll see this is for the best. Tell Sarah I'll get in touch with her after a while. She's been more than my best friend, and nothing will ever change my feelings toward her. Tell her, though, that Darius loves her more than she knows. I don't think she realizes that.

Go back to your work, Jon. Think of the lost novel as an exercise in discipline. You did it once, you can again.

When I'm able to talk coherently, I'll be in touch.

Sarah stared at the round, childish handwriting, and thought about Cecily's unexpected wisdom. Perhaps those who observed life, rather than participated in it, were the sages. Sages . . . the word lingered in her mind. What had Darius said? *Score one for the old sage . . . the cure for love is marriage.* He'd unwittingly summed up Charmain's philosophy of life. Did he believe it was also Sarah's? She had to get to him, make him understand how much she loved him and wanted to be his wife.

Jonathon raised his head at last and looked at her with drowned eyes. "What am I going to do? I loved her, Sarah, I did love her, her quiet dignity, her courage. How could I have driven her away? Oh, God, what am I going to do without her? She was the one who kept me going. I'd never have written my novel without her. I'd have given up. I did give up. Time after time. And now I don't even remember what I said to her. I was worried because you wanted us to leave. One of the workers brought me a bottle of tequila. I don't remember what I said to her!"

"Drink the coffee, Jon," Sarah urged him, pushing the cup closer.

He looked at her, blinking as though trying to bring her into focus. "I didn't . . . oh, God, surely I didn't—"

"Tell her about me?" Sarah finished for him. Cecily's note hinted he might have, yet there'd been no resentment directed at Sarah. "Jon, if you loved her, why did you string me along? I'd have got over you a lot faster if I'd known you really loved Cecily. I thought—"

Jonathon gulped a mouthful of coffee, choked and fumbled for a handkerchief. He blew his nose and said,

"I wanted you, Sarah. I still do. You're beautiful, exciting, but—"

"Lacking in the qualities you loved in Cecily? Funny how none of us appreciate what we have until we've lost it." Sarah sat down opposite him, wanting the table between them. "Listen, Jon, I've got to leave right away. Because of this whole rotten mess I stand to lose Darius. Well, I'm going after him, I'm going to fight for him. I suggest you go after Cecily and do the same."

"I wouldn't know where to go, how to—"

"Dammit, neither do I. But sitting here isn't going to bring them back."

She stood up, but he caught her wrist. "Sarah, do you think Danny might have . . . she and Danny . . . do you think they . . . made love?"

"You told me you and she didn't. How should I know about her and Danny? He didn't exactly take me into his confidence about anything."

"Maybe that's why I lost her. I couldn't see her as a sexual object. A saint, a madonna, but not a . . . a—"

"Jonathon, if you say what you're thinking, I'll slap your face, because that would imply that's how you saw me. Now let go of my wrist, drink your coffee, then get going."

She strode toward the kitchen door, stopped and turned to look at him. "I'm going to tell Ramon that if you're still here tomorrow morning, he's to refuse service. Goodbye, Jon. I hope things work out for you."

"Sarah, wait! Don't just walk out on me like this, please. For the sake of all we've been to each other . . ."

The sound of his voice followed her as she ran down the hall to her bedroom. She grabbed her bags and hurried out through the front doors. She had already said goodbye to Charmain, who was now making up for lost sleep.

Ramon had the jeep running. He helped her with her bags, then offered his hand. There was deep sadness in his dark eyes. *"Vaya con Dios,* Sarah. I will take care of everything here, do not worry. I will be waiting when you come back. But my Charmain . . . I think she will be gone. I do not think I can keep her here."

Sarah shook his hand, then hugged him. "I know, Ramon. I'm sorry. Charmain never wanted to be tied down. But you had her for a little while, didn't you?"

As I had Darius for a little while, she thought as she drove down the desert road, and Jon had Cecily. And none of us knew it wouldn't be forever.

Chapter 30

Sarah sat in a hotel room in New York, twisting the gold bangle Darius had given her, sliding it back and forth on her wrist, unable to bring herself to take it off. She had sold all of her other jewelry, including the brooch Charmain had given her.

It was just no use. She'd have to take a job. She'd exhausted all of her resources trying to find Darius, who had vanished without a trace. Calls to his answering service, his friends in Paris and England, even shipping agents who might have handled the shipment of his antiques, all had proved fruitless. No one knew where he was. Mrs. Mason, his Surrey housekeeper, stammered that she hadn't heard from "the master" since he left with Sarah. The French housekeeper told her he'd stayed briefly at his Paris flat, refusing all calls, until his mechanics came to tell him the new racing car was ready.

Sarah was numbed by fear at this news. But Darius's

name did not turn up on the roster of any known road or track race. Besides, the car was designed for desert racing, and it was too late for the Baja winter race, too early for the summer Baja 500.

She called his villa in Morocco and found it was in the charge of a man named Hashim who said he was the "houseman." He was living at the villa in the absence of his master, although the residence was officially closed for the summer.

Weeks had slipped by since she left Mexico. In desperation, Sarah had hired a firm of private investigators to find Darius for her. They were no more successful than she had been.

The New York Times lay on the bed beside her. She fingered it, thinking about job hunting. Suddenly the phone rang and she grabbed it, hoping it might be Charmain. Sarah's mother came on the line. "Sarah? You're still at a hotel? Have you decided what you're going to do?"

"Hello, Mother, how are you?"

"I'm fine, dear. I don't suppose you've found your husband? No? Sarah, why don't you just give up and come home? I was talking to Buck and Estelle the other day, and they agreed with me we should all let bygones be bygones. They had a call from Cecily, you know. She got a Mexican divorce from Jonathon and promptly married that young chauffeur, what was his name. Anyway, they're living somewhere in the Southwest, I forget where, and apparently they're very happy. At least that's what she told her mother, but you know, after the scandal of the whole thing, she'd have to say that. Jonathon came back here. He didn't stay long. He went to see Buck and Estelle, and the next day left town. Sombody said he'd gone to Hollywood, hoping to get a job as a screenwriter, but somebody else said he was hoping to teach, I don't know—"

"Mother! Listen, I won't be coming back for a while. I still have a hotel in Mexico to look after, you know.

I'll be going back there in the fall for our grand reopening if—" She hesitated, *if I haven't found Darius by then.* "Mother? Are you still there? I heard from Cecily and Danny too. They're truly happy, no pretense. They're both working hard and saving to open a motel with complete facilities for wheelchairs and other handicapped guests."

"Oh, I see. My goodness, this urge to run hotels does seem to run in the family, doesn't it? But Cecily . . . *working?*"

"And loving it. She's a receptionist in a nursing home. Mom, listen, I was just leaving. Say hi to Dad for me."

Sarah replaced the receiver, wondering whether she should try to call Charmain again. The last she'd heard, Charmain had left Mexico, stopped briefly in Palerville to see how her Early Americana museum and adjacent park were being run, then headed for her old haunts in Europe.

A minute later, as Sarah was preparing to shower, there was a knock on her door. Opening it, she could hardly believe her eyes when Charmain swept into the room. "Darling child! How are you, dear? You look pale and wan. Definitely wan. But cheer up, your fairy godmother is here with wonderful news."

"I thought you were in Europe, old bean," Sarah murmured weakly. Charmain was resplendent in powder blue, from head to toe, her flaming tresses gleaming under a tiny concoction of feathers and flowers. Sarah was enclosed in a perfumed hug.

Charmain took the only chair in the room, looked around her with slightly raised eyebrows. "What a depressing dump, dear! No wonder you look so defeated. Lord, I'm alliterating, aren't I? Now, toots, aren't you going to ask me my wonderful news?"

"What's your wonderful news, Charlie?" Sarah smiled, glad to see her and feeling instantly more cheerful.

"I know where Darius is!" Charmain announced triumphantly.

Sarah's breath quickened. She waited as Charmain savored the moment, her blue eyes sparkling. "I went to Paris, love, and I knew that if anyone could tell me what happened to Darius it would be those mechanics who work on his cars. Of course, they'd been sworn to secrecy. But there was this darling older man in charge, hmm, fortyish—just right for me. It took a few evenings of dancing and dining and—"

"Charlie, old girl!" Sarah shouted, "Where *is* Darius?"

"He was at his villa in Morocco three days ago."

"But when I called, his man Hashim told me the villa was closed for the summer."

Charmain raised a perfectly formed eyebrow. "Sweetie, this will come as a surprise to you, I know, but some people have been known to tell small lies. Especially Darius's people. Well, come along, get your things together. I've arranged our flight to Tangier. That was all I could get at such short notice. We'll get a flight from there to Marrakech."

Sarah ran to the closet and pulled out her suitcase. "You're coming with me?"

"I wouldn't miss this reunion for the world," Charmain assured her.

Hashim proved to be a formidable figure. Fierce black eyes regarded Sarah over prominent cheekbones that rose like bony hills beside a hawk's beak of a nose. His beard was streaked with gray, but there was no hint of aging in his movements as he led her into the villa, or in his stance as he turned to face her. He wore a striped garment unlike any Sarah had seen before, perhaps because it was caught at the waist by a rough sash into which was tucked a large curved knife in an ornate sheath. There were several stones in the hilt that could have been precious gems. Hashim had bowed and bid her, *"Salaam aleikum,* you are a hundred times welcome," but there was little welcome in those ferocious eyes.

Behind her, Charmain said, "I remember you, Hashim. Good Lord, I thought you were dead years ago! Oh, dear, do forgive me! How tactless of me—jet lag you know, love. Sarah, Hashim isn't a servant, I'm sure. He was a friend of Darius's father. We met somewhere, I know we did. I'd never forget a man who looked like him."

Hashim's lips parted, revealing startling white teeth. "How may I serve you, Miss D'Evelyn?" He wasn't smiling, Sarah noted. His lips had curled back in the manner of an animal giving a warning growl. His voice, however, was soft, pronouncing the English words slowly but flawlessly.

Charmain walked around him in a wide circle, her brows knitted in concentration. "Here! It was here at the villa I met you. Philippe brought you here. No, that night at the cafe. The night of the dancing boy. I remember now, you were one of the men in the cafe. He wanted you to ask your father's permission to allow a race to take place in his sheikhdom. But I never heard that it did."

"My father is dead. My elder brother now rules in his place." Eyes like obsidian moved from Charmain to Sarah. "Some mint tea, perhaps, to slake your thirst after a tiring journey?"

"Yes, thank you. That would be great," Sarah said, sending a warning glance at Charmain.

Hashim bowed, touched his forelock and left the room on silent feet.

"My God, sweets, did you see that knife in his belt? You don't suppose he's done poor Darius in, do you?" Charmain said in a stage whisper when Hashim's magnificent body disappeared through the arched door.

Sarah looked around the room. All the furniture was covered with white dust sheets except for a small couch grudgingly uncovered by Hashim and offered to them. "No, I believe he is just keeping an eye on the place. But I think either he expects Darius back soon or knows where he is. He doesn't want us to hang around. Are you certain that mechanic in Paris said Darius was coming here?"

Charmain sat down gingerly on the edge of the couch. "I'm positive. I was with him when he called the villa to tell Darius the car was ready."

"Then what? Do you remember what else he said?"

"Not really . . . well, something about Aden. Arranging shipment to Aden, I believe. I didn't listen, once I was certain he had called the villa and Darius was here."

Sarah thought about this. "You said Hashim talked at length with Darius's father about the possibility of a car race in his father's sheikhdom. The mechanic mentioned a shipment to Aden. Could he have been shipping Darius's race car, the dune buggy thing, to Aden? Did you notice how Hashim quickly said the sheikhdom is now ruled by his brother?"

Hashim appeared suddenly in the doorway, a tray of frosty glasses and a pitcher of mint tea on a tray. Charmain stifled a gasp. Sarah jumped too, but recovered more quickly. She exclaimed, "Put that down, Hashim, and come here." When he hesitated, she snapped, "I am *Mrs.* Darius Descartes. In his absence, this is my house."

The tray was placed on a sheet-covered table, and Hashim approached her. She challenged him. "Why are you here while my husband is preparing to race in your brother's sheikhdom?"

He gave her a baleful stare but didn't answer.

Sarah took a step closer to him. "How do I know, in fact, that you are here by invitation? My husband said nothing to me about you coming to stay here. Perhaps I should call the police—"

"My brother the sheik and I have a blood feud. I

cannot go to his country under pain of death. I am an exile. I came here to discuss the terrain, the best route, the difficulties, with the son of my old friend. I could not accompany him, so he suggested I stay here and wait."

Sarah's heart had begun to thump painfully against her ribs. "And when will this race begin? Why has there been no word of it?"

"Your husband and three of his friends who have built desert racing cars wanted to see if it were feasible. They will race against each other, privately."

"When?"

"The race begins the day after tomorrow."

"You, Hashim, who claim to be his friend, have sent him to his death," Sarah declared, her voice shaking.

The fierce countenance looked shocked. "No! He has special car. He has raced many times."

"Never over desert sand. Besides, he doesn't know it, but his car is unsafe." Sarah had no idea whether this was possible, but it was obvious from Hashim's expression of dismay that he believed it was. She plunged on, "We have just come from the mechanics. They left out a vital . . . uh . . . rod. We must fly to your brother's sheikhdom at once."

He backed away in alarm. "No! I cannot go there. I told you, my brother would have me killed."

"Then tell me how to get there. I must take the . . . rod . . . to my husband."

"Send someone else. A woman cannot make such a journey."

"This woman can. And I have no intention of letting anyone else be responsible for my husband's safety. I *will* go, Hashim, with or without your help."

His hand strayed to the hilt of his knife, closed around it. There was another flash of white teeth as he chewed thoughtfully on his lower lip for a moment. At last he said, "Your husband's father once saved Hashim's life by interceding with my father when my brother demanded my death."

Charmain leaned forward. "Fascinating! Tell us, Hashim, what sin were you guilty of?"

He turned to answer her, but Sarah had the uncanny sensation that he was still looking in her direction. He said softly, "I took my brother's favorite wife. In our faith the crime of adultery is punishable by death."

Sarah swallowed hard. "Will you please make me a map showing the sheikhdom?" Out of the corner of her eye she saw Charmain's hand fly to her throat at Hashim's confession.

Hashim said, "There is no need. I will take you there. Perhaps it is kismet."

Chapter 31

The specks in the distance slowly materialized into stark islands. Then a mud-colored coastline jutted into the green-blue water of the Red Sea. Sarah's plane circled Hodeida before landing on the airstrip north of the city.

She felt slightly queasy, extremely disoriented from lack of sleep and not a little uneasy in Hashim's menacingly silent presence. Having left all of the arrangements to him, she wasn't sure if they were taking the most direct route to his brother's sheikhdom or whether he was trying to elude possible assassins.

They had come by way of Aden, which, Hashim told her, some Europeans called the hellhole of the world. Sarah had vague memories of a busy harbor churning with liners, tankers and bumboats, of the impact of sunlight like a scimitar crashing through the searing sky. Neither the Baja desert nor Marrakech had prepared her for the heat, or the flies. She had never seen so many flies. They hurled themselves at any stationary object, clung to her face and clothing.

Hashim had insisted she rest before the next leg of their journey to Yemen. She took a hotel room and was given a suite on the top floor. From her windows she could see a shimmering sweep of water, dazzling salt basins, and to the south, the Indian Ocean simmering in the heat. Down from the north came blasts of air so hot they could have been wafting from an oven. Sarah was too keyed up to sleep, though, and tossed and turned all night.

When they boarded the next plane, she pressed Hashim for information about his country and, grudgingly, he responded. Sarah wasn't sure how old Hashim was, but she had the distinct impression that time had stopped for him when he was still a young man. Either that or there had been little progress in his part of the world in the last thirty or forty years.

"The sheikhdoms encircle the rim of Arabia," he said, "from the head of the Persian Gulf along the coast of Yemen. Despite the heat, much of the land along the seaboard has freshwater springs and much vegetation. Before the British came, it was the home of Arab pirates, pearl fishermen, dhow builders and traders. The sheikhdoms are remote, exotic, rushing headlong, one English wag said, into the thirteenth century."

Sarah smiled, but her amusement faded before Hashim's stern glance. "The part of my brother's land where your husband and his friends plan to race is barren—an inferno."

Sarah leaned back against the seat and closed her eyes, some of her resolve faltering. I'm just tired, she told herself. I stood up to summer in the Baja, didn't I? So it's hotter here. Once the temperature goes over a hundred, does it matter by how much?

She dozed and was awakened by Hashim. He placed a paper-wrapped parcel on her lap. "Go now to lavatory and put this on."

The brown paper came away to reveal a black silk *abeyah,* that voluminous, all-enveloping robe worn by the women of the region. Sarah blinked. "You surely don't expect me to wear this? I'm American, why should I cover myself completely?"

"If you do not, you will be pointed at, spat upon, insulted by all who see you. Only bad women travel in public without the *abeyah* and veil. I have arranged for a friend to fly us in a small plane to an oasis which is to be the finishing point of your husband's race. My friend will not fly a bad woman."

So it was that Sarah found herself swathed in black silk, being buffeted by unstable air as the ground below the twin-engined plane disappeared in a sandstorm.

She clutched Hashim's arm. "How can he land in that?" She had to shout over the roar of the engines, which seemed to be laboring against the wind.

Hashim shrugged. "Wind and sand make a storm. It happens too often to worry about. It is Allah's will."

Sarah looked down at the swirling clouds of dust, and wondered how the racing cars would fare in such conditions. They had been built to travel over the dunes, but could any vehicle withstand the onslaught of dust and sand blown with such ferocity? She said a silent prayer that they would arrive in time to persuade Darius to give up the mad idea. The plane was to land at the finishing point. When she had asked Hashim why they were not going to the starting point, he had turned scathing black eyes on her and replied, "Because the starting point is the palace of Sheikh Abdullah al-Za'im, my brother who has sworn to kill me on sight. I will take you to the oasis on the edge of the Empty Quarter, and you will pray to your God that your husband and his friends have others, mechanics perhaps, waiting there to take you to him."

The plane hit another air pocket and dropped, then lurched sideways. The pilot spoke no English, but appeared to be singing or perhaps chanting in Arabic. Sarah had the uncomfortable feeling he was praying.

Suddenly the air around them cleared, and they were again flying in brilliant sunshine. Sarah gave a sigh of relief. It had evidently been only a localized sandstorm.

Just before they landed, bouncing down heavily on an uneven airstrip, Hashim glanced out of the window and remarked, "*Badu* caravan at the oasis."

The Bedouins, their camels and a few straggly palms were all Sarah could see in the vast emptiness of the sculpted sand dunes. She clutched the black silk *abeyah* awkwardly as Hashim helped her down from the plane. They had landed, she saw, on a salt flat.

"Hashim, I don't see any cars or jeeps," she said apprehensively. Heat rose from the ground in fierce waves, and she was glad she had taken time to buy sturdy leather hiking boots. Under the smothering black silk she wore khaki cotton slacks and shirt. "Hashim, what about the plane? Will he stay, wait for us? You did tell him to stay?"

"He will stay. I will speak with the *Badu* chieftain. Perhaps his caravan has passed through my brother's land and he will have news. You," he exclaimed, glaring down at her from his impressive height, "will remain silent."

Hashim strode toward the oasis, making no move to relieve her of her travel bag, so she struggled with the bag and the voluminous black silk, which she had to hold at strategic points since there were no fastenings. Her boots crunched on the gravelly sand as she ran to keep up with him.

When they reached the small encampment around the oasis, gaunt men and shriveled children greeted them with the long speeches of a desert welcome. Women were kept hidden from the stranger's eyes.

Sarah shuffled from one foot to another, uncomfortably hot, tired and fighting growing impatience as she waited for the speeches to end so she could find out what they knew about Darius and the other racers. Perhaps the whole thing had been called off and this harrowing journey had been for nothing?

At length Hashim turned to her, his face grave, and translated. "Men and vehicles—I think perhaps mechanics—were here when the *Badu* arrived. They left an hour ago, as soon as the storm passed, to search for the racers."

"What do you mean *search* for them? They haven't started the race yet—"

"They were to have finished today. The cars arrived sooner than expected and there had been predictions of a storm late today or tomorrow. They decided to start sooner to avoid it. They should have reached the oasis by noon today."

Sarah's heart skidded. She looked down at her watch. It was almost five in the afternoon. The *abeyah* slipped from her hand, and she let it fall, twisting out of it until it was a black pool on the sand. "To hell with the blasted thing," she yelled at Hashim. "They can think what they like about me. Go, quickly, tell the pilot to take off and search for the cars. He can cover a lot more territory than anyone on the ground."

When Hashim hesitated, she grabbed his arm and shook him. The Bedouins gathered around to watch the spectacle. For an instant she was afraid Hashim would strike her, but he shoved her away from him and began to run toward the plane.

After the agonizing heat of the day, the night chilled the bones. Sarah huddled under her *abeyah* and a blanket as close to Hashim's campfire as she could get, refusing the Bedouins' offer to allow her to join their women in a tent on the far side of the muddy water hole. The plane had returned before dusk with news that there was no sign of any vehicle between the oasis and the sheikh's palace, which was to have been the starting point of the race.

There was nothing to be done but wait for daylight, Hashim told her sternly. The pilot had landed to refuel, spoken with Sheikh Abdullah al-Za'im. May Allah protect his humble brother Hashim if the pilot had told

of his presence here! The sheik had promised to send
out searchers, radio for more planes to come. Morning
was sure to bring one or more vehicles back to the
oasis, or an airplane to the salt flats.

Hashim served her a flat omelette that tasted like
leather and lay heavily in her already upset stomach.
Sarah watched the sky turn into a blazing tapestry of
flame and scarlet as the sun set, then the cold darkness
fell. Hashim wasn't inclined to talk, but he answered
her question as to what the *Badu* were doing to their
camels.

"They force balls of flour paste, like giant pills, down
the throats of the beasts. This gives the animals more
strength, as well as making them drink more water so
they can withstand the crossing of that sandy sea. You
are watching the last of a diminishing number of desert vagabonds. It is rare to see a *Badu* caravan these
days."

"They're getting ready to leave?" Sarah asked.

"At dawn. They will travel to my brother's village."

Despite the coldness of the desert night, Sarah's
eyelids drooped and she was soon asleep. Her last
thoughts had been of Darius, a prayer that he would be
found alive, but hovering in the back of her mind was
the heartbreaking story Charmain had told about Philippe. *Please,* Sarah prayed, *don't let history repeat itself.*

She awoke just before dawn to an eerie silence. The
stars hung in the sky, looking near enough to touch.
Beautiful planet Venus faded, and a clear silver beam
of light came over the unadorned rim of the earth,
flooding the cool sands, shading the subtle variations of
the desert landscape into geometric relief, warming the
dust-etched faces of the sleeping Bedouins.

They began to stir. Sarah saw that the women had
already prepared food for the men, who ate alone.

Sarah sat up slowly, caught in the magic of the
sunrise, spellbound by the fragile beauty of the endless
dunes. In that moment, when the light of the new day
shone on the stark uncluttered scene, it seemed as if her

mind was also swept clean of every unnecessary thought. She knew exactly what she must do.

Hashim was awake, preparing to light a fire. Sarah slid her heavy gold bracelet down her arm and unbuckled it. She had thought she had worn it because she wanted to please Darius, but now she saw another purpose for the bangle. "Hashim, I want you to take this bangle to the Bedouin chief. It is very old, very valuable. It belonged to a great sheik, and there is a legend that the woman to whom he gives it will forever be his. Tell the chief that I want to ride with their caravan."

He looked at her as if she'd gone mad. "They will not take you."

"Please! Ask them. Tell them this is only a fraction of what they will receive if they find my husband. Hashim, quickly, before they leave. I must go with them." She pushed the bracelet into his hand.

He looked down at it, turned it around, reading the Arabic inscription. Then he looked at her again. "You must love your husband a great deal. That is good. But the planes will come. You can ride with the pilots. Or wait until a car comes. If you go with the *Badu* you must ride a camel. The caravan will travel by the most direct route, the chief will allow two, perhaps three, men to detour from the main group to help you search."

"I'd rather take my chances with them than wait here and do nothing. Besides, they've been crossing the desert since the beginning of time. They may see something that a plane in the air wouldn't."

Hashim sighed deeply. "Very well. I will go with you."

"No! You can't. You told me you can't let your brother know you're here. Please, Hashim, the worst that can happen to me is that I pay an unexpected visit to the sheik. I'm less likely to get lost traveling with the Bedouins than I am if I go out in a tow truck or a jeep."

After a moment of consideration, Hashim ap-

proached the chief. Sarah watched as the gold bangle
was passed from one to the other and the negotiations
were completed. Hashim returned to her side. "They
will help you search. But you must wear the *abeyah* and
veil. They are afraid if you do not and your husband is
found alive, he will kill you, and they think this would
be a waste of a brave woman."

Sarah smiled for the first time since leaving her
husband's villa. "How soon till we leave?"

"You will become sick on the camel's back," Hashim
predicted sourly. "And your husband will flay my back
when he arrives at the oasis and you are not here, but
wandering in the desert with the *Badu*."

Chapter 32

Nothing had prepared Sarah for the incredible discomfort of riding a camel. Not only did she have to
maintain a hunched position to remain on the animal's
back, but the swaying motion of its gait quickly brought
on a nausea akin to seasickness. A boy with a camel
stick was assigned to walk with her until she became
accustomed to the tricky balancing act. She would stay
with the caravan while scouts rode out in search of any
trace of the missing men. The scouts would return for
her if they found anything.

The forbidding vistas of the vast and barren dunes
had a stark and compelling grandeur. Sarah found
herself gazing, trancelike, as mirages floated on the
shimmering, heat-hazed horizon. At first she had taken
frequent sips of water from the goatskin bag the

Bedouin chief had given her and she had considered shedding some of her clothes, especially the hated *abeyah*. But she saw that the Bedouins did not drink. As the sun became hotter, they huddled more deeply into their garments until only their dust-flecked eyes were visible. They rode. They didn't waste energy on anything else. Sarah called softly to the boy prodding her camel, then pointed to his camel. He gave her a grateful grin and ran to untie his mount from the camel leading it.

Sarah licked her dry lips and regretted the impulse when they instantly felt more parched than before. Sand and sky and sun blurred and she began to drift. Sensing her inattention, the camel lurched over to a small clump of desert grass and bowed his great neck to nibble. Sarah was flung rudely from its back and landed with a jolting thud amid a cloud of dust.

The Bedouins were amused. Dust cracked on their faces as they grinned. The boy slid from his camel and rushed over to help her to her feet, then coax the camel into a kneeling position so she could remount. The camel turned and regarded her malevolently, dribbling bright green saliva with an unbelievable stench.

"You miserable sullen beast," Sarah said under her breath. Darius, if you're dead after all this . . .

There was a shout from the rear of the caravan, and she turned to see two of the scouts thundering down the dunes, waving their arms and yelling. They caught up with her and expertly cut her camel from the caravan, and she was suddenly galloping across the sand at a breakneck pace. Coming up over the rim of a dune, she saw the approaching dust clouds and said a silent prayer of thanks. Vehicles—trucks, dune buggies, cars—at least five or six were approaching.

The lead vehicle stopped as the three figures on camels came toward them. Sarah was behind the others. The scouts had already dismounted and were surrounded by men and trucks by the time she reached them. They all turned to watch her as she slid from the camel. "Darius? Where's my husband?" Her voice cracked horribly.

One of the men broke away from the rest. He wore oil-smeared overalls and a dusty towel tied turban fashion over his hair. He grabbed her arm as she started to run toward the others. "Mrs. Descartes? No, wait! He isn't with us. I'm your husband's chief mechanic. Listen, please, the racers got caught in a severe sandstorm. We found the others, but there was no trace of your husband. We've covered every inch of ground. It's like he fell off the earth."

Sarah screamed, "You're not leaving! You've got to go back! Search some more. He can't just have vanished without a trace."

"I'm sorry, but men and camels have been known to disappear. The sand blows into huge unstable piles. Sometimes it covers cracks and crevices and forms pools of quicksand that could swallow a house. Mr. Descartes was way ahead of the others when the storm hit. We've no idea whether he stayed on course. Sometimes electrical disturbances in the air drive compasses crazy. Besides, we've got to get back to the oasis, we all need water and food and rest. The search planes should be arriving here soon, we radioed for help."

Sarah fought the urge to hit him. "Do you have an interpreter with you? I need someone to explain to the Bedouins that I must continue to search for my husband."

Darius moved his neck cautiously, turning his face to seek the small spot of light over his head. His arms were trapped in sand, hands still locked to the steering wheel. Even if he could have moved, which he couldn't, he was afraid any motion would bring down tons of smothering sand, cutting off the one sustaining shaft of air.

There was no pain now that the numbing cramps had subsided, but the raging thirst tormented him almost as much as his realization that he had endangered his friends with his recklessness.

At least the storm had passed. He estimated that when the wind blew his car over he had been on the unseen edge of a dune. The car had flipped over, landed on its side and brought loose sand down like a concealing blanket. He thought he had heard distant engines earlier that day. And he was certain a plane had flown over him the previous afternoon. Searchers wouldn't find him unless they came close enough to hear him shout. Even then, he wasn't sure his parched throat would allow him to be heard over the sound of throbbing motors.

Damn his stupidity. Both Hashim and the sheik had warned him that racing in the Sahara meant certain death. Even his own father, they pointed out, had recognized the danger and given up the idea.

"I've built special cars," he'd told them in his arrogance. "The heat of the summer isn't here yet. I'll have mechanics at the oasis and at the palace. We'll be in radio contact all the time."

His radio was somewhere in the sand.

He had tried moving various parts of his body, but each movement caused the sand to shift dangerously. In a few hours he would probably succumb to thirst. Better to go down fighting! So he began to spread his fingers, trying first the right and then left hand. Movement was easier for the left. He concentrated on raising his left arm, easing it up with agonizing slowness through the imprisoning sand.

A shower of stinging particles sprayed his face and he stopped working his arm, choked and coughed. He lay still for a minute, his breath ragged.

The sun climbed in the sky. Now the small spot of light over his head became a torch beam, searing his eyes. He let dust-coated eyelids close, willing himself to stay awake, fearing sleep might lead to unconsciousness. He examined his thoughts carefully. The desire to live was foremost in his mind. How could he ever have imagined it would be otherwise? Or that his father's death had been anything but accidental?

Despair, like every other human emotion, could be borne until it gave way to knowledge of its cause. Would he ever accept the fact that Sarah didn't love him? He supposed he would in time—if he would have that time. He'd come to accept the fact that she had always loved Jonathon Conway and probably always would. Knowing the hopelessness of trying to end an obsession, Darius pitied Sarah. They were both caught in the trap of loving someone who didn't return their love. Conway was too torn with frustration and self-pity to love anyone but himself.

Thoughts of his rival sent another surge of adrenalin pumping along Darius's veins. He began to work his fingers again, flex the muscles of his shoulder and rotate his elbow to try to free his arm.

He should have stopped the car. Found some sheltering dune and waited for the storm to pass. But they were so close to the oasis—at least, he was. He had left the others behind. The storm had begun as a mud-colored cloud hovering on the horizon, which separated suddenly into three distinct whirlwinds of sand towering high in the air as they raced toward him. The dreaded jinn of the desert—the demon storm—was upon him in seconds. Dust and swirling air masses exploded around him like a host of roaring gods descending from the skies in vengeful wrath.

His vision was instantly blocked by a thick coating of sand on his windshield. The next second the car flipped over. Fool, he told himself again. Idiot! You asked for this. He worked his arm furiously, and suddenly it came free. At the same moment the spot of light went out. He opened his eyes in complete darkness, felt his face with his stiff fingers. The car had shifted in the dune again, cutting off the one shaft of air and light. His head must be in a small pocket of trapped air. How long could the air last?

He scraped at the sand around his other shoulder, felt down his right arm until he touched the top of the steering wheel. His arm was wedged under it. Resting, he began to pant with both exertion and lack of air. His tongue was swelling. *I'm not going to be able to shout, even if rescuers come.*

There was a muffled sound somewhere far away. The crunch of someone . . . something . . . walking with a heavy tread on the sand above him. The car moved again. This time the sand came down over his face in a gritty choking mass.

He couldn't speak or breathe. His head was exploding. Then suddenly hands were scraping away the sand from his face, other hands were digging around his body. The sunlight blazed, and for a split second he thought he saw Sarah's face, a halo of light bronzing her hair. Then he felt a leaden hand squeeze the breath from his lungs, and he slipped away to the oblivion that had been waiting to claim him.

Sarah worked frantically, scooping the sand from Darius's mouth with her finger, tilting his head forward, then back, so she could force air into him, then bending to give him the kiss of life, her own breath. The two Bedouins were still working to free him from the buried car as she breathed life-giving air into his lungs.

They pulled him free, carried him away from the shifting dune to a heat-baked hollow. Sarah still pressed her lips to his, blew air into his mouth, but he didn't respond. Her eyes burned. She would have wept tears of frustration, but it seemed every drop of liquid in her body had dried up. In her anguish she beat on his chest with her fists. "Damn you, Darius, don't you dare die! I won't let you! Not after what I've been through!"

He choked, coughed and blinked his eyes.

She held him in her arms until he was breathing

normally, then opened the goatskin bag and moistened a piece of cloth torn from her shirt. Dabbing his cracked lips and wiping the dust from his eyes, she said, "Oh, Darius, you frightened me."

He took a sip of water and blinked again. "Am I hallucinating?" The words were a whisper. She had to bend low to hear him. His hand came up slowly, touched her hair. "Sarah . . . are you really here?"

For answer she kissed his cheek, his forehead, his dust-coated eyelids. One of the Bedouins had whipped off his robe and propped it up with his camel stick to make a pocket of shade over Darius's head. Sarah pulled off his helmet.

She gave him more water, then began to feel his arms and legs to see if anything was broken. "Do you hurt anywhere?"

He shook his head weakly, still staring at her in disbelief. There was dried blood in his hair matting along one temple and abrasions on his face and hands, but miraculously there didn't seem to be any broken bones. "Try to move your legs," she said.

"Stiff . . . just stiff. I can move them. Sarah, it's really you. What are you doing here?" His voice was a dry croak. She gave him another sip of water before answering.

"Looking for you, of course. It's evident you need someone to keep an eye on you—'look after you.'"

"You saved my life!"

"Better credit the Bedouins with that. They recognized the outline of the car in the sand. I wouldn't have. Sand had blown over all your tracks. And they dug you out."

"Would they have been here without you?" Darius looked at the two Bedouins squatting beside him, and spoke to them in Arabic. They answered, gazing admiringly at Sarah, then looking away, while the dialogue continued rapid-fire until Darius seemed satisfied.

His cracked lips parted in a ghost of a smile as he

turned his head to her. "They compliment me on my choice of a woman. They say you are brave as a warrior, beautiful as a flower . . . but I should tame your temper."

The effort to speak exhausted him. He closed his eyes and nodded. Sarah huddled beside him in the sparse shade, moistening his lips with the wet cloth until he regained consciousness. He looked up at her wonderingly. "I thought I'd dreamed you . . ."

"Darius, we have to get you onto a camel, get you back to the oasis."

His eyes flew wide open. Suddenly he was alert. "A camel! You mean you rode a *camel?*" He began to make sputtering sounds. "And you're wearing an *abeyah!*" He waved his freed arms wildly.

Sarah was alarmed. He seemed to be choking, but she realized after a moment he was chuckling. The two Bedouins came to help as he struggled to his feet, uncoiling stiff limbs and wincing as a turban was tied onto his head. He swayed on his feet for an instant, then recovered. Moments later he was seated on a camel with one Bedouin holding him up. They began the slow trek back to the oasis.

They were within sight of the oasis when the Bedouin brought his camel to an abrupt halt. He turned and spoke rapidly to his companion. Darius shielded his eyes against the sun's glare to stare at the distant palms.

"What is it? What's wrong?" Sarah asked as her camel loped into position beside them.

"We must go on without our friends. Bid your camel a fond farewell. We have to walk the rest of the way."

"But why? It's just across that plain. You're not strong enough to walk."

"I'll manage. Come on." Darius slithered down the side of the camel. Puzzled, Sarah followed suit. "I promised their chief a reward for helping me find you."

Darius spoke to each of the two men at length,

offering his hand in gratitude. Then he said to Sarah, "They'll be rewarded. They're journeying to the village, and I'll radio my friend Sheikh Abdullah al-Za'im to furnish them with camels and provisions. I just hope the imperial guards at the oasis aren't searching for a member of their tribe on some felony charge."

They waved as the two Bedouins rode back across the dunes, leading the camel Sarah had ridden. "Magnificent rogues," Darius said softly.

"What do you mean, imperial guards at the oasis?" Sarah asked.

"The Bedouins have eyes sharper than eagles. They've spotted a large force of guards circling the oasis. From their positions, they are trying either to keep someone from getting in or getting out. The Bedouins fear the wrath of the sheik. If one of their number has angered him, they want to find out. And they'll want to put distance between the guards and themselves if there has been some trouble. They're hurrying back to the caravan to see what happened."

Sarah stopped dead in her tracks, an uneasy suspicion forming. "Hashim!" she said. "The sheik could have found out about Hashim."

Darius stopped too, his face full of fear for his friend. *"Hashim?* He's *here?* Then . . . that's how you knew. Oh, no!" He pressed his fist to his forehead, as though trying to drive away the fog of weakness and comprehend what had happened. "Sarah, you shouldn't have let Hashim return. His brother will have him killed."

"I wanted to find you. I'd have done anything to find you. Darius, listen to me, don't get any wild ideas about dashing to your friend's rescue. You aren't strong enough. Look at you, you're swaying on your feet, you're dehydrated. You may have injuries you don't know about. Darius, I love you, oh, I love you so much. I didn't know it until I lost you. I won't lose you again, *I won't—*"

He caught his breath, stared at her with a bright

flame of hope in his eyes. "Sarah, do you really mean it?"

She slipped her arms around his neck, gazed up at him, imploring him with her eyes to believe what she said. "I love you. I want to be your wife."

He played with a tendril of her hair that had escaped from her turban. "And what about Jonathon Conway? You know that Cecily divorced him. He's free to marry you now."

Sarah wanted to scream with rage, but she said as calmly as she could. "Darius, I've flown through a sandstorm, been eaten alive by flies, ridden through the desert on a camel—and been tossed off the miserable beast's back—frozen to death at night, nearly died of thirst, to say nothing of wrapping myself up in a hundred yards of black silk so the Arabs wouldn't think I was a bad woman. Do you think I went through all that for *fun?* So I could go home and fling myself at Jonathon? Darius Descartes, what do I have to do to convince you that I *want* to forsake all others. Oh, Darius, I really do . . ."

She couldn't muster tears, but dry sobs came crackling up her throat and she pressed her face to his chest, shaking with frustration. He enfolded her in his arms and held her as she stammered, "I . . . can't . . . even cry . . . properly . . . no moisture left . . ."

"Don't cry, my darling. Don't ever cry over me again. I love you, Sarah, I've never loved anyone else. I never will. I'll spend the rest of my life making up for what you've been through. Darling, please, don't cry, I can't stand it. Do you know, this is the first time I've seen you cry?"

Sarah raised her head, her lip still quivering. "What did you think I was—some kind of super woman?"

He smiled. "Yes. I'm glad to know you're mortal, like me. Come on, we must get to the oasis before the midday sun finishes off what the desert couldn't accomplish."

Sarah hesitated. "What about the sheik's soldiers? What about Hashim?"

"Our turning to bleached bones out here isn't going to help him, is it?" He took her hand and they began to walk toward the oasis.

As they neared it a land rover left the ranks and drove toward them. Darius greeted the driver who helped Darius and Sarah into the vehicle. She said, "I see the sheik's men have modern equipment."

"Oil," Darius whispered. "The sheikhdom is a cesspool of oil."

The land rover passed a row of turbaned soldiers, then drove to the edge of the rise above the water hole. When it stopped, she saw that the other racing cars and mechanics' vehicles were parked near a cluster of palms. The area was guarded by several men with guns who were prepared to ward off any attack. Almost simultaneously, Sarah saw the man striding toward the land rover. He was an older version of Hashim, tall, ferociously handsome, a jeweled dagger in the silk sash entwined about his waist. There was no need for Darius to tell her who he was. Sheikh Abdullah al-Za'im seized Darius by the shoulders, then pulled him close in a fierce hug of greeting.

Sarah waited for the long speeches in Arabic, but the greeting was cut short as Darius turned and extended his hand to bring her closer, apparently to introduce her to the sheik. Black eyes went over her in careful appraisal, then Abdullah launched into a stream of rapid Arabic and pointed toward the water hole and the crouching figures behind the incongruously streamlined racers.

Darius turned to Sarah. "He knows his brother is down there. He's given my people until nightfall to send him up here. They refused. Abdullah has now closed his borders to Western traffic—planes, rescue vehicles—until Hashim is delivered to him. They can't get in, we can't get out."

"Will they attack us?" Sarah glanced at the sheik out

of the corner of her eye. There seemed little doubt he would.

"I'm going to his tent to talk. One of his women will take care of you. Don't worry, Sarah, you'll be safe, no matter what happens."

"No, I want to stay with you. This is the twentieth century! They're surely not going to spill blood because someone rolled in the hay with someone else's wife?" Sarah grabbed Darius's arm and hung on.

He disentangled her fingers gently. "Every day, somewhere in this part of the world, some outraged father or husband or brother kills an adulterous woman and her paramour, if they can catch him. Western mores don't apply here. There is no justice other than that dispensed by the sheik. Now, if you don't go with the women, you'll cause me to lose even more face, which isn't going to help my negotiations for Hashim's life."

Sarah turned reluctantly to go toward the tent set up a distance away from the land rovers. Halfway across the sand separating the women's tent from the encampment of the sheik and his guards, Darius called after her. "Sarah, do you remember that day in the Baja when we encountered the rattlesnake? Sometimes it's advisable to be aware of whose territory we're trespassing on."

She looked back at him. "All I can say is that for a little while I thought we were going to have a happy ending. I didn't think we'd lose everything over a thirty-years-ago adultery."

"Sarah, *we* have our happy ending, no matter what. We love each other."

She watched as Darius and Abdullah walked together toward the sheik's tent, deep in a conversation that appeared angry but controlled. Then Sarah went to the women's tent.

Within the tent the women had discarded *abeyahs* and veils, and they rested on pillows, wearing vivid colored skirts and blouses, throats and wrists encircled with gold jewelry. Sarah thought a little wistfully of her own gold bangle, soon to be presented to a Bedouin bride.

A very young girl with kohl-emphasized eyes and the tattoo of a white flower visible on the top of one breast stepped forward and smiled shyly at Sarah. She offered her a drink of cool sweet liquid and a platter of dates. Sarah accepted the refreshments, as well as the silk pillow brought to her by a second young woman. Dropping her *abeyah,* which was now dusty and wrinkled, she felt dozens of disapproving eyes stare at her shirt and slacks.

"This is the twentieth century, you guys. Women's liberation. The Equal Rights Amendment!" Sarah promptly wondered if she were losing her mind. The strain, she decided, had definitely affected her. The sheik's women couldn't understand what she said, and maybe it was just as well. She and Darius were in enough trouble. And poor Hashim who was about to die for a spot of harmless pleasure he couldn't even remember. Why had she dragged him here? Surely she could have found her own way? But, of course, she couldn't have.

The minutes dragged by, measured by her heartbeats. After the women had satisfied their curiosity about her, they closed their eyes and dozed in the afternoon heat. Flies buzzed lazily over their heads, often landing on their faces and at the corner of their eyes. When they did that, Sarah had the horrible feeling the flies were drinking. She shuddered and batted at them as they cruised in her direction.

She wasn't sure how much time had passed when there was a sudden shout outside that grew rapidly into a babble of yelling voices. Grabbing the tent flap, Sarah flung herself outside in time to see Darius racing from the sheik's tent to the top of the rise above the water hole. She ran after him, slipping on the loose sand.

Sarah fell heavily a few inches from the top of the

dune. She pulled herself up on her elbows and looked down at the oasis. Hashim was walking slowly toward the sheik's soldiers as the others entreated him to return.

Darius called out, "Hashim, go back!"

Hashim raised his head and looked at Darius. "It is Allah's will. Either I die with my friends, or I die alone. In any case, I am dead. Do not blame your wife for this, old friend. It was written."

The sheik had now reached Darius's side, and half a dozen guards formed a line beside him, their rifles cocked and pointed at Hashim. Abdullah's arm was raised to signal a volley of bullets. Darius's cry, "No!" still hung in the air. For Sarah everything had frozen into a deadly tableau. She tried to move, but couldn't.

Then Darius was hurtling down the sandy slope toward Hashim, flinging himself between his friend and the roar of gunfire exploding like the wrath of Allah.

Chapter 33

Sarah walked slowly across the moonlit terrace of the villa, still warm from the Moroccan sun. She wore a deep green dress of silk chiffon that whispered over her body as she moved. Her hair was loose, blowing around her face in a gentle evening breeze that sighed in the date palms.

Over her head the stars hung in a velvet sky, close enough, it seemed, to reach out and touch. She paused beside the magnificently gnarled branches of an olive tree, caught in the heartbreaking beauty of the desert night, her mind filled with memories. The rustling leaves seemed to murmur ghostly music that called insistently to her senses, and the fragrance of jasmine compelled her to relive another such night.

She could almost feel the beat of the tango in her blood. It was easy to conjure up the first time she had come to the villa, the first time she had danced with Darius. Looking back, it seemed incredible she hadn't fallen madly in love with him at once. What a lot of time they'd wasted because she'd been unable to let go of the past.

"Darling!" Charmain exclaimed, rising from a wooden chaise on the far side of the terrace. "There you are! You look lovely. You're beginning to get an interesting expression on your pretty face. You've lost that blank look of youth. Experience is leaving its mark on you. I'm proud of you, love, I think you've managed to combine the best qualities of my generation and your own."

Sarah smiled at her and returned her kiss. "I'm sorry I wasn't here when you arrived. How are you, old bean? You look marvelous. White always was your color. And what's this? I don't remember seeing that ruby pendant before, or those earrings."

Charmain blushed prettily. "The maharaja has been *more* than generous. But tell me all your news! Why, I haven't seen you since you left on that gallant but foolish rendezvous with Hashim's brother."

They sat down and regarded one another fondly across the aged tile of the terrace. Sarah said, "Six months ago. Now I can look back and think the time has flown. But, of course, it didn't, at first."

Charmain leaned forward and caught Sarah's hands in hers. "I know, pet. I did come to the hospital, you know. But you were so distraught I don't suppose you knew I was there. I remember the old sheik pacing back and forth, wringing his hands and almost wailing in his anguish."

"I suppose he couldn't have known the impact the sight of his brother would have on him after all those years. I'm sure that at the instant he signaled for his men to fire he regretted the gesture. Or perhaps all of Darius's pleading had reached him."

"What had Darius said to him, do you know?"

"I think something to the effect that his brother couldn't have stolen Abdullah's wife if she hadn't wanted to be stolen. That women, whether men liked it or not, made choices too."

"How ironic that Hashim should come through the whole thing unscathed while Darius . . ."

Charmain broke off as the first haunting strains of a tango filled the night air. The two women turned toward the white-suited figure emerging from the arched doorway. Darius said, "Charmain, *belle dame,* if ever anyone deserved a bullet in his shoulder, I did. Besides, I thoroughly enjoyed having Sarah fuss over me while I recovered."

He crossed the terrace swiftly and pulled Sarah to her feet. Something gleamed in the moonlight as Darius held her hand and slipped a cold smooth object onto her wrist. She gasped with surprise and pleasure. "Darius! It's my gold bangle! The one I traded to the Bedouin chief! How on earth did you get it back?"

Darius smiled and kissed the back of her hand as he fastened the buckle. "I've had old Abdullah's men following the caravan all over the Empty Quarter, searching for it. After all, it was the least they could do. Didn't we reunite two old men who can now spend their days exchanging lies about their lives? Besides, no other woman in the world wears that bracelet with greater flair than you do, my love."

He seized her waist and they swayed to the beat of the tango, then moved across the terrace, dancing with effortless grace, as though a single will guided their bodies. The music reached its crescendo, and Darius bent her backward over his arm, his lips closed over hers in a kiss of mounting passion. For Sarah the only reality was the man in her arms, the love they had for each other and all the dreams that now would come true. She kissed her husband, responding to his touch, his nearness, and saw out of the corner of her eye that Charmain had slipped away, leaving them alone under the vast canopy of the desert sky.

About the Author

Katherine Kent is the pseudonym of a prolific writer of romances and mysteries. She was born and educated in England but fell in love with an American—and then with America. Although as a child she was steered toward a career as an artist, she always knew she was a born storyteller, and her successful writing career proves this. Katherine and her husband live in California with their three children. She has written two other Richard Gallen Books: *Waters of Eden,* an historical romance, and *Dreamtide,* another contemporary romance.